Totally Bound Publishing books by Hannah Murray

Perfect Taboo

The Shame Game
Sharing His Submissive
In His Hands
The Sadist and the Brat

Collections

Naughty or Nice?: Santa Daddy
Sun, Sea and…: Sun, Sea and Satisfaction Guaranteed
Dark and Deadly: Show Me Something Good

Perfect Taboo

THE SADIST AND THE BRAT

HANNAH MURRAY

The Sadist and the Brat
ISBN # 978-1-80250-563-4

Interior text design by Claire Siemaszkiewicz
Totally Bound Publishing

Published in 2023 by Totally Bound Publishing, United Kingdom.

Totally Bound Publishing is an imprint of Totally Entwined Group Limited.

THE SADIST AND THE BRAT

Dedication

For all the brats.

"It's easy to take off your clothes and have sex. People do it all the time. But opening up your soul to someone, letting them into your spirit, thoughts, fears, future, hopes, dreams…that is being naked."

—Rob Bell

Chapter One

Sadie Bloom shifted on her chair, sipped her virgin strawberry daiquiri, and took in the scenery.

The annual Halloween party and BDSM open house was in full, and though it was nearly midnight, showed no signs of slowing down. A round of demos had just ended, sending the crowd wandering back to the vendor booths to look at ball gags and zip ties and everything in between. The mummification booth was getting a lot of traffic, aided no doubt by the pair of very pretty submissives on display. Wrapped head to toe in cling wrap, they looked oddly like wax statues, only the strategic cutouts for breathing and fondling giving them away.

The woman had cutouts around her breasts and vulva, and the booth operator—her Domme—was encouraging curious passersby to touch. The other submissive had similar cutouts around his genitals, probably to give his testicles room. They were hanging lower than usual, thanks to the ball stretcher and weights, and his Dom was using a crop to tap at his engorged cock.

"Poor guy."

Sadie grinned at her friend. Olivia was perched on the chair next to her, sipping her own virgin cocktail, her eyes glued on the mummification booth. Every time the crop hit cock, she winced.

"If the state of his dick is anything to go by, the 'poor guy' looks like he's having the time of his life," Sadie pointed out.

Olivia laughed even as she winced again. "He does, doesn't he?"

"Don't get me wrong, it's not my thing either," Sadie went on, "but far be it from me to yuck anyone else's consensual, risk-aware yum."

"I'll drink to that." Olivia tapped her glass against Sadie's and pursed her lips. "What do you think Cade would do if I tried taking a crop to his dick?"

Sadie choked on her daiquiri. "Since when do you have a death wish?"

Olivia grinned. "He loves me too much to kill me."

"True, but you probably wouldn't sit down for a month."

"That is very likely." Olivia angled her head, her honey-blonde hair swinging around her shoulders. "Might be worth it to see the look on his face, though."

"I think being blissfully in love has rotted your brain."

Olivia sniffed. "You're just jealous."

Sadie slurped up the last of her drink. "You have a sexy man who loves you and does horrible, wonderful things to you. Of course I'm jealous."

"He does the dishes, too."

"You're such a bitch."

Olivia snorted out a laugh. "I take it things are not going well with what's his name?"

"Who? Oh. You mean Paul." Sadie set her empty glass on the table in front of her. "That's not really a thing. He doesn't even live in St. Louis. He just pops in every couple of weeks for work."

"I thought that's what you liked about him."

Sadie leaned back and crossed her legs. "It is."

"Do you ever get tired of dating guys whose most attractive quality is their absence?" Olivia asked.

"It's not his *most* attractive quality," Sadie protested, feeling for some reason as though she should defend the absent and lackluster Paul. "He's fun in bed. Eats pussy like a fiend."

Olivia made a vague sound and continued sipping her piña colada.

"He's too passive, though," Sadie went on. "Kinky, and enthusiastic, but too egalitarian. When I say 'no' or 'stop' during sex, do you know what he does?"

"What?"

"He stops." Sadie flung her hands up, then let them fall. "Just...stops. I had to remind him that he's not supposed to do that unless I use my safeword, but he can't seem to help himself."

"Ensuring consent is not a bad thing," Olivia began.

"No, but still. Once I squealed, because he bit my neck while he was doing me from behind? And he *stopped fucking me to ask if I was okay.*"

Olivia snickered. "Damn, that's awkward."

"Right?" Sadie sighed. "He's a good guy, but I think we've had all the fun we're going to."

Olivia reached over to pat Sadie's knee. "I'm sorry if you are."

"I'm not, really. I'll miss the beatings, and the regular sex, but that's why God invented vibrators."

"What about the beatings?"

"Eh."

"Eh?" Olivia's eyebrows shot up. "What does 'eh' mean?"

Sadie shrugged. "I haven't been that interested in playing lately. I'm…bored."

"Really?"

"After a while all the spankings start to blur together, you know?"

"Um, no."

"Oh, what do you know? You're blissfully in love."

"And my man is inventive," Olivia said with a smug smile.

Sadie shook her head. "Such a bitch."

"You know, maybe it's not the spankings that are boring," Olivia ventured.

"I know. It's the men."

"I don't think it is, actually."

"Surely you're not suggesting *I'm* boring."

"Not exactly."

"Not exactly?" Sadie repeated slowly and narrowed her eyes in mock menace.

Olivia's lips twitched, but her gaze was steady. "It's kind of hard to have anything more than a superficial experience if you never let yourself connect with someone."

"I connect," Sadie protested.

"But do you let yourself be vulnerable?"

"I'm a single submissive," Sadie said, trying not to sound defensive. "I have to be careful."

"No argument," Olivia said. "But if you want more than pickup scenes and fuck buddies, you're going to have to trust someone."

"It's not that easy," Sadie protested.

"I know," Olivia said, a wealth of understanding in her hazel eyes. "I know it isn't."

"Shit." Sadie blew out a breath. "How did we even start talking about this?"

"You said 'eh'."

"Well, I won't do that again." Sadie grabbed her empty glass, just to give herself something to do with her hands, and spotted movement at the bar. "I think you're being hailed."

Olivia turned to look. "Whoops. Guess my break is over."

Sadie waved at Cade across the room as Olivia drained the rest of her drink. "It's not a very imaginative costume, but he carries it well."

"Doesn't he?" Olivia plucked the glass from Sadie's hand and rose. "We're going to play pirate and wench later."

Sadie considered Cade's eye patch, billowing white shirt, and very tight leather pants. "Pictures or it didn't happen."

"Not a chance."

"Party pooper." Sadie stood to give her friend a brief hug. "I'm going to go find Nikki. I promised to be a friendly face in the crowd for her demo."

"What's she doing again?"

"Pervertables."

"Oh, yeah. Cade's bummed to miss that one. He was looking forward to getting some new ideas."

"From what you've told me, I don't think he needs any help in the creative Dom department."

Olivia's grin was both delighted and satisfied. "He really doesn't."

"All right, now you're just bragging. Get out of here before I start to hate you."

Olivia just laughed. "Give Nikki a good luck kiss from me."

"Will do," Sadie promised, and Olivia hurried away.

Sadie watched Cade greet his lover with an enthusiastic kiss and a smack on the ass. Ignoring the all too familiar twist of envy the sight invoked, she turned away from the happy couple to survey the room.

She didn't see Nikki—no small wonder with so many people around—so she began to wander, enjoying the wide variety of costumes on display. She spotted a pair of slutty fairies wearing nothing but wings and pasties, a vampire in six-inch platform heels, an old-fashioned English bobby leading a serving wench in handcuffs, and at least three sexy nurses, one whose costume was completely see-through.

"I love Halloween," she murmured, then turned when someone called her name.

She grinned with genuine pleasure at the man in black leather shorts and a harness making his way toward her. "Hey, Sam."

"Love the costume," he said, bending to kiss her cheek. "Wicked Witch of the East?"

"Slutty Witch of the Midwest," she corrected.

"It's great," Sam enthused and flicked the wide brim of her pointed hat. "But I almost didn't recognize you with so many clothes on."

"I know, right?" Sadie looked down at her costume. Her dress was black, long sleeved and fitted, and opened in a deep vee from neck to navel. It fasted over her belly button with three tiny hooks before flaring open to flutter around her thighs. By vanilla standards, it was downright risqué—especially since the fabric was sheer, and the only thing keeping her from being totally on display were the pasties over her nipples and the skimpy G-string that had barely enough fabric to qualify as underwear. But since she usually attended play parties naked—or close to it—it was definitely a change.

"I feel like I'm wearing an overcoat or something," she confessed. "And my hair feels funny."

Sam gave one of her loose strawberry-blonde curls a tug. "Because it's not in pigtails?"

She wrinkled her nose. "Exactly."

"Well, you look great."

"So do you," she replied, looking him over. His summer tan was long gone, the black leather of the harness he wore providing a sharp contrast to the white of his skin. It showed off his lean build, and the thighs he'd built by riding his bike to work every day strained the leather shorts to their limit. He had close-cropped dark hair with streaks of silver at the temples, a clean-shaven jaw, and a hint of devil in his smile. "Love the harness."

He ran his hands over it with obvious delight. "Me, too. Where are you off to?"

"I'm trying to find Nikki. I promised to be a friendly face for her demo."

"Right, pervertables." Sam nodded. "Colette was going to volunteer us for that, but I wasn't sure I'd be able to get the night off."

Sam's job as an emergency room nurse kept him away from a lot of club events, especially since he'd switched to the night shift.

"How's work going?"

"Bloody, stressful, and exhausting."

"You love it."

"Every minute," he said with a smile. "I better go. I'm supposed to be fetching Colette a drink."

She flicked a gaze over his shoulder at the bar, and the line that now wound halfway through the room. "If you can get Olivia's attention, she'll shuffle you to the front of the line."

"I just might do that. When are we doing WWW again?"

WWW was short for Whine & Wine Wednesday, the semi-regular gathering of submissives she hosted in her apartment. "This Wednesday is Halloween, so next week?"

"I'm off that night, so it's a date." He kissed her cheek. "Don't get into trouble at the demo."

Sadie laid a hand on her chest and forced her eyes wide. "Who, me?"

"Yeah, you." He flicked a finger down her nose. "And don't bother with the Little Miss Innocent look, because I'm not buying it."

Sadie wasn't sure if she should laugh or be offended. "I do know how to behave in public, you know."

"Except when you have a chance to annoy Jack."

"I'm just being me," she countered. "It's not my fault he's so easily annoyed."

"Right."

She narrowed her eyes at his grin. "Stop provoking me and go get your lady her drink."

"Yes ma'am," he drawled, and snorted when she crossed her eyes at him. "Be good."

"Said the pot to the kettle," she called after him, and took a minute to admire the flex of his ass in the leather shorts as he walked away.

"Sadie, there you are."

Sadie turned with a smile for the very grown-up, very sexy Wednesday Addams hurrying toward her. "Hi, Rebecca. Great costume."

"I need your help," Rebecca said, ignoring the compliment, and grabbed Sadie's hand. "Come with me."

Sadie fell into step beside her. "What's up?"

"It's Nikki," Rebecca said, sounding uncharacteristically grim, her stride eating up the floor. Sadie had to hustle to keep up. "I need you to help me convince her to go home."

"She's supposed to bottom for Jack in the pervertables demo." Sadie dodged a naked woman with a rainbow tail and a unicorn horn being led on a leash by someone dressed as Deadpool.

"I know, but she can't." Rebecca frowned after Deadpool and the unicorn. "I don't get that."

"I'll explain later. Why can't Nikki do the demo?"

"Because she broke her ankle today." Rebecca stopped at the edge of one of the conversation areas that had been set up around the warehouse for the event. Perched on the velvet sofa, her mouth tight with pain, was Nikki.

Sadie saw immediately that Rebecca was right—there was no way Nikki was up to bottoming. Her pretty face was strained and drawn, her eyes dull with pain. Her normally glowing olive complexion held a tinge of gray, and she had her booted foot propped on the low table in front of the sofa. Though her makeup was flawless and her dark hair was carefully done in a crown of braids, her exhaustion was plain.

"I'm fine," Nikki said.

Sadie eased down next to her. "What happened?"

Nikki sighed. "I was at work this morning in the warehouse, and one of the guys was coming through with a pallet jack. He ran into my ankle."

Sadie winced in sympathy. "How bad is the break?"

"It's not, really, but I have to wear the boot for eight weeks, and I can't work," Nikki said, and Sadie saw the worry in her eyes. "I should get some disability pay, but I don't know…"

"Don't worry about that," Sadie said, and saw Rebecca's nod out of the corner of her eye. If disability didn't cover what Nikki needed, they'd figure something out. "You can't do the demo, Nik."

"I have to," Nikki said, grim determination hardening her delicate features. "I promised Jack."

"Jack will lose his shit if you try to play like this," Rebecca declared.

"I'm not actually playing," Nikki countered. "It's a demo, not a scene. And there's no reason I can't do it. I didn't take any of the pain pills they gave me, so I'm not altered."

"I can tell." Sadie tapped a gentle finger under Nikki's eye, where she'd tried and failed to cover up the dark circles. "I can also tell you need one."

"I promised Jack," Nikki repeated, her mouth set in a stubborn line. "It's too late for him to find someone else."

"He'll understand," Rebecca insisted.

Nikki just shook her head, and Sadie exchanged a look with Rebecca.

"How about I go get Jack?" Rebecca offered.

"I don't want him to be mad at me," Nikki said softly.

Sadie mouthed "*Go,*" then turned back to Nikki as Rebecca dashed off. "Honey, he's not going to be mad at you for something that isn't your fault."

"I don't know," Nikki began. "He's pretty stern."

"Stern, yes. Asshole, no. He's not going to let you play—or demo," she amended, anticipating Nikki's protest, "with a broken ankle."

"I just hate canceling at the last minute."

"Of course you do." Sadie patted the younger woman's hand. "But if you try to play in this shape, you won't sit for a month."

Nikki's eyes widened. "You think he'd paddle me?"

"If he doesn't, I will," Sadie said, pleased when Nikki laughed. "Now, let's figure out how to get you home. Did you drive yourself?"

Nikki shook her head, her crown of braids gleaming in the overhead lights. "I took a rideshare."

"Then you need a lift home."

"Oh, I can just take another rideshare." Nikki bit her lip as Sadie started looking around. "I don't want to put anyone out. I'll be fine."

"You'll forgive me if I don't trust your judgment, Miss I Can Play With A Broken Ankle," Sadie said, and lifted a hand to wave at the top dressed as a cowhand by the bar. "Kody!"

"Oh, no," Nikki moaned.

"Something wrong with Kody?" Sadie asked, keeping her voice low, and noted with interest that Nikki's cheeks turned pink at the question.

"I kind of have a crush on them," Nikki whispered back and lifted a hand to her hair. "Do I look okay?"

"Adorable," Sadie assured her and looked up with a smile as Kody approached with a jangle of spurs. "Hello, Your Grace."

"Oh, so you *do* have some manners," Kody drawled, amused, and hooked their thumbs in the pockets of their blue jeans. They'd gone all out with their costume, accessorizing the jeans and pearl-snapped western shirt with boots and spurs, leather working gloves, and a straw cowboy hat. There was even a whip coiled on their belt. "Next time you holler at me from across the room like that, I'm going to assume you need a reminder to use them."

Sadie lowered her eyes respectfully and tried to sound demure. "Yes, Your Grace. I apologize."

Kody nodded, a short jerk of their head. "All right, then. Something I can do for you?"

"Nikki needs a ride home." Sadie swallowed a grunt when Nikki's elbow made contact with her ribs. "Are you available?"

Kody's eyes, a faded blue that nearly matched their shirt, narrowed on Nikki's booted foot. "What happened?"

Sadie stayed silent, and after a moment, Nikki said, "I got hurt at work."

"She was supposed to bottom for Jack's demo," Sadie offered, taking pity on her friend. "But has now realized that would be a terrible idea."

Kody's frown deepened. "Jack was going to do a scene with you like this?"

"He doesn't know yet," Sadie offered, and the killing light in Kody's eyes faded a bit. "She was hoping she could power through."

"Thanks a lot," Nikki muttered, her shoulders hunching as Kody turned a stern gaze on her.

Kody stared at her a moment, radiating disapproval, then gave a short nod. "I'm glad you realized that wasn't a good idea."

Nikki sagged with relief, and Sadie cleared her throat to bring Kody's attention back to her. "She took a rideshare here, but I thought it'd be better if someone drove her home."

"You thought right. Let me go get my phone, and I'll be back. Do you have crutches?"

"Um. No." Nikki bit her lip. "It's a walking boot, so I didn't think I'd need them."

Kody's eyes went fierce. "Stay right here," they commanded and waited, eyebrows raised.

Nikki ducked her head, her cheeks going pink again. "Yes, Your Grace."

Kody gave one sharp nod, aimed a look at Sadie that clearly said *stay with her until I get back,* and strode off.

"Hot," Sadie commented, watching Nikki watch Kody leave.

"Stop it," Nikki muttered, her cheeks scarlet, and sighed. "They don't even know I'm alive."

"Well, you'll have a whole car ride home to remind them that you are," Sadie told her. "And knowing Kody, they'll probably help you inside, make sure you take your pain pill, and tuck you into bed."

"Oh, no."

"What?"

"I was going to do laundry this morning, but I was running late." Nikki pressed her hands to her cheeks. "There are piles of dirty clothes all over my bed. Will you stop laughing?"

"I can't help it," Sadie teased. "You're just so cute."

"And what if I mess up their pronouns?" Nikki fretted. "I don't want to offend them."

"How often do you use someone's pronouns when you're talking to them?" Sadie asked gently.

Nikki's expression turned sheepish. "Oh. Right."

"And if you do mess up, just apologize and correct yourself," Sadie continued, and patted Nikki's thigh. "It'll be fine."

"What'll be fine?" a deep voice rumbled, and Sadie looked up to find Jack looming over them, Rebecca hovering a step behind.

His eyebrows formed straight slashes over dark brown eyes, and his chestnut hair, glinting with red and gold highlights, spilled in waves to his shoulders.

His jaw was covered in a full beard in the same gorgeous color and was clenched so hard she could see it even through the thick pelt.

And of course, his face was fixed in his usual 'resting-dick-face' expression, like the world was on his last nerve.

It was an almost distressingly handsome face, even with the scowl, and she wondered idly how gorgeous he would be if he didn't always look like he was about to get a prostate exam.

She swallowed a giggle at the thought and cleared her throat. "Going home instead of doing your demo."

He spared her a brief glance, then circled the low table to Nikki's other side. His leathers creaked when he squatted down and laid one big hand on Nikki's knee. "What happened?"

"Work accident," Nikki said with a sigh. "I can probably still do the demo—"

"No, you cannot," he interrupted. "You're going home, putting your foot up, and taking a pain pill."

Sadie let out a sigh of relief, then blinked when Jack frowned at her. "What?"

"You didn't actually think I'd let her do the demo like this?" he asked, and he sounded so pissed off that she forgot herself and scowled back.

"Of course not," she began hotly, and bit back a curse when his eyes narrowed in warning. She gritted her teeth and made an effort to keep her tone respectful. "But she was too worried about disappointing you to believe me."

"I feel bad bailing on you," Nikki admitted, and her voice was so small Sadie put an arm around her for comfort. "I know it's important."

His tone was firm. "It's not more important than your health, or your safety."

Nikki bit her lip. "You'll have to cancel it."

"I'll make it a lecture instead of a demo," Jack said. "It won't be as fun, but it'll do the job."

"There, see?" Sadie gave Nikki's arm a pat. "Problem solved."

"But it's on the schedule as a demo," Nikki said, displaying the stubborn streak that lurked beneath her shy exterior. "People are expecting it, and James said there's been a lot of interest."

Jack's expression had shifted, and he was regarding Nikki with an almost thoughtful look on his face. "This is important to you."

Nikki shrank a little under his steady gaze but nodded. "I don't want to be the reason it doesn't happen."

"You're not," he said, and Sadie was a little impressed that he could sound compassionate and absolutely implacable at the same time. "It's my decision, not yours."

Nikki sighed. "Yes, Sir. I'd just feel better if you were able to find a replacement."

"Maybe I can do it," Rebecca put in. "I'm sure Nick wouldn't mind."

"Aren't you and Nick supposed to be on the role-play panel?" Sadie reminded her. "It's the same time as the demo."

"Oh, right. I forgot." Rebecca winced. "Well, I'm sure someone can do it. What about Amanda?"

Sadie shook her head. "She did a pretty hard scene earlier, she's not going to be up for it."

"Olivia?"

"She's on bar duty."

"Excuse me," Jack said, and Sadie looked at him. She was surprised to see amusement in his expression. "Didn't I just get done saying this was my decision?"

"We're just trying to help," Sadie said and tried not to notice how damn good he looked. She could usually ignore the ridiculous level of hotness he walked around with—the whiskey and cigar voice, the tight ass, the romance novel hero shoulders—because he was always such a crab ass. But with a half-smile on his face and a warm, almost mischievous twinkle in his teddy bear eyes, he looked not only handsome but approachable.

Frankly, it was upsetting.

He looked at her, and while he didn't stop smiling, the look in his eye went from a warm twinkle to a nerve-inducing glint. "You want to help?"

What the fuck did he think she was doing here, knitting a tea cozy? "Nikki's my friend. Of course I want to help."

"Good." His smile turned sharp. "You can do it."

"She can?" Rebecca said, shocked.

"You can?" Nikki squealed in excitement.

"I can do what?" Sadie asked, then the hammer fell. "Wait, what?"

"This is a perfect solution," Rebecca enthused, and Sadie swung around to stare at her friend.

"I don't know about perfect," Sadie began, narrowing her eyes at Rebecca.

"Sure it is," Rebecca said, completely unaffected by Sadie's death glare. "You're comfortable in front of an audience, and an experienced submissive. You're probably already familiar with everything Jack's going to use in the demo."

"Well, I do have some surprises," Jack put in drily, his eyes all but dancing now. "But none of it too advanced."

"And with you filling in, Nikki can leave with a clear conscience and get some rest," Rebecca continued, and aimed a gleeful look at Sadie. "Which is what we all want her to do."

I hate you, Sadie thought, and only resisted sticking her tongue out at Rebecca because Jack was there to see it.

"Would you, Sadie?" Nikki asked, and Sadie stopped shooting daggers at Rebecca long enough to look at her. She had her hands clasped between her breasts, her eyes shining with hope. "I'd feel so much better about going home if I knew Jack didn't have to cancel."

Shit. Sadie forced herself to smile. "For you? Of course, I will."

"Oh, thank you," Nikki gushed, and wrapped her arms around Sadie in a grateful hug. "I can't tell you what a relief this is."

Shit, shit, shit. "You're welcome." Sadie patted Nikki's back. "Just promise me you'll take a pain pill and elevate that ankle, okay?"

Nikki pulled back, beaming. "I promise."

Shit.

"Then it's settled," Jack said, and he sounded so satisfied that Sadie had to bite her tongue to keep from sticking it out at him. "Sadie and I will handle the demo, and you handle getting better. All right?"

Nikki nodded, looking much calmer than she had a few moments ago. "Yes. Thank you, Sir."

"You're very welcome," he replied, and pressed a kiss to the crown of her head. "Now. How are you getting home?"

"I got her a ride." Sadie ignored Jack and his very un-Jack-like expression—why was he still smiling?—and watched Nikki's face go bright red when Kody stepped up next to Rebecca.

The smile she aimed at Kody was so full of naked longing that Sadie wasn't surprised to see an answering flush on Kody's cheekbones.

They cleared their throat. "Ready to go?"

"Ready, Your Grace," Nikki said and started to push herself up.

Jack let out an exasperated huff and scooped her up. "I'll carry you out to Kody's car."

"Um. Okay." Nikki put her arms around Jack's neck, her eyes wide. "Thank you."

"You're welcome," he said with a gentle smile before aiming an arched eyebrow at Sadie. "Sadie, we'll talk when I get back. Stay here."

Sadie opened her mouth to answer, but he was already gone, striding for the exit like he was carrying a pillow instead of an full-grown person. She watched for a moment—she was only human, after all—then aimed a glare at Rebecca. "Just what the hell did you think you were doing?"

Rebecca dropped onto the sofa next to Sadie with a grin. "Helping?"

"You and I," Sadie declared, "are no longer friends."

Rebecca just snickered. "Hey, Jack started it."

"And you had to follow his lead?"

"Well, yeah," Rebecca said and laughed when Sadie cursed. "You have to admit it was the perfect solution. Nikki went home with barely a fuss."

"Except now I have to do a demo with Resting Dick Face."

Rebecca choked. "You've got to stop calling him that."

"Why?"

"Because he's going to find out."

Sadie wanted to scrub her hands over her face, but she didn't want to wreck her makeup. "So?"

"So, it's not a good idea to piss off the Dom you're about to play with."

"I am not *playing* with Jack. Being a stunt bottom for a demo is not playing. It's…acting," she decided.

"Uh-huh. Acting. Tell me, do you subscribe to the method school?"

"Oh, shut up," Sadie muttered and pushed to her feet. "I'll be right back."

"Where are you going?"

"I didn't bring my play bag with me, so I need to get a couple of things."

"Um, Jack told you to stay put."

That made her laugh out loud. "I'll be right back."

She walked away on Rebecca's squeak of dismay—*serves her right, the traitor*—and headed to the bar. The line was even longer now, people scrambling for drinks before the next round of demos started, but she pushed past it without a qualm and leaned over to get Olivia's attention.

"Sadie, you can't jump the line," she admonished, and shot a look over her shoulder where Cade was scooping ice into a glass. "You're going to get me in trouble."

"I'm not here for a drink. Do you have any emergency aftercare kits left, or are they all gone?"

Olivia scooped a cupful of frozen pineapple out of a bag and dumped it into a blender. "We still have some. Why, do you have a crashing submissive on your hands or something?"

"No, it's for me."

Olivia set the blender to whirring, her eyes brightening with interest. "Did you find someone you want to play with?"

"I'm doing Jack's demo."

Olivia blinked, and the blender ground to a stop. "You're what?"

"Nikki's hurt, so she can't do it, and somehow I ended up agreeing to fill in."

"How the hell did that happen?"

"I'll let you know when I figure it out," Sadie muttered under her breath.

A shout from Cade on the other side of the bar made Olivia jump. "Shit. Don't go anywhere," she told Sadie, quickly pouring the contents of the blender into the cups she had lined up and waiting. She garnished the mocktails with slices of fruit, laid them out on the bar for waiting customers, then began shoveling ice and frozen fruit into the blender again. "Okay. What exactly happened?"

"That's a much longer conversation than we have time for." Sadie glanced behind her, noting that while Jack hadn't returned yet, Rebecca was getting agitated. "*Get your ass back here,*" she mouthed, and Sadie rolled her eyes. "Listen, I'll fill you in later, but I need the aftercare kit now."

Olivia reached under the counter. "Do you want nuts or chocolate?"

"Both," Sadie decided, and took the small baggies. "Thanks, Liv."

"You got it. Do you still want a ride home?"

She'd carpooled in with Cade and Olivia and had planned to get home the same way. "Of course. Why wouldn't I?"

Olivia's eyes twinkled. "Maybe Jack will want to take you. You know, for aftercare."

Sadie snorted. "No, he won't."

"Stranger things have happened," Olivia sang and burst out laughing.

"What's so funny?"

"Nothing, nothing," Olivia said, waving her hands, and laughed harder.

"Go back to work, weirdo," Sadie said, and with Olivia's laughter still ringing in her ears, headed back to the conversation pit. She was halfway there when someone stepped into her path.

"Hello, Sadie."

Sadie gritted her teeth and made a concerted effort to keep the sneer out of her voice. "Joel."

He went from smiling to scowling in an instant. "Excuse me?"

Tool, Sadie thought and inclined her head. "Forgive me. *Sir* Joel."

"That's better," he said, the smile blooming once again. He raked his gaze down her body. "You look lovely tonight. Appropriate costume."

"Thank you," she said stiffly. Joel was handsome in a generic white-boy way, with gilded blond hair and a gym-fit physique, but he always left her feeling like she needed a shower—and not in a good way.

"Where are you off to?" he asked, licking his lips.

Ew. "I'm on my way to rejoin Rebecca," she said and shifted to move around him. "If you'll excuse me, Sir."

"You can gab with your friends anytime," he said, blocking her sidestep. "I've got the spanking bench reserved tonight."

"Then have a good scene," she replied and tried to step around him again.

"I reserved it for us." He reached for her arm. "Come on. We'll give the newbies a show."

"No, thank you," she said, twisting to avoid his grab, and waited a deliberate beat before pointedly adding, "Sir. As I said, I have other plans."

His face twisted into a sneer. "Your *friend* can spare you for an hour."

"She could," Sadie allowed, noting the way he spat the word *friend* as though it left a bad taste in his mouth. "If I wanted to do a scene with you. But I don't, so you'll have to excuse me."

She didn't wait for his reaction, simply scuttled around him and hurried over to Rebecca.

"What was that all about?" Rebecca asked as Sadie resumed her seat.

"Joel has reserved the spanking bench for us," Sadie said.

"Ick." Rebecca wrinkled her nose. "I assume you told him no."

"I'd have told him fuck no, but he'd try to get me into trouble for it."

Rebecca shook her head. "I don't like that guy. He's..."

"An asshole?" Sadie ventured.

"A big one," Rebecca agreed, frowning at Sadie's hands. "What'd you get at the bar?"

"I didn't bring my play bag, which means I don't have my aftercare kit." She held up the two small bags. "I snagged a couple of the emergency kits they stocked for the night."

"Almonds and chocolate, good choice." Rebecca nodded. "I like meat and cheese, myself."

Sadie started to consolidate the contents of the two bags into one. "Well, if I were placing an order, it would be a full charcuterie plate, but beggars can't be choosers."

"I should make more specific aftercare requests," Rebecca mused. "A cheeseburger would be awesome after a scene, don't you think?"

"My favorite is fondue," Sadie said. "It's warm and buttery and there's just a little bit of booze. Perfect."

"I'd either burn myself or stab myself with a skewer if I tried to eat fondue after a scene," Rebecca admitted.

"Life is full of risks."

"Speaking of..." Rebecca raised an eyebrow. "Playing with Jack."

"It's a demo," Sadie reminded her, and zipped the full baggie closed with a scowl. "Don't you have to get back to Nick?"

"And miss this? Hell, no."

"I need better friends," Sadie muttered. "Oh, look. Resting Dick Face returns."

"Shhh!"

"He's halfway across the room, Rebecca," Sadie pointed out drily. "He can't hear me."

"Doms hear everything," Rebecca hissed, her lips barely moving. "Sooner or later."

"You're paranoid."

"And you're reckless," Rebecca shot back. "One of these days you're going to meet a Dom who you can't boss around, then you'll see."

"I doubt it," Sadie groused and ignored Rebecca's curious glance. "He looks weird tonight."

"What do you mean?" Rebecca narrowed her eyes. "I think he looks good. The leathers really suit him, don't they?"

Sadie refused to look, focusing her attention on his face as he moved through the crowd. "Why's he smiling?"

"People do that, you know."

"Jack doesn't. At least, not at me." Sadie watched him approach, unease building with every step he took. "I didn't even know his face could move like that. He looks almost...happy."

"Maybe he is," Rebecca said. "After all, he tricked you into playing with him."

"He didn't trick me," Sadie protested. "And we're not playing."

Rebecca turned to grin at Sadie, laughter dancing in her gray eyes. "Whatever you need to tell yourself, sweetie."

"I hate you," Sadie said, and, ignoring the flutter in her belly as Jack drew closer, reached out and pinched Rebecca's thigh.

Rebecca pinched her back, making Sadie flinch, but there was no time to retaliate because Jack was there, towering over them with his arms crossed over his chest, that odd little smile on his face. It made her nervous, so she ignored it. But that meant she either had to look away or look at the rest of him. And since looking away would be like holding up a neon sign reading *Hey! I'm nervous!*, she looked at the rest of him.

Rebecca was right—the leathers suited him.

She'd gotten used to seeing him in business clothes, since he often came to parties and events straight from his job as head of a liquor distribution company, and he looked good in a suit. But the black leather pants were...*whew.* They rode low on his hips and clung to his thighs, and the leather had the supple look that came from years of wear and care. The urge to reach out and see if they were as soft as they looked had her curling her fingers into her palms. *Bad Sadie, no touch,* she reminded herself, and tried to find fault with the shirt he'd chosen.

Unfortunately, the white dress shirt looked perfect, a bright, crisp contrast to the leathers. He'd left the neck open to show off the column of his throat and several delicious inches of hair-sprinkled chest. He'd rolled back the sleeves too, in a blatant display of forearm porn. The sight of well-defined muscles and the dusting of reddish-brown hair would have been appealing enough, but the tattoo on his right arm made it downright mesmerizing. The twisting black lines rippled as the muscles in his forearms flexed, and she bit back a curse.

They're just arms, she reminded herself, and shifted her focus to someplace benign, like his hair.

He wore it long, just past his shoulders, thick and wavy. The rich dark-brown color was streaked with red and blond, contrasting with the summer tan that still clung to his skin, even though it was October. His beard was neatly trimmed and looked as thick and soft as a mink pelt—she had to dig her fingernails into her palms again to keep from finding out.

He wore his hair down unless he was playing, when he put it in either a ponytail or a man bun to keep it out of his way. She'd never been a fan of man buns, finding them silly looking on everyone who wasn't Jason Momoa, and it was absolutely irritating that Jack seemed to be the exception to the rule.

He wore heavy silver rings, two on his left hand and one on his right. He had tiny silver hoops in both ears, and a leather bracelet wrapped around his right wrist.

He cleared his throat, with a kind of *look at me, little girl* growl at the end of it that made her want to roll her eyes and drool at the same time. Instead, she fixed a bland smile on her face and looked up.

His eyes were dark and thickly lashed, but instead of the irritation or exasperation she was used to seeing they looked almost...amused?

Bite me, she thought, and scowled before she could tell her face to behave.

The amusement deepened. Without breaking eye contact he said, "Rebecca, where's Nick?"

"Um. The last time I saw him he was talking with James and a couple of visitors," Rebecca replied, and she sounded so gleeful that Sadie pinched her again.

"Why don't you go find him. I need to talk to Sadie."

"Oh," Rebecca said, clearly disappointed. "Well. Okay. Unless Sadie wants me to stay."

Normally Sadie would've asked her to stick around, if only to irritate Jack. But since Rebecca was only offering for her own entertainment, Sadie fluttered her lashes and smiled. "Aw, you're so sweet. But you can go. I'll be fine."

"I can totally stay." Rebecca turned so Jack couldn't see her face and aimed pleading eyes at Sadie.

Sadie reached out and patted her hand. "Totally unnecessary."

Rebecca scowled. "Fine." She stood, shoulders slumped in defeat, and began to walk away so slowly a snail could've run laps around her.

Sadie rolled her eyes at the slow retreat, then turned to find Jack still staring at her. It threw her off, and before she could think better of it, she snapped out, "What?"

"Hang on," he said, and without looking away called out, "If you're not out of eyesight in five seconds, Rebecca, I'm going to have a chat with Nick about the way you follow orders."

Rebecca squeaked and shuffled away so fast Sadie wouldn't have been surprised to see skid marks, and she couldn't help but laugh.

"Your friends are loyal," Jack remarked.

"My friends are nosy," she corrected, and reluctantly turned to look at him. His arms were no longer crossed over his chest, his hands hanging loose at his sides, but he looked no less imposing, and no less gorgeous. It was irritating and loosened her tongue. "What's the deal?"

One dark eyebrow quirked up. "The deal?"

"You know what." Sadie kept her eyes on his so she didn't have to see his lips curl into that disconcerting smile again. "Why'd you tell Nikki I'd fill in for her?"

"She would've spent the whole night fretting if I'd canceled the demo."

"You could've told her you'd find someone else. It didn't have to be me."

"True," he acknowledged. "But she trusts you, and you fit my criteria for a demo bottom."

She started to fold her arms across her chest, but she didn't want to seem defensive. "And what criteria is that?"

"Experience, comfort in front of a crowd." He angled his head so the light caught his hair. "Being an interactive player is a big plus."

"An interactive player?"

"Not quiet," he elaborated, and shocked her to her toes by grinning. "I assume your mouth doesn't stop running when you're playing."

"You assume correctly," she managed, and let out a careful breath. *Holy crap.* He was hot when he scowled, but that grin was *potent.*

"I need someone who isn't afraid to talk during the scene," he was saying, and she forced herself to pay attention. "As much as the audience is watching what I'm doing, they're also watching how the bottom reacts."

"Nikki's quiet," Sadie pointed out.

"Nikki volunteered for the demo because she's trying to get more involved in the scene, and she's trying to build her confidence around playing in public." He shrugged. "And I can usually get a reaction out of even a shy bottom."

"I'll bet," she muttered, and he smiled again.

It wasn't a gentle smile, or even a happy one. It was the kind of smile that nature documentaries captured on sharks and crocodiles right before they devoured their hapless prey. It made the breath catch in her throat and the hair on the back of her neck stand up and launched a thousand butterflies in her stomach.

Holy crap, she thought, and tried to hear over the pounding of her heart.

"Well?"

"Well, what?" she managed.

"Am I canceling, or are you filling in?"

"You're actually giving me a choice?"

"You're an adult, Sadie. I can't actually make you do something you don't want to do."

"I'm aware," she snapped, the hint of mocking in his tone putting some starch back in her spine. "You don't want me to do this, anyway."

"I don't?" He looked intrigued, and faintly amused. "Why not?"

"You think I'm a brat."

His expression didn't change. "You are a brat."

"And I think you're a stuffed shirt," she shot back.

He smiled wider, making his eyes crinkle and a dimple pop in his cheek. The damn thing was so deep she could see it through the thick pelt of his beard. "And you don't play with stuffed shirts."

She ignored the dimple and the crinkles and crossed her arms over her chest, not caring anymore if she looked defensive. "This isn't a scene, it's a demo."

"If it's not a scene, then what are we arguing about?"

Well, I backed ass first into that one.

"Are you afraid I'll hurt you?" he asked, looking serious for the first time, and she couldn't bring herself to lie.

"No." He wouldn't hurt her. He'd annoy her, and he'd make her feel things she didn't want to feel, but he wouldn't hurt her. And she knew better than to say what she said next, she really did. But she was feeling off balance and cornered and the words just spilled out before she could stop them. "But I'm not interested in being bored."

The gleam that came into his eyes had her stomach dropping to her knees. "Bored?"

Shit, shit, shit. "I just meant we're incompatible. Kink wise. Play wise."

"Incompatible," he murmured, the light of challenge in his eyes not fading even a little bit.

"So really," she went on, desperate for a way out, "it would be better if you found someone else. I'm sure Nikki would understand."

"You don't think I can make it fun for you."

It wasn't a question, but it was clear he was waiting for an answer. And since she couldn't tell him the truth, she lied to his face. "No."

"Hmmm."

She waited, but he didn't say anything else. He just watched her, silent and stoic, the gleam in his eye threatening to stretch her nerves to the breaking point. She tried to stare him down, but meeting his gaze was making her even more jittery. With excuses circling in her head and a sinking sensation in her belly that felt alarmingly like disappointment, she started to stand.

She was almost on her feet when he said, "What if I can?"

She sat back down. She had to—her knees had turned to water. "What?"

"What if I can?" he repeated. "What would you give me?"

"Give you?" she repeated, confused. "What, like a trophy?"

"I wouldn't mind a trophy," he mused, the gleam in his eyes still shining bright. "But I had something else in mind."

Don't ask, don't ask, don't ask. Fuck it. "What?" she asked.

"If you do the demo—and you have fun—you owe me a real scene."

"Are you…" He wasn't. He couldn't be. "Are you saying we should make a *bet*?"

"Why not?"

There were several very good reasons why not. The fact that none of them immediately came to mind was immaterial. "That's the most ridiculous idea I've ever heard."

"Why?"

"Because it is," she said, and stuck out her chin. "I'm not doing it."

He shrugged, unperturbed. "All right, then."

"It's juvenile," she told him.

"No question."

"And irresponsible."

"Probably," he agreed.

His tone was so bland she could've used it as wallpaper paste, but his eyes were still glinting and his expression was smug. *Resting Smug Dick Face.* She resolved not to take the bait.

She lasted ten seconds.

"And besides, a bet has to have two parts," she told him.

"True."

"So what happens if you *don't* make it fun?" *Jesus, Sadie, stop talking!*

"I'll owe you a favor of your choice."

That got her attention. "Whatever I want?"

"Within reason," he allowed. "I'm not moving to Antarctica."

She didn't know how to respond to that without possibly crossing the line from sassy to disrespectful, so she ignored it. "I hope you don't think 'fun' equals 'orgasm'."

The smile only deepened. "You don't think orgasms are fun?"

Oh, I am not going there. "You know what I mean."

"Don't worry," he assured her. "I have no intention of getting you off tonight."

She drummed her fingers on her knee, eyes narrowed. "Is that right?"

"It's not a problem if you do," he told her with a wink that made her want to punch him. "But it's not my goal."

"What is your goal?"

"To demonstrate how to take an ordinary household object and turn it into a BDSM toy," he said simply. "And have some fun."

She stared at him, trying to figure his angle. She didn't for a minute think he was sincere about wanting to do a scene with her, which meant this was some kind of power play. She couldn't see the end game, though, and that was unusual. People were transparent, their motives and agendas never as hidden as they thought they were, and most of the time she could see the end game before the first move.

But she couldn't see his.

Clearly unbothered by her narrow-eyed stare, he glanced at the clock on the wall. "Clock's ticking, pet."

"I'm not your pet," she said, keeping the snap out of her tone through sheer effort.

He inclined his head. "Clock's ticking, Sadie. If you're in, we need to get set up for the demo. If you're not, I need to make the announcement that it's canceled."

He held out a hand, palm up. "What's it going to be?"

This is a terrible idea, she told herself, staring at his hand. *Absolutely the worst.* If she had any sense, she'd tell him to eat bees and go sit at the bar to watch Olivia make virgin cocktails until it was time to leave.

And that was exactly what she planned to do, right up until she opened her mouth. "I assume you have rules."

"I have one rule."

"Just one?" If that was true, she'd eat her couch. "What is it?"

"Obey me."

She snorted before she could help it. "That's it?"

"I like to keep it simple." He cocked an eyebrow, hand still extended. "Well?"

She didn't know if he actually meant to sound challenging or if she just took it that way, but either way, the result was the same. She slipped her hand into his, allowing herself to be pulled to her feet.

She saw a brief flare of triumph in his dark eyes, but he only nodded. "Demo starts in fifteen," he said, cool as a cucumber, "so we better get going."

Trapped by her own ego and by his firm, warm grip on her hand, she fell into step beside him and wondered what the hell she was getting herself into.

Chapter Two

Jack strode across the warehouse, Sadie at his side. He didn't need to hold on to her—though she was all but vibrating with energy, he knew she wouldn't run. She'd given her word, not just to him, but to Nikki, and one thing he knew about Sadie Bloom was that she was loyal to a fault, and she kept her promises. She'd made the bet, and she'd follow through no matter how much she was mentally kicking herself for letting her ego override her common sense.

Thank God for competitive subs.

But he liked touching her, so he kept his hand on hers as they wove through the crowd, the light tap of her footsteps echoing his on the concrete. She walked lightly, which he appreciated—most people stomped like elephants without even realizing it—and her steps had an easy rhythm to them. He could picture the movement of her hips in the slight pause between steps, the slow, almost lazy swing of them.

He was most familiar with the rear view. The woman spent an inordinate amount of time walking away from him.

But she was walking with him now and, thanks to a broken ankle, a strong sense of loyalty, and an inability to back down from a challenge, would in very short order be bound and under his hands.

At last.

He'd been wanting to get his hands on her since the first time he'd seen her, looking like a perverted dream come true in her Catholic schoolgirl uniform. She'd worn a crisp white blouse with her tits bursting out, and a skirt so short there was no missing the fact that she hadn't considered panties to be an essential part of the uniform. Her bright hair had been in pigtails, the ends curled to bounce on her shoulders, her lips painted a deep cherry red. But he'd been late to the party, and she'd already found someone to play angry professor to her sassy student. So someone else had left handprints on her ass and left with her cherry-red lip print on his cock.

Thanks to a work schedule that had gone unexpectedly haywire, it had been months before he saw her next. By the time he'd got things under control and started coming to parties again, she'd become an integral part of their kinky little community. An enthusiastic submissive with a fondness for role-play and costumes, she had no shortage of play partners, and seemed happy to go from Dom to Dom and scene to scene. But over the last month or so, he'd suspected she was getting bored. She'd been spending her time at parties socializing instead of playing, and when she did play, she looked more like she was performing than enjoying herself.

He'd debated asking his friends if they knew what was going on but had decided against it. He'd made the mistake a few months back of telling them he felt ready to find a partner and settle down, and the teasing had started up immediately. Which didn't bother him—it was par for the course in a small, insular community like theirs—but the offers to set him up had struck fear into his heart.

The last thing he needed was his friends—or their partners—playing matchmaker. If they knew he was interested in Sadie, speculation would run wild, and he wasn't quite ready to tip his hand yet. To anyone, but especially to Sadie.

He'd spent enough time observing her to see the pattern. She favored hookups, for scenes or sex or both, and shied away from deeper connections—he'd never seen her stick with a romantic partner for more than six weeks. It baffled her friends, and while it could be that she genuinely wanted to stay unattached, he had a different theory.

He could be wrong, of course. He didn't know her well enough to say for sure that it was a fear of genuine intimacy keeping her single. But if he was right, and she had any inkling how much he wanted her, she'd never let him near her.

So he'd bided his time, keeping his eyes peeled for the right opportunity, and it had finally come.

Now, he just had to not fuck it up.

There was already a crowd gathered around the demo area, almost every chair filled. He moved through the throngs, past the ropes that marked off the scene space, and with a gentle tug on her hand, urged her forward.

She dropped his hand and turned in a circle, taking in the setup. There was a rope dangling from a ceiling beam, the leather cuffs attached having been set for Nikki's height. He eyed her boots, noting the high heel, and decided to forgo adjusting them until he had her barefoot.

There was a table set up a few feet away from the cuffs, its surface laden with the items he'd brought to demonstrate. He'd laid them out meticulously in the order he'd planned to use them and covered them with a black sheet. He'd planned to unveil them in a bit of showmanship for the crowd, but now he'd be doing it for Sadie as well.

He bit back a smile when she trailed her fingertips over the sheet, fingers toying with the edge. He saw the quick, side-eye glance she shot his way, the calculation as she weighed her curiosity against the possible consequences of peeking. He had no objection to her looking, but she didn't know that, and basic protocol would dictate that she either ask, or wait for permission.

But Sadie almost never did the expected, so he waited for her to decide.

She held his gaze for a moment, fingering the sheet, then dropped it and turned back to the cuffs. She lifted one, stroking her thumb against the soft leather. "I take it those are for me?"

"Yes." Jack kept his voice mild and controlled with an effort. The surge of excitement he'd felt watching her try to decide whether to be bad or good had him fighting to appear unaffected. "Cade checked out the beam, and it's safe for suspension. Not that we have time for that."

"Thank God."

"You don't like suspension?"

She shrugged and flicked the cuffs, sending them spinning. "I don't know. I've never done it."

"Why is that?"

She turned away from the cuffs. "I have trust issues."

"Hmmm," he said, and bit back a smile when she narrowed her eyes.

"Again with the *hmmm?*" she asked, and he had to swallow another smile at the sardonic bite in her tone.

"It's a good word. Versatile."

"Hmmm," she said, and he laughed.

She turned to face him fully, a look of shock on her face.

"What?"

"Nothing," she squeaked, and cleared her throat. "I just don't think I've ever heard you laugh before."

"Maybe you haven't been paying attention." He jerked his chin at her hand, curled in a loose fist at her side. "What do you have there?"

"Oh." She unfurled her fingers to display the contents. "I wasn't planning to play tonight, and I didn't bring my aftercare kit, so I got one from the bar."

He frowned. "You bring your own aftercare kit?"

"Sure." She jiggled the bag in her hand. "Most Doms have a blanket and a bottle of water ready to go, but sometimes I want something specific. A pair of fuzzy socks, lip balm, good dark chocolate. So, I bring it with me."

"You should tell your play partner what you need," he told her, still frowning. It bothered him that she was supplying her own aftercare. "And they should get it for you."

She shrugged. "I don't have a regular play partner, and most of my scenes are pickups. It's easier to just bring what I need."

"Trust issues," she'd said. Making a mental note to revisit that statement, he held out a hand. "I'll put it with the blanket and the bottle of water."

Her lips twitched, and she took the two steps necessary to put it in his hand. "I know you said you only have one rule, but I'd feel better if you gave me some guidelines for this."

He crossed to the table and placed it on top of the toy bag he had stashed beneath. "Fair enough. I want you naked with your hair out of the way."

The way she blinked told him the order took her off guard, but she reached for the trio of small buttons holding her dress together without hesitation. "I don't have anything to put it up with."

He always kept elastics on hand for himself—he didn't like his hair in his face when he played—so he crouched and reached into his bag. He rose to his feet just as she peeled the dress off her shoulders and tossed it aside.

He shook his head when he saw the details on the pasties covering her nipples. "Only you."

"What?" She glanced down at herself, delight lighting her expression. "Aren't they awesome?"

"Where did you even find pasties shaped like spiders?"

"I didn't," she confessed, and tossed the hat after her dress. "They're just regular stickers with body glue added to hold them in place. I glued the googly eyes on, too."

"Inventive," he drawled, and watched her breasts sway—and the googly eyes jiggle—as she bent forward to peel off her boots.

"I like costumes," she said, grunting a little as she tugged first one, then the other boot off and tossed them aside.

"I noticed." He twirled a finger in the air. "Turn, please."

She wanted to roll her eyes—he could tell—but she simply turned to give him her back.

She was in good shape, muscles flexing subtly under soft white skin. She had a smattering of freckles across her shoulders, and a small cluster decorating her left buttock, bared by the G-string. He eyed her ass critically, his mind on the impact toys he'd planned to demonstrate. It was firm and round, as were her thighs, and her hips…

"I'm going to put my hands on you," he warned her, and reached out to cup her hips. They were nicely padded, the bones shielded by a good layer of muscle and fat, and he grunted with satisfaction. He slid his hands down her legs to feel the muscles there, pausing when she shivered.

"Are you cold?" he asked mildly, careful to keep the satisfaction out of his voice. The room was warm, and though he had more muscle mass than she did—and more clothes—he didn't think her reaction had anything to do with the temperature.

"No," she said, and twitched again under his hands. "Just a little ticklish."

"That's not the kind of thing you should say to a sadist," he advised, his amusement deepening.

She snorted. "Good note."

His eyes were locked on her ass. That little cluster of freckles was vaguely heart shaped, and he gave into the urge to trace his thumb over them. "Are you okay with non-penetrative genital contact?"

"That's fine." She twisted around, peering over her shoulder at him. "Is there something wrong with my ass?"

"Nope." He lingered for a heartbeat more before dropping his hands and stepping back. "Continue, please."

She turned back around and hooked her thumbs in the thin strings over her hips. She shoved the panties down and off with brisk efficiency that shouldn't have been the least bit enticing. And the sight of her naked was nothing new—it was actually far more rare to see her clothed. But when she tossed the panties on top of her boots and dress and reached for the pasties, he couldn't help but stare.

Her tits were round, her pussy waxed bare, and every inch of her looked so damn soft, he just wanted to sink his teeth into her.

"Ow," she muttered, pulling his attention back to her face. She was tugging at the sticker on her left breast and wincing. It clung to her skin, clearly unwilling to let go.

He couldn't blame it.

"Want a hand?" he asked.

"I've got it," she muttered, and gave it a solid yank. It came free, leaving behind dried glue and reddened, puffy skin. She grabbed the other one firmly, ripping it off with one swift motion.

Her nipples were a pale pinkish brown—the same color as those beguiling freckles—and looked as soft as the rest of her until she began rubbing at them. "Sore?"

"Itchy," she replied, and peeled a small string of dried adhesive from her skin. "I used too much glue."

Her nipples were pebbling, their color deepening when she rubbed harder. "Do you need something to get it off?"

She bent her head to examine her nipples and her hair fell forward, partially obscuring his view. "No, I think I got it all."

"Good." Her hair slid over her skin, pink gold against porcelain. Reminding himself that staring was bad manners—and that he was on the clock—he held out the hair ties he'd dug out of his bag. "Two braids, please."

Her eyes—hazel now, though he knew they could just as easily appear brown—glanced around as she sectioned her hair and began to braid. "Tell me about the demo."

"It's a little bit of everything. A lot of impact and bondage, wax, clamps. Any issues there?"

"No, that's all fine."

"What about gags or blindfolds?"

"Fine," she said, then stopped, her fingers pausing in her hair. "Wait, you're going to gag *and* blindfold me?"

"I'm going to demonstrate several ways to do both with common, inexpensive items," he corrected. "But you won't stay that way."

"Oh." She resumed braiding. "Okay."

"We don't have time for a thorough negotiation, but is there anything you specifically want off the table?"

She finished the first braid and wound the elastic around the end. "Minor bruising or light marks are fine, but I don't want anything heavy or long lasting."

He skimmed his gaze down her body again. Her skin was pale, but she played regularly enough that it would probably take some effort to raise a bruise. "Do you mark easily?"

She began to separate her hair for the second braid. "My ass and thighs, no. Non-impact zones will bruise easier."

He nodded, filing the information away. "Any past traumas I need to know about, physical injuries or impairments?"

"I rolled my right ankle a few months ago, and sitting on it still hurts sometimes. Other than that, no."

He glanced at her feet, pale and freckled with sparkly orange toenails, and made a mental note to put a pair of fuzzy socks in his toy bag. "You won't be kneeling. Will ankle cuffs be a problem?"

"Shouldn't be."

"What's your safeword?"

"I use the stoplight system. Green for good, yellow for slow down and check in, red for stop."

"Use them if you need to. I'll be talking to the audience a lot, telling them what I'm doing and why. I'm going to be checking in with you, but if anything is too much, don't wait to tell me."

She began weaving the second braid. "Okay. Is that it?"

"No. I want the audience to see how you react, so don't be afraid to be vocal."

She slipped the elastic over the end of the braid. "Can I swear at you?"

He cocked an eyebrow. "Do you usually swear at your Dom?"

"Sometimes." She tossed the braid over her shoulder and planted her hands on her hips. "When it fits the scene."

"Hmmm."

"Is that a yes?"

"That's a 'you can do whatever you want, but there will likely be consequences'," he replied.

Her eyes went round. "Well, duh. That's why I do it."

He fought back a grin. "You know, your mouth is going to get you into trouble one of these days."

"I keep hearing that," she drawled, her lips turning up in a smile that matched the gleam in her eyes. "But everybody around here seems to be all hat and no cattle."

His lips twitched at the phrase. He would've been happy to show her just what kind of trouble she was courting, but time was running short. He gathered up her clothes and tucked them under the edge of the table with his toy bag. "One of these days," he warned again, and held out a hand. "Ready?"

She nodded, the ends of her braids brushing against her breasts. "Ready, boss," she said with an impish twinkle in her eye and slipped her hand into his.

He led her to the edge of the roped-off section. The crowd immediately began to quiet, the folks that had been milling around returning to their chairs, and within thirty seconds everyone was seated, their attention squarely on him.

"Wow," Sadie breathed. "I gotta learn how to do that."

He gave her hand a warning squeeze. "Welcome, everyone," he said, pitching his voice to the last row. "My name is Jack, and I'll be giving tonight's presentation. The lovely woman next to me is Sadie, and it's her I'll be presenting on."

Laughter ran through the crowd, and Sadie curtseyed with a smile and a rapid flutter of eyelashes.

"This demo is about pervertables—those everyday objects and items that can be repurposed for kinky fun. BDSM toys and equipment can be expensive, and while there are definitely areas where you should make sure to buy quality, dedicated equipment, everything I'll be using today was purchased from grocery stores, all-purpose retailers like Walmart or Target, hardware stores, and even the dollar store. You can have a lot of fun without spending a fortune, and that's what this demo is about. So let's get started."

With Sadie's hand still in his, he turned to walk to the center of the platform, pleased when she allowed him to lead her into position under the dangling cuffs, facing away from the audience. "Arms up, please, Sadie."

She obeyed, and he buckled first one cuff then the other around her wrists. As he'd suspected, there was too much slack in the rope, so he gathered up the slack and tied it off few inches above her wrists. She still had enough room to bend her elbows and rest her arms, but her wrists weren't sitting on her head anymore.

He ran a finger between the cuff and her soft skin. "Cuffs feel okay?"

She flexed her arms and wiggled her fingers, testing the restraints. "They're good."

"All right. Let me know if anything starts to pinch, or if your arms need a break."

"Yes, Boss," she quipped.

"Brat," he shot back, but he was smiling when he turned back to the audience.

"First up," he announced. "Impact toys."

Sadie lost track of the number of things he hit her with. Rulers, wooden spoons, spatulas, belts, cutting boards, a shoe—she was pretty sure she'd be sporting the tread from his size twelves on her ass for the next few days—and a miniature souvenir St. Louis Cardinals baseball bat were on the list. He used a handful of zip ties as a makeshift cat-o'-nine-tails on the backs of her thighs, and an electric fly swatter on her ass. The sting from that had put her on her toes, squealing and dancing to escape the biting sparks. The audience had laughed along with Jack, and his deep rumble had launched a fleet of butterflies in her belly.

He tickled the sensitive skin on the backs of her knees with a feather duster, then rubbed the coarse bristles of a dollar-store hairbrush against her skin for contrast. He put a plastic chair mat on the floor upside down and made her stand on the little plastic spikes. She cursed at him when he did that, because he'd put a sleep mask over her eyes first so she couldn't see it coming, and the 'you bastard' just slipped out. But he'd just laughed, the rich chuckle sending the butterflies dancing again. Even his declaration that the mat would remain as punishment for her insolence had been delivered with amusement, throwing her so off balance she'd almost forgotten to curse him again.

By the time he turned her around to face the audience, she was floating on a sea of endorphins. Even the plastic spikes under her feet weren't awful, and she normally *hated* having her feet played with. In fact, she was a little disappointed when Jack knelt in front of her to remove it.

He glanced up at her, his dark eyes assessing, and after a moment a little smile curled his lips. "Step wide," he told her, and she obeyed, adjusting her stance so he could pull the mat from between her feet. But when she started to bring her feet together again, he tapped her leg.

"Stay put," he ordered, then stood and grabbed something long and black from his prop table.

"This isn't something I picked up at Walmart," he began, holding the object up for the audience. She squinted, trying to see what it was, but the light was in her eyes. "But all the components—except for the cuffs—were sourced at the hardware store. PVC pipe, a length of chain, and two carabiners. There are other ways to make a spreader bar, and a lot of commercially available ones that are very reasonably priced. But this is simple to put together, and I don't know about you, but I like to hear the rattle of chains."

The audience laughed, but Sadie's eyes were locked on Jack as he knelt in front of her again, the spreader bar in one hand and a set of thick cuffs in the other. He dropped the bar between her feet and wrapped her right ankle in the soft, supple leather, thickly padded to provide ample cushion between her skin and the hard edge of the PVC. He checked the fit and gave the D-ring a testing tug before moving on to her left ankle. With the second cuff secured, he lifted the pipe and snapped the carabiners into the D-rings.

"Anything pinching, pulling, uncomfortable?"

She took her eyes off the bar, which looked impossibly sexy between her widespread bare feet, and looked at him. He was still kneeling, a traditionally submissive position that didn't detract at all from the aura of power he wore like skin. He'd tied his hair back and opened a few more buttons on his shirt, and the medallion he wore around his neck glinted dully against the bronze skin of his chest.

He had no business looking that good on his knees, and she had no business noticing that he looked that good.

"Sadie?" he prompted, and she refocused on his face, his forehead furrowed in concern. "How does it feel?"

Sexy, she thought.

"Suspicious," she said.

Amusement lit his eyes, and his low chuckle mingled with the laughter from the audience.

"Clever little submissive." He rose and stepped to the table that held all his treasures. He picked up a package of...was that...?

"These are hair clips," he said, holding the package up to the audience. "They're small, and as you can probably guess by the pink sparkles and unicorn shape, designed for children. They're not meant to hold a lot of hair, so they're not strong enough to work as, say, a nipple clamp. But there are other areas where I find them to be charmingly useful."

He pulled the hair clips off the cardboard placard holding them, one by one, until he held all eight of the glittery pink clamshell clips in one hand. Then he got on his knees in front of her again.

"Oh, balls," she said, and his delighted laughter rang out.

"Deep breath, now," he advised, and without giving her any time to obey, attached a clip to her labia.

The small plastic teeth bit into the tender flesh, and she flinched at the sharp discomfort. But the spring on the clip wasn't strong enough for it to clamp down very hard, and after a moment that first pinching sting faded. She sighed with relief, then realized what she'd done.

"Oh, shit," she said, and looked down into Jack's laughing eyes.

"Well, I think that means we can do the rest," he enthused, and picked up another clip.

He put three on one side and three on the other, watching her face carefully. Sadie concentrated on breathing through the initial pinch of pain and riding the wave of arousal as it faded into a spreading warmth. The first hadn't hurt too much, but the cumulative effect of five more clips was more intense than she'd expected, and more arousing. Eyes watering and heart pounding, she tilted her head back and tried to ride it out.

When she looked down again, Jack was watching. He searched her face for a moment, and whatever he found must have pleased him. He relaxed, some of the intensity fading from his expression, and a glimmer of a smile reappeared. He shifted, angling his body to half face the audience.

"Two left," he said, and holding her gaze, arched an eyebrow. "I wonder where they should go?"

"Oh, no." She shook her head, the ends of her braids bouncing across her chest.

"No? Are you sure?"

"Very sure," she said firmly, scowling at the audience when they erupted into a chorus of disagreement. "Hey, whose side are you all on?"

Jeers and cheers erupted, and Jack's eyebrows went up. "I think they're on my side."

"Don't do it," she warned, swallowing the laugh. She wiggled to try to get away, but the spreader bar kept her from being able to move her feet, and the wiggling made the clips already attached to her pussy shift and pinch, and with her hands cuffed she couldn't push him away. All she could do was watch with increasing trepidation and rising excitement as he picked up a clip, pinched it open, and aimed it at her clit.

"No, no, don't you dare, don't you—" The rest of her words died in a yelp when he let the clip go, the sharp little prongs digging in on either side of her clit, trapping the engorged nub in a tiny plastic cage.

"Fucking sadist," she managed between pants, not caring that she was cussing him out in front of a full house.

"True," he said cheerfully and rose to his feet. "But you knew that."

She didn't bother to respond, the pressure on her clit taking all her focus. Then he held up the last clip, angling it so the light bounced off the glittery unicorn horn.

"Duct tape is one of my favorite things to use as a gag," he said, keeping his eyes on hers. "But it has drawbacks. Skin damage is the main one, and you can work around that by adding a thin layer of lotion or Vaseline to your partner's skin to protect it. It won't stick as well, of course, but that's the trade off."

Distracted by what was happening between her legs—the sharpness had faded to a throb, accompanied by a wonderful pressure and a spreading heat—she wondered dimly why he was talking about duct tape when he was holding a hair clip.

"Now, I'm a sadist, so I don't normally mind taking a bit of skin off," he went on. "But sometimes it's just not practical. So if you want to gag your submissive without leaving marks—or removing a layer or two of skin—there are other options. A scarf, a bandana. Using a piece of your or your submissive's clothing, like a necktie or a pair of stockings, can be especially erotic. Or even…"

He paused, and the smile that curved his lips was so joyfully sadistic it had warning bells clanging in Sadie's head. "A hair clip. Open wide."

Her mouth had gone bone-dry. "You are kidding."

"'Fraid not." He tapped her chin with the clip. "I'm only going to ask one more time. Open up, please."

In spite of the please—or maybe because of it—the warning came through loud and clear. She'd either open her mouth, or he'd open it for her. With no other choice, and with her throbbing clit reminding her just how precarious her position was, she parted her lips.

"Good girl. Now, stick out your tongue."

Eyes narrowed, and muttering curses under her breath, she obeyed, and he slipped the last clip onto the tip of her tongue.

It didn't hurt, at least not much, but to keep from knocking it off, she had to keep her tongue out, and that was both awkward and annoying. The clip wasn't strong—a sharp flick of her tongue would send it flying, and she was tempted to do just that. But she knew if she knocked it off, he'd just put something else there.

"You motherfucker," she muttered, only it came out sounding like *oo mudda puppa,* which unfortunately for her, wasn't quite garbled enough.

Jack cocked his head, eyes gleaming. "Sorry, what was that?"

She hesitated a moment, her self-preservation instincts warring with her sense of humor, then she thought, *oh, what the hell.* "Oo. Mudda. Puppa," she repeated slowly, throwing caution to the wind and tugging the tiger's—or in this case, the sadist's—tail.

"That's what I thought you said," he replied, his lips curving into a smile that she felt all the way to her toes. And in certain parts along the way that she was currently doing her best to ignore.

"If you're going to gag your partner," he said, pitching his voice to the audience, "you'll want to make sure they still have a way to safeword. So Sadie's safeword is now three hoots. Demonstrate for our friends, please."

Feeling ridiculous, and with embarrassment and arousal warming her cheeks, Sadie let out three short hoots.

"Thank you, Sadie," Jack said, lips twitching, and turned to stride to the table that held all his bargain torture devices. "Now, as I said, the hair clips don't make very good nipple clamps. But I've got something else that does."

Son of a bitch, Sadie thought, and with her pussy throbbing and her tongue going dry, braced herself for more.

Jack glanced at the clock, then refocused on Sadie. Her left nipple sported a wooden clothespin, and the right was trapped between two wooden chopsticks held in place by the elastic hair bands he'd wound around the ends. He'd placed a dozen smaller, plastic clothespins on the tender undersides of her breasts, and used a wooden yard stick to flick them off.

Her screams, though garbled, had been highly satisfying. And though it had been a bit difficult to decipher with the hair clip still on the end of her tongue, he was certain he'd heard the phrase "dick weasel". He gave her points for inventiveness, and an extra flick of the yardstick as a reward.

The tiny red marks left behind by the clothespins weren't the only indignity her breasts had suffered. One of them was reddened and swollen from repeated slaps of a miniature spatula, and wax clung to the smooth slope of the other, dripped from the single candle he'd lit to splash onto her skin.

She'd squealed when he'd done that, squirming and writhing so the chain in the spreader bar rattled while her eyes shot fire. They'd changed colors like a chameleon as he'd worked her over, going from hazel to brown to green and back to hazel, and watching them change with each new sensation had been unexpectedly fascinating.

They were a soft hazel now, and still spitting fire. Her skin was flushed, her breathing slightly ragged, and her mouth was no doubt dry with the clip on her tongue. He was surprised it was still there, as he'd have bet money on her flicking it off immediately. The fact that she hadn't pleased him enormously.

If he'd thought to negotiate it beforehand, he would've rewarded her with an orgasm.

Since he hadn't, he put the idea out of his mind and turned his attention to the table. He'd demonstrated almost every tool he'd brought on her, from feathers to zip ties, and the only things he hadn't were the ones he'd brought only to show the audience. Tiger Balm, a finger of ginger root, plus a few other things that could wreak havoc on the delicate mucous membranes of a pussy or anus. Nikki hadn't been comfortable with that level of exposure, and though he'd thought about including them for Sadie, he'd decided to stick with the original plan and simply explained the various ways to use them.

Though when he'd peeled the ginger with his pocketknife, her mumbled threats and fierce glare had been so entertaining that he deeply regretted that it was going back into his crisper drawer instead of her asshole.

He laid a hand on her lower back, wanting the connection of touch. Her skin was damp and warm, muscles rippling under her skin. The signs of arousal were there in her flushed cheeks and dilated pupils. He could attribute the hardness of her nipples to the implements currently attached to them, but the gleam of wetness on her thighs was an unmistakable sign that even the most novice of Doms couldn't miss.

The urge to continue was strong. He wanted to draw it out, give her a little pain, a little pleasure, increasing the intensity each time to see how much she could take. To push her right to the edge of what she thought she could handle, then hold her tight as he eased her over it, so he could feel every shudder and jerk, every pulse and throb of pain, of pleasure that wound through her.

But they hadn't negotiated a scene, and he was out of time.

"Our time together is about up," Jack said to the audience and savored the flash of disappointment in Sadie's eyes. "I hope you enjoyed the demonstration, and thank you all for coming. I'm going to get Sadie undone and settled with a snack, then I'll be happy to answer any questions you might have. Even if you don't have questions, I'd recommend sticking around for a minute. This is the fun part."

He turned to face Sadie, delighted with the suspicion in her narrowed gaze, and reached for the clip on her tongue. "Coming off," he warned and popped it free with one quick movement.

She winced, pulling her tongue back into her mouth and working her jaw.

"All right?" he asked.

"No," she mumbled, her shining eyes defying the grumpy tone, and licked her lips. "Need water."

He bit back a chuckle at the garbled demand. "Let me get the rest of this off you first."

He didn't wait for her acquiescence before reaching down and without warning, plucking the clothespin off her nipple. Her eyes flared briefly with relief, then the pain came flooding in as the blood rushed back into the tortured little nub. She yanked at her hands, instinctively trying to reach for the pain to rub it out. But she was still cuffed, so all she could do was writhe and mumble curses.

Enjoying himself, he removed the chopsticks from her other nipple, and this time she let out a muffled scream.

He crouched to deal with the hair clips on her labia. Half of them were already gone, unable to stand up to all the wiggling, and he quickly removed the rest. Ignoring her squirming, he ran his fingertips over her to assess the damage. She was slick with arousal, and though the clips had left little dents in the tender flesh, they hadn't caused any real damage.

He plucked the last clip from around her clit. It was engorged, and he was tempted to slide his finger through the wetness coating her labia and give it a stroke.

Forcing himself to focus on the task at hand, he unclipped the carabiners from the cuffs at her ankles, pulled the spreader bar out of the way and rose to his feet.

Her cheeks were even more flushed now, and the loss of the spreader bar had her wobbling. He wrapped one arm around her waist to hold her steady, then flicked open the quick release hooks on her wrist cuffs and drew her arms carefully down.

She swayed and reached out with one hand to grab the collar of his shirt. "Whoa."

He cupped her cheek, tilting her face up so he could see her eyes. "Talk to me, Sadie."

She blinked up at him. "That hurt, you sadist."

"You're welcome," he told her, and laughed when her eyes lit. He scooped her up, ignoring the way she went stiff with surprise, and carried her a few feet away. He lowered her to a seated position on the floor, bracing her back against his bent knee, then picked the blanket up off the top of his toy bag and draped it around her shoulders. When she grabbed the ends, he picked up the water bottle, unscrewed the top, and handed it to her.

She snorted. "See? Bottle of water and a blanket."

"Smart ass," he chided, and tapped the bottle. "Drink."

"Bossy," she shot back, and tipped the bottle to her lips.

"Hold the water in your mouth for a second before swallowing," he instructed. "It'll help your tongue feel better."

She obeyed, her eyes sparkling at him. "You put a unicorn hair clip on my tongue."

He smiled at the accusation. "I did."

"It was pink. And sparkly."

He didn't bother to hide his delight. "It was."

She ran her tongue around her teeth. "I have glitter in my mouth."

"Well, what do you expect from dollar-store hair clips?" he asked, and tsked with exaggerated disapproval when she stuck her tongue out at him. "That's not the kind of behavior that gets rewarded with chocolate."

"I was just showing you," she said, her eyes going innocently wide.

"Uh-huh." He picked up the baggie and offered it. "Is that the story you want to stick with?"

She worked an arm free of the blanket and reached into the bag, digging out a few almonds. "Yes."

He looked her over while she munched the snack, searching for signs of a post-scene crash. Her color was good, her eyes bright, and she was having no trouble holding the water or feeding herself—or plotting revenge for the hair clip, if the look in her eye was anything to go by.

He'd expect nothing less.

He scanned the rest of her. The blanket had slipped down on one side, baring her breast and the candle wax that still decorated the smooth slope almost to the nipple. "Looks like I missed something," he remarked mildly, and reached out to peel it away. The marks left behind were bright pink against her pale skin, and he traced them with one finger, noting the increase in warmth where the wax had been. "Does it hurt?"

"No."

Her voice was tight and strained, and he lifted his gaze to her face. She'd gone still, the almond she'd been bringing to her lips forgotten in her hand, and her eyes were heavy. He shifted to cup her breast, holding the weight in his palm, and stroked his thumb over the largest of the marks. "You sure?"

"Do you want it to hurt?"

"Little bit, yeah."

"Maybe it stings a little," she admitted in a voice gone raspy with arousal.

He stroked his thumb over the mark again, slowly, just to watch her eyes darken. Then he forced himself to pull away and reached for his bag. "I've got a burn gel that should help."

"I have some in my aftercare kit."

"You didn't bring it," he reminded her, and held up the tube. "May I?"

"Um. Sure."

He cupped her breast again to hold it steady and smoothed a thin layer of gel over the small burns. She was still under his touch, like a small prey animal trying not to draw attention to itself. But she couldn't quell the pulse fluttering in her throat, or the way her nipple went from soft and pale to tight and flushed. And when he could linger no longer and dropped his hands, the breath she let out sounded suspiciously like disappointment.

"All done," he announced, and tossed the tube of gel back into his bag. "Any other ouchies that need attending to?"

"No," she squeaked, and he knew she was in rough shape when she didn't smirk at him for saying *ouchies.*

"You sure? The clothespin was pretty tight on your nipple." He tapped the nipple in question, watching her face carefully. She jerked slightly at the contact, her breath catching and her eyes flaring in either pain or pleasure. Maybe both. "Sore?"

"Some," she said in a thin and throaty rasp. "Nothing I can't handle."

"Hmm." He traced a finger around it gently, watching the areola pucker even further before nudging the blanket aside to expose her other breast. "What about this one? I didn't tighten the chopsticks as much as I could have."

"It's fine."

He knew she didn't mean it as a challenge, but he had a hard time not taking it as one. Promising himself that there would be plenty of time to test both of their limits later, he shifted his attention to the tiny little welts on the undersides of her breasts, their edges already turning blue. "These will bruise," he told her, and skimmed his fingertips over them. Her breath hitched at his touch, making her breasts bounce lightly. "Some anti-bruising cream will help."

"I have some at home," she said, and he nodded. He had a tube in his bag, but he still had a Q&A session to get through, and he'd probably pushed her enough for one night.

"I'm going to go do the Q&A. Finish the water, and the almonds, then you can have the chocolate."

A spark of her usual defiance joined the arousal in her eyes. "It's cute that you think you're in charge."

"It's cute that you think I'm not," he countered and tapped the end of her nose in admonishment. When her mouth dropped open in surprise, he turned and walked back to the crowd. Most of the audience had dispersed, but a good dozen people remained. He snagged an empty chair and turned it around to straddle it. Forcing Sadie to the back of his mind, he smiled. "Thank you for your patience, everyone. Are there any questions?"

Chapter Three

Sadie almost decided to skip the nuts and go right to the chocolate, just to see what he'd do. The demo had left her feeling edgy, aroused and restless, and she was tempted to push it. But she wanted the protein, and Jack made her just nervous enough to hesitate. So she dutifully finished her water and all the nuts, then dug out the first piece of chocolate.

She rolled it around in her mouth, savoring the bittersweet flavor as she watched him take questions from the small group that had remained. She was too far away to hear what anyone was saying, but she could read body language well enough. He was attentive, listening to questions with focus and answering with an easy smile, Resting Dick Face nowhere in sight. He looked relaxed, a state she envied.

She was too horny to relax.

She reached for another piece of chocolate and tried to ignore all the places on her body that wished the demo wasn't over. Her breasts felt heavy and tender, her pussy swollen and slick. She had little twinges and throbs on her thighs, back, and butt from all the slaps and smacks and hits—even her feet were sensitized from standing on the plastic mat, and it annoyed her to realize she didn't hate it. Her whole body buzzed with arousal, and since she wasn't in the mood to put on a show, she was going to have to wait until she got home to do anything about it.

And on top of that, she'd lost the bet.

"Who knew Resting Dick Face had it in him?" she muttered and shoved the last piece of chocolate into her mouth.

"Who had what in them?" Jack asked.

She squeaked in surprise, nearly choking on the chocolate, and scrambled to her feet. And promptly tripped over his toy bag.

"Whoa." Jack reached out to steady her. "Easy."

She shook her foot to dislodge the strap she'd stepped in and swallowed the chocolate before clearing her throat. "I'm fine. Q&A over?"

"All done." He kept his hand on her elbow. "You okay?"

"I'm fine," she repeated, and tried to ignore how warm and firm his hand felt on her arm. "Um. Did you see where my clothes went?"

"I've got them." He dropped her elbow and crouched, reaching under the table and pulling out a neatly folded bundle of clothing. He dropped it onto his toy bag, then plucked her dress from the pile and stood, looking at her expectantly.

"What?"

"Don't you want to put this on?" he asked, holding the dress out.

"Oh." Feeling foolish, she put her right arm through the sleeve, then the left. He lifted the garment into place, smoothing his hands across her shoulders.

Warmth seeped through the thin, diaphanous material and made her want to sink back into him.

"Get it together, Bloom," she muttered, and rolled her shoulders so his hands dropped away.

"What was that?"

"Nothing," she said, and keeping her back to him, reached for the trio of fasteners. "Thank you."

"You're welcome." He stepped around her to reach for the pile and came up with her panties in his hand. "Do you want to put these back on?"

"If I don't, I'll have to hold them for the rest of the night." She gestured to her dress. "It's not like I have pockets."

"Good point," he said, but when she reached for the G-string, he slid smoothly to his knees in front of her. "Step in."

"I can do it myself," she protested.

"I know," he said, and waited.

Stuck, she lifted a foot. "This feels weird."

"Does it?"

"You're on your knees," she pointed out, wobbling a little.

"So? Put your hand on my shoulder for balance," he ordered.

She obeyed, trying not to notice how his shoulder felt under her hand—hard and warm and more than capable of holding up her ankles, an image that popped into her head and did nothing to make her feel any steadier—and slipped her foot into the leg hole. "You don't feel submissive on your knees like that?"

"I never feel submissive, because I'm not," he replied. "Do you feel dominant right now?"

She slipped her other foot into the panties, his shoulder hard under her hand and his breath warm against her thighs. "Not exactly."

"There you go." He slid the panties up her legs. She winced when they scraped over her tenderized butt. "Sore?"

"A little," she told him and took a step back.

He stayed on his knees. "So? What'd you think?"

She was off balance, edgy and aroused, and spoke before she could think better of it. "What do you want, a review?"

"Sure," he said, and smiled. "It'll help me plan our next scene."

She stared down at him and struggled to think. Her mind felt like it was full of cotton candy, and he was still on his knees, which wasn't helping. "Next scene?"

"You owe me one, don't you? If you had fun." His eyes were dancing as he picked up one of her boots and held it out. "Want some help with these?"

She just stared at him, for once in her life genuinely speechless.

His smile spread, waking up the butterflies in her belly. "Give me your right foot."

She complied, watching the light play in his hair as he worked the boot over her foot and zipped it up. When he reached for the second boot and held out a hand, one eyebrow raised in demand, she gave him her left foot without a word.

He slid the boot on and zipped it, his touch no more personal than a shoe salesman's, and rose smoothly to his feet. "So?"

She slipped the elastic off the end of one braid and began to unwind it, just to give herself something to do. "I had a…not terrible time."

"Please, you'll turn my head with such effusive praise."

His tone was so dry she snorted out a laugh before she could stop herself. "Okay, it was fun."

"There now, was that so hard?"

You have no idea. "I guess I owe you a scene."

"I guess you do. One week."

"For what?" she asked, going to work on the second braid, then froze. "Wait. You want to play in a week?"

"We're going to play in a week," he corrected. "Saturday night, my place."

"Hold on," she began, and frowned when he flipped a business card out of his pocket and held it out. "What's this?"

"My email. Send me your limits list—a current one," he amended when she just stared at him. "By Wednesday."

"That's not a week," she protested weakly.

"I need time to go over it," he reminded her. "We'll negotiate in person, too, but the list will give me a starting point."

She stared at the card, held between his fingers, and struggled to think. A week wasn't enough time. And at his place? "I don't play privately with new people."

He looked pointedly at the pile of toys he'd used on her during the demo. "I'm hardly new."

"This doesn't count."

"No?" He cocked his head, his smile going smug. "Your pussy was awfully wet for something that doesn't count."

She bit her tongue to keep from snapping back. If she denied it, she'd just look foolish. "I'm not playing with you alone."

He nodded, serious now. "All right. Who do you trust to play DM?"

"James."

"And if he's not available?"

"Nick," she decided. "Or Cade. If none of them can do it, you're shit out of luck. And I'm not coming to your house."

He shrugged. "I don't mind coming to yours."

"Oh, hell no," she blurted out, panicked at the thought of him in her cozy apartment. "Neutral ground."

He eyed her for a moment, considering, then nodded. "I'll handle it." He bent to pick up her hat, tucking the card he still held under the ribbon circling the brim before setting it on her head. "By Wednesday, Sadie."

She wanted to say *Or what?* But she was afraid she wouldn't like the answer. She took a step back, unable to help herself, and could only be grateful she didn't stumble. Her legs still felt wobbly, and the last thing she needed was him having to catch her.

He watched her for a moment, dark eyes assessing. For a moment she thought he'd reach for her and braced herself. But he didn't. He simply smiled, a full smile that showed teeth and dimples and eye crinkles, then picked up his toy bag. "Thanks for filling in. I know Nikki appreciated it."

"Nikki is very welcome," she said, emphasizing *Nikki*.

"I appreciated it, too," he said, unperturbed. "I'll show you how much on Saturday."

And with one last eye-crinkling smile, he turned and walked away.

"Well, shit."

She stared after him until he'd disappeared into the crowd, then dragged the hat off her head with a huff. The card fell off, fluttering down to land at her feet.

Curious, she bent to scoop it up. The plain white cardstock had his name in simple black print on the front, and nothing else. Frowning, she turned it over. There was a phone number, and an email address.

"Jack at RestingDickFace dot net," she read aloud, and laughed until she thought she'd pee her pants.

Chapter Four

She put it out of her mind.

On Sunday, Sadie skipped family dinner at her parents' house in favor of takeout Chinese and worked up a budget for the home improvements she'd been considering. Most of her regular massage clients preferred that she come to them, but enough wanted to come to her that it made sense to spruce up her single bathroom to give it a more spa-like feel, and to turn her tiny second bedroom into a dedicated treatment room.

Working the numbers—and hauling her desk and file cabinets out of the small bedroom and rearranging the rest of her furniture to make room for it—took up most of the day. The result was a slightly more cluttered than was comfortable living room, but she gained a seat with the addition of the desk chair, and it wasn't like she needed room for dancing.

Drinking, yes—dancing, no.

On Monday morning she had her two early morning, start-the-work-week-off-right massage clients, then she went to the hardware store to look at paint chips. She narrowed her choices down to two and bought a sample quart of each before heading back out to meet a new client. It was the only other thing on her calendar for the day, but first appointments always ran long. There was paperwork to fill out, and the getting to know you chatter always ate up more time than it should. Sadie didn't mind—the more information she got about a client's lifestyle, the better, and sometimes things popped up in casual conversation that they just didn't think to mention on the assessment form.

After the appointment, she went home and scarfed down a peanut butter and jelly sandwich—she really needed to remember to hit a grocery store or she was going to be down to hot water and bouillon cubes—then started prepping the walls in the newly cleared-out bedroom for paint.

With the walls washed and wiped down, she dug out a brush and painted a swatch of each sample to compare side by side. She was trying to decide which she liked better, the warm, pale gold with shimmery undertones or the light blue-green that reminded her of the ocean when she heard a knock on her door.

Wiping her hands on the too-many-holes-to-wear-in-public yoga pants she kept around for cleaning days, she headed for the front door. Her stomach rumbled, the peanut butter and jelly long gone, and she was contemplating her takeout options when she opened the door.

Olivia, Rebecca and Nikki stood there, Nikki balanced on a pair of crutches and Olivia and Rebecca each holding a paper sack.

"What are you all doing here?" Sadie asked, her nose twitching at the scent wafting from the sacks. "Is that Phở?"

Olivia sent Rebecca a smug look. "I told you."

"Told her what?" Sadie asked, her attention on the takeout. Her stomach growled so loud it echoed in the hallway.

Rebecca stepped forward, handed the bag she held to Sadie, and headed for the kitchen. "She told me if we brought Phở you'd let us in."

"I'd let you in for Hot Pockets," Sadie called after her. "I haven't been to the grocery store in two weeks."

"Where are your bowls?" Rebecca called back from the kitchen.

"Cabinet above the fridge." Sadie eyed Nikki, swinging forward on her crutches. "Looks like you're getting the hang of those things."

"Yeah." Nikki smiled. "But my armpits hurt."

"And the ankle?"

"Sore, but better."

"Good. Go sit." Sadie shut the door and turned to see Rebecca coming back from the kitchen, her hands full.

"I found wine," she announced, and set the bottle and a large bowl on the coffee table.

"Did you find glasses, or should we just pass the bottle around?" Olivia wanted to know.

"Keep your pants on," Rebecca said, and trooped back to the kitchen.

Sadie dropped her bag on the coffee table next to the bowl then crossed the room to grab her desk chair. She wheeled it over in front of Nikki, now sitting on the sofa. "Here, prop your foot up."

"It's fine," Nikki began.

"Don't argue." Olivia said, unpacking the takeout. "Or I'm not giving you your salad rolls."

"That's just mean," Nikki complained, but lifted her booted foot onto the chair.

Rebecca came back in with glasses. "Somebody pour the wine. I'm going back for napkins."

"Get me a spoon too, will you?" Sadie asked, and reached for the open bottle of red. She glanced at Nikki. "Are you still on pain pills?"

"Yes, and don't worry." She pulled a bottle of sparkling water from her shoulder bag. "I'm not drinking."

"What about you?" Sadie asked Olivia.

"One glass. I'm driving." Olivia finished unloading the food and set the bags aside. "Did you rearrange the furniture in here? It looks different."

Sadie handed Olivia a glass of wine and gestured to the corner where the desk now lived. "I moved the stuff out of my office so I can turn it into a massage room."

Rebecca returned with a handful of napkins and a spoon. "That explains the outfit."

Sadie glanced down at her yoga pants and the Garth Brooks concert T-shirt that would've come to her knees without the knot she'd tied at the hip. "What, you don't like Garth?"

"I like him," Nikki piped up. "He's my dad's favorite singer."

"That would make me feel old, except I stole this shirt from *my* dad," Sadie said, accepting the container of broth and bag of ingredients from Olivia. "Did you get it with tripe?"

"Yes."

Rebecca grimaced. "I don't know how you can eat that."

Sadie grabbed a set of chopsticks and settled into a chair. "It's just meat, Rebecca."

"It's gross," Rebecca countered, and sat down on the couch. "Where's my bánh mì?"

Sadie pried the lid off the container of broth and poured it into the bowl, then dumped in the meat and noodles. She started to tear the basil leaves, remembered that she'd been washing walls and painting, and dashed into the kitchen to clean up. By the time she got back, Nikki and Rebecca had dug into their food and Olivia was sitting cross-legged on the floor.

"I can get a chair from my bedroom," she offered.

Olivia shook her head and flipped open the takeout container in front of her. "I'm good on the floor."

Sadie sat and began to shred the bundle of basil leaves. "What'd you get?"

"Peppered salted calamari." Olivia took a bite. "And it's excellent."

Sadie finished doctoring her bowl of Phở, settled cross-legged in the chair, and inhaled the fragrant steam. "God, I needed this. Thanks, pals."

"Don't thank us yet," Rebecca warned and plucked a sliver of carrot from her sandwich. "We have ulterior motives."

Sadie shook her head and mumbled "I don't care" around a mouthful of noodles and meat.

"Don't be too sure," Nikki cautioned.

"What happened Saturday night with you and Jack?" Olivia demanded, and Sadie was grateful she'd already swallowed.

"And don't try to convince us that nothing did," Olivia told her. "I could tell by your face Saturday night. It was weird."

Sadie twirled her noodles and tried to act nonchalant. "My face was weird?"

"You know what I mean." Olivia gestured with her chopsticks, a chunk of fried squid clamped between them. "Even Cade noticed. He asked me if you'd had Botox."

"Has he ever seen someone who's had Botox?" Nikki wondered.

Olivia shrugged. "Not that he'd notice. So? What happened? Start with before the demo."

She knew if she didn't tell them, they'd keep badgering her, and it would be impossible to enjoy her dinner. It also occurred to her that talking to her friends about this wasn't the worst idea. "We…had a conversation."

"That's all?"

"Pretty much."

"Oh, I very much doubt that," Rebecca said over Olivia's snort of disbelief.

"A conversation about what?" Olivia wanted to know.

Sadie shoveled a pile of noodles into her mouth and mumbled, "About the bet."

Nikki frowned, peanut sauce dripping off her salad roll. "About your hat?"

Sadie swallowed her mouth full of food, took a fortifying sip of wine, and said, "Not hat. Bet."

"What bet?" Rebecca demanded, and Sadie sighed.

"The one I made with Jack."

"Oh, boy." Olivia gave a little butt wiggle. "I *knew* this was going to be good!"

"It's not a big deal," Sadie began.

"If that were true, you'd have already told us about it." Olivia bit into a chunk of fried squid and jabbed her chopsticks in the air. "Come on, spill it."

"Fine." Sadie took another gulp of wine. "We were discussing the demo, kind of bickering a little—"

"Because he tricked you into it," Rebecca put in.

"He did not."

"Um." Nikki cleared her throat, an impish smile on her pretty pixie face. "He kind of did."

Sadie scowled. "Do you want to hear this story or not?"

"Fine, he didn't trick you," Rebecca soothed. "*Totally tricked her,*" she mouthed at Olivia, who snickered and promptly choked on her calamari.

"Serves you right," Sadie muttered.

"You were saying?" Nikki prompted, passing her water to Olivia.

Sadie reached for her wine. "Anyway, I said something about not wanting to be bored, which in retrospect, was probably unwise."

"Probably?" Olivia wheezed.

"Then he asked if I didn't think he could make it fun for me, and I said no."

"Were you *drunk*?" Nikki asked, mouth open in shock.

"I wasn't thinking straight," Sadie admitted. "Anyway, it just kind of...evolved from there."

"Into a bet?"

Sadie nodded. "He said if I won—if I didn't have fun—he'd owe me a favor."

Nikki leaned forward, eyes bright. "And if you *did* have fun?"

"I'd owe him a real scene."

The three of them stared at her for a moment, wide-eyed and silent, then Rebecca said, "This is *fantastic.*"

"Oh, shut up," Sadie said and drained her wine.

"When are you playing?" Nikki wanted to know.

"Why do you assume I lost?" Sadie demanded and scowled as all three women began to laugh.

"I hate all of you," she declared, and reached for the bottle to refill her glass.

"Sorry, sorry," Nikki said, and made a valiant attempt to stop giggling. "I meant, did you lose? And if you did, when are you playing?"

"If I decide to go through with it, you mean?"

"If you decide?" Nikki asked. "Isn't it kind of a done deal?"

"Not exactly," Rebecca put in.

"What does that mean?"

"It's complicated. I mean yeah, she lost a bet—"

"This has not yet been established," Sadie mumbled around a mouth full of noodles.

"—but it's not enforceable. Exactly."

"I'm lost."

"Bets can be fun," Olivia put in. "Especially for scenes. Playing with the power dynamic, you know?"

Nikki's expression went dreamy. "Yeah."

"But it's really easy to go too far. Ego," Olivia explained with a pointed look at Sadie—which she roundly ignored—"can get in the way, and consent gets fuzzy."

"So while technically Sadie lost the bet," Rebecca chimed in, "Jack can't *make her* pay up. She has to do it willingly."

Nikki nodded. "Consensually."

"Exactly."

Sadie paused with her wine glass halfway to her lips when all three of them turned to stare at her. "What?"

"Are you going to pay up?" Nikki wanted to know.

Sadie set her wine down. "I haven't decided yet."

"Because he tricked you?"

"He didn't—" Sadie scowled at Nikki's grin. "Fine, he tricked me, and no, that's not why."

"Is it because you don't like him?"

Sadie leaned forward to put her bowl on the table. "I don't not like him, exactly. He just always struck me as…well, an asshole."

"He can come off that way," Rebecca agreed. "But he's just, I don't know, reserved. Once you get to know him, he's a good guy—warm, funny, generous."

"And hot," Olivia put in. "Don't forget hot."

"She said from experience," Sadie drawled and snatched the piece of calamari Olivia threw before it hit her in the face. She popped it in her mouth with a grin. "You're right, that is good."

"Bitch," Olivia said with a laugh.

"Hold on." Nikki raised her hand again. "Did you hook up with Jack?"

"It wasn't exactly a hookup," Olivia hedged.

"Cade asked Jack and Nick to help him out with an interrogation scene," Rebecca explained.

Nikki's eyes widened. "Oh. That sounds…"

"Hot," Olivia finished. "And believe me, it was."

"Let's not lose our focus, people," Rebecca said. "We are here to discuss Sadie's future sexual exploits with Jack, not Olivia's past ones."

"I wouldn't mind hearing more about Olivia's past sexual exploits," Nikki complained.

Olivia winked. "I'll tell you later."

"What else?" Rebecca asked Sadie.

"What do you mean?"

"I mean, if it was just the asshole thing, you wouldn't be this twisted up. You'd say no and be done."

"That's true," Olivia agreed.

"So?"

Sadie shifted to curl up in her chair. "I can't figure out why."

"Why, what?" Olivia asked.

"Why he wants to play with me."

Olivia turned to Rebecca. "Is she kidding?"

"I don't think she is," Rebecca murmured back, then turned to Sadie. "Why wouldn't he want to play with you?"

"Well, let's see." Sadie gestured with her wine glass. "He never smiles at me or talks to me unless it's to tell me I'm doing something wrong."

"Well, he's a sadist," Nikki said with a shrug. "Isn't a stern image part of the package?"

"I guess," Sadie allowed. "But Nick is stern, and he doesn't come off as chronically constipated.

"And," she continued while Rebecca choked, "he thinks I'm a brat."

"But...you are a brat," Nikki pointed out.

"Which I know isn't for everyone," Sadie went on. "I'm an acquired taste, and that's fine."

Olivia exchanged glances with Rebecca. "You don't think he likes brats?"

Sadie shrugged. "I don't know if he likes brats, but it seems pretty clear he doesn't like me. So I don't know why he'd want to play with me."

"Did you ask him?"

"No," Sadie admitted. "But I will."

"His answer should be interesting," Olivia murmured, and cleared her throat. "You said you've been bored lately. Were you bored last night?"

Sadie shook her head. She'd been a lot of things last night—aroused, confused, annoyed—but she hadn't been bored. "No."

"Do you have concerns about his skills as a Dom, or that he might not respect your limits?"

"No, nothing like that."

"Are you attracted to him?"

Sadie bit her lip. "Just between us?"

"Absolutely," Olivia said.

Rebecca held up three fingers. "Scouts' honor."

"Cross my heart, hope to die," Nikki said somberly, and leaned forward.

"I want to climb him like a tree and sit on his face," Sadie admitted and gulped the last of her wine.

"Damn," Nikki breathed.

"I knew it," Olivia crowed.

"Where'd you leave it with him?" Rebecca wanted to know.

"I'm supposed to get my limits list to him by Wednesday."

Rebecca frowned. "At James and Amanda's party?"

"No, he gave me his card so I can email it," Sadie said and, remembering, laughed. "Which is another thing."

"What's another thing?" Olivia asked, and Sadie rose and headed for the desk in the corner of the room.

She opened a drawer, plucked out the little white card, and returned to her seat. "Here."

Olivia took it and stared at it with a frown. "It just has his name."

Sadie settled back in her chair. "Turn it over."

Olivia flipped it over, blinked twice, then began laughing.

"Well, don't keep us in suspense," Rebecca said and leaned over to snatch the card out of Olivia's hand. "Oh, my God!"

"What does it say?" Nikki asked as Rebecca collapsed into laughter.

"His email address is Jack at RestingDickFace dot net," Sadie told her.

"Which Sadie is always calling him," Rebecca put in between giggles.

"Someone must have filled him in." Sadie frowned. "I wonder who?"

"Everybody knows you call him that," Rebecca told her, and tossed the card on the coffee table.

"Did you look at the web page?" Olivia wanted to know.

"Yeah." Sadie picked up her wine. "It's just a picture of his face, in full resting dick mode."

"You're kidding." Rebecca's eyes had gone round with delight. "That's *fantastic*."

"It kind of is," Sadie admitted.

"So, to recap—he's a trustworthy Dom, he's hot as fuck, and he knows how to laugh." Olivia waited a beat. "So why aren't you climbing him like a tree and sitting on his face?"

"Fear," Nikki said, and everyone turned to look at her. "What?"

"You're not wrong," Sadie admitted, and had all three faces swiveling her way again. "It does feel scary."

"Good scary, like 'this could be fun but I've never done it before so I'm nervous', or bad scary, like 'my lizard brain is trying to protect me'?" Rebecca wanted to know.

"I don't know."

"I think you should go for it," Rebecca declared.

"Me, too. Carpe the…what's Latin for dick?" Olivia wondered.

"I'll look it up," Nikki offered.

Rebecca plucked Sadie's phone from the coffee table. "I'll email him your list."

"No, you won't," Sadie said, unfazed. "It's password protected."

Rebecca set the phone back down. "Since when?"

"Since I accidentally called one of my brothers while I was fucking Paul."

"Which brother?"

"Brian, the younger one. We've vowed never to speak of it again, but he still can't look me in the eye."

"I can't find Latin for dick, but penis is pēnis, which is just the same word with a little thingy over the 'e'." Nikki looked up from her phone. "Apparently it originally meant 'tail', and eventually became slang for dick."

"Language is so interesting," Olivia mused.

"So, are you playing at James and Amanda's party on Wednesday?" Rebecca wanted to know. "Is that why he wants the list by then?"

Sadie shook her head. "He wants to play on Saturday."

"Then can you do me a favor and play chaperone for a guest?"

"You're bringing a guest?" Olivia asked. "Who?"

"Kit," Rebecca said, and at Olivia's blank look, elaborated, "She's Nick's assistant."

"Oh."

"He doesn't know she's coming, and she doesn't want him to."

Olivia nodded. "Yeah, that might make work awkward."

"If you could stick with her, help her steer clear of Nick for the night, it would be a big help," Rebecca told

Sadie. "I told him I want to play at the party, so I should be able to keep him occupied for a while."

"Slut," Sadie said and leered to make her friend laugh. "I'd be glad to help."

"Really?"

"Sure." *It'll give me an excuse to avoid Jack.*

"Thanks, Sadie. I'll send you her number so you can coordinate arrivals."

"No problem."

"And now back to you," Olivia interjected and pinned Sadie with a look. "What are you going to do?"

"I don't know, but I guess I'll figure it out."

"If you want my advice—"

Sadie snorted. "Do I have a choice?"

"—I say, go for it," Olivia finished. "You regret one hundred percent of the dicks you don't ride."

"That is an utter lie," Rebecca declared while Sadie sputtered with laughter and Nikki choked on her water.

"Okay, maybe that was a bad way to put it," Olivia admitted. "But I think you regret the dicks you don't ride more than the ones you do."

"Okay, that might be true," Rebecca mused. "I still wonder what it would've been like to bang Dennis Fisher. He was my dad's golf buddy."

"Your *dad's* golf buddy?" Sadie managed, still laughing.

"Younger than my dad, but only ten years older than me," Rebecca remembered with a sigh. "Looking back, it's probably a good thing he moved to Florida when I was sixteen."

"I think we're getting to the origin of Rebecca's daddy kink," Olivia said, "but back to the matter at hand. Carpe pēnis, my friend."

"Carpe the hell out of it," Rebecca agreed. "I wonder if Dennis is on social media. I bet he's still hot."

"It was twenty years ago," Olivia reminded her. "And Nick might object to you getting in touch with the object of your teenage lust."

"Yeah, he would." Rebecca sighed, then brightened. "But I bet he'd be willing to play golf pro and caddy."

"You guys are weird," Olivia declared. "Can we get back to Sadie's issue?"

"Fine." Rebecca nudged Nikki. "What's your vote?"

"I say go for it," Nikki said. "For what it's worth, he was really nice when we were negotiating for the demo. Kind and patient."

"I'll keep that in mind," Sadie told her. "And now, if we're done discussing my potential sex life, I'd like to move on to yours."

Nikki blinked, brown eyes wide. "Mine?" she squeaked.

"Yours," Sadie repeated and raised an eyebrow. "Kody drove you home Saturday night. How'd it go?"

"Um." Nikki swallowed, her cheeks turning a charming shade of pink. "It was fine."

"Oh, do you like Kody?" Rebecca clasped her hands together in glee. "That's great!"

"No, it's not," Nikki wailed, and covered her face with her hands. "I was a total dork."

"Honey." Olivia reached out and patted the younger woman's knee. "I'm sure you weren't."

Nikki peeked through her fingers. "I accidentally threw a laundry basket full of dirty underwear at them."

Sadie bit back the laugh and pasted a sympathetic look on her face. "I'm sure they found it charming."

"No, they didn't." Nikki dropped her hands with a sigh, looking so forlorn that Sadie just wanted to cuddle her like a sad little puppy. "What am I going to do?"

"What do you want to do?"

Nikki looked at Olivia with wide eyes. "I want them to ask me out."

"Maybe you should ask them out," Sadie said.

Nikki bit her lip. "I wouldn't even know what to say."

"We'll help," Rebecca said, and, as they talked strategy, Sadie put Jack out of her mind.

Chapter Five

On Wednesday night—or rather, early Thursday morning—Sadie dipped her roller in a pan of paint and applied it to the wall. She hadn't been sure of the color, worried that the gray-tinged blue would be too dark for the small bathroom, but it worked. She'd have to repaint the trim, as the standard apartment off-white didn't provide a sharp enough contrast, but that was easily done. She wouldn't even have to buy more paint, since her mother had some left over from the kitchen remodel they'd done last year and was more than happy to share.

She dipped her roller back in the pan, hips moving to the beat of the song playing on her phone. She'd lost her earbuds again, so the small space was filled with Adele's big voice. She sang along with gusto, trying and failing to hit the high notes. She was tired, but she knew if she tried to go to bed, she'd just stare at the ceiling with her brain spinning in useless circles. So she let the monotony of the physical labor do its job and hoped that by the time the room was painted she'd be able to sleep.

The song finished, and Sadie was reaching for her phone to find something else to listen to when she heard a knock on her front door. She checked the time, wincing when she saw it was past two. Hoping the music hadn't disturbed her neighbors, she wiped her hands on her yoga pants and hurried to the door.

She rose on her toes to check the peephole out of habit.

Jack, his image distorted through the fish eye lens, stared back at her.

"Oh, hell," she muttered under her breath.

"Hello to you, too," Jack said, his deep voice carrying easily through the door.

She angled her head to try to see him more clearly through the peephole. He wore a camel-colored overcoat and leather gloves the color of chocolate, with a matching scarf draped around his neck. He had one hand tucked in the pocket of the coat, and in the other…

"What's in your hand?"

He held it up. "Package for you. It was sitting in front of your door."

"Tampering with the mail is a federal offense," she informed him.

"It's only tampering if it's actually in a mailbox," he replied. "On the floor doesn't count."

"I don't think that's true."

"Look it up," he suggested. "Are you going to open the door?"

"Not until you tell me what you're doing here."

"I didn't get your email."

Since he couldn't see her, she made a face at him. "I didn't send an email."

"That would explain it." One dark eyebrow quirked up. "Want to tell me why?"

Shit. She knew she'd have to deal with this at some point. She just hadn't pictured doing it at two a.m. "It's late, Jack. Can't this wait until tomorrow?"

"Coward."

She scowled at his image, then dropped back to her heels, flipped open the locks and opened the door. "Stop calling me a coward."

"Stop acting like one." His gaze skimmed over her. "Nice hat."

She reached up to yank off the bandana she'd tied over her hair to protect it from paint spatters. "I was painting."

His gaze dropped to her chest. "Something blue, I gather."

She glanced down, saw the splotch of paint covering Garth's face. "Dammit."

"There's a streak on your face, too," he said, eyes crinkling as he tapped his own cheek with a gloved hand.

She did not have the mental fortitude to deal with eye crinkles at two in the morning. They scrambled her brain, which was probably why she blurted out, "I haven't decided if I want to play with you yet."

To her relief and disappointment, the crinkles went away, and he nodded. "Fair enough."

She narrowed her eyes, suspicious of his quick agreement, then nodded. "Good night."

She started to close the door when he said, "Let's talk about it."

She swung the door back open to stare at him. "Now? It's two in the morning."

Amusement flashed in his dark eyes. "So? We're both awake, and there's an all-night diner down the street. I'll treat you to a slice of pie. Or," he continued when she just stared at him, "did you just plan to avoid me forever, like you did at the party tonight?"

She bit back the wince. She'd spent most of James and Amanda's Halloween party playing hostess to Rebecca's friend, as promised, and had a brief spanking scene with an old lover. When the scene was over, she realized Jack had watched the whole thing, and not wanting a confrontation, had thought it prudent to avoid him for the rest of the night.

Apparently, she'd just postponed it.

"Fine," she muttered. "Wait here."

She shut the door in his face and, ignoring the laugh that drifted through the door, went down the hall for her phone. She thought about stepping into the bedroom for a bra—in fact she was tempted to take her time getting ready just to see how long he'd wait for her. But she was too tired for games, so she shoved her feet into her snow boots, grabbed her coat and purse, and opened the door again.

"That was fast."

She dug out her keys to lock the door and tried to ignore the fact that he was standing way too close. "I want pie."

"You forgot your package," he said, holding it out.

She took it, feeling the distinctive shape of a bottle through the padded envelope. Probably the almond massage oil she'd ordered for one of her clients, she thought, and shoved it into her purse. Shrugging into her coat, she bypassed the elevator and headed for the stairs.

He fell into step beside her. "My car is parked around the corner."

"It's two blocks," she pointed out, making her way down the stairs.

"Walking it is," he said and followed her down.

Jack studied his companion. They'd passed the two-block walk in surprisingly companionable silence, and though Sadie hadn't seemed entirely comfortable, she'd been at least somewhat relaxed. She'd greeted the waitress with a smile, addressing her by name, and they'd been directed to a corner booth. By the time they'd shed their coats and settled in, the waitress had appeared with two steaming cups of coffee. She engaged in a bit of small talk, eyeing him with undisguised curiosity, and took their orders before disappearing to deal with her other customers.

"You come here a lot," he guessed, and tried not to salivate when she shrugged, making her breasts bounce under her shirt. She hadn't put on a bra, and the well-worn cotton didn't hide much.

"A few times a month," she confirmed. "Usually for breakfast. They make a good omelet."

"I'll remember that." He picked up his coffee and took a sip, eyeing her over the rim. She shifted in the booth, wincing, and he remembered just what she'd been doing at the party instead of talking to him. "Sore?"

"I'm sorry?"

"From your spanking earlier," he elaborated, and watched her cheeks go pink. "Nate looked like he did a thorough job."

"Do you know Nate?" she asked warily.

He shook his head. "Met him tonight. Do you?"

She shrugged, toying with the handle of her coffee cup. "We hung out a little last summer."

So James had informed him after the party. He set down his coffee. "He seemed fairly preoccupied with the new girl. Kit, was it?"

"Yeah." Some of the tension went out of her as she smiled. "She's Nick's secretary. I think they've got a thing going."

"Well, if they didn't before, they do now. They were in the mirror room for almost an hour."

"I know." She grinned, her whole face lit with delight. "I have to remember to call Rebecca tomorrow and get the scoop."

"Hmmm," he said, and bit back a smile when her eyes narrowed. "So."

"So, what?"

He reached into the inner pocket of his coat and pulled out a small flask. "You said you haven't decided if you want to play."

She nodded slowly. "That's right."

He twisted the cap off the flask. "What's your hesitation?"

She didn't answer, just watched him add a splash of amber liquid to his coffee. "What's in the flask?"

"Whiskey," he said, and held it out. "Want some?"

She reached for the flask, her fingers skimming over his. She fumbled a little, making him want to smile, and raised it to her lips for a sip. Her eyes went wide. "Wow."

"Is that a good 'wow'?"

"Yes." She took another sip, her eyes unfocused. "That doesn't taste like the whiskey I'm used to."

"What kind is that?"

"The kind I can get at the grocery store for less than twelve bucks."

"Then, no," he said drily. "This is not the whiskey you're used to."

She handed him the flask and picked up her coffee. "You're a booze snob."

"I run a liquor distribution company," he reminded her. "Occupational hazard."

"Hmmm."

He grinned, enjoying her, and tucked the flask away before picking up his coffee again. She had her bright hair pulled back in a loose ponytail that trailed down her back, leaving her face unframed. Her skin was pale, except for the faint flush the whiskey had left behind, and there were delicate shadows under her eyes.

"You're staring," she accused and drank her coffee.

"You're beautiful," he replied.

Her blush deepened. "Um. Thank you."

"You're welcome. You haven't answered my question."

"I'm not sure how," she admitted and looked up when the waitress reappeared. "Oh, that looks great. Thanks, Janie."

"You're welcome," Janie replied, sliding plates off her tray. "Y'all holler if you need anything else."

"Thank you," Jack said and waited until Janie had walked away. "Well?"

She kept her eyes cast down and picked up her fork. "Will you answer a question for me first?"

"If I can."

"Why?"

He paused, his fork poised over the slice of key lime pie on his plate. "Why, what?"

"Why do you want to play with me?"

He lowered his fork. She was still looking down, and while her posture was relaxed, the tension in her voice was as clear as a bell. "Look at me."

She wanted to refuse. He could tell. But after a long moment, she lifted her head. Her gaze had gone wary and guarded, the vulnerability he heard in her voice well shielded.

"You want to know why I want to play with you?"

Her gaze darted to the side, her throat working as she swallowed, then she squared her shoulders and met his gaze head-on. "Yes."

Pleased that she'd found the courage to face him, he pushed his pie aside and leaned forward.

"Because," he said softly, making sure his voice wouldn't carry to the other diners close by, "I want to see that sassy mouth put to good use, and hear the sarcastic bite in your tone fade into screams of pain and pleasure."

Her eyes went wide, the gold flecks in the hazel so bright they all but glowed, and he allowed himself a small, feral smile. "I want to work you over until you can't remember my name, and make you come so hard you can't remember yours. And when we're all done, when you're lying at my feet in a puddle of sweat and tears and come, I want to do it all over again."

He stayed where he was, holding her gaze for a moment, then eased back, slid his pie in front of him again, and picked up his fork.

"Shit, Jack."

He forked up a bite, enjoying the combination of tart and sweet on his tongue. "Now that I've answered your question, how about you answer mine?"

"What was it again?"

He didn't bother hiding his smile this time. She looked thoroughly befuddled. "What's your hesitation?"

"Oh." Sadie picked up her fork, running it through her fingers. "I thought you didn't like me."

That got his attention. "And why is that?"

She shrugged and stabbed at her slice of lemon meringue. "You think I'm a brat."

"You are a brat," he replied, amused now.

"You don't like brats," she mumbled around a mouthful of pie.

"Who told you that?"

She swallowed. "I inferred. You know, from all the glaring and head shaking and disapproving frowns."

He took another bite of pie, chewing slowly to give himself time to consider. She was watching him with narrowed eyes, but he could see the vulnerability—and the fear—lurking in her gaze.

He didn't mind the vulnerability, but the fear had him treading carefully.

"You know what they say about making assumptions," he drawled, and forked up more pie.

"It's not an assumption, it's an observation," she told him.

"Hmmm."

"Don't start that again," she warned him, but she was smiling behind her coffee cup. "Okay, I'll play with you."

"Just like that?" he asked and tried not to grin with sheer delight.

She picked up her fork and went back to work on her pie. "Would you like a formal engraved invitation?"

"Not necessary." He nudged his plate aside and reached for his coffee. "The limits list I requested, however, is."

She started to roll her eyes, then seemed to think better of it and reached for her purse. "I'll send it to you now, all right?"

He enjoyed his doctored coffee while she rummaged through her purse. "Is it current?"

"I updated it at the end of the summer." She frowned into her bag. "Dammit, where's my phone?"

He watched, bemused, as she began taking things out of her purse and piling them on the table. A small makeup bag, keys, a bright pink wallet, two tubes of lip balm, a handful of pens and the package he'd found at her door were accompanied by a veritable avalanche of receipts.

"Aha!" She held up her phone, triumphant, then set it aside and began to shove everything back into her bag.

"Do you need all these receipts?" he wondered, plucking one from the pile. It was from a drug store, dated a month ago, with condoms and a Snickers bar the only purchases.

"No," she said, distracted. "I shove them in there just in case I have to return something and forget about them."

He let the receipt flutter to the table. "So why are you putting them back?"

"I can't leave them on the table," she said, and this time she didn't abort the eye roll.

"They have a trash can," he pointed out.

"Too much trouble." She scooped up the pens and lip balms and dropped them into her purse. "Although..."

He raised an eyebrow when she just stared at the pile of debris on the table. "What?"

She grabbed the package. "I can empty this, put all the receipts in it, then toss it when I get home."

"Do you think you'll remember?"

"Ha, ha." She ripped the padded envelope open and pulled a bottle out. "Oh, hell."

Damn, she was cute when she scowled. "What?"

"What the hell am I supposed to do with sixteen ounces of anise extract?" she asked and turned the bottle so he could see the label.

"I have no idea," he admitted. "What is anise extract?"

"Licorice flavoring." Sadie set the bottle on the table and reached back in the packaging.

He grimaced. "I hate licorice."

"I don't mind it, but it's not the almond massage oil I ordered." She pulled a slip of paper out of the padded envelope to frown at it. "I should be able to return it."

"The receipt hoarding finally pays off," he remarked drily, and began to gather the loose papers.

She put the bottle and the receipt into her purse, then stared at the papers in his hands. "How'd you get them all in a neat pile like that so fast?"

"Magic."

"Funny." She held out the padded mailer, waited until he'd slipped the pile inside, then folded it and put it in her bag.

"What would you bet that's still in there come Saturday?"

"I'm not betting with you anymore," she said firmly.

He grinned and, picking up her phone, held it out. "Limits list."

"Okay, okay." She took it and spent a few moments scrolling and tapping. "There, it's sent."

He nodded. His phone was in his pocket, but he'd already felt the quiet buzz of an alert. "Let's talk limits."

"I just sent you my list," she reminded him, her fingers fluttering on the edge of the table. She wasn't as calm as she appeared, he realized, and felt a quiet surge of satisfaction.

"And I'll look at it later," he assured her, keeping his expression neutral. "But since we're both here, tell me what you like about BDSM."

Surprise flared in her wary gaze. "I like what everyone likes about it. Orgasms."

"You can get orgasms without BDSM," he pointed out.

"Yeah, but they're not as much fun."

He couldn't dispute that, as he felt exactly the same. "Is it the physical aspect that appeals to you most, or the mental?"

"I like giving up control," she replied slowly and dropped her fluttering fingers to her lap. "That's mental, and more important than the physical, I think."

Then she smiled, a slow curve of that lush, unpainted mouth. "But I like the physical a lot."

He chuckled. "So do I," he assured her and switched gears before she could get too relaxed. "Are you aroused by pain?"

"I don't think I'm a masochist," she said, a hint of panic in her tone. "But certain kinds of pain, yeah."

"Do you want sex to be part of our scene?"

Her cheeks turned pink, but her grin was instant. "If there's no sex in your violence, what's the point?"

"I'll take that as a yes." He tapped his fingers on the table. "Oral, vaginal, anal?"

"Oral and vaginal, no anal."

That surprised him. "You're taking anal play off the table?"

"No, I'm taking anal *sex* off the table," she clarified. "Anal play is fine."

"I'm confused."

She sighed. "Have you ever been fucked in the ass?"

His lips twitched. "I can't say that I have, no."

"Well, when you repeatedly drive something into the rectum—say, a dick—and that dick goes back and forth, back and forth, back and forth in a fucking motion, a great deal of air can get trapped in there."

He coughed to cover a laugh. "Is that so?"

"And eventually, it has to come out."

He had to pause for a moment to make sure he could speak. "You're saying anal sex makes you fart."

"Like a dog who eats nothing but raw broccoli and baked beans." She sighed forlornly. "It sucks, because I really do love butt sex."

He gave up trying not to laugh.

"What?" she demanded as he shook with mirth. "It's awful."

"I believe you." He cleared his throat. "Top three erogenous zones."

She blinked. "Aside from or including genitals?"

"Aside from. Exclude breasts, too."

She chewed her bottom lip thoughtfully. "This is off the top of my head, and I reserve the right to revise this list."

He ignored her mouth and the urge to bite it. "Understood."

"My tentative answer is upper back, neck, and thighs."

He filed that information away. "Top three things you hate that aren't hard limits?"

"I'm not telling you that."

"Why not?"

"Because any time a Dom says 'tell me what you hate', it's guaranteed he's gonna do it."

"If you won't tell me, I'll be forced to discover it on my own."

She scowled at him, then huffed out a breath. "Fine. I hate tickling, having my teeth licked, and having my ears nibbled."

He blinked. "Having your *teeth* licked?"

"My college boyfriend thought it was sexy to lick my teeth when he kissed me." She shuddered. "Spoiler alert—it is not."

"And the ear nibbling?" he asked, chuckling.

"It always sounds so *wet*, and not in a good way."

"Good to know," he managed. "Any other limits you want to emphasize?"

"No humiliation, no permanent marks, and I'm still not playing with you alone or at your house."

"James has offered his basement," he told her, sucking some of the righteous wind out of her sails. "And agreed to play DM, per your request."

"Oh. Good."

He pulled out his wallet. "If I have any questions after I read through your list, I'll text you."

"You don't have my number," she pointed out, frowning as he dropped enough cash on the table to cover their pie, plus a generous tip.

"Of course I do," he countered and slid out of the booth.

"Of course you do," she muttered.

He shrugged into his coat. "Come on, I'll walk you home."

He thought she might protest, just for form, but she just grabbed her coat and purse and stood.

He helped her on with her coat, which had her eyeing him suspiciously again, and laid a hand on the small of her back as they made their way to the door.

She was tense under his hand, even as she waved cheerfully to the waitress. He kept his hand on her once they hit the sidewalk, wanting to see if she'd shake him off.

She didn't, though she didn't quite relax, and they made the two-block trek back as they had before, in silence.

When they reached her building, she turned to face him. "Thanks for the pie."

"You're welcome." He tapped a hand on her purse. "Don't forget to throw out the trash."

"Yes, Boss," she said, and let that full eye roll loose again.

"Brat," he growled, and she was grinning when he moved. He grabbed her chin in firm fingers, and the startled squeak she let out when he jerked her head up was music to his ears.

Moving slow to give her time to stop him and savoring the panicked arousal in her suddenly wide eyes, he leaned forward. He kept his eyes locked on hers, delight flooding him as heat replaced the panic in her gaze. Holding her steady, he caught her plump lower lip between his teeth and bit down, absorbing her flinch. He let it go, then slicked his tongue over it before pulling back.

He straightened, dropping his hand from her chin, and calmly buttoned his overcoat. "See you Saturday," he said, his voice once again mild as milk, and, grateful the overcoat hid the erection tenting his slacks, walked away.

Chapter Six

"Then what did he say?"

"He said he wanted to do it all over again."

Rebecca's eyes, a soft dreamy gray, were bug-wide. "That's so hot I think my panties just melted."

Sadie blew out a breath. "Oh, good. It's not just me."

"It very much is not." Rebecca shifted on the couch, wincing when the Velcro on her orthopedic boot caught on the seat cushion. "Goddamn this thing."

"Does it hurt?"

"No, it's just annoying. I can't believe I fell off a stepladder and spent the whole party at urgent care."

"Sorry, sweetie. At least it's not broken, like Nikki's."

"Small comfort. Nick's so worried about hurting it further, he won't fuck me."

Sadie snickered. "It's only been two days."

"Three," Rebecca grumbled, then brightened. "But he says as soon as my ankle's better, I'm getting a paddling for playing matchmaker with Kit and Nate behind his back."

"Something to look forward to," Sadie said with a laugh.

"By the time it happens, I'll be so horny I won't care how hard he spanks me." Rebecca sighed. "Anyway, back to you. What else happened with Jack?"

"We had a kind of impromptu negotiation, he walked me home, kissed me—"

"He kissed you?"

"Well, it was more of a bite and a lick than a kiss," she confessed.

"I love that move."

"Me, too. Then I went upstairs and masturbated for an hour."

"I don't blame you. You haven't heard from him since?"

"I got a text this morning," Sadie said. "It said to be at James and Amanda's at eight-thirty, wearing comfortable clothes, and to bring my aftercare bag."

"Why are you frowning?" Rebecca asked. "You said you wanted James to DM."

Sadie plucked at a loose thread on a throw pillow. "Yeah, that was a mistake. I should've known he'd be on Jack's side."

Rebecca snorted. "Doms stick together."

"Like shit on a shoe," Sadie agreed and pushed to her feet. "Do you mind if I get myself a drink?"

"There's a bottle of white wine in the fridge," Rebecca told her, and Sadie headed across the spacious loft to the kitchen. "Get me one too, will you?"

"You haven't taken any pain meds, right?" Sadie asked, pulling down a pair of glasses.

"No, just over-the-counter stuff," Rebecca assured her. "And before you ask, Nick didn't tell me not to. He told me not to walk any more than necessary and keep my damn foot elevated, but he didn't say boo about drinking."

"More fool, he." Sadie came back to the sofa with two full glasses, passing one to Rebecca before resuming her seat on the couch. "Where was I?"

"Shit on a shoe," Rebecca said and sipped her wine.

"Right." Sadie contemplated the golden liquid in her glass. "Amanda texted me to tell me I was welcome to stay in the guest room, if I didn't feel up to driving home after…well, after."

"I think you should take her up on it." Rebecca snuggled deeper into the corner of the sofa, laying her head back so her hair spread out over the pillow, black on red. "At least pack a bag so you can stay if you need to."

"Maybe." Sadie sipped the wine. "What if Jack wants to spend the night with me?"

Rebecca shrugged and closed her eyes. "Morning sex?"

Sadie would've kicked her, but the only part she could reach was her booted foot, and that just seemed unsporting. "Be serious."

"You don't like morning sex?"

"Of course I do. That's not the point."

Rebecca opened one eye. "You're really nervous."

"Because it's weird." Sadie bit her lip. "Isn't it?"

"You playing with Jack?" Rebecca tapped a fingernail against her glass. "I thought so at first, but now I think it's kind of perfect."

Sadie blinked, baffled. "Why?"

"Well, he's not going to put up with your usual shenanigans—"

"Because he's a humorless goob," Sadie pointed out.

"Excuse me, but putting a picture of his face on RestingDickFace dot net invalidates that argument."

"Okay, that was funny," Sadie conceded.

"But all the testing and pushing you do with other Doms? He's not going to let you get away with that."

Sadie frowned. "I don't test."

"Please. You push them to see how hard they'll push you. None of them have pushed back hard enough, but I bet Jack will."

Sadie drank her wine. "I don't know if I want Jack to push me."

"Then you better not do the scene, because he's going to."

"Shit." Sadie drained the rest of her drink. "I need more wine."

"Bring the bottle back," Rebecca told her, and Sadie went to fetch it.

"You don't think he'd hurt me, do you?" Sadie asked, filling her glass as she walked back to the couch.

"Of course not." Rebecca held out her glass. "I mean, he's a sadist, so he might hurt you. But he would never *hurt* you."

"I don't know anybody who's played with him before." Sadie filled Rebecca's glass, then set the bottle on the end table and resumed her seat on the couch. "Aside from Olivia, and that was under special circumstances."

Rebecca pursed her lips. "Nick says he doesn't play as much as he used to. I guess he was really busy at work for a while, and he's only started coming back around regularly in the last year."

"That's what Amanda said."

"She would know." Rebecca struggled to sit up, dragging her booted foot over the sofa cushions. "Did she say anything else?"

"Just that if James had to choose someone to look after her, Jack would be at the top of the list."

"High praise."

"I guess I'm just…uneasy," Sadie decided. "Off balance, you know?"

"Which is probably right where he wants you," Rebecca pointed out.

Sadie blew out a breath. "God, I hate him."

Rebecca snickered. "Does it help to tell yourself that?"

"Not at all. I'm fucked, aren't I?"

"Yep."

"Then I might as well enjoy it," Sadie decided, and drained her wine.

Rebecca just laughed and raised her glass in a toast. "Here's to enjoying it."

* * * *

Jack stood in James' basement, looking over the large guest bedroom he was planning to use for the scene. "This'll work for the role-play scenario I've worked out. Do you still keep supplies in the nightstands?"

James nodded. "Lube and condoms, plus a few other odds and ends."

Jack circled the bed and opened the top drawer. "Clover clamps. Nice."

"I often think so."

"I have my toy bag, but those might come in handy." He shut the drawer.

"If she shows up."

"Oh, she'll show up," Jack said confidently. "She's got too much pride not to."

James led the way out of the bedroom. "Is that how you got her to agree to this?"

"Pretty much." Jack flicked off the lights and followed James into the main basement.

"You know you can't actually hold her to the bet, right?"

The mild tone didn't fool Jack. One of the more experienced members of their group, James often took on the role of protector. He looked out for the submissives and had a particular soft spot for Sadie.

"I do," Jack said. "She knows it, too."

"I have no doubt." James walked over to the bar that occupied one side of the finished basement. "Join me?"

"Sure." Jack settled into one of the club chairs flanking the fireplace on the other side of the room. He took the glass James offered with a murmur of thanks.

"So." James settled in to the chair opposite Jack. "Sadie."

Jack met his friend's gaze head-on. "It surprises you."

"Not at all," James said, and Jack blinked in surprise. "I've been wondering when you'd make your move."

Jack let out a chuckle. "I've been waiting for the right moment."

"The bet," James said.

Jack grinned into his Scotch. "Best idea I've had in a long time."

"She's a brat," James pointed out.

"That's at least half of what I like about her."

"And the other half?"

"I'm still figuring that out."

"Which brings me to the big question."

Jack sipped his Scotch. "Which is?"

"Is this play date just a play date, or something more?"

"That'll be up to Sadie," Jack hedged, then thought, *what the hell*. "But I want her. And I like her."

"Does she like you?"

"Not yet," Jack allowed and smiled. "That's what tonight is for."

"Well." James lifted his glass in a toast. "I wish you luck."

"I feel like there's an unsaid 'but' there."

"But you've got your work cut out for you," James said. "There are some deep issues under all that sass."

"I noticed that." Jack eyed his friend. "She doesn't trust a lot of people, does she?"

"Her friends, yes. Men?" James shook his head.

"She trusts you," Jack pointed out.

"I'm not a threat," James reminded him. "I'm married, and she's not sexually attracted to me. That makes me safe."

"I guess I should take the fact that she doesn't trust me as a good sign, then. Thanks for agreeing to DM, by the way."

"I'm glad to help. Speaking of, what's your plan?"

"For the scene?"

James nodded. "You mentioned role-play?"

"She's familiar with role-play, and I want her to be comfortable," Jack explained, and smiled. "To a point."

"Oh, I'm very glad I'm going to get to see this," James said with a grin, and leaned forward. "Tell me what you have in mind."

* * * *

Sadie stepped up onto James and Amanda's front porch and rang the bell at precisely eight-thirty. She had on her snow boots for warmth, and her most comfortable pair of yoga pants that didn't have holes in them. Her big puffy coat—also for warmth and not armor at all—hid a faded sweatshirt she'd had since college. She had packed a bag, just in case she decided to stay the night, and she'd brought along her aftercare kit, as ordered.

She was on time, bathed and buffed and ready to play. And nervous. Very, very nervous.

"This is ridiculous," she muttered, staring at her feet. Her boots were starting to look a little ragged, she noticed. She would probably need new ones before the winter was over. "It's just a scene. He's just a Dom. It's no big deal."

"Hi," Amanda said, and Sadie nearly fell into the rose bushes.

"Jesus, Amanda." She scowled. "Scare me half to death, why don't you?"

"Sorry." Amanda leaned in for a hug. "I assumed since you rang the doorbell, you'd be expecting someone to answer it."

"Ha." Sadie returned the hug and stepped over the threshold. "Hey, great hair."

"You think?" Amanda raised a hand to her hair. The sleek dark bob she usually wore had been transformed with a shaggy cut with a hint of curl. "It's not too young for me?"

Sadie shook her head. "It makes your grays look amazing."

"Amazing grays are not a thing." Amanda said with a smile. "But thanks. I just did it today, and I'm not sure it works."

"It looks great," Sadie assured her, and dropped her bags to shrug out of her coat.

"Here, I'll get that." Amanda took the coat and crossed the foyer to the closet, then came back for the boots Sadie had slipped off. "I'm supposed to let you use the bathroom if you need to, then take you right downstairs."

"Right." Sadie wasn't sure if the feeling in her belly was anticipation or nausea. "Any idea what's in store for me down there?"

"Please, like they'd tell me." Amanda gave her a nudge toward the powder room. "Go on."

"Fine," Sadie muttered and went to pee.

"Aren't you going to remind me that I don't have to do this if I don't want to?" she called through the door.

"Do you need me to remind you?" Amanda called back.

"No," Sadie admitted. Business taken care of, she nudged the door open so she wouldn't have to shout and began to wash her hands. "But Rebecca and Olivia both said it, so I figured you'd be next."

Amanda picked up Sadie's bags. "You wouldn't be here if you didn't want to be."

"Your bedside manner sucks," Sadie informed her, turning off the water and reaching for a towel.

"It's not *my* bedside manner you need to be worried about." Amanda told her, blue eyes laughing, and started down the basement stairs.

With few choices—and none that wouldn't make her look like a screaming coward—Sadie followed.

The basement was a large, open space that somehow managed to be cozy and cavernous at the same time. There was plenty of room for equipment and people, which was why so many club parties were held there. But it was also warm and inviting, with soft carpets and comfortable furnishings, and Sadie had always felt safe there.

Well. Until now.

She didn't see Jack, but James was standing by the pool table Amanda had gotten him for Christmas the year before, a cue in his hand. He looked up when they walked in, a smile creasing his handsome face. He was in what Amanda called his 'at home uniform' of jeans and a sweater in pale blue that brought out the color of his eyes. He had salt-and-pepper hair, a leanly muscled build, and a gentlemanly air that hid the beast beneath.

Amanda reached him first, and he leaned down to plant a soft kiss on the side of her neck. "Hello, beautiful."

"Sir," she murmured with a dreamy smile that had envy curling in Sadie's stomach.

"And Sadie," James said, turning his attention to her. He laid his pool cue on the table and placed both hands on her shoulders, kissing each cheek in turn.

"Hello, James."

"I see you followed instructions," he said, glancing at her sweatshirt and yoga pants. He glanced at the bags Amanda still held. "Which of those is your aftercare kit?"

"The small one."

He nodded at Amanda. "Go ahead."

Sadie watched, curious, as Amanda turned and walked to the big bedroom with both bags. The door was slightly ajar, and Amanda slipped through. "What's she doing?"

"What she was told," James said, his eyes flashing with amusement. "Now, how are you feeling?"

"Fine," she said, squirming when he just continued to look at her in his calm and steady way. "A little nervous."

He nodded. "Understandable, with a new play partner. Have you had any alcohol tonight?"

"No, of course not."

"Taken any medication?"

"No."

"What did you have for dinner?"

"A loaded baked potato," Sadie replied, perplexed. "And a salad. What's with the questions?"

He raised an eyebrow, and she winced. Her tone had been less than respectful. "I'm sorry. That came out wrong."

He patted her shoulder. "Apology accepted. And to answer your questions, I'm determining if you're fit to play. Any caffeine?"

"A Coke," she replied, still confused. "I am still playing with Jack, right? He didn't outsource me to you?"

He chuckled. "No," he began, turning when the bedroom door opened and Amanda emerged. She pulled the door shut and crossed the room with a smile.

"All done, Sir."

He nodded. "Thank you, Amanda. You can head upstairs now."

"Yes, Sir." Amanda leaned over and pressed a kiss to Sadie's cheek. "See you in the morning, sweetie."

"Bye."

"I'm taking care of some of the logistics," James explained, pulling her attention back to him. "Which brings me to my last question. Are you here because you want to be?"

She frowned. "I don't understand."

"I'll rephrase. If you're only here because you lost the bet and you have no genuine desire to play with Jack, I'll call off the scene and take you home."

"Oh." She swallowed the lump in her throat. "No, I want to be here."

His eyebrows rose. "You're sure?"

He was so sweet, playing protector. And so devious, making her admit what she didn't want to. "I'm sure."

"Good enough. In that case." He held out an envelope.

"What's this?"

"The rest of your instructions." James nodded at a door on the other side of the pool table. "Take it into the small bedroom and read it. It'll answer all your questions."

She turned the envelope over in her hand, noted her name scrawled across the front in slashing black ink. She looked up at James. "What's with all the cloak and dagger?"

"Mood," he said cryptically and nudged her forward. "Go on, now."

"I'm going, I'm going," she muttered under her breath and, ignoring James' low chuckle, went into the small bedroom and shut the door.

The room looked the same as it always had. Queen-sized four-poster bed, soft carpet. The walls were painted a quiet gold, the color picked up in the metallic threads running through the creamy white duvet and tasseled throw pillows. But the two black garment bags laying on the bed were new.

She stepped closer. They were plain, the kind of garment bags that come with a rented tux, identical but for the tags on the hangers. The one on the left was marked *A*, the other had a *B* written on its tag.

"Eat Me, Drink Me," she murmured, and lowered the zipper on *A*. A snowy white button-down shirt was inside, the kind she sometimes wore when she was in naughty-schoolgirl mode, and when she lowered the zipper all the way she saw the green and blue plaid skirt that would complete the look.

She spread the garment bag open, noting there was a package of knee-high socks and a pair of shiny black Mary Janes in the bottom. He got points for thoroughness, she thought, if not for imagination.

"Well, that's Eat Me," she murmured, and reached for the bag marked *B*. "Let's see what Drink Me brings to the table."

At first, when she brought the zipper down, she thought the bag was empty. But the light bounced off something wet-looking, and when she put her hand inside she felt the cool slickness of PVC. "What in the…?"

She tossed the envelope onto the bed and reached in the bag with both hands, pulling the garment out and spreading it on the bed. It was a catsuit, she realized, long-sleeved with a hood and a zipper that went from crotch to neck.

"Drink Me, I think I love you," she said out loud, skimming her fingers over the slick fabric. She'd gone shopping for a catsuit last year, but the good ones were too expensive and the cheap ones were too low-quality, so she'd given up.

She glanced at the envelope. Instructions, James had said and, with a sense of anticipation that she hadn't felt in far too long, she tore it open.

Sadie, she read. *In the garment bags on the bed, you'll find two outfits, each corresponding to a different role-play scenario. Please read through the descriptions below carefully, as you'll be the one choosing which scenario we do.*

He was giving her a choice? That was unexpected. She read on.

In Bag A you'll find a school outfit – shirt, skirt, stockings and shoes. If you choose this scenario, you're a student breaking into her professor's home to steal the answers to an upcoming test. Unable to find an office, you'll go into the large bedroom to continue your search, where you'll be discovered and appropriately punished by your professor.

Not bad, she mused. She could see the possibilities, and even though she'd done the schoolgirl thing so often she could script it in her sleep, this was an angle she hadn't played with before. It could be fun, if option B was a dud.

Eager to find out, she read on.

In Bag B is a catsuit. If you choose this scenario, you're a cat burglar.

Even as she snickered, her interest sharpened.

You'll dress in the catsuit and matching boots –

Wait, there were boots? She went back to the garment bag, shoving her hand into the bottom and pulling out a pair in the same black PVC as the suit. They were pull-on, with a high, tapered heel that made her roll her eyes. *No cat burglar would ever wear high heels – talk about fantasy*. But since fantasy was the point, and the boots would make her ass look fantastic, she ignored the lack of realism and picked up the letter again.

You'll dress in the catsuit and matching boots, and when you leave the bedroom, James will turn off the basement lights. There's a black pouch in the bottom of the garment bag for your 'loot', and a penlight that you'll have to use to make your way to the big bedroom to burgle it. The homeowner will catch you in the act and will attempt to capture you. You will try to evade, and if you fail, the consequences will be dire.

"Dire, huh?" she murmured, a shiver running up her spine at the thought. Shaking it off, she refocused on the letter.

The choice of which scenario we play out is up to you, and I'll take my cue from your clothes. As soon as you leave the bedroom, the game is on.

-J

She let the letter fall to the bed and eyed her choices. On one hand, naughty schoolgirl was a classic choice, and a safe one. Even with the slight curveball of the scenario he'd laid out, it was familiar. Comforting.

On the other hand—catsuit.

It wasn't even a contest.

She shed her clothes, tossing her yoga pants and sweatshirt across the bed. She hadn't bothered with a bra or panties—mostly because she hadn't wanted to waste clean underwear. Naked, she picked up the catsuit and began to wiggle into it.

It was snug, but the inner fabric was surprisingly soft and slid over her skin with ease. She tugged on the legs like a pair of tights, smoothing as she went, then worked her arms in. The zipper she'd thought ended at the crotch actually went between her legs and up the crack of her ass to end at the base of her spine. There was a tab at each end, enabling it to be unzipped from either direction. She could appreciate the versatility of the design, for both practical reasons—she wouldn't have to take the whole thing off to pee—and more pleasurable ones. She had a brief flash of being bent over, unzipped, and unceremoniously fucked from behind.

Flushed at the thought, she zipped it up to the base of her breastbone, then bent forward to jiggle her boobs into place. When she straightened, she crossed to the mirror to check out the view.

She looked sleek and sexy, the PVC gleaming in the lights, her tits half exposed in the deep V of the open zipper. They looked as though they were half a breath from bursting free but stayed put when she bounced on her toes. She bent this way and that, testing the limits of the fabric, pleased when it moved with her without pinching or bunching.

Eager to see how the rest of it came together, she dragged on the boots. They might not be what a real burglar would wear, but they definitely added to the effect. Her ass looked amazing, her tits even better. She grabbed the hood and dragged it up over her head, letting her hair spill forward. The strawberry-blonde was bright against the slick and shiny black, the ends tickling the bare skin between her breasts in a subtle tease.

She grabbed her phone out of the kangaroo pocket of her sweatshirt, and after a slow spin in front of the mirror, struck a pose. After snapping a couple of quick selfies, she tossed the phone on top of her sweatshirt and dug back in the garment bag.

She found the bag he'd mentioned in the letter—a small velvet pouch with drawstrings—and opened it up. There were a few pieces of costume jewelry inside, the kind one might find in a child's dress-up box. Still, he got points for the effort, and for making the role-play as realistic as possible.

She picked up the letter and skimmed through it again, wanting to make sure she hadn't missed anything. *Catsuit, check. Boots and bag, check.* She didn't have the flashlight, she realized, and went back to the garment bag. She found it way at the bottom, a slender bit of plastic that really did look like a pen, and clicked it on. It emitted a surprisingly strong beam of light for such a little thing and, satisfied, she clicked it off again.

She wound the strings of the pouch around her left wrist and kept the pen light in her right, then stepped to the door, opened it a crack and stuck her head out.

James was sitting in one of the chairs by the fireplace across the room, his attention on the book in his lap. But he heard the door open and lifted his head, smiling when he saw her.

"All set?" he called softly, and she gave him a thumbs-up.

He put the book aside and rose from the chair, crossing to the light switch beside the staircase. He lifted his hand, sent her a wink, and with a flick of his wrist plunged the basement into darkness.

Chapter Seven

Even though she'd been expecting it, the sudden lack of light was so disorienting that Sadie froze for a moment. The room was like pitch, the only hint of light a small red dot on the wall security panel, and she realized dimly that James must have hit a master switch of some kind, because he'd killed the lights in the bedroom behind her, too. She couldn't see anything, and for a second, she panicked. Then she remembered the flashlight.

She fumbled it on, flinching when it hit her full in the face, and quickly directed the beam to the floor. Blinking the spots out of her eyes, she tried to think what she would do if she was actually trying to rob the place.

Since she'd never actually met a burglar or tried to rob anyone, she had no idea what that was. But books and movies had given her more than a few examples, so she channeled her inner villain and slowly swept the light across the floor.

The letter had said her goal was to burgle the big bedroom, so she aimed her light in that direction. The door across the room was slightly ajar now, clearly visible in the wide beam of light. With her eyes on the prize, she started forward.

And promptly walked into the pool table.

She let out an *oof* and stumbled, flinging out her arms for balance, and the pen light went flying out of her hand. It careened through the air, the wildly flashing light momentarily blinding her again. She slammed a hand down on the pool table's felt top for balance, sending balls clattering as the light hit the wall and fell, with the tiniest of muffled thumps, to the floor.

"Fuck a duck," she muttered, and pushed off the table with a grunt. The light was only a few feet away, pointing at the wall with its beam half buried in the carpet. She made her way over to it carefully, one hand rubbing at her hip—that was definitely going to bruise—and scooped it up.

With the light trained in front of her—she didn't think there was anything else between her and the bedroom, but she wasn't taking any chances—she started forward again. Even with the carpeting her footsteps sounded loud, the noise amplified in the dark. She shifted to the balls of her feet in an attempt to stay quiet, and with her heart pounding in her ears and the light guiding the way, crossed the room.

She made it to the bedroom door without incident, which struck her as a little odd. With one hand on the doorknob, she turned to sweep the light behind her. The beam was bright enough to illuminate even the farthest corner, revealing...nothing. The room was empty—even James had disappeared—and unless he was hiding under the pool table, Jack wasn't here either.

Her stomach did a little top-of-the-roller-coaster flip as she swept the room again. Her heart was pounding with excitement and anticipation, her skin all but tingling. If this was what real cat burglars felt when they plied their trade, she could understand the appeal.

Satisfied that the basement was empty, she laid a hand on the door and pushed. The door swung open and she slipped inside, closing it behind her. She swung the pen light around the room, making sure it too was empty, then started forward. She was here to fake-rob the man, so she might as well have some fun with it.

Jack's ribs hurt from holding in his laughter, and James wasn't doing any better. They stood on the stairs, four steps up so they couldn't be seen from the basement, eyes locked on the monitor in James' hand. There were no security cameras in the basement, and though James had offered to relocate one of the exterior house cameras for the night, Jack had opted for the baby monitor. He'd used it before, for scenes where he wanted a submissive to think they were alone, and though the camera resolution wasn't perfect, it was clear enough for them to see Sadie go stumbling into the pool table.

Her muttered "*fuck a duck*" had come through loud and clear, and he'd had to bite the inside of his cheek to keep from laughing out loud. She'd straightened and retrieved her light, rubbing at the hip that had made contact with the pool table, but he couldn't see any sign of further injury. She moved easily, creeping across the basement like, well, like a cat burglar.

He watched her do another sweep of the room—clever girl—before slipping into the bedroom. When the door clicked shut behind her, he let out a whispering wheeze. "Holy shit."

James' shoulders shook with laughter, and his eyes were wet with tears. "Is she all right?"

"I think so." Jack said, keeping his voice low. He doubted she could hear them from the bedroom, but he didn't want to risk it. "She hit her hip pretty hard, but she was moving well."

"Good." James wiped his eyes. "What's your plan?"

"Well, once I've lost the urge to laugh—"

James snorted. "Good luck with that."

"—I'm going to walk down there and turn on the lights like I'm coming home from work and catch her in the act."

James nodded. "Where do you want me?"

"Stay on the stairs," Jack decided. "When she runs—and she will run—"

"Agreed."

"—that's where she'll go," Jack continued. "I'm going to try to catch her before she gets there, but just in case."

"She won't make it far in those heels," James predicted. "Nice touch, there."

"I need some advantage," Jack explained. "Once I get her back in the bedroom, you can follow us."

"Do you want me to stay out of sight?"

Jack shook his head. "She specifically requested you as DM, so let her see you."

James nodded. "It's your show."

Jack switched off the monitor and set it down, then picked up the briefcase he'd brought along and headed down. He forced himself to walk slowly and casually, the way he would if he was coming home after a long day at the office, and when he reached the bottom of the stairs, hit the switch.

The lights came back on, illuminating the empty basement, and he started across the room. He could hear her banging around in the bedroom—she'd never be a real cat burglar making that much noise—and forced himself to maintain his pace when everything in him urged him to rush.

With anticipation simmering, he paused outside the bedroom. The thick carpet had muffled his footsteps, and since the noise from inside hadn't abated he assumed she hadn't heard his approach. There was a muffled bang, followed by a triumphant "Aha!" and he wondered what she could've found to elicit that reaction.

He thought about making some kind of noise to warn her—making his phone ring, or dropping the briefcase—but decided against it. He had the element of surprise on his side, and he wasn't going to waste it. So he laid a hand on the doorknob, turned and pushed, and stepped into chaos.

Sheer shock had him stumbling to a halt only a few feet inside the door. The tidy guest room he'd stowed his gear in earlier looked like it had been hit by a hurricane. The bed linens had been stripped and lay crumpled on the floor, dresser drawers pulled out and tossed aside, their contents spilling out. The nightstand on the far side of the bed was tilted sideways, leaning drunkenly against the wall, and the drawers of the other had been pulled out, their contents emptied onto the bed. The closet doors were open, the extra blankets that James and Amanda kept on the top shelf in a pile on the floor in front of them, and the chair that James had moved into the room so he could sit and observe had been tipped forward to lay face down on the floor.

He couldn't see Sadie, but the occasional thump and mutter from the other side of the bed gave him a good clue as to her whereabouts.

"What the fuck?" he said loudly and dropped the briefcase to the floor with a thud.

There was a sharp crack, a muttered "Shit!" and Sadie's head popped up to peer across the mattress.

Her eyes were big and round, her cheeks flushed with either excitement or exertion, and her unpainted mouth formed a delicate and enticing *O*. For a second, she looked like a trapped rabbit, panicked and vulnerable, then her eyes lit and she scrambled to her feet.

He wanted to take a moment to appreciate just how good she looked in the catsuit—the grainy resolution on the baby monitor hadn't done her justice—but he couldn't afford to. She was already moving, dancing back a few steps as her eyes flicked to the door, gauging her chances of escape. Reminding himself to stay in character, he forced a scowl and started forward. "You fucking bitch."

She let out a trilling laugh, her eyes bright with challenge. He was coming around the foot of the bed, cutting off the only direct route to the door, but he should've known she wouldn't give in that easily. She sprang forward, leaping up onto the mattress just as he rounded the bed. He spun around, but she was across the bed and running out of the door before he could take two steps.

He sprinted after her. She had a head start, running full out for the basement stairs, but his legs were longer and he wasn't wearing heels. James, who had been sitting on the bottom step, stood up when she was about halfway there. She let out a squeak of dismay and pinwheeled to a stop.

Her head whipped around, the hood falling off and her hair flying free, and he got a glimpse of her flushed, determined face before she darted to the left.

He changed direction to follow, slowing down slightly when he saw where she was heading, and came to a stop when he reached the pool table. She stood at the other end, the length of the table between them. She was panting from the run, eyes bright and cheeks flushed, and he could've devoured her whole.

He planted his hands on the table. "Gotcha."

Her lips were curved in a smug smile, her eyes dancing as she mirrored his pose. "Oh, honey," she drawled. "I think you've got delusions of grandeur."

Goddamn, this was fun. He made a show of looking around. "The exits are covered, sweetheart. You've got no way out."

"There's *always* a way out," she countered, her eyes narrowing to slits. "You think you can keep me here? In that suit?"

Jack grinned. Since he was supposed to be coming home from work, he'd worn his usual office attire. He'd even added a tie, which he normally didn't bother with, just so he could gag her with it.

"Don't let the Armani fool you, sugar tits," he advised.

Her eyebrows shot up at the term. "Excuse me?"

He deliberately lowered his gaze to her breasts, all but bared by the deep vee of the zipper. They were barely constrained by the snug material of the catsuit, ready to pop free at a shrug of her shoulders. "Seems like a fitting term."

"Oh, he's a misogynist," she said, icy sweet. "What a surprise."

"I don't hate women," he returned mildly. The verbal sparring match had his blood pumping, forcing him to reach for calm. There was a plan, and he needed to stick to it. "Unless they break in and trash my fucking house."

"Aw, poor little rich boy came home to a mess," she whined with an exaggerated pout. "What, is it the housekeeper's day off?"

"You know, I was just going to call the cops," he said, conversationally. "Have you thrown in jail. But now, when I get my hands on you? I'm taking that mess out on your ass."

"I'm trembling," she drawled.

"You should be," he countered, deadly serious, and watched the first hint of unease flicker into her eyes. "You have no idea what I'm capable of."

"Oh, I knew you were a sick fuck when I went through your nightstands," she countered, rallying to sneer at him. "What's the matter, can't get it up without props?"

He merely smiled. "I'm going to give you one chance to hand over the bag and sit quietly like a good girl until the cops get here."

She snickered, and though the uneasiness in her gaze had brightened into fear, lifted her chin defiantly. "Or what?"

"Or you can take your chances with me."

She raked her gaze over the bespoke suit, the silk tie. "You don't scare me, rich boy."

"I will," he promised, and pushed off the table. He stood straight, his arms loose at his sides. "Last chance."

"Fuck you," she said, and lunged to her left.

He knew it was a feint—the way her eyes went right as her body went left was a dead giveaway—but he went for it anyway, rounding the table to intercept her. She crowed, triumphant, and switched directions on a dime to dart down the other side of the table, hair flying as she turned to laugh at him.

He had the singular pleasure of watching her eyes widen with shock when he planted a hand on the felt and vaulted over the table.

She squeaked and put on a burst of speed, but he was already on her, slamming into her back. Momentum carried them forward into the wall, the air leaving her lungs in a whoosh when he pushed her into it. She went still, the wind knocked out of her, and he grabbed her wrists, pinning them to the wall on either side of her head. "Gotcha."

She had her breath back, and it was coming fast and ragged. She jerked her arms. "Get the fuck off me."

He tutted into her ear and carefully tightened his grip. He didn't want to bruise her wrists if he could help it, though with the way she was squirming, it might be inevitable. "Temper, temper."

"Fuck you," she replied, and kicked out.

He sidestepped, barely avoiding a heel to the shin, then stepped into her. He'd held back when he grabbed her, not wanting to slam her into the wall, but now all bets were off. He pressed her into it, using his weight to quell her struggles, and waited. After a few moments of bucking and twisting and increasingly inventive curses, she went slack.

"That's more like it," he said, softly mocking, and grinned when she bucked again. "You're a feisty one, aren't you?"

"And you're an ass," she countered, breathless, and tried to head butt him.

He avoided it easily—with the way she was pressed into the wall, she hadn't been able to put much on it—and made a mental note to ask her if she'd had any martial arts training. "So feisty," he mocked, and she twisted her head to look at him.

Her eyes snapped at him through the curtain of her hair, hanging wild and tangled in her face. Her cheeks were flushed, her breath coming in sharp pants—though that could be due as much to the way he was pushing her torso into the wall as exertion—and her lips were curled in a sneer.

"Fine, go ahead and call the cops," she said, and gave a defiant toss of her head. "Won't be the first time."

"Oh, no, sweetheart," he said, chuckling when her eyes narrowed at the mocking endearment. "You had your chance for the cops. Now we do this my way."

Her eyebrows rose. "You're going to bore me to death?"

"You won't die," he promised with a low laugh. "Probably."

"I'm shaking," she began, then, "Hey!"

He yanked her right arm down, pinning her wrist to the small of her back, then did the same with the left. Using one hand to hold them in place—and leaning into her for extra emphasis—he yanked his tie loose with his free hand.

"What are you doing?" she demanded when he slipped the silk over her hand.

"Securing the prisoner," he replied, pulling it snug before wrapping it around her other wrist. He had them secured in moments, tied loose enough so as not to cut off her circulation, but tight enough that she couldn't easily wriggle free.

He hoped, anyway.

"There," he declared, satisfied, and spun her around to face him. He took a moment to appreciate the view—the tumble of silky hair, flushed cheeks. Her eyes were bright, sparkling with defiance, her mouth lush. She'd bitten the lower one at some point—he could just make out the teeth marks—making it swell and flush with color, and he had to fight the urge to bite it himself.

She sucked in a breath, drawing his attention to her chest. She'd arched her back to take the pressure off her bound hands, shoving her tits forward so the inner curves were pressed against the edge of the zipper. Her skin was damp with sweat, tits lifting with every ragged breath. They were a wiggle away from spilling out of the catsuit, and he almost reached down to help them along.

Then she said, "What the fuck are you looking at, rich boy?" and he remembered the plan.

"The spoils of war," he said, and bent to put his shoulder into her belly. He hoisted her up, one arm clamped firmly around the backs of her knees, and started for the bedroom.

Damn, Sadie thought, hanging upside down, her hair bouncing at the edges of her vision as Jack walked across the room. *He really does have a nice ass.*

And hard shoulders, she added, and drew a careful breath. She still could, which was a relief, but her breathing was definitely compromised by the hard shoulder in her belly, so she wiggled a little, trying to find a spot where it didn't dig in so much.

A hard hand landed on her ass. "Be still, or I'll take my piece out of your ass and still call the cops," Jack said, and she remembered she was supposed to be playing a part.

It wasn't usually so difficult for her to remember her role, but normally she wasn't this horny.

It would've been embarrassing, how wet she was under this catsuit—seriously, she was half afraid that when he finally got her out of it there would be a waterfall—if he wasn't just as aroused as she was. Thirty seconds ago, when he'd had her pinned to the wall, his dick had been so hard against her butt she'd actually thought he might have a weapon in his pocket.

A big one.

She made a mental note to tell Olivia she'd been right, then tuned back in to the moment at hand. What was she supposed to be doing? *Oh, right. Resisting, with attitude.*

"How 'bout fuck you, Richie Rich?" she said and sank her teeth into his back.

It was awkward, because she had to turn her head almost sideways, and there wasn't much to grab. He was pretty lean, and what there was to grab onto was muscle. But still, she managed to find flesh under the suit jacket, vest, and shirt, and he let out a very satisfying yelp.

"Dammit," he snapped, and his hand landed on her butt again, much harder than before. Undaunted, and spurred on by the short burst of pain and the spreading heat that followed, she bit him again.

"I'm going to fuck you up," he promised in a deep, rolling growl that couldn't quite hide the laugh lurking underneath.

She grinned into his suit jacket. "Promises, promises," she taunted, then the world was spinning again.

She found herself dropped to her feet and jerked around. She stumbled, disoriented, and was caught and steadied by hard hands. She tossed her head to get her hair out of her face, eager to start snarking at him, but one of the hands gripping her shoulders moved to her head, gathered her hair in a fist, and pushed her down and forward.

She didn't see the mattress until she landed on it with a grunt, the pillowtop enveloping her in a cloud of softness from pelvis to chest. She blinked her eyes open, found herself looking at the headboard through the curtain of her hair, and realized she was bent over the footboard. Hard hands jerked at her wrists, loosening the tie around them, and as soon as they were free, she planted them on the mattress and pushed up.

A hard hand on her back shoved her down again.

By the time she'd spat out the mouthful of mattress and hair, he'd dragged her left wrist behind her. She jerked her head around to look, taking in the soft leather cuff now wrapped around her wrist—the same ones, if she wasn't mistaken, that he'd used for the demo last week. There was a short chain attached to the D-ring, a small carabiner on the end, and before she could blink, he had it clipped to an eyebolt in the bedpost.

She yanked her arm, making the chain rattle. "What the hell is this?"

"This?" He grabbed her right hand, holding it firm while securing the second cuff. "This is called 'the consequences of your actions'."

"Fuck you," she snarled, and tried to yank her arm free.

He just yanked it back, holding the chain firmly despite her continued attempts to gain her freedom. "You know, most people in your position would be friendlier," he commented and, with a click, locked carabiner to post.

"I'm not most people," she countered, and tried to kick him.

She missed, but she didn't think it was by much, and his low chuckle gave her a better idea of his location so when she kicked out a second time, she connected solidly with his shin.

"You're just begging for it, aren't you?" he ground out, his voice tight with pain.

She shook her hair out of her face and craned her neck to try to see him. She couldn't, not quite, but she could see the corner of the room now, and the wing-back chair where James sat. For a second she was confused—why was he there?—then she remembered she'd asked for a DM, something that seemed a little silly now.

He gave her a subtle nod but said nothing, and she knew he wouldn't interfere with the scene unless he had to. Forcing herself back into character, she cleared her throat. "I'll make a deal with you, pretty boy."

"Oh, yeah?" Jack stepped into her line of sight, and she had to bite her lip to keep from drooling.

His hair was tangled, his dark eyes flashing. He'd stripped off the suit jacket and vest and was unbuttoning the cuffs of his black dress shirt. Moving quickly, with a brisk efficiency that didn't make it any less hot, he rolled up first one sleeve, then the other before folding his arms across his chest. "What's that?"

She couldn't take her eyes off his arms, the swirls of ink over the flexing muscles. "Huh?"

There was a snicker from the corner, and heat flooded her face. Her gaze darted up to Jack's, and the knowing gleam in his eyes made her blush harder. *Pull yourself together,* she admonished herself. *They're just forearms.*

"Let me go," she said, forcing arrogance and confidence into her tone, "and I won't hurt you."

He eyed her with amusement, one dark eyebrow cocked. "You see the position you're in, right?"

"Oh, I see it," she told him, and rattled her chains for emphasis. "And I'm pretty sure this counts as kidnaping. Or at the very least, unlawful restraint."

"You weren't worried about the law when you broke into my house," he pointed out.

"I'm warning you," she began, and he threw back his head and laughed.

She'd seen him amused before, but it had always been a subtle thing. Even during the demo, when he'd so clearly been enjoying himself, he hadn't done more than chuckle in a quiet, contained way. This was a belly laugh, full and uninhibited, and it transformed him. Resting Dick Face Jack was hot—all that brooding and smoldering intensity just worked—but Laughing Jack was *whoa.*

"You're warning me," he repeated, still laughing, his grin so wide she could practically count his teeth, even with the beard. "That's rich."

"Asshole," she spat out and, turned on and frustrated, yanked at her chains again.

"Oh, sweetheart." The laughter faded from his face and he leaned down, putting his face mere inches from hers. He wore an expression of such menace that she flinched, and his eyes gleamed with satisfaction. "I haven't begun to show you how big an asshole I can be."

Her mouth went dry. "Is that a threat?"

"A promise," he corrected, and straightened.

He moved out of sight, his footsteps muffled by the thick carpeting, and she craned her neck to try to follow. But her position made it impossible, so all she could do was listen and wait.

She heard a zipper, and the sounds of someone rummaging around. There was the thump of wood on wood, and she imagined him looking in the dresser drawers she'd left strewn on the floor.

It seemed as though she lay there, ears straining, forever, but it was probably only a matter of seconds before she heard him coming back. Still, she wasn't expecting the hand that wrapped around her ankle, and she flinched.

"Jumpy," he observed, and pulled her foot to the side. "What's the matter, sweetheart? Nervous?"

She didn't answer—her mouth was too dry, and she was very much afraid her voice would betray her—so she tried to kick him instead.

"So feisty," he jeered, his fingers tightening on her foot. Something wrapped around her ankle, and she realized he was cuffing her to the bedpost.

He moved swiftly, locking the cuff in place before she could try to kick him again, then he was grabbing her other foot. He jerked it to the side, forcing her stance wide and taking away the support of her legs, and she sank even farther into the bed. It made her feel horribly, deliciously vulnerable, the butterflies in her belly going berserk, and she bucked against his hold.

His chuckle was low, the delight in it unmistakable. "Fight all you like, sugar tits. Makes no difference to me."

"I'm going to gut you like a fish when I get out of this," she warned and bucked again.

"When you get out of this, you'll be lucky to be conscious," he replied, and smacked her ass so hard she lost her breath.

That wasn't his hand, she realized dimly as the pain and the heat spread, bright and hot and hard. It covered too much real estate, hitting her with equal force across her spread buttocks, and it was too firm – no give at all. It had to have been some kind of paddle, probably wood or plastic, and just as the pain had begun to fade, he did it again.

"Fuck!" she cried, bucking against the blistering heat. "What the fuck are you hitting me with?"

"Just one of my 'props'." He hit her again and again, laying stinging blows across her ass one right after the other with barely a pause in between.

She lost count at five, and when he finally stopped her face was wet with tears and her lip was bleeding where she'd bitten it. Her ass was on fire, a thick and heavy pulse of pain that should've obliterated everything else, but every throb and twinge sent shocks of pleasure right to her clit. Her pussy was throbbing too, the tender opening fluttering and pulsing in a shallow mimic of the rhythmic pull and clench of an orgasm.

She wiggled, desperate for friction, but with her legs spread and her pelvis at the wrong angle, she couldn't get it.

"Had enough?" Jack taunted.

"Fuck you," she managed, and half hoped he'd hit her again.

"Not yet, sugar tits," he drawled, and there was a muffled thump that she assumed was the paddle—or whatever he'd been using to tenderize her ass—hitting the floor. "Got a few things to do first."

She opened her mouth, a taunt on the tip of her tongue, then shut it again when he grabbed the tab of the zipper over her tailbone. He began to draw it down slowly, carefully, and she held her breath.

The way her legs were spread meant there was no slack in the PVC, and the zipper was snug against the damp, needly flesh between her legs. If she moved unexpectedly or he yanked too fast, he could catch her tender labia in its teeth, and that was a level of discomfort that she didn't want. So she kept as still as possible while he drew the tab down between her legs, letting out her breath in a soundless sigh of relief when he slid the zipper past her pussy and up her belly. His forearm brushed against her pussy, coarse hairs tickling the bare, damp flesh, and she shuddered.

"Well, well," he murmured, a sinister note in the quiet words. "What have we here?"

He slid a finger over her pussy, tracing the outer labia with a delicate, almost gentle touch. But his fingertip was rough, and she was swollen and sensitive, and he might as well have touched her with a cattle prod.

"You like getting your ass beat, sugar tits?"

"Of course not," she croaked. "You sicko."

He chuckled, low and rich, and she shivered at the dance of his breath across her heated skin. "Takes one to know one."

She was trying to come up with a suitable rejoinder—somehow, *I'm rubber and you're glue* didn't seem to fit the mood—when he gripped the sides of the open zipper and pulled them apart so the teeth dug into the juncture of her thighs and her ass was bared.

"Look at that ass," he marveled.

Her skin was tender and sensitive, like a fresh sunburn, and when he spread his fingers and squeezed, renewed pain made her hiss.

"I do love a redhead. All that pale skin just waiting to be marked. You're glowing like a stoplight, sugar tits."

His thumbs were so close to her pussy, empty and yearning, she could barely think. "Sadist," she managed.

"You say that like it's an insult." He lifted one hand and brought it down on the already tenderized skin, and she cried out.

"Oh, I like that," he said, his voice rich with approval and pleasure. "Do it again."

"Bite me," she snapped back, and immediately wished she hadn't.

"I'm afraid you'll have to wait for that, too," he drawled, and gave her ass a firm, grinding squeeze before releasing her.

He was rummaging around behind her again, and she tensed with every new noise. She tried to relax, knowing there was nothing she could do but wait, but she couldn't keep from straining to identify each sound. The clatter of wood, the clink of metal, the faint rustle of his clothes as he moved. She pictured him sifting through the toy bag she hadn't had a chance to dig through and wondered what he was going to do next.

She wouldn't have to wonder long.

Jack advanced across the room, lube in one hand and the heavy glass butt plug in the other. Sadie's ass was like a beacon drawing him forward, round and lush and glowing red. He'd decided to paddle her hard, without a warmup, to see how she'd handle the pain. She'd taken it with hardly a sound, and though he'd gotten the *tears* signal from James, who was well positioned to see her face, she'd bounced back fast and with her usual sass.

And her pussy, when he'd unzipped the catsuit, had made it clear that she didn't mind this particular kind of pain at all.

She was waxed bare, and so wet he could see her glistening halfway across the room. Her labia were swollen, the thick outer lips flowering open to reveal the deeper pink folds beneath, and the temptation to forgo the plan and fuck her now was strong. But he wanted more than a fuck, and so did she, and he wasn't about to disappoint either of them.

So he slipped the butt plug into his pocket, and standing between her widespread thighs, popped the cap on the tube of lube.

She flinched at the sound, her head jerking up. He laid his left hand on the small of her back, both to hold her steady and to remind her who was in charge, and unceremoniously squirted lube into the crack of her ass.

"Cold!" she cried, and tried to jerk away.

"Hold still," he demanded, and swiftly slapped one reddened cheek. She squealed, jerking again, and he repeated the slap on the other side and slid his thumb into her ass.

"Fuck," she wheezed, and froze.

He laughed, watching the back of her head carefully. She'd pressed her forehead into the mattress, her hair falling forward, shielding her face from James' view. So he moved slowly, pumping his thumb into her asshole once, twice, before pulling free, adding more lube, and sliding it deep again.

She groaned this time, her hole clamping down on him, and he'd have sworn he felt the first warning flutters of an orgasm.

"You know, sugar," he drawled, leaving his thumb buried deep, "if I didn't know any better, I'd say you like having my thumb up your ass."

She lifted her head, turning it to the side to try to see him. She couldn't—he was too far behind her—but he could see a bit of her expression now, and the mix of pain and pleasure was a joy to behold.

"Dream on, asshole," she rasped and closed her eyes.

Jack flicked a glance at James, who nodded and gave a subtle thumbs-up. He had a good view of her face again and would signal if he thought she was nearing her limit. Reassured that he still had room to play, Jack pulled his thumb from the warm clutch of her ass and reached into his pocket for the plug.

He'd wanted something special for this evening, knowing how much Sadie enjoyed anal play, and he'd found it in the sculptured piece of tempered blue glass. It was thicker than he'd have normally used during a first scene, with a wide flared head and an only slightly narrower midsection that would keep her anus distended past what most people would find comfortable. But Sadie was an experienced butt plug enthusiast, and he'd wanted to see if she could take it.

And he'd bought a more reasonable version that he could bring out if this one proved to be too much.

When he set the cold, hard tip against the slick skin of her anus, she froze.

"Deep breath now, sugar tits," he drawled, and waited until he heard her suck in air before he began to push.

The breath she'd just taken came out in a hiss, but he didn't stop. He pressed forward with steady pressure, and after the initial moment of resistance, her anus began to give way. It spread around the wide, flared head of the plug in a graphic and obscene display that he found absolutely delicious.

"Look at that hungry little hole," he remarked and grinned when her buttocks clenched. Delighted to have an excuse, he gave her a hard smack. "None of that, now. Take it like a good little bad girl."

"Fuck you," she muttered and sucked in another breath. "Christ, what are you shoving up there, a Buick?"

He chuckled and nudged the plug a little further. It was almost to the widest point. "Don't act like you don't love it. Your asshole is practically sucking it in."

She was panting like a woman in childbirth, breathing through the discomfort. He pulled it back slightly, watched her asshole spasm, then shoved it forward again. The flared head popped though, and the ring of muscle clamped down on the slightly narrower neck.

She yanked at her hands, making the chains rattle. "Oh, God."

She was shaking, fine tremors making her ass jiggle and her legs wobble. Her asshole was clenching at the plug, making it dance, and just below her pussy was so wet she was all but dripping. He thought she might be coming, but when he looked at her face to confirm, he couldn't see her through the cloud of hair.

He looked to James questioningly. His friend was watching Sadie with a small smile on his face, and when he glanced up at Jack, nodded in confirmation.

"You little slut," Jack growled, returning his attention to the quivering, quaking woman in front of him. "You love this."

She shuddered though the last spasms and went limp on the bed. "Do not."

"A liar as well as a thief," he drawled. "You think I don't know an orgasm when I see one?"

"I think fuck you," she managed on a gasp.

"Oh, you will," he promised, and, leaving the plug in her ass, crouched to undo her ankle restraints.

Chapter Eight

Sadie tried to resist when he pulled her off the bed, but her arms felt like noodles and her legs didn't want to work and every time she moved, the log in her ass made her pussy clench and scattered her wits, By the time she'd gotten it together and was ready to put up a fight, she was on her knees at the foot of the bed, her wrists shackled to her ankles, staring at Jack's crotch.

Olivia had definitely been right, she thought hazily and shook her head. That mini orgasm had barely taken the edge off, and she wanted more. But she was supposed to be in character, so she ignored her needy pussy and her full ass and gave the restraints a yank. "Let me go."

He laughed, a deep rumble that didn't do anything for her concentration. "I don't think you're in a position to make demands, sugar."

She rattled her chains again, wincing when her butt sang in protest. She was sitting on her feet, the edges of the open zipper cutting into her bruised flesh, and when she shifted, her bootheels knocked into the base of the plug. The plug was big, the glass slick with lube, and the neck wasn't narrow enough to keep it from shifting. Every time it moved, her pussy clenched and her clit pulsed and she lost the script.

"I'm going to make you pay for this," she warned, still staring at his crotch. Jesus, was he wearing a cup?

"That threat might have more punch if you weren't drooling," he remarked, and reached for his zipper.

"I'm not drooling, I'm sneering," she retorted and lost the thread again when he pulled his zipper down. He hauled out his cock, stepped forward, and tapped the fat head on her lips.

"Open," he said, and without even a pretense of resisting, she did.

He lay heavy and hot on her tongue, the tip slick with pre-come, so she licked it off. She didn't love it—come wasn't generally her favorite thing, at least not in her mouth—but she liked sucking cock, and it was better than the taste of latex, so she'd learned to ignore it. She swirled her tongue around the glans, then gently scraped her teeth against the thick ridge. He stiffened above her, his dick jumping in her mouth, and she did it again, just a little harder.

"Brat," he growled, and reached down to grab her hair in his fists. "Wider."

She dropped her jaw and sucked in a breath, anticipating him, and wasn't disappointed when he smoothly drove his cock to the back of her throat. She gurgled when he hit her gag reflex, unable to help it, and his hands tightened in her hair.

"I like that," he said, pulling back to rest on her tongue. "Do it again."

"You do it again," she mumbled around his dick, then he was pushing forward and she was gurgling again, her throat spasming when he tried to push past it.

He kept at it, pulling back and shoving forward so she gasped and gurgled and choked around him, spit dripping from her open mouth to coat her chest. He ignored it and kept fucking her face, using her hair as handles to yank her forward and back. She relaxed into it, letting him do the work, and tilted her head to get the angle right. On the next forward thrust, he slipped into her throat, and she gagged hard.

"Don't you dare fucking puke on me," he warned, holding her steady with his cock wedged in her throat. Her throat spasmed around him and her eyes watered, and when he finally pulled out, she sucked in a desperate breath.

"Again," he demanded, and shoved himself into her throat again.

When he finally pulled free and took a step back, her face was streaked with tears and her throat felt raw, her neck and chest soaked with drool. She blinked to clear her vision, her eyes locked on his cock. It seemed even thicker than before, and so hard she could actually see it throb. The front of his slacks was soaked with her spit, and she wondered idly if it would stain.

"Something funny?" he asked, and she realized she'd giggled out loud at the thought of him having to explain drool stains to his dry cleaner.

"Just picturing you in jail," she shot back, and wished she'd put on a full face of makeup for the evening. Lipstick on the front of his pants would've been perfect, but she hadn't bothered with it. However, she had worn eyeshadow and mascara. Not much, just

Saturday running errands level makeup, but with the amount of crying she'd been doing, maybe…

She leaned forward suddenly, and before he could move out of the way, rubbed her wet and ravaged face against the front of his slacks. He cursed and tried to yank her away, cursing again when his dick got caught in the tangle of her hair. By the time he'd worked himself free and shoved her back, most of her eye makeup decorated the front of his pants.

He looked down at himself, then scowled at her. "You're going to pay for that."

She smirked back at him, not even bothering to smother the laugh. He looked almost comically ridiculous, standing there in his Armani suit with his dick hanging out, black streaks decorating the wet spot on pants that probably cost more than her rent. "Fuckin' sue me."

"Oh, I'll do more than that," he vowed. He reached down and unclipped her wrist cuffs from her ankle cuffs, then hauled her to her feet. Her legs buckled, and with something akin to amused horror, she felt the plug start to slip from her ass.

"Um…" she began, but it was too late. Too thick and wet for her anus to hold and too heavy to defy gravity, it hit the carpet with a thump and rolled under the bed.

"Did you just drop my butt plug?" Jack asked, a silken note of menace in his voice that almost covered the laugh.

"I told you it was too big," she managed, still shuddering. Her anus was pulsing, the sensitive ring of muscle struggling to close back down after having been held open so long, and every twitch made her clit buzz.

"Your ass didn't think it was too big," Jack replied, backing her up until she was braced against the bed. "That slutty little hole wanted more."

Sadie tried to come up with something sassy to say to that, but she was too horny to think of anything.

He tugged at her arm, and she looked up. He was attaching her wrist cuff—now with an added length of chain—to an eyebolt in the bedpost about a foot from the top, stretching her arm out. He did the same on the other side, then stepped back.

The mattress pushed into the backs of her knees, and she leaned into it, grateful for the support. Her legs weren't quite steady, and her toes were starting to pinch in the boots, but she barely felt it. When Jack turned to rummage in a black bag on the floor, she thought about trying to escape, or maybe planting her boot in his ass, but she couldn't focus enough to decide. She could barely remember she was playing a role, and that almost never happened to her. She was a bratty schoolgirl or a defiant cat burglar to the end, no matter how horny she got.

Except she wasn't sure she'd ever been this horny before, and that meant she was currently much more interested in another orgasm than she was in performative defiance.

"Still with me, sugar tits?" he asked, and she blinked at him. He was standing in front of her again, something shiny in his hand, his fathomless gaze locked on her face.

"Right here, salty dick," she replied, and snickered.

His beard twitched and his eyes crinkled—God, he was cute when his eyes crinkled—but he didn't laugh. "Feeling sassy, I see."

"So are you," she commented, and looked down at his dick. He'd lost a degree or two of stiffness, pointing toward the floor instead of the ceiling now, but it still looked delicious, and her pussy twitched in response. "You gonna do something with that besides wave it around like you're conducting a choir?"

"What's the matter, sweetheart? That pretty little pussy feeling needy?"

"Please," she scoffed, completely unconvincingly.

"I do like it when a woman begs," he drawled. "But I think you can do better. We'll work on it. But first..."

"First what?" she asked when he trailed off and squirmed when his eyes crinkled again. Dammit, he had to stop doing that. She liked it way too much.

"First this," he said, and opened his hand.

She blinked at the set of clover clamps that lay in his palm, the chain connecting them falling to dangle between his fingers.

"Is that all you've got?" she scoffed, even as her nipples puckered in response.

"Oh, don't you worry, sugar," he assured her and reached for the tab of the zipper. "I've got plenty more up my sleeve."

He began to draw the zipper down, and she dropped her head to watch. With her arms out wide, the suit was already stretched to its limit, and as he lowered the zipper inch by slow inch, the PVC peeled back from her torso to bare her breasts. He paused when they bounced free, and she swallowed when she saw how hard her nipples were, standing out like pencil erasers against her pale skin.

She thought he was going to put the clamps on and held her breath in anticipation. But after a moment he continued on, pulling the zipper tab down until it met the end he'd unzipped earlier, just below her belly button.

Her tits were out and so was her cunt, but her arms and legs and sides were still firmly encased in PVC. It was an odd sensation, making her feel more exposed than if she'd actually been completely naked, but she didn't have much time to contemplate it, because he bent and sucked her nipple into his mouth.

She jerked, a squeal on her lips, and braced for pain. But his mouth was soft, his tongue circling gently before he began to suck, and it felt so lovely that she sighed and sagged against the mattress.

But after a moment she began to squirm. He was being so delicate she could hardly feel him, mouthing her breast with barely any suction and not even a hint of teeth. What had started out as soothing was quickly turning annoying – she needed friction, dammit!

She squirmed and wiggled and bucked, trying to get him to nibble or suck harder, but he paid her no heed. Just when she thought she'd scream from frustration, he shifted his attention to the other breast and treated it with the same soft, gentle nuzzling.

"Jack," she said, the word coming out with a distressingly pleading note instead of the firm rebuke she'd intended, but he didn't even twitch. He just kept working her nipple like a dying goldfish and finally, in desperation, she let her head fall back and let out a loud, rumbling snore.

He froze, head still bent to her breast, and she did it again, making sure to drag air hard through her nose for maximum noise.

He picked his head up. "Am I boring you, sugar?"

"Huh? What?" She shook her head, blinking as though coming out of a deep sleep. "Oh. You're still here. I wasn't sure."

There was a snicker from the corner, and she turned to look at James. He shook his head, blue eyes dancing, and she sent him a wink before dropping her head back and letting out another bone-rattling, air-sucking snore.

"Hey. Wake up," Jack said, and slapped her breast. Hard.

"What the fuck?" she yelled, head whipping around to look down at her breast. There was a handprint, bright pink, covering half of the pale globe. "That hurt."

"Good," he said, and slapped the other one just as hard. "Maybe it'll keep you awake."

"I'm awake, I'm awake," she managed, gritting her teeth against the sting.

"Let me just make sure," he said, and slapped both breasts at the same time, his hands swinging in to catch the outer curves. She yelped and he did it again, making her tits bounce and her skin burn. Then, with his glittering eyes locked on hers, he licked the fingers of both hands and brought them down—*crack!*—right on her nipples.

If she hadn't been literally chained to the bed, she'd have fallen to the floor. Pain swam through her system, smothering her senses so his rumbling laugh sounded like it was coming from far, far away.

He laid a hand on her belly, warm and hard and rough against her soft skin, and she tried to focus on it, to center herself. But then something pinched her left nipple, and she looked down at the gleaming clover clamp pinching it tight. He gave the attached chain a tug, pulling the clamp tighter, and she let out a whimper.

"Still bored, sugar?" he asked, low and hard and with an edge that made her shiver, and attached the second clip to her right nipple before she could answer.

Pain enveloped her breasts, bathing them in fire. The lingering sting from the slaps, the hard, cruel pinch of the clamps. Instinct had her holding her breath, but experience told her that would just make it worse. She had to get ahead of this if she was going to be able to handle whatever came next—and there would be a next, no way he was stopping at the clamps—so she sucked air in and blew it out, and kept doing it until the bright, sharp spears of pain faded into a manageable throb.

It merged with the beat of her heart, rattling her ribcage and pounding in her nipples, in her clit until she wasn't sure where pain ended and pleasure began. Maybe it didn't, she thought dimly, and tried to get her whirling senses under control. Maybe they were the same.

"I assume I have your fucking attention now," Jack drawled, pulling her focus from the pain swimming through her system to his face. He wasn't crinkling now, and his beard didn't twitch. His eyes were like ice, cold and hard and black as coal in the low light, not even a hint of warmth in their fathomless depths. For a moment she felt real fear, brighter and sharper than the pain, and *yellow* trembled on the tip of her tongue.

Then he smiled, a slow, sly curl of his lips, and pleasure—genuine and true—slipped into his eyes. "Does it hurt, sugar tits?" he asked, and there was so much anticipation in his voice, so much eager lust that she answered honestly before she could think of a lie.

"Yes."

Her voice was harsh, almost guttural with the pain, and his eyes flared brighter. "Good," he replied, low and soft and smooth as silk. "Is your pussy wet?"

Was it? Her entire body felt like one big, fat, throbbing nerve—with harsher, heavier beats in her breasts and cunt—so she thought it probably was. But she couldn't tell for sure.

She licked her lips, surprised at how dry they were and how much effort it took to talk. "Why don't you…see for yourself?"

His hand still lay on her belly, hard and heavy, so he slid it down, past the spot where the zippers collided, down to the bare folds between her thighs. She shuddered when his hand made contact, fingertips gliding smoothly through the heat and the wet. She could actually hear him touching her, and when he lightly slapped her pussy, it sounded like he'd dropped his hand into a puddle.

"Yeah, you're fucking wet," he growled, and slapped her harder. Her hips jerked, shoving her cunt into his hand. "You like a little pain, don't you?"

"Don't be ridiculous," she managed, and rolled her hips, hoping for firmer contact. The heel of his hand was lying right over her clit, and if she could get just a little more friction…

"I wouldn't want to be ridiculous," he scoffed and pulled his hand away.

"Dammit," she muttered, and sagged against the bed. "If you're not going to do the job, the least you could do is untie one of my hands so I can do it myself."

He trailed his wet fingertips back up her belly, and both hands came up to cup her breasts. "Nobody's getting untied, sugar tits. Your punishment isn't over yet."

Her breasts felt swollen and heavy in his hands, her nipples pulsing dully. He squeezed, pushing them together until the clamps clacked against each other, and she lost her breath in the wave of sensation. His grip was punishing, bruising, forcing blood into her trapped nipples, and it hurt. But it made her clit pulse and her pussy gush, and she wanted his dick inside her so badly she was close to begging.

Get a grip, she admonished herself, and sucked in air. "Get on with it, will you? I've got shit to do."

He laughed and stepped closer, his hands tightening on her tits. He was so close that his cock dragged over the bare skin of her midriff, thick and hot and hard. "You do like pulling the tiger's tail, don't you, sugar?"

She could barely think with his dick trying to punch a hole through her belly button. She wondered what he'd do if she lifted her legs, wrapped them around his waist, and tried to impale herself.

If she could've grabbed onto the bed posts for leverage, she might have tried. But the wrist cuffs didn't give her enough support, so she settled for angling her pelvis forward and rubbing herself against him. "Tiger's tail?" she repeated, grinding against his dick. "More like a tabby's tail."

He leaned into her, forcing her back against the bed, his dick like a brand against her skin. "A tabby?"

He was so close she could count his eyelashes, his breath hot on her face. "Declawed," she breathed, and snapped her teeth as close to his nose as she dared.

He jerked back, a look of stunned shock on his face, which was highly satisfying. But his hands jerked back too, yanking her tits with them. She yelped and stumbled forward, her arms jerking painfully when the chains brought her up short.

"Serves you right," he ground out, and shoved her back. He let go of her breasts, but her relief was short lived when he picked up the chain connecting the clamps and yanked it up. She yelped again as the dull throb in her nipples morphed into screaming agony, and it took her a second to notice the chain he held in front of her face.

"Open," he demanded.

There was only one reason he would be asking her to open her mouth, and she wanted no part of it. "No."

He slapped her breasts, first the left then the right, hard and fast. "I said open your mouth, Sadie."

Tears sprang to her eyes, blurring her vision, but still she shook her head.

"If you don't open your mouth," he warned in a low rasp, "I'm going to torture your tits until you beg, then jerk off on them and leave you with your hands tied all night so you can't reach that need, greedy, wet as the fucking Everglades pussy."

Oh, my God. "What?"

"You heard me." He raised one dark eyebrow. "Well?"

"I hate you," she whispered, torn between wanting to avoid the pain and needing the orgasm they'd been working toward all night.

He smiled, a full beard-twitching, eye-crinkling grin of pure delight. "I know. Now for the last time, open your fucking mouth."

She swallowed hard and parted her lips.

"Wider."

Glaring, she obeyed, and he slipped the chain between her lips. "Close," he ordered, and she did.

"Good girl," he said, his eyes glittering with satisfaction and heat and so much lust it almost stopped her heart. "Keep that chain between those pretty cock-sucking lips, now."

"Or what?" she mumbled, the tang of metal on her tongue.

He bent to brush his lips across her ear. "Or I'll cut those pretty tits to ribbons," he whispered, then turned and walked back to the duffel on the floor.

He wouldn't, she told herself, watching the muscles in his ass flex when he crouched to rummage through the bag. She'd very clearly stated on her limits list that while she was good with knife play, anything beyond a scratch was a hard limit. And James was there, making sure Jack followed the rules. But as threats went, it had teeth, and though part of her was tempted to drop the chain just to see what he'd do, she kept it clamped between her teeth and concentrated on breathing.

Her ass was on fire, her nipples throbbing. Every beat of her heart deepened the torment, the pain bringing with it an almost unbearable pleasure. It was the fly in the ointment, the wrench in the works, because while she could manage the pain, push past the ache and the burn, her throbbing clit and the deep, insistent ache deep inside were too big, too heavy to ignore.

Still, she tried. She couldn't help it, the wanting to win, even though her body was screaming for her to give in. If she gave in there would be relief, and pleasure. If she stopped fighting, he'd fuck her, spear her pussy with his thick, heavy cock. The pain would intensify the orgasm that she knew was coming, and the orgasm would erase the pain, at least for a little while. She'd be feeling it tomorrow, and probably every time she sat down for the next few days, but for those brief, blissful moments, it wouldn't matter.

She was so caught up in the inner battle she didn't see him until he was on top of her again, his face so close she could taste his breath. She blinked to bring him into focus, gasping in shock and pain when his hands clamped onto her ass and lifted her.

"Don't lose that fucking chain," he warned her, stepping between her legs. His cock dragged against the soft skin of her thigh, the rub of latex making her wince, then he was shoving into her, hot and hard and heavy, going balls-deep in a single thrust that would've had her singing hallelujahs if she'd had any breath left in her lungs.

"Jesus," he ground out, fingers digging into her ass. He held her still while he pulled back, dragging his cock through her tender, swollen channel, and shoved forward again.

She cried out, and the chain slipped from her teeth to rest on her bottom lip.

"You just can't fucking follow directions, can you?" He shifted his grip, angling her hips, and on instinct she lifted her legs to wrap them around his waist.

Struggling to think through the flood of sensation, she licked her lips, pushing the chain down to her chin. "You're not the boss of me."

He laughed, a genuine burst of humor that made his cock dance inside her. "You don't think so?"

She shook her head, the chain slipping down to pool at the base of her throat. His dick felt huge inside her, stretching her wide, and she wanted to move—rub against it, ride it, use it to make herself come—but he wasn't moving, and he was holding her too tightly for her to do it.

She had to get him to move.

"Fuck you," she gasped, and snapped her teeth at him again.

"Oh no, baby," he drawled. "Fuck you."

He bent his head, gathering the chain in his teeth, and leaned back. He pulled it taut and kept going, tightening the clamps on her brutalized nipples. She lost her breath in a silent scream, back arching to try to take the pressure off, and her pussy went fist-tight.

He rumbled something that she couldn't quite understand, not with the chain between his teeth and the blood rushing in her ears. He leaned forward, letting the chain dangle between them for a moment, then jerked back again, and her cunt spasmed anew.

She saw literal stars, exploding behind her eyes like sparklers on the Fourth of July, and tasted the sharp coppery tang of blood.

"Open your eyes, Sadie," he demanded, and she realized she'd closed them. She forced them open, blinking to bring him into focus. His face was taut, and there was a glitter in the dark chocolate depths of his eyes. Heat and lust and the cool calculation of a Dom's assessment, making sure she was okay to keep going even though she hadn't even hinted at her safeword. She stared back at him, too far gone to be able to keep her feelings hidden, her ability to censor herself washed away in the flood of pain and the promise of pleasure.

With his eyes locked on hers, he tightened his grip on her ass and began to move.

He fucked her with hard, heavy thrusts that made her legs shake and her tits bounce. The chain was still caught in his mouth, yanking the clamps on her nipples with every bounce, the silver glinting against the gold-flecked mahogany of his beard.

Every heavy, hammering thrust brought a sunburst of pleasure, heightened by the pain in her nipples, in her ass. Her thighs ached from trying to hold on to his hips, her arms from being stretched overhead. She wanted to bitch at him about it, to whine and brat it up, but for once she didn't have the insults. There was nothing in her brain but the need for more, however she could get it.

She started to fuck him back, pumping her hips into his thrusts, and he laughed around the chain.

She didn't care.

The pleasure was gathering in her belly, the need getting stronger with every slide of his cock into her pussy, every bump of his pelvis against her clit. She wanted the promise of that pleasure, the explosion of pressure and tension and need that would burn and cleanse like fire, leaving nothing behind but peace.

She wiggled in his grip, using the little strength she had left in her arms to take a little of her own weight and push it back at him. It helped, but it wasn't nearly enough. She twisted against him, seeking more, and one of his hands slipped and sent his middle finger skidding inward to press against her anus.

Her choked cry, and the accompanying spasm of her pussy around his cock, made him smile around the chain. "That what you need?" he muttered, bouncing her to adjust his grip so the middle fingers of both hands connected with her fluttering anus. He dug in and pulled, spreading the tender hole enough for both fingers to slip into the slight gape.

The orgasm hit her like a lightning strike, white hot and sudden, crackling through her. A scream tore from her throat that he swallowed when he kissed her. She tasted metal and blood and a hint of minty toothpaste when his tongue thrust into her mouth, tangling with hers around the chain in an almost desperate kiss. She bit his tongue as the spasms in her pussy went on and on, and cried into his mouth when he bit back. The chain tightened, bringing a burst of pain that set off another round of spasms.

He wrenched his mouth from hers, the chain falling to land on her chest. He followed it down, sinking his teeth into the upper swell of her breast with a growl, his hips speeding up to hammer into her even harder.

She closed her eyes, bouncing and shaking in his grip as he pounded her, floating on a sea of endorphins. He stiffened between her thighs, his cock swelling and pulsing inside her as he came.

She kept them closed when he softened his grip on her ass and unlocked his teeth from her breast, when he slid his still hard cock from her swollen cunt and set her gently on her feet. She swayed when he released her arms, sagging against him when he scooped her up and laid her on the bed, and when she finally opened her eyes and saw him staring back at her with concern and what could only be described as affection, she wondered what the hell she'd done.

Chapter Nine

Jack closed the door gently behind him.

"How is she?"

He looked up at James, seated by the fireplace with a drink in his hand. "Asleep."

"I'm not surprised. That was…"

"Intense," Jack finished, and collapsed on the sofa.

"It was that," James agreed, and held out a glass. "Here. I took the liberty."

"Thanks." Jack took the tumbler of whiskey, swirling the glass so the amber liquid danced in the firelight.

"You're going to need to have those pants cleaned," James remarked.

Jack dropped his gaze to his lap. His slacks were no longer damp, but there were definite stains, and not just from Sadie rubbing her face all over his crotch. "Yeah. My dry cleaner is going to have questions."

James chuckled. "Worth it?"

Jack lifted his bare feet to the hearth, letting the dancing fire warm his toes, and sipped his drink. "Oh, yeah."

"And on that note..." James rose, glass in hand. "I'm going upstairs to fuck my wife."

"Enjoy," Jack said with a smile. "And thanks for playing DM."

"Happy to help." James headed for the stairs. "Feel free to help yourself to anything you need in the kitchen and ignore any noises coming from the second floor."

"Will do. 'Night."

Alone, Jack turned his gaze to the flames dancing in the fireplace. He was loose and relaxed from the scene and the sex, but his mind felt almost painfully alert, and he wouldn't sleep for several hours yet. He didn't feel like turning on the television, so he settled back into his chair, inched his feet closer to the fire, and went over the scene in his mind.

She'd liked the pain, he mused, staring into the flames. He'd given her plenty, with the ass beating and the breast torture, and though it had shocked and scared her, she'd soaked it up like a dry sponge. He'd forced himself not to push her too far, too fast, but he'd wanted to see how she'd react to real pain, and couldn't be more pleased with the result. There was no doubt in his mind she could take more, though he didn't know if she realized it, or would believe him if he told her so.

She didn't trust him yet, and though it was frustrating, he couldn't blame her. As an unattached submissive, she was smart to be careful, though he thought most of her reticence had more to do with a desire to keep him at a distance rather than any real concerns about her safety. Still, her boundaries were hers to set, and he would respect them.

Which is why he hadn't objected to her demands for a neutral play space, or her insistence on having James act as DM. Building trust was a process, one that couldn't be rushed, and he already knew building Sadie's trust in him was likely to be a long, complicated one.

It didn't bother him. Whatever she needed to feel safe, he'd make sure she got, and hopefully, she'd eventually realize her safety and well-being was as important to him as it was to her. It might take a while, but he wasn't going anywhere.

He'd been waiting for this chance for too long to waste it.

"Hi."

He turned at the soft sound. He'd been so lost in his own thoughts he hadn't heard the door open, and she was already halfway across the room. She was wrapped in the thick green robe he'd left draped over the foot of the bed, so big it all but swallowed her up. Her hair was loose, hanging past her shoulders in tangles and snarls, and her eyes were sleepy. Her cheeks were free of the tear tracks and makeup smears she'd been sporting when he tucked her in, so he surmised that she'd managed a trip to the bathroom before seeking him out.

"Hey," he replied, his voice coming out gruffer than he'd intended. She looked so vulnerable and small, wrapped in his robe with her face scrubbed and glowing, and he was struck by the competing urges to cuddle and comfort, or tie her down and fuck her up again.

He cleared his throat and reminded himself that he was trying *not* to spook her. "Having trouble sleeping?"

She shrugged, lifting a hand to brush at her hair as she shuffled closer. Her sleeve fell away, revealing the soft white skin on the underside of her forearm. "I dozed, but I'm not really tired."

Her voice was husky and thick, but she didn't sound distressed. "Did you drink the water I left for you?"

"Yes, Daddy."

"Careful," he warned. "I don't care how bruised your ass is, I'll still paddle it."

"The hell you will," she warned him, eyes flashing. They were hazel right now, he saw, and soft with contentment despite the bite in her tone. "I'm going to be lucky to be able to sit tomorrow as it is."

He chuckled, unfazed. He'd gotten a good look at her butt when he'd tucked her in, and he'd bet a bottle of fifty-year-old Scotch that she'd be eating standing up through Monday. "I know."

She rolled her eyes, but her smile was shy. "Um, Amanda invited me to stay here tonight."

He nodded. "I know."

"Are you staying?"

"I was planning on it," he said, treading carefully. He couldn't read her face. "But if you'd rather be home, I'm happy to drive you."

"I was going to stay," she told him, and he let out a quiet breath of relief. "Is it okay if I hang out here for a while?"

"Sure," he said, and kept his hands at his sides when she came closer. He wanted to reach for her, but her eyes were wary. "I can move to a chair."

"You're fine," she told him, and lowered herself gingerly to the cushion at the other end of the sofa. She lay on her side, curling up in a loose fetal position, and he saw her feet.

"You found the socks."

"Oh. Yeah." She lifted her foot, wiggling her toes inside the fuzzy tiger-striped socks.

"Are they okay?"

"Perfect."

Testing, he drew her feet into his lap. After an initial jerk of surprise, she didn't resist. "Feeling okay?"

"A little loopy." She shifted, twisting her torso so she faced him more squarely while still lying on her hip.

"That's normal." He reached out and patted her butt, smiling when she jerked and hissed. "How's your ass?

"It hurts." She said it with a scowl, but her eyes were shining.

"Yeah?" He grinned. "How much?"

"On a scale of one to ten?" She grabbed a throw pillow and wedged it under her head. "Seven and a half."

"I went too easy on you."

"Believe me," she said fervently, "you did not."

"Are you going to tell me you didn't like it?"

"I'd like to tell you that." She shifted, wincing when her butt hit the back cushions. "But aside from the part where you were gumming my nipples like a dying goldfish—"

"Like a *what*?"

"—I really liked it," she finished, and her eyes drifted closed on a sigh. "I don't think I've come that hard in…ever."

"Well." He sat back, surprised. "That sounds suspiciously like a compliment."

Her eyes stayed closed. "I assume that squeaking I hear is the sound of your ego expanding."

That surprised a laugh out of him. "Does your mouth ever quit?"

"Not really," she said, and yawned.

She looked so small bundled up in his bathrobe, her hair tangled on the pillow and her lashes casting faint shadows on her flushed cheeks. Stripped of mascara, they were the same strawberry-blonde as her hair, and for some reason he found that fascinating. Her mouth was soft and swollen, the lips parted to give just a glimpse of strong white teeth. He smiled when he remembered her snapping at him, and wondered, if given the chance, she'd actually bite him.

The robe covered her from neck to ankle, her hands pulled inside the sleeves. She shifted her feet, one of them bumping up against his crotch. Her eyes popped open, and she pulled them back an inch. "Sorry."

"It's fine," he assured her. "Are you cold?"

"No, but…"

"What?" he prompted.

"Can I put my toes under your leg?"

He raised an eyebrow, curious at the sudden shyness in her gaze. "Sure, if you want."

"They're not cold," she assured him, wedging her toes under his thigh. "I just like sleeping with something on my feet."

"The socks don't do the trick?"

"I need something heavy. I usually put a pillow over them," she admitted, the pink on her cheeks deepening. "I know, it's weird."

"I've seen weirder." Her toes wiggled against his leg, more of a poke than a caress, but he nonetheless felt the beginning stirrings of arousal. "You sure you're not cold? I can get a blanket."

She shook her head, her eyes drifting closed again. "I'm fine."

The words were faint, and slightly slurred, so he wasn't surprised when a moment later, her breath puffed out in the slow, deep rhythm of sleep.

And watching her, he wondered what came next.

* * * *

"Then what happened?"

Sadie shrugged and reached for her wine. "Nothing. I woke up in the bed and he was gone."

Olivia frowned. "He left?"

"About seven-thirty," Amanda confirmed. "That's what James said, anyway. I was still sleeping, too."

"It's no big deal," Sadie said, glancing around the room at her friends. They were all crowded around the coffee table, Olivia and Rebecca crammed in next to her on the couch, Sam and Amanda in the chairs opposite. "It's not like I needed aftercare at that point."

"I always need aftercare the morning after a hard scene," Olivia put in and reached for the plate of cheese and crackers on the table. "Even if it's just extra cuddles."

Sadie shrugged and sipped her wine. It might have been nice to wake up to cuddles, but she didn't expect it. "He put a pillow on my feet. That was enough."

"Did he call you at least?" Rebecca wanted to know.

"He texted me Sunday afternoon," Sadie said. "To check in."

"He called James, too, to make sure you ate breakfast before you left our house."

Sadie blinked at Amanda. "He did?"

"Has he called you since Sunday?"

"No." Sadie turned to look at Rebecca. "Why would he? It's not like we're going to play again."

"You're not?"

"No."

Rebecca grabbed the plate of crackers from Olivia. "You don't sound very sure."

Sadie smothered a wince in another sip of wine. "Well, he didn't *say* anything about playing again."

Sam popped up to snag the bowl of grapes, then sat back down. "Do you want to play with him again?"

Sadie pondered the question. She'd thought of little else since she'd woken up alone on Sunday morning, and she still wasn't sure what the answer was.

"I don't know," she admitted. "I mean, I had a good time—"

"That sounds like the understatement of the year," Rebecca muttered.

"—but we're completely incompatible."

"You sound pretty compatible to me," Olivia said around the wedge of cheese she was nibbling.

"I'm still kind of shocked he planned a role-play scene," Amanda put in. "I don't think he's ever done that before."

Sadie frowned. "Do you think he did that just for me?"

"Well, not *just* for you," Amanda gestured with her wine glass. "He got something out of it, too."

"I know, but…"

"He probably came up with it because he knew you'd enjoy it," Rebecca said. "Which I think is sweet."

"Very sweet," Amanda agreed, and the others murmured their assent.

"I also think he enjoyed the hell out of it," Rebecca continued.

"He did laugh a lot," Sadie murmured, remembering.

Amanda leaned forward, eyes sharp. "Really?"

"Not mocking laughter, or like something was funny. It was more…joyful," she decided.

"Happy sadist laughter," Sam put in. "That's what Collette calls it when she's having so much fun she just can't hold it in."

"Nick does that sometimes," Rebecca said with a nod. "It's hot."

"Very," Sam agreed.

"It scared me a little," Sadie admitted and laughed. "And yeah, it was hot."

"But you don't want to play with him again."

Sadie looked at Amanda and sighed. "Truth? I do. And that scares me, too."

"It's about damn time," Amanda said.

"Hear, hear," Rebecca said and leaned across the coffee table to tap her glass against Amanda's.

Sadie's mouth dropped open in shock. "You *want* me to be scared?"

"Of course not." Amanda reached over to pat her hand. "But if you're scared, then it matters."

"And that *is* something we want for you," Rebecca said. "Because we love you."

"Um. Thanks, I guess?"

"You're welcome."

Olivia reached for another piece of cheese. "Why did he put a pillow on your feet?"

"Because I can't sleep unless there's something heavy on my feet."

Rebecca's gray eyes went dreamy. "Aww."

"That's fucking adorable," Sam decided.

Amanda nodded, eyes sparkling. "Hallmark channel-level cute."

"Hey, did you hear that Nikki has a date with Kody?" Sadie asked brightly.

"Smooth," Olivia said, and Amanda snickered into her wine.

"That is a very obvious ploy and normally we would not let you get away with it," Rebecca admonished. "But I'm very invested in this Nikki-Kody thing. When are they going out?"

"Friday," Sadie supplied.

"Scene or date?" Sam wanted to know.

"Date." Relieved to be talking about something other than her suddenly very confused feelings about Jack, Sadie plucked a handful of grapes out of the bowl Sam still held. "She told me Kody said they should get to know each other before they discuss playing."

"That's sweet," Rebecca decided.

"It is," Olivia agreed. "Kody comes off as kind of a hard ass, but they're kind of a marshmallow."

"I don't know about marshmallow," Sadie said. "You've seen them do a needle scene, right?"

"Right." Rebecca gave a delicate shudder. "Nick wants to learn, but I'm not so sure I'm ready to be a human pincushion."

"It's fun," Sam said, and as the conversation shifted to the pros and cons of needle play—pros, endorphins! Cons, blood—Sadie tried not to think about how much she wanted Jack to call her again. Or what she would do if he did.

* * * *

"Like a what?"

Jack took his shot, waiting until the four ball had landed with a satisfying clatter in the side pocket before he answered. "A dying goldfish."

Nick was laughing so hard he had to lean on the pool table for support. Cade wore a look of wide-eyed fascination, and James was grinning into his beer.

"Excuse me." Cade lifted a hand. "She said that mid-scene?"

"After," Jack clarified and circled the table to find his next shot.

"Mid-scene she pretended to fall asleep," James told them, and sent Nick off into gales of laughter again. "Snoring like a congested moose."

Jack crouched to eye the five ball. It was partially shielded by the seven, but maybe a bank shot would work. "She wasn't snoring for long."

"I bet," Cade muttered, but he was smiling. "I'm actually sorry I missed that."

"Me, too," Nick wheezed.

"It was all I could do to keep from laughing," Jack admitted, and rose to take his shot.

He sank the five, but he fouled by hitting the seven ball first. Taking it philosophically, he handed the cue to Nick. "Your turn."

Nick frowned at the table. "What am I supposed to do with this mess?"

Twisting the cap off a beer, Jack settled into a chair. "Your meager best."

"Bite me," Nick muttered and bent to examine the setup.

"So, is this going to be a regular thing?" Cade sank into the chair next to Jack, a soda in his hand. "You and Sadie?"

"Yeah, right," Nick scoffed and, repositioning the cue ball to his advantage, lined up his shot. "Six, side pocket."

Jack watched him sink the ball with amusement. "You don't think Sadie will play with me again?"

"You had to win a bet to get her to do it the first time," Nick reminded him. "I'm still surprised she went through with it."

"Maybe my sparkling wit and sunshine personality won her over."

"No, that's not it. Seven, far corner."

"Olivia said Sadie told her she's been bored lately," Cade put in.

"That could be it," Nick allowed and shot his cue forward.

Jack cocked an eyebrow as balls clattered. "Are you saying she only played with me because she had nothing better to do?"

"Or pity," Nick offered. "That's another possibility. Nine off the eight, near corner."

"I don't think it was pity, or boredom," James put in, rising to cross to the bar. He popped the top on a fresh beer and poured it into the pilsner he held. "It wasn't even the bet, because nobody would hold her to that."

"That's true," Cade mused, looking thoughtful. "I have to admit, I'm at a loss."

"Did it ever occur to either of you chuckle fucks that she did it because she wanted to?"

"Oh, she definitely wanted to." James returned to his seat with his fresh beer. "I haven't seen her that excited in months."

"That was probably the role-play," Nick offered, eyeing the only ball left on the table besides the cue ball. "Or the catsuit. You let her keep it, right?"

"Right."

"Definitely the catsuit, then. Eight ball, that corner."

"You'll never make that shot," Cade warned him.

"Fuck off." Nick drew back his cue. The string of curses he let out when the cue ball went sailing past the eight without touching it made Jack smile.

Cade shook his head. "Told ya."

"You can't do it."

Cade rose smoothly to his feet and took the proffered cue. "Hold my Coke."

Nick took the can and collapsed into Cade's vacated seat. "Where was I?"

"It was the catsuit," Jack prompted.

"Nah, it couldn't have been that," Cade said from the other side of the pool table, cue ball in hand. "I mean, sure, they're expensive, and I bet she's happy to have it, but if Sadie really didn't want to play with you, you could offer her a gold-plated catsuit with a diamond-studded zipper and she'd tell you to shove it up your ass."

"This is true." Nick frowned. "Shit. She really must have wanted to play with you."

"Thank you," Jack said drily.

"I gotta admit, this is blowing my mind."

"Yeah? Well, brace yourself. I want her."

"Well, that's not news," Nick said.

"No, I mean I *want* her. As my submissive."

Nick stared, uncomprehending for a moment, then his eyes went wide. "You *want* her?"

"As your *submissive?*" Cade echoed and shot the cue ball clean off the table.

"Dammit, Cade." James got to his feet. "If you've torn the felt..."

"The felt is fine," Cade said, laying his cue down without even looking at it, his eyes locked on Jack. "I'll pay for the felt. You want her as your *submissive?*"

"Is that so strange?" Jack wondered.

"Yes," they chorused in unison.

"I don't think it's so strange." James shrugged when both Cade and Nick turned to gape at him.

"Thank you, James," Jack said.

"You're welcome, Jack."

"Why?"

Jack didn't pretend to misunderstand Nick's question. "Why not?"

"She's a brat," Nick pointed out.

"I like brats."

"She's not a masochist," Cade added.

"No, but there's a pain slut hiding in there," Jack countered, enjoying himself. "You just have to push the right buttons."

"Are you in love with her?"

Jack eyed Nick over his beer, considering. "We don't know each other well enough for me to say that yet."

Nick's eyes went bug-wide. "*Yet?*"

"Well, damn." Cade leaned back against the pool table. "I did not see this coming."

"Do you have any idea what you're getting yourself into?" Nick demanded. "This is Sadie we're talking about. She's...well, she's..."

"Beautiful? Funny? Sexy? Loyal?" Jack supplied.

"And fragile," Cade put in with a frown. "She comes off like a ball buster, but that's an act."

"Not all of it," Nick protested, then conceded, "but some of it."

"There's a lot of fear hiding under all that swagger," James agreed quietly.

"Major intimacy issues," Nick agreed, frowning at Jack. "If she finds out you're thinking about a serious relationship, she'll bolt."

Jack nodded soberly. "I know."

"You got a plan?" Cade wanted to know.

Jack looked at the three of them, considering. These were his friends, as close to him as brothers. They were the people who, aside from family, knew him best—in some ways, knew him better. "It's pretty bare bones. I wouldn't mind getting some opinions on it."

Cade took his Coke back from Nick and resumed his position against the pool table. "Tell us whatcha got."

Jack leaned forward, waited for Nick and James and Cade to do the same, and filled them in.

Chapter Ten

When the phone rang on Saturday morning, Sadie scowled. Though her Saturday schedule usually held one or two client appointments, she'd cleared her calendar so she could spend the day finishing her redecorating projects. But she'd gotten into a groove yesterday and worked late into the night, and when she'd fallen into bed at three-thirty in the morning, both the bathroom and her new massage room were client ready.

She planned to celebrate by staying in bed as late as possible, getting up only to pee and eat, then climbing back into bed. Whoever was calling at the ungodly hour of—she opened one eye to squint at the bedside clock—ten-thirty in the morning was interfering with that plan, and she didn't appreciate it.

She wanted to ignore it. But she had parents who were getting older, and siblings with small children, and emergencies happened. So she fought one hand out of the covers, grabbing for the phone on the nightstand, and managed to somehow hit the right spot on the screen to answer. "H'lo."

There was a beat of silence before a low, smooth voice said, "Did I wake you?"

Her eyes flew open in surprise, then slammed shut again against the sunlight streaming through the window. "Oh, God."

"Good morning to you, too."

She couldn't get her bearings. The light burned her eyes, and now that she was conscious her bladder was demanding attention. And for some reason she was talking to—

"Jack?" she rasped.

"So you are awake," he replied, the amusement in his voice deeper now. "I wasn't sure."

"Barely." Her voice was a hoarse croak, her mouth dry. She'd have given her new catsuit for a bottle of water. "What are you doing?"

"Talking to you," he replied. "What are you doing?"

"Sleeping."

"Late night?" he asked.

She grunted, rolling onto her side. She'd been sleeping on her stomach, but her bladder wasn't having that anymore. "I'm sleeping in. It's Saturday."

"So it is."

Sadie yawned, her attention drifting. With the need to pee momentarily muted, fatigue was creeping in again, and she was almost asleep again when she realized Jack was talking. "What?"

"Maybe I should call back when you're awake," he said with a chuckle.

"No, it's fine," she mumbled, and fought back another yawn. "What were you saying?"

"I said, what are you doing later this afternoon?"

"Nothing." She forced her eyes open and stared at the window, hoping the streaming sunlight would keep her awake. "Why?"

"Want to do something?"

Wariness kicked in, a beat too late. "Like what?"

He chuckled again. "So suspicious. You can relax, I'm not asking you on a date."

Relief came first, followed by a sense of disappointment that she didn't care to examine too closely. "What *are* you asking me for?"

"A favor."

"Okay." She waited, but he didn't say anything else, and she was starting to get irritated. She wanted to get up to pee so she could go back to sleep, and she couldn't do either until she got off the phone. "Are you going to tell me what it is, or am I supposed to guess?"

"You're not much of a morning person, are you?"

"No." She fought off a yawn. "Either tell me what the favor is or go away so I can pee and get back to sleep."

He chuckled. "Fine. I have a bondage class this afternoon—"

"Since when do you teach bondage classes?" she interrupted.

"Since Cade asked me to fill in for him. He's got a family thing today."

"Oh." The light was too bright to keep staring at it, so she closed her eyes. "Sorry, go on."

"It's an hour class, basic bondage ties. I demonstrate a few of them with you, then the students pair off and practice on each other."

"Hmmm," she said, drifting again, then her eyes popped open. "What? What do you mean, demonstrate them with me?"

"That's the favor," he explained, sounding amused again. "I want you to do the class with me."

Sadie sat up and shoved the hair out of her face. She clearly needed to be more alert for this conversation. "Why?"

He chuckled. "Well, that's blunt."

She winced. "Sorry. That came out wrong. I meant...why me?"

"Why not you?" he replied mildly. "I need someone to demonstrate on, and while I could probably use one of the students, they don't know me."

"And I do?"

"More than they," he pointed out. "You're experienced, comfortable in front of a crowd—"

"This is sounding familiar," she muttered.

"What was that?"

"Nothing. Go on."

"The class meets at one of the student's homes," he said, "and everyone keeps their clothes on. The class lasts an hour, but I figure with travel and setup, it'll take about two hours of your time."

Sadie rubbed a hand over her eyes. "What time does it start?"

"Two o'clock. Are you interested?"

"I don't know yet. Gimme a minute."

"Take your time," he said and fell silent.

Sadie tried to think. She knew if she said no, he'd accept it, no questions asked. The trouble was, she wasn't sure she wanted to. It had been a week since they'd played in James and Amanda's basement, and she was feeling...antsy. Her bruises had healed, all evidence of the scene erased by the passage of time, and it bummed her out every time she looked in the mirror. It was always a bit of a let-down when marks faded after a hard scene, but she always knew there were more to come. The next scene, the next spanking. The next Dom. But it was unlikely she'd ever wear Jack's marks again, and for reasons she refused to examine too closely, the knowledge was disheartening.

An hour's worth of fully clothed bondage wasn't going to get her a bruised butt or teeth marks on her nipples, but it was better than nothing. She'd been horny since she'd woken up alone on Sunday morning, and her vast and varied collection of porn and sex toys hadn't done much to take the edge off. Maybe an afternoon of being tied up—even an R rated version—would be the catalyst for finally finding some relief.

"All right," she said finally. "I'll do it."

"Good," he said, as though he'd known all along she would. "Wear comfortable clothes, preferably something with some stretch, and leave your hair down. I'll pick you up at one-thirty."

"Fine," she said, hiding her rising excitement behind a cool, disaffected tone. She felt like the sun had just come out after a long and heavy rain, but he didn't need to know that.

"Make sure you eat something at least an hour before. I don't want you passing out on me."

"Yes, Boss," she said, and since he couldn't see her, stuck her tongue out. "Anything else?"

He just chuckled. "Don't be late."

He disconnected without another word, and Sadie rolled her eyes. "Goodbye to you, too," she muttered and fought her way out of the covers and hurried into the bathroom to pee.

"It's a demo," she reminded herself as she washed her hands. "Just another demo, and no big deal at all."

Then she grinned at her reflection. "But I'll shave anyway."

* * * *

Four hours later, Sadie was lying on the floor in a hogtie while Jack circled the room, checking on everyone's practice ties.

She was pretty comfortable. The carpet was nice and thick, and the leggings she'd worn were snug but stretchy so nothing was pinching, and though he'd gathered her hair in a ponytail and attached it to the ropes holding her wrists and ankles, she had enough slack to lay her cheek on the pillow someone had thoughtfully tucked under her head.

There were half a dozen couples in the class, most of them in their thirties or forties, and their enthusiasm was charming. And she had to admit, Jack was a good teacher. He was calm and clear in his instructions, and he answered questions or made corrections with patience, kindness and humor—no Resting Dick Face to be seen.

She still wasn't used to him smiling. It was weird, but she couldn't say she didn't like it.

She wiggled a little on the floor, flexing her hands to keep the blood flowing. He hadn't tied her very tight, the ropes just snug enough to keep her in the hog-tie position, and she could feel the knots when she ran her fingertips over the ropes. For a moment she toyed with the idea of trying to get out of them, just to see what he'd do, then discarded the idea with a sigh. This wasn't a scene, and it wasn't about her.

"You doing okay down there?" Jack asked, and she looked up to see him crouched in front of her.

He wore all black, jeans and a Henley with the sleeves shoved to his elbows, and his hair was tied back in his habitual man bun. He'd had a beard trim sometime in the last week, and when he smiled, she could all but count his teeth.

"I'm fine," she assured him, and tried not to drool. He looked really good, and the ropes pressing into her bare arms combined with the restricted position were making her horny again. "How's everyone doing?"

"Good," he said, glancing around. "They're a good group, eager to learn."

"They seem like it." Sadie smiled when laughter broke out across the room. "They're having fun, anyway."

"That's the whole point." He looked back down at her. "How about you?"

"I'm enjoying myself," she replied, and it was true. Though she'd be enjoying herself more if she was naked and he was naked and he was using those pearly whites on her neck.

Get it out of the gutter, Sadie, she admonished herself, and refocused on his face. "Well, as much as I can being stuck on the floor."

"I think I like you on the floor," he mused.

"That's because you're a pervert," she informed him.

He flicked the end of her nose. "Takes one to know one."

She wrinkled her nose. "Rude."

He just chuckled and pushed to his feet. "All right, everyone," he called out, and the chatter and movement stopped as all eyes turned to him. "Now that the riggers have gotten comfortable with a hog tie, let's give the rope bottoms something to work on—getting *out* of a hog tie."

Sadie lifted her head off the pillow. "Hello."

A titter went through the room, and Jack aimed his fathomless eyes at her. "Want to give it a shot?"

She eyed him warily. "I'd say yes, but I don't know if I trust you."

He just watched her, both eyebrows up and a smile on his mouth. "Go ahead, try to get out of that."

"I notice you didn't say I could trust you," she said, still eyeing him with suspicion.

"Sometimes you've just got to roll the dice, darling," he said, and turned his attention to the couple closest to him. "Lucas, let's see how well Melanie's knots hold up."

Sadie waited a beat, but he didn't look back, so she began to feel along the ropes wrapped around her wrists. When she found no knots, just layers of rope, she switched her attention to the rope tethering her wrists to her ankles, and there struck gold. But the knot was just out of her reach, her fumbling fingers unable to hold it. So she arched back, bringing her heels closer to her head. With some slack in the rope, she found the knot again and, able to grasp it firmly now, went to work.

She kept a careful eye on Jack as she untied the first knot, then moved onto the next. He'd left Lucas and Melanie to their own devices and was now deep in conversation with Francine and Kara. Francine had made short work of the ropes, so Jack was giving Kara some extra pointers before moving on to the next pair.

Her attention on Jack faltered as her fingers encountered a particularly difficult cluster of rope between her feet. She tried to extend her feet and twist her head to see, but she hadn't yet managed to undo the knot holding her hair in place. Extending her feet gained her nothing but a sore neck, and the only thing she could see was the ceiling. So she pulled her feet into her butt once more and, using the tips of her fingers, felt carefully around the cluster to see if she could tell how it was put together.

The rope under her fingers moved, the slightest loosening. Encouraged, she plucked at the knot, excitement rising as it began to unravel. The bindings on her wrists went slack, and she twisted her arm to work her hand out of the loop. She stifled a shout of triumph and reached for the tie around her hair, then squeaked in shock when a fist closed over her ponytail, trapping her fingers, and yanked her head back.

She blinked away the sparks that danced across her vision and looked up into Jack's amused face. "Having fun?"

"Oodles," she purred, and batted her eyelashes.

He chuckled, his grip on her hair easing, and after a moment the tension on her hair loosened, and the thin rope he'd used to bind it fluttered to the floor. "I think we're about out of time," he announced and continued to loosen the knots she hadn't been able to. "If your rope bunny is still tied up, go ahead and untie them. Does anyone have any questions?"

Sadie vaguely heard someone ask about quick release knots, but she didn't follow the answer. She was too busy enjoying Jack's hands on her.

She'd tried to ignore it at first, when he'd begun tying her up at the beginning of the class. But she was too horny, and she remembered too clearly just what those hands could do, so after a few minutes she'd stopped fighting it and allowed herself to enjoy it. She'd savored every brush of his fingers over her skin, every layer of rope he wound around her wrists. When he'd gathered her hair to tie it up, she'd resisted, just so he'd pull harder, and had almost bitten through her tongue to keep a moan from slipping free.

The last bit of rope fell away from her ankles, and Jack's hands were gone. She sat up as he crossed the room and watched him crouch next to Melanie over a still prone and bound Lucas. She rubbed absently at her wrists, feeling the impressions left behind by the rope, and tried not to sigh with disappointment. To distract herself, she picked up one of the piles of rope lying on the floor around her. She ran the treated hemp through her hands, somehow soft and rough at the same time, and began to coil it up. When the thirty-foot length was in a tight, tidy bundle, she set it aside and reached for the next.

"Well, aren't you helpful?" Jack crouched in front of her and picked up one of the neat bundles to examine it. "Not bad. Thanks."

She handed him the last bundle with a smile. "You're welcome."

He bounced the rope in his hand, eyeing her thoughtfully. "Do you do this a lot? Bundle rope after a scene?"

She pushed her hair back, wincing at the tangles. She should've brought a comb. "Sometimes, but mostly I just practice with my own."

His eyebrows rose, ever so slightly. "You have rope?"

"I have a toy bag, same as you," she said, amused now.

"Is that right?" He laid the rope down, his eyes on hers. "Is this like carrying your own aftercare supplies?"

"A single submissive has to be prepared. What if I'm playing with someone who doesn't have their own nipple clamps?"

"God forbid," he murmured, a faint smile curving his lips. "What else is in this toy bag of yours?"

"The basics." He was watching her so intently that she began gathering rope bundles just to have something to do.

"Like what?" he prodded.

"Rope, wrist and ankle cuffs, nipple clamps. Some candles, a paddle, vibrators and the like. I had a Wartenberg wheel, but I lost it somewhere." She paused, rope in hand, and scowled. "It was medical grade, too."

"Ouch."

She added the bundle she held to the pile on the floor. "Tell me about it."

"How often do you have to get into it?"

"Into my toy bag?" She shrugged. "More often than you'd think."

"Hmmm."

"Don't start that," she warned him.

"You had fun today."

She glanced around. All the couples were packing up, chattering easily amongst themselves as they gathered rope. "I did."

"We've been invited to stay for cocktail hour," he told her. "Apparently it's part of the regular programs."

"That's nice."

"But?"

Of course he'd heard the but. *Friggin' Doms.* "I'm not really in the mood to socialize," she admitted. "But if you want to stay, I can catch a rideshare."

"I'm not feeling very social, either," he said, and rose smoothly to his feet. His rope bag in one hand, he extended the other. "But I wouldn't mind getting a cup of coffee."

She looked at his hand, then up at his face. She didn't want coffee—she wanted him, and she was tired of pretending she didn't. "Instead of coffee, could you take me back to your place and fuck me?"

Though his eyes widened slightly in surprise, he didn't miss a beat. "Can I tie you up again first?"

"Can I try to get out of it?"

"Yes."

"Good." She put her hand in his and let him haul her to her feet. Her heart was beating fast, her mouth was dry, and she was glad she'd remembered to wear underwear otherwise she might have left a wet spot on Lucas and Melanie's carpet. "Let's go."

* * * *

Twenty minutes later, she was standing naked in Jack's living room while he laid out the ground rules.

"The second floor is off limits," he said, pushing a large square leather ottoman into the wide space between two sofas. He'd already dumped his rope bag out onto the couch, piling it high with multi-colored hemp. The sight of all that rope—and knowing what he intended to do with it—made her feel overheated, despite her nudity. Her thighs were wet, her pussy dripping thanks to the earlier bondage and anticipation, and she had to force herself to pay attention. "You set foot on those stairs, and you'll earn a punishment."

He looked almost unbearably hot, standing there in his black Henley and black jeans. Silver glinted at his throat and ears, visible with his hair still up, and his feet were bare. She was grateful he'd only removed his shoes—if he'd taken off anything else, she probably wouldn't have heard a word he was saying. What had he said? *Oh, right.* "What kind of punishment?"

"Whatever kind I choose," he said and smiled.

It was his predator's smile, and seeing it made her nipples tighten and her belly clench and her thighs grow even wetter. And from the way the gleam in his eyes brightened, she was pretty sure he knew it.

"Right." She swallowed and forced herself to look around. He lived in a loft, a large, open space with a wall of windows and exposed ductwork that had been painted black. The wood floors were cool on her bare feet, but she was so overheated it barely registered. There was minimal furniture—a dining table at the far end, tucked between an open kitchen and the stairs to the second floor, the two couches at the other.

There was a floating wall on the far side of the sofas, behind which sat an office, and another past the dining table that hid a small guest bedroom and bath. The second floor held the main bedroom, and she was a little disappointed that she wouldn't get to see it.

All the furniture was black, which didn't surprise her—even the granite counter that ran the length of the open kitchen was black. But there was color in the art on the walls, in the rugs and bits of sculpture and knickknacks set out. It was, despite the stark, modern style, a surprisingly warm and inviting space.

Focus, Sadie, she admonished herself and cleared her throat. "So I have the whole first floor?"

"Minus the office," he qualified. "And try not to crash into the bar."

She looked around, confused, then spotted a low cabinet positioned under the windows. It was mid-century modern, wood with brass handles and narrow legs. It looked like an old console television, and a tray with glasses and a shaker rested on top. "You mean that?"

He nodded. "I don't care about the glasses but breaking the bottles inside will earn you another punishment."

"Got it." She wanted to ask what kind of booze he kept in there that was so special, but that wasn't going to get her any closer to an orgasm. "Anything else?"

He shook his head. "Your turn. Anything you want to declare off limits?"

She nodded. "No anal sex."

Curiosity and humor joined the heat in his expression. "Is this the farting thing again?"

"No—well, yes, but also..." She thought for a moment, trying to decide just how to phrase it. "You know how when you're expecting company, you clean your house?"

"Yes," he said, confused now.

"I wasn't expecting company."

He blinked, then barked out a laugh. "Fair enough. What about plugs?"

"That's fine," she decided.

"Okay. Anything else?"

"No orgasm denial," she added. "I know you're a sadist, but there are lines."

"Speaking of sadism," he said, still amused, "what kind of pain do you want?"

"The kind that gets me orgasms," she answered promptly.

"I meant, what level of pain," he clarified with a chuckle. "If on a scale of one to ten, our last scene was a five..."

"Oh." She thought for a minute. The pain he'd given her in James' basement had been shocking, and in the moment overwhelming, but there also had been moments when she'd wanted more. "Maybe a seven?" she finally said.

"You don't sound sure."

"I'm not, not really." She had to fight not to fidget. She was already so aroused, so ready, that she was tempted to call off the scene and just ask him to fuck her. But she knew a simple fuck, while fun, wouldn't be satisfying. "I think I want a little more, but I don't know how much."

He nodded. "All right, baby steps."

"How about toddler steps," she suggested, alarmed that he might soft peddle it, and he chuckled.

"Don't worry," he assured her. "I'm going to be plenty rough with you."

Twin emotions of relief and trepidation flooded through her, "Oh. Good."

"You want a head start?"

"Yeah." She rolled to her toes, bouncing a little. "Give me three seconds."

"That's not much of an advantage."

"I'm not actually trying to get away," she reminded him.

His eyes gleamed. "Good. One-Mississippi..."

She turned and sprinted for the stairs before he had *Mississippi* out of his mouth, ducking behind them and taking a sharp left to dart behind the partition wall that separated the guest room from the dining area. She looked around, searching for a hiding space. The bed was huge, and there was enough space between the duvet and the floor for her to see that there was space under the bed.

Her heart pounding, she scrambled under, belly-crawling until she was centered under it, and waited.

She couldn't hear anything over her own panting breaths, and realized if she thought she was loud, he could probably hear her. She remembered reading somewhere that it was easier to breathe silently through an open mouth, so she let her lips part, concentrated on breathing as silently as possible, and listened for footsteps.

She didn't know how long she was under the bed, not a sound reaching her straining ears. It felt like an eternity, her body tensed and flooded with adrenaline, her heart pounding so loud in her ears that the sound all but drowned out the pants she couldn't seem to control. She was so tense and on edge that when a hand finally clamped over her ankle, it was almost as much a relief as it was a shock.

Instinct took over and she screamed, loud and long, and tried to jerk her foot free, drawing her knee up toward her body. But her leg was yanked back, hard enough to make her grunt, and the unmistakable sensation of rope wrapping around her ankle registered a beat too late.

She tried to scramble forward, clutching at the rug with her fingers and digging in with the toes of her free foot, but he was too fast, quickly looping rope around that ankle as well, then began dragging her back.

She tried to find purchase, to resist, but the rug was old and thin, with almost no pile to speak of, and her fingernails simply skidded over it. Pain flared in her thighs, her belly, her breasts as he dragged her back, the thin weave like sandpaper against her tender skin. Her nipples, already sensitized, felt like they were going to be ripped off. She tried to push up on her elbows to make some space, but he was moving too fast, and when her elbows skidded out from under her, she hit her chin on the floor.

It snapped her teeth together, momentarily stunning her, and her chin burned. By the time she shook it off he'd dragged her out from under the bed, flipped her over and was wrapping her right wrist in rope with a gleefully sadistic grin.

"Asshole," she snarled, and drew her knees back to her chest, preparing to kick.

He simply leaned into her, pressing his chest against her feet and pinning her knees to her chest. "That's 'sadist asshole' to you."

She twisted her right hand in his grip, found it implacable, and struck out with her left. She missed, the punch skidding off his shoulder instead of his face, and before she could try again he had that hand, too, and pinned both to the floor.

"No face hitting," he admonished.

"That wasn't one of the rules," she protested feebly, her voice a thin wheeze. The way he was leaning on her made it hard to draw a deep breath, and a lick of panic tickled her throat.

"I know." He looked bemused. "I forgot who I was dealing with."

She concentrated on breathing shallowly and took stock of her body. Her nipples felt like they'd been run through a cheese grater, her hips were screaming from the almost bent in half position he had her in, and her chest felt as though there was a full-grown man resting on it. Which there was. The panic was still there, dancing slyly at the edges of her senses, but it wasn't overwhelming. In fact, it was turning her on.

That was a surprise, as Sadie had never been the kind of submissive that got off on being scared. She wasn't unfamiliar with the concept, of course. Several of her friends enjoyed it, and she'd had Doms attempt that kind of play with her before. But she'd always found it unbelievable, and therefore boring. They weren't really going to hurt her, and if they tried, she had her safeword, so how could she possibly be scared?

But with Jack…

She wasn't exactly afraid of him, because she knew he wouldn't cause her real harm. He was too responsible, too ethical a Dom for that. But he *was* a sadist, and much more willing to hurt her than anyone she'd ever played with before. And despite her experience, she couldn't seem to anticipate him.

It was exhilarating.

She wiggled under him, testing. But his grip on her hands was firm, his weight on her solid. "Can't breathe," she wheezed, and put a touch of panic in her tone.

"You don't think that's going to work, do you?" he asked, amusement gleaming in his eyes. "You disappoint me, Sadie."

She narrowed her eyes, a pithy retort on her tongue, then let out a shocked gasp when he suddenly lifted off her. She didn't have time to do anything but suck in a single, convulsive breath before she was on her stomach and he was straddling her hips, dragging her hands behind her.

He had her wrists bound almost before she could catch her breath, then the heavy weight of him shifted off her butt. She tried to take advantage of her momentary freedom and managed to roll over halfway before he shoved her back onto her stomach, one hard hand on the back of her head. She spit out a chunk of hair, grunting when his weight settled on the backs of her thighs. When he let go of her head, she wasted no time looking over her shoulder.

She had to blow the hair out of her face to see him, then blinked in surprise. He was facing her feet, and for a brief, confused moment she couldn't figure out why. When the rope around her left ankle loosened, she realized he was retying them. She considered trying to buck him off, but it wouldn't get her anywhere, so she decided to conserve her energy for whatever was coming and settled in to enjoy the view.

The muscles in his back flexed as he worked, and when he leaned forward, the hem of his shirt rode up to bare the skin beneath. It was almost unbearably sexy, that thin band of flesh, and she would've reached out to touch if her wrists hadn't been tied. He twisted a little, leaning to the side to pick up another bundle of rope, and the shirt slid up even more, revealing the edges of his tattoo.

She knew he had tattoos, of course—the one on his forearm made her mouth water every time she saw it, and she'd known he had others. But since she hadn't seen him naked yet…

She blinked, surprised. She hadn't seen him naked yet. In fact, now that she thought about it, she remembered that he hadn't even taken off his pants during their scene last week, much less his shirt. Not that she had any complaints. That scene had been...*woof.* And she understood why some Doms didn't like to get naked when they played—it made the power imbalance starkly, glaringly obvious, and added to the tone of the scene. But that strip of skin looked warm and smooth, and she had a sudden yearning to feel it against hers.

She was wondering how he'd react to a polite request for nudity when he rose smoothly to his feet, grabbed something off the bed and stuffed it into his back pocket, then bent down and grabbed her arms. "Up you go."

She squeaked, panic flaring when he pulled her up. For a moment she was hanging in the air, her bound ankles making her legs useless, his grip on her arms the only thing keeping her from falling and smashing her face on the floor. The sense of utter helplessness made her stomach lurch, but then he was setting her on her feet, steadying her with firm hands, and the moment passed.

She tossed her head back to get her hair out of her face, squeaking in alarm when she wobbled. His grip on her arms tightened, keeping her upright, and *thank you* was on the tip of her tongue until she remembered she was supposed to be resisting.

Funny how it didn't seem important to do that anymore.

Still, she had a role to play, so she ignored the urge to lean into him and worked up a scowl. She opened her mouth to snarl at him when he lifted her up by her arms, turned her to face the open doorway, and plunked her back onto her feet. He dropped his hands, forcing her to balance on her bound feet, and she'd barely managed to steady herself when he slapped her ass and said, "Walk to the living room, please."

The smack caught her unaware, and she swayed dangerously before steadying again. When she was sure she wasn't going to fall flat on her face, she risked a glance back at him. Her hair had fallen back into her face, but she didn't dare try to flick it out again or she'd probably fall into the wall. "Excuse me?"

"You heard me." He slapped her other cheek, hard, making her wobble again. "Walk."

"What are you, dense?" she asked, doing her best to sneer at him through the curtain of her hair. "I can't walk with my feet tied together."

"Hmmm."

Her eyes were mostly hidden by her hair, so she figured it was safe to roll her eyes.

"That is a problem," he continued, stroking his beard with one hand as he stared thoughtfully at her feet. "What you need is motivation."

"What I need is my fucking feet untied," she shot back, then frowned when he pulled something from his back pocket. "What's that?"

He held it up, a plastic wand about the length of a ruler that fit easily in his hand. It was black on one end and red on the other, with the red end tapering down to a point. "You've never seen this before?"

Nerves jumped in her belly. "No. What is it?"

"Some people call it a zapper," he replied and laid the point on her flank. "I call it motivation."

She flinched, but nothing happened. At first. Then he pressed a button on the handle, and with a loud zapping noise and a flashing spark, a sharp, tingling pain hit. "Hey!"

"You're well hydrated," he observed, and hit the button again.

The buzz and the spark made her jump as much as the jolt of pain, and she teetered dangerously. He grabbed her arm with his free hand, holding her upright, and zapped her again.

"Cut that out!" she cried and squealed when he hit the button a fourth time.

"Better get walking, darling," he said, one eyebrow raised and a devilish glint in his eye. He dragged the wand up so the point pressed into her right buttock, firmly enough that she could feel the metal prongs at the end of the plastic. "You keep standing here, you're going to get zapped."

He wasn't bluffing. If she didn't move, he'd zap her until she did. It hadn't actually hurt that much, all things considered—a cane was worse. But she had no idea if there was a higher setting, and she couldn't be sure he'd confine his 'motivation' to her butt. She wasn't familiar with electrical play, but she seemed to remember reading it was best to stick to fleshy areas. That left quite a few possibilities, some of which she was eager to keep electricity-free.

The idea of him slipping that thing between her thighs and giving her pussy a jolt—her bare, tender, and very wet pussy—was enough to have her shuffling her feet forward a couple of inches.

"Atta girl," he encouraged, and stepped with her, keeping the zapper pressed to her skin. "I knew you could do it."

She gritted her teeth to hold back the string of insults that leapt to her tongue and concentrated on moving forward. He'd tied her ankles tightly, leaving barely any slack between them, so the best she could do was slide one foot forward, then the other, gaining an inch, perhaps two each time. It was painfully slow, and she figured it was only a matter of time before he decided she wasn't moving fast enough.

"You're not moving fast enough," he said.

She heard the buzz and crackle of the electricity before she felt it, the noise almost worse than the sting. She tried to quicken her pace, but without her arms for balance she was afraid if she moved too fast, she'd fall flat on her face.

"I can't move any faster," she told him, breathless from both the effort of shuffling forward in inch increments and the anticipation of the inevitable jolt. "I'll fall."

"Well, then," he said, somehow sounding delighted and resigned at the same time and aimed the next jolt at her left buttock.

By the time she'd reached the dining room table she was jittery from half a dozen more jolts and starting to perspire. She could feel the skin at the small of her back growing damp, and worried that if she got too sweaty it would make the zaps hurt more. And though her mind was starting to go fuzzy, she had enough of her senses to recognize that that could be a very bad thing.

"You're starting to sweat," he announced behind her with unmistakable glee, not missing a trick. "And you've got about...oh, thirty feet to go. This could get interesting."

She looked down at her ankles. She'd hoped the shuffling would've loosened the ropes, but they were snug as ever. Her skin was faintly red, abraded by the friction produced by her ungainly shuffle, but she barely felt it. Abrasions were the least of her problems at the moment.

She was just past the dining room table when he zapped her again, this time delivering it to the tender—

and damp—skin where ass met thigh, and the jolt was so much sharper and harder than the ones that came before that she reacted without thinking, leaping forward with a shriek. She went airborne, and for a split second her mind went white with panic. Then instinct kicked in—along with four years of childhood gymnastics—and she bent her knees, crouching low for balance, and stuck the landing.

"Well, damn," Jack said, and she looked back. He was two feet behind her, a surprised grin on his face. "You've been sandbagging."

She hadn't, but she wasn't about to tell him that. She merely gathered herself and hopped forward again.

She didn't go far, not wanting to risk a fall with no way to catch herself, but it was farther than the shuffle method had gotten her. So she did it again, and again, hop after hop with barely a pause between. When she reached the ottoman, she hopped in a half circle and plopped down on it with a grunt.

Then Jack stepped in front of her, and she realized the sound she'd been hearing wasn't her heart pounding in her ears. He was laughing.

His deep, rich belly laughs filled the air, one hand on his abdomen as though he wanted to feel them shake out of him. It was…well, it was kind of awesome.

She found herself smiling, watching him bend forward, his hands braced on his knees as tears of mirth streamed down his face. She didn't even care that he was laughing at her. In fact, that just made it better.

When the laughs had faded to wheezing chuckles and the occasional guffaw, she cleared her throat to get his attention. "So glad I could amuse you."

He wiped his streaming eyes. "Me too," he gasped and, walking up to her, took her face in his hands and kissed her.

She jerked, surprised, but he held her steady, rubbing his lips over hers. The soft, almost sweet caress was a stark contrast to the rough way the scene had begun, and it threw her off balance. Wary, she held herself still, her scrambled brain trying to figure out his angle. But his lips were firm and warm, and she could smell the subtle spice of whatever he put in his beard to make it so soft, and it was hard to remember that she was supposed to be resisting. After a moment of agonizing over whether to stick to the script or go with the flow, she parted her lips in invitation.

He smiled and moved his hands, tunneling them into her hair to cradle the back of her head. He slipped his tongue smoothly past her lips to glide silkily against hers, and the frantic thoughts swirling around in her head just drifted away.

She'd expected him to devour—instead, he savored. She'd expected an assault—he gave her a seduction. Slow strokes of his tongue, the gentle scrape of teeth. When he closed his teeth gently on her lower lip, biting down just hard enough to make her breath catch, the wave of heat that spread through her left her dizzy.

With a last nibble, he drew his mouth from hers, sliding across her cheek to nibble along her jawline. "You scared the hell out of me."

Her head felt so heavy, and it was so easy to just let it fall back into his cradling hands. "I did?"

"Mmmm." His tongue slid down her neck, leaving a tingling trail in its wake. "When you made that first leap, I was too far away to catch you if you fell."

"Oh." She blinked her eyes open to stare hazily at the ceiling. "Oops."

He laughed softly into the hollow of her throat. "You stuck the landing, though."

"Gymnastics," she managed as he scraped his teeth against her collarbone, hard enough to make her flinch. When he flicked his tongue over the tiny hurt, she sighed with dreamy pleasure. "Four years."

"Yeah?" He kissed his way back up her throat to nip at her chin. "That's good to know."

Something in his tone had a twinge of apprehension fluttering to life inside her, and she tipped her head down to look into his face. He was smiling, laughter still dancing in his eyes. But there was something else, just a hint of wildness lurking behind the mirth that made her throat go thick with sudden panic. "Why is that?" she asked faintly and tried to swallow it down.

His gaze darted down to her throat, watching it work. When it lifted to meet hers again, that faint hint of wildness had turned into a savage blaze, and, too late, her survival instinct kicked in.

He smiled, and this time she saw the devil in it. "I'll show you."

Chapter Eleven

Her eyes flared with alarm, hazel darkening to brown, but she offered not a hint of resistance as he dropped his hands to her wrists and swiftly dealt with the rope. Keeping one hand firm on her unbound wrists, he leaned into her, urging her back onto the ottoman with his chest against hers. When she lay flat, her arms pinned beneath her, he reached for the cuffs he'd set out before going after her.

"You're going to give me your left wrist," he told her, putting some steel in his tone. "If you try to get away or do anything other than give me your left wrist, I'll zap your pussy."

Alarm flared in her eyes, and her throat worked as she swallowed. But she dragged her hand from behind her back and offered it.

"Thank you." He wrapped the padded leather around her wrist. He'd wanted to use rope—it had been clear during the demo that she loved the feel of it against her skin—but he'd been afraid she'd be too wiggly, too resistant to get it on her safely.

Delighted that the threat of electricity applied to her pussy was so effective, he ran a finger under the edge of the cuff, making sure it wasn't too tight. Satisfied, he positioned her arm so her elbow was bent, her hand up by her head. Pleased with the position—she'd be able to move, but not enough to hit him—he ran a length of rope through the D-ring and tied it off to the leg of the ottoman.

"Right hand, please," he asked, and she silently slid it out from under her back and laid it in his waiting palm.

He applied the second cuff, positioned her hand so it mirrored her left, and tied it off. With both arms secure, he eased back, one knee planted on the ottoman.

She immediately gave her bonds a yank, making him smile. She didn't look panicked or particularly scared, though wariness gleamed in her gaze as she tested her range of motion. She gave a second, harder yank, making her breasts wobble, and he dropped his gaze to her chest. Her upper chest was as flushed as her face, and her nipples were bright red.

Part of that was from dragging her out from under the bed. Her breasts, belly and thighs were abraded from the rug, the scrapes bright red against her fair, freckled skin. They weren't bad enough to require immediate attention, and he made a note to apply some aloe later. For now, though…

He traced a finger around one puffy, reddened areola, pleased when it tightened at his touch. He did the same to the other, with the same results, and she squirmed.

He raised his gaze to her face. Her eyes had darkened, and the flush on her cheeks and chest had deepened. He lifted a hand to her face, wanting to feel the heat there, and she turned her cheek into his hand with a little mew of contentment even as she yanked against the ropes again.

Amused at the contradiction, he chuckled and leaned down for another kiss, lingering over it. Her mouth was soft under his, and hesitant at first, but when he tilted his head to take the kiss deeper, she opened her mouth for him eagerly.

When he drew back, she tried to follow, her eyes half closed and dazed, only to come up short against the cuffs on her wrists. His amusement deepened when the soft, sexy expression she wore immediately morphed into a frown.

"My back hurts," she complained, and he wondered if she knew how close she was to pouting. "Can I bring my knees up?"

He straightened, keeping his knee planted on the ottoman next to her hip, and considered. The position she was in—flat on her back with her feet on the floor—would put strain on her lower back, and he liked that she'd asked for permission. But the request lacked something.

"Can I bring my knees up, what?"

She blinked at him, confused. Then her expression cleared, and she gave a little laugh. "Can I bring my knees up, Boss?"

He didn't bother to hide his amusement. "Boss?"

"Sir is boring," she told him, a sparkle in her eye that told him she wasn't quite ready to surrender yet.

"Wouldn't want you to be bored," he drawled and watched the gleam in her eye turn wary. "Put your feet up on the ottoman."

She obeyed, her eyes locked on his, and he saw relief shimmer across her face as the pressure on her back eased. "Thank you."

"Thank you…?"

"Thank you, Boss," she parroted, and smirked.

"You're welcome, brat," he countered and, sliding into a crouch, began to unwrap the rope from around her ankles.

She sighed. "Oh, that feels nice."

"Was it too tight?" he asked, running a hand around the marks the rope had left behind. They weren't deep, and though some spots were red from the friction induced when she'd shuffled her way across the room, they weren't any worse than the rug burn on her thighs.

"No." She flexed her feet, making the candy-apple-red polish on her toes gleam. "But it always feels good when it comes off, you know?"

He lifted her right foot so it rested on his chest and reached for another length of rope. "Hmmm."

"You're not going to start that again, are you?"

He did a quick loop around her ankle, tied it off, and slowly pushed her foot back until her heel met her thigh. Pleased with her flexibility, he drew the end of the rope around the top of her thigh. "Start what again?"

"The 'hmmming'," she said, flexing her foot.

"Be still," he admonished and to drive the point home, flipped the zapper out of his back pocket and gave her a quick jolt.

She jerked, her high-pitched squeal echoing around the room. "God, that thing is evil."

"That's what I like about it," he told her, and continued winding the rope up her bent leg in a spiral.

"You're a terrible human being."

Pleased to have an excuse, he zapped her again, this time on the inner thigh, dangerously close to her bare, wet pussy. "Keep it up," he warned over her sharp cry, "and you'll find out just how terrible I can be."

With her panting breaths filling the air, he tucked the zapper back in his pocket and tied the first knot on the inside of her knee, locking the top loop of rope into place before moving down to the next. When the third and final loop had been locked into place, he passed the working ends between heel and thigh and started up the other side.

He worked quickly, knotting the loops in place so she wouldn't be able to straighten her leg, then checked the tension. Satisfied that it was snug enough without being dangerously tight, he gave her leg a pat. "How's that feel?"

She tried to flex her leg, a combination of wariness and delight crossing her expression when she couldn't. "Restrictive."

"Good," he said, and reached for a second length of rope to start on her other leg.

"Sexy," she continued, and he paused to look at her face. She was watching him with heavy eyes, her cheeks bright pink. Her fingers had curled into loose fists, and her pulse fluttered in her throat.

"Well now, that kind of honesty deserves a reward, doesn't it?" he said softly, and without warning or fanfare, dipped his head and gave her pussy a long, slow lick.

She jerked against his mouth, hips rising in search of more. And he was tempted to give it to her—she tasted like sin and sunshine, and he wanted to eat her alive—but instead he lifted his head, ignored her dazed, wide-eyed stare, and began securing her other leg.

"Jack," she whined.

"Who?" he asked, not pausing in his work.

"Boss," she amended, and from the corner of his eye, he saw her lick her lips.

"Better," he allowed. He wound three loops up her bent leg, then began to tie them off. "Something you need?"

She licked her lips again. "More."

"You'll get it," he promised with a low chuckle.

"When?" she demanded.

He finished the last knot and checked it as he had her first leg. "When I'm ready to give it to you."

He rose to his feet, ignoring her frustrated wiggle, and circled the ottoman so he stood behind her. He wanted her legs apart, but wasn't sure if he wanted to pull them straight back, toward her head, or out to the edges of the ottoman.

"You seem plenty ready to me," she said, and he glanced down to find her staring at his crotch.

"Behave, or I'll jack off on your face and leave you like this," he warned, and having made his decision, picked up a bundle of rope and moved to her side. He ducked down to loop rope around the leg of the ottoman, drawing it up through the one binding her leg and slowly pulling her knee to the side. He didn't need to pin her leg down, just keep it out of his way, so once that was accomplished, he tied it off.

Grabbing another section of rope, he knee-walked around to the other side and repeated the process with her other leg.

Rising to his feet, he surveyed his handiwork with satisfaction. Her knees were up and out to the side, leaving her pussy spread open and delightfully vulnerable. A glance at her face told him she'd realized just how vulnerable—worry and excitement reflected in her wide, cautious eyes.

Deciding he'd teased both of them enough, he reached down and grasped the sides of the ottoman. "Hold on."

"To what?" she wondered.

"I guess that was a poor choice of words," he allowed, and grabbed the sides of the cushion. Ignoring her surprised squeak, he dragged it across the room until he could perch on the sofa with her bound form laid out like a buffet in front of him. "Well, now that we're comfortable—"

"Speak for yourself," she muttered.

"—let's get on with it."

"Oh, please let that mean fucking."

He laughed. "Not yet."

"What's a girl gotta do to get laid around here?" she moaned and yelped when his hand landed firmly on the inside of her thigh.

"Obey," he replied.

"That's not exactly one of my strengths," she pointed out.

"That's what this is for, darling," he said, and pulled the zapper out of his back pocket.

"Oh, shit," she whined, and he would've bet the bottle of fifty-year-old McCallan in his liquor cabinet that she would've rolled right off the ottoman if she hadn't been tied down. "Keep that thing away from my pussy."

He raised an eyebrow. "Excuse me?"

"I mean it." She squirmed, but the ropes held her firmly in place.

"That sounds like you're giving me orders," he mused, and drew the tip of the wand gently up her thigh. She jumped, panic widening her eyes. "Is that what you're doing, Sadie?"

She shook her head wildly, her hands curling into fists as she yanked on the ropes. He wasn't even sure she registered that he hadn't hit the button, that it was only the cool metal prongs pressed against her skin.

"That's good." He slid the wand up her thigh, inching closer to her pussy. She tried to close her legs, but the ropes kept them apart. She could do nothing but writhe helplessly as he trailed the zapper up, up, up to the deep pink folds. "I'd hate to think you were trying to top from the bottom."

She let out a high, thin whine, the muscles in her belly rippling when he gently tapped her labia, and the fear that leapt into her eyes was like a hot fist squeezing his cock.

"You wouldn't top from the bottom, would you, Sadie?" he asked, sliding the wand down until he was sure she couldn't see it. He stopped it on the tender skin between pussy and asshole and wasn't at all surprised when she shut her eyes, squeezing them tight.

"No, no." She held her breath, her eyes squeezed so tightly they almost disappeared. "I won't, I promise."

"Because if you did," he went on mildly, "well, I'd have to punish you."

He lifted the wand away from her skin and hit the button. The zapper flashed and sparked, emitting the loud buzz that accompanied the burst of electricity, and she jerked so hard the ottoman actually moved.

He laughed, delighted with her, and hit it again. The yelp she let out cut off abruptly, and her eyes popped open to stare at him.

He waggled the wand, held up between her knees where she could clearly see it, and grinned when she scowled. "Gotcha."

"That was mean," she accused.

Amused, he laid the wand back on her thigh and cocked an eyebrow. "I can be meaner."

"I believe you," she said fervently.

"Are you going to behave?"

She bobbed her head, eyes locked on the zapper. "Yes."

"Yes, what?"

She swallowed. "Yes, Boss."

"Then I don't need this," he said, and laid the wand next to him on the couch. "But I'll keep it close by, just in case."

"Oh, goodie," she muttered.

He laid his hands on the insides of her thighs, absorbing the quiver of her muscles. Partly from the stretch of the position, but there were nerves, too. "You be a good girl while I play, and you'll get what you want. Can you be a good girl for me, Sadie?"

Her eyes widened. He could see everything in them, fear and lust and worry and need. So much need. "My track record in this area is not stellar."

He chuckled and patted her thigh. "Well, then it's lucky I'm not giving you a choice, isn't it?"

Sadie swallowed hard and told herself there was no reason to be afraid. She had a safeword, and he knew her limits. Hell, they'd even gone over the parameters of the scene ahead of time, and she trusted him to stick to them. So there was no reason to be scared.

But when he rose to his feet, crossed to a low cabinet under the window, and began rummaging through the contents…if she hadn't been tied down, she would've bolted for the door.

Or maybe not, she thought, and licked her lips. Somewhere between hopping across the room to avoid his evil little zapper and now a switch had flipped inside her. Except for the desperate arousal, it was almost like she was at the end of a scene instead of the beginning. All the sharp edges inside her had smoothed away, leaving behind desire and need and a strange, inexplicable craving to see him smile again.

She was so used to Resting Dick Face that seeing him smile still gave her a little jolt, a sort of knee-jerk *what the fuck* reaction, then a strange warmth would spread through her and she'd smile back, wanting to share it. And when his smile faded, as smiles inevitably did, she found herself yearning to do something to bring it back.

Which was very, very weird. Since when did she care if Jack smiled?

She was pondering that when he came back, settling onto the couch again, and she thought absently that it was a shame she didn't have her phone, because it would make a great picture. Her tied and spread legs framing him between them, leaning forward with his elbows on his knees, that sly, baby-you're-in-for-it-now smile that made her belly flip. Of course, even if she did have her phone, she couldn't use it, because her hands were tied. It really was a shame.

He laid a hand on her shin. "How you doing?"

"I'm horny," she said, and tried to wiggle enticingly. It was difficult, trussed up as she was like a Christmas turkey, but she managed to get her boobs to bounce a little. "Is it time to fuck yet?"

"Every time you ask me that, I'm adding ten minutes to your wait time."

She gasped in genuine horror. "You *are* a sadist."

"And that ten minutes," he continued, eyes dancing with a combination of laughter and evil, evil intent, "will be filled by an alternative activity of my choosing."

That didn't sound good. "What kind of alternative activity?"

"A painful one."

"This violates my limits," she protested.

"Does it?" He angled his head. "How?"

"No orgasm denial, remember?"

"You can come whenever you want," he promised, his smile going sharp. "Now, hold still."

"Do you think I have a choice?" she asked, rattling her cuffs for emphasis, then jerked in shock when something cold and wet hit her upturned asshole.

He slapped her thigh, making her jerk again. "I said, hold *still*."

"Sorry," she gasped, and fought not to squirm. The lube he'd squirted on her asshole was like ice, and the shock of it had barely begun to fade when he popped his thumb inside.

She wanted more than anything to fuck back against his hand, to push hard against it, but she didn't dare. So she stared at the ceiling and panted her way through the urge, gritting her teeth against the demands to go faster, do it harder, make her come, goddammit.

"You're awful quiet," he commented, the words accompanied by another icy squirt of lube before his thumb was back, pushing it in. "Nothing to say?"

"I'm being good," she informed him, the words a strangled gasp. It felt so good, and she desperately wanted to move, but she was terrified of doing anything that would delay getting his dick inside her.

He laughed, a deep rumble that jiggled his thumb in her ass and had her gritting her teeth again. "You don't have to keep quiet. The apartment is soundproofed."

He pulled his thumb out of her ass, and the breath she hadn't been aware of holding left her lungs in a woosh. "I'm trying not to beg."

"Why?"

He sounded genuinely perplexed, and she lifted her head to scowl at him. "Because you told me not to!"

"I told you not to ask me to fuck you," he corrected, and picked up something from the floor. There was a faint crinkle of plastic, like a package being opened. "Begging, on the other hand, is always allowed."

"What's the difference?" she wanted to know, trying to sit up further to see what he had in his hand. But the ropes would only let her go so far, and he held it too low.

"A semantic one, I suppose," he allowed, glancing up. "But I'll tell you if you go too far."

"By then it'll be too late," she pointed out.

"I know." He winked at her. "Lie back."

She grumbled, but obeyed, her heart pounding. She could feel it everywhere—her fingers, her toes, her nipples, and especially in her pussy. Her clit felt like one big, exposed nerve.

"This is a little bigger than the plug I used last time," he said, his tone almost conversational, and she felt a cool pressure against her asshole. "But since it's silicone rather than glass, I'm sure you can take it."

"How much bigger is 'a little'?" she asked, alarmed. The plug he'd used before had been almost more than she could handle. Sure, part of that was because glass was solid, with no give, but size had plenty to do with it. If this one was bigger…

"A trifling amount, really." The pressure increased. "Hardly worth mentioning."

"My ass," she choked out and began to pant.

"It certainly is," he said with a chuckle. "Breathe, Sadie."

She sucked in air and blew it back out, trying not to hyperventilate as the plug advanced. He was going slowly, and her asshole was well trained, but he hadn't been kidding about big. "Shit, shit, shit."

"That's not a safeword," he reminded her, and advanced it a few millimeters more.

"Yellow, you bastard," she choked out, blinking furiously to clear her vision. She was panting like a sprinter, her hands clenched into fists, brain buzzing with a confusing mix of pain and pleasure. "Give me a minute, please."

"Take all the time you need," he soothed, holding the plug still. "I'm not going anywhere."

"Okay. Okay." Knowing that fighting would only make the pain worse, she forced her hands to unclench, her muscles to relax. Breathing through the discomfort, she focused her attention on the tight ring of muscle. It was fluttering, spasming as it tried to adjust to being forced open. But after a few deep breaths, it relaxed enough for the pain to fade away, leaving in its wake only a deep, pulsing pleasure.

"There you go," he murmured, one hand coming up to stroke the outside of her thigh. It wasn't a sensual touch, but a comforting one. "That's a good girl."

She relaxed even further, her muscles going lax and allowing her to sink into the ottoman. A sneaky warmth spread through her chest, not unlike how she felt when she made him laugh. Not wanting to examine it too closely, she blew out a shaky breath and lifted her head. "Please tell me it's almost in."

His eyes were soft, gleaming with something she couldn't quite name. "You're at the widest part."

"Thank fuck," she breathed and lay back once more. "Okay, I'm ready."

"Deep breath, darling," he warned, and waited for her inhale and, with a final push, sent the plug home.

She squirmed, the sensation of fullness making her pussy pulse anew. There was still pain, little jolts as her muscles continued to adjust, but it was an enhancement to the pleasure now instead of an impediment.

"How does it feel?" he asked, and she blinked back to the moment.

"Full."

"I'll bet," he chuckled. "Hurting?"

"A little," she said, and gave an experimental wiggle. Her asshole clenched down in response, and the resulting spasm of pain made her pussy pulse and her clit throb. "It's good, though."

"So I see," he murmured and she suddenly remembered that her pussy was on display, and she lifted her head to see him staring down at her, his face mere inches away. "You like the pain."

"Yes," she managed, for once incapable of playing games. He was staring at her with an absorbed look on his face, as though he was looking at something amazing. She'd never had someone look at her like that before.

He lifted a hand to run a finger, light and soft, over the delicate skin around her opening. "I could see it here, in this pretty little hole. It was pulsing."

She knew it. She could feel it. But knowing that he could *see* it made her feel small and exposed, and God, so fucking horny. "I know."

"I wonder," he murmured and looked up, his eyes meeting hers. "Will that happen with other kinds of pain?"

She couldn't speak. He looked like a hungry wolf that had just come across a helpless deer, and she knew, in some small, rational corner of her mind, that it should scare her. But the only thing she felt was desire.

"I don't know," she finally managed. "I'm not usually looking at it."

A small smile curved his lips. "Well, then. Let's find out."

A trickle of unease worked its way through the haze of lust. He turned away, reaching back, and she tensed, wondering what toy or tool he was retrieving. But he only laid the tube of lube on the sofa beside him and turned back, settling back between her spread legs.

"What are you going to do?" she asked, the words trembling with anticipation.

He smiled. "Whatever I want."

Chapter Twelve

The first blow came before the words had even faded, hard and sharp and square on her right butt cheek. It was followed closely by one on her left, the crack of it mingling with her startled cry. She jumped, an instinctive twist to try to evade. It made her muscles flex, which in turn tugged on the plug embedded in her ass and set off a round of spasms in her pussy.

"Now, that's charming," he observed with obvious delight. "Absolutely charming."

She wanted to say something like, 'Glad you think so', but she couldn't seem to get enough breath to form the words.

"But I do wonder," he continued, "if it's the pain that causes that reaction, or the way you jump when you get hit. What do you think?"

It took her a moment to answer. "I don't know," she finally managed. "Does it matter?"

"Not at all," he said cheerfully, and this time brought his hand down on the inside of her thigh. The sting was sharper there, more focused, and dragged a short, sharp cry from her lips.

"Hmmm." He frowned, his eyes trained between her legs. "That didn't seem to have the same effect."

"Sorry," she said, and hoped he'd hit her again.

"No worries," he said, waving a hand as though she was apologizing for stepping on his foot. "I think I know what the problem is."

She gave a short, gurgling laugh that had him glancing up. "I know I'm going to regret this, but I'm going to ask it anyway."

His eyes gleamed at her, laughter and lust dancing in them, with that hint of evil lurking beneath. "That's my girl."

She ignored the little fission of delight and tried to focus. "What..." She had to pause to catch her breath. God, she wanted to fuck, but she didn't dare ask. "What do you think the problem is?"

"What a good girl you are," he enthused, and to her surprise, leaned down and planted a smacking kiss right on her clit. She shrieked, the spasm of pleasure making her hips jerk in search of more, but he was already sitting back. He said something else, but she couldn't hear it over the buzzing in her ears.

She shook her head to try to clear them. "What?"

"Never mind." He let out a chuckle that would've done any cartoon villain proud. "I'll show you."

He reached down to pick something up off the floor, and she wanted to keep her head up to see what it was. But her neck was getting sore, and she'd find out soon enough, so she let her head fall back to rest on the ottoman.

"I need you to look at me, Sadie."

She lifted her head obligingly, but her neck twinged in protest. "My neck is starting to get sore," she said, raising her gaze to his. "Could I have a pillow, Boss? Please."

"Of course." He shifted smoothly to his feet, lifting a plump velvet pillow from the couch, and circled the ottoman. He slipped a hand behind her head, lifting it for her, and slid the pillow into place. "Better?"

"Much," she said, sighing with relief at the support. "Thank you, Boss."

"You're welcome, brat," he replied, and laid a brief kiss on her mouth before moving back to his seat on the couch. "Can you see me?"

The pillow put her at the perfect angle, though she couldn't see anything below the edge of the ottoman. "Yes, Boss."

"Excellent. You have a choice to make," he said, and held something up. It dangled from his fingers, glinting in the light as it swayed, and after a moment she realized it was a pair of nipple clamps, connected by a chain. "This is a set of alligator clamps. You're familiar, I assume?"

"Yes." Alligator clamps were her favorite kind because the little screws made them easily adjustable. And unlike clover clamps, they didn't get tighter the harder they were pulled.

"Good. You'll notice," he continued, picking up the end of the swinging chain so he held a clamp in each hand, "that one of the clamps has had its teeth coated in plastic. The other has not."

She could see that. The clamp in his right hand had a thick red coating that would act as padding, allowing the user to tighten them down without the teeth biting in. The clamp in his left hand was bare, tiny steel points gleaming in the light.

"What I like about the coated side," he went on blithely, seemingly unaware of the increase in both her heart rate and her trepidation, "is that I can tighten them down quite a bit without risking damage. And what I like about the uncoated side is that I can do quite a bit of damage without having to tighten them down."

He smiled, and she knew he hadn't missed a thing. "Which would you prefer?"

"What?"

"I'm going to put these on you," he explained, allowing the chain to dangle from one hand again. "And I want you to choose which end."

"Oh, fuck me."

"Is that a formal request?" he asked silkily.

"No, no." She shook her head frantically. "That was an expression of…of…"

"Dismay?" he offered.

"Yes." She nodded, head bobbing frantically. "Dismay."

"Hmmm." He eyed her for a moment, considering, then relented. "All right, you get a pass on that one."

Her sigh of relief was audible. "Thank you, Boss."

"But you still have to make a decision." He set the chain to swaying. "What's it going to be, Sadie? Teeth or padding?"

She bit her lip. Padding was the obvious choice, because those teeth were vicious, and her nipples were sensitive. But with the padding, he could crank the pressure to the maximum, causing serious pain without drawing a drop of blood.

"Is 'neither' an option, Boss?" she asked hopefully.

"Since you asked so nicely, I'll tell you that choosing neither will be considered a choice for both," he said, and smiled his cartoon-villain smile.

"Figures," she muttered.

His smile widened, getting, if possible, more sinister. He held up his phone, the screen facing her so she could see the clock app, set to a thirty-second timer. "You have thirty seconds to decide." He tapped the screen to start the countdown. "If the timer goes off before I have your answer, I'll make a choice for you."

Shit, shit, shit. She closed her eyes, trying to focus past the instinctive panic. It was a choice between pressure or punctures, and that meant it was no choice at all. While the potential for intense pressure scared her, thinking about those sharp little teeth digging into her nipples was just—wait a minute. He'd said, "I'm going to put these on you", but he hadn't specified where.

Her eyes flew open. "Hang on."

One dark eyebrow rose. "Yes?"

She ignored the numbers ticking down on the screen. "Where exactly are you planning to put the clamps?"

"Well, well," he purred. "You're just asking all kinds of good questions tonight, aren't you?"

She fought the urge to squirm. He'd gone past cartoon villain and right to comic book supervillain. "Are you going to answer it?"

"Of course," he said smoothly. "Whichever end you don't choose will be attached to the rope around your thigh."

She swallowed, very much afraid she knew where this was going. "And the other end?"

"Will be attached to your labia," he said, and glanced at his phone screen. "Along with three other sets of clamps. Ten seconds."

Three other sets of clamps? She stared at him, stunned and momentarily frozen in shock.

"Five seconds," he announced. "Four…three…"

"Padded!" she shouted, drowning out his two-second warning. "I choose padded!"

"One," he finished, and smiled as his phone chimed. "Just made it under the wire."

"Shit," she wheezed and slumped back against the pillow. "I think I hate you."

"You might want to reserve judgment on that until all the facts are in," he said and, with the smile she was coming to dread, held up four sets of alligator clamps.

She swallowed so hard he heard the click. "I don't know if I can take that," she said, her voice thin with fear.

He laid a hand on her belly and waited until her eyes flicked back to meet his. "Will you try?"

For a moment he thought she'd say no. But she nodded, trust and fear and desire in her eyes. "Okay."

"Good girl," he whispered and brushed a kiss on the inside of her knee. He heard her breath catch, felt the muscles of her belly quiver, and had to pause a moment to keep his own emotions in check. When he was sure he could continue, he lifted his head. "All right, darling, here we go. Don't forget to breathe."

Several minutes later, Jack sat back, keeping an anchoring hand on Sadie's abdomen. Her breathing was ragged, the muscles rippling under his palm, neither reaction unexpected. After all, he'd just attached four clamps to her labia.

"Breathe, darling, that's it," he crooned, watching her carefully. Her eyes were closed, her face flushed and damp. The hair at her temples had turned dark with sweat and the tears that leaked from her eyes. He didn't mind them—just the opposite, in fact—but he needed to guide her through the intense pain to the endorphin rush waiting on the other side in order to make them worth it.

"Keep breathing," he instructed, leaning forward to slide his hand up between her breasts. Her heart hammered under his palm, a steady and rapid thump. "In and out, that's a good girl."

Her lashes fluttered, and after a moment she opened her eyes. Pain swam in their depths, nearly edging out the arousal. It was still there, though, and his relief at seeing it would've brought him to his knees if he hadn't already been sitting down.

"Give me a color, Sadie," he said, putting some snap in his tone to get her attention.

She blinked, and he could almost see her brain kick back into gear. "Yellowish green," she finally said, her voice hoarse and thick. "You're a fucking sadist, Boss."

"So I've been told," he said, masking his relief with a chuckle, and with his hand planted between her breasts as an anchor, looked down at her pussy.

The clamps were attached to her labia, two on the left and two on the right. Her pussy was slick with arousal—the butt plug had had more of an effect than he'd realized—and he'd had to tighten the screws more than he'd first estimated to keep them in place. That had made her writhe, little cries breaking from her throat with each turn of the screws, but she'd been handling it, breathing deep and maintaining eye contact.

Then he'd extended the chains, pulling them slowly to the side to attach the clamp at the other end to the ropes around her thighs. With two clamps on each side, the DIY pussy spreader held her wide open, every inch of tender pink skin visible, and it had the added benefit of being stunningly, shockingly painful. He imagined she'd had clamps on her nipples any number of times, but if she'd ever had her pussy clamped, he'd eat his shoe.

"I've never..." she began, licking her lips, "had clamps...on my pussy before."

"I could tell," he said, pleased that she was more alert. For a moment there, he'd been a breath away from taking off the clamps, cutting through the rope, and bundling her off to a hot bath. "Well?"

She blinked. "Well, what?"

"What do you think?

"It hurts," she told him baldly.

He chuckled. "Of course, it does. That's why I did it."

She managed a choking laugh through labored breaths. "So? What...now?"

"That depends on you, sweetheart. What's your color now?"

"Greener," she admitted. "But still more underripe-banana than Kermit."

He shook his head, amused. "Trust you. All right, I'm just going to ask. Do you want to keep going, or do you want to stop?"

"I don't want to stop," she said in a rush and bit her lip, her eyes clouding over with worry. "But I don't know how much more I can take."

"Beautiful girl," he murmured, swamped with emotion. She was trying so hard to take the pain, for nothing but the promise of pleasure – and because he'd asked her to. "Do you want to come?"

She nodded, need shining in her eyes. "Yes, please."

"Can you stand a little more pain for that?"

"How much is a little?" she demanded hoarsely.

He laughed, enjoying her. "Hardly any at all."

"I'm going to need specifics," she insisted.

"I'm afraid you're just going to have to take my word for it." He stared her down, watching the emotions flit over her face. *Disbelief, outrage, wariness.* Then finally, a grudging acceptance tinged with arousal and a delicious sheen of fear that made him want to devour her whole.

"You promise I'll get to come?"

He swiped his finger over his heart. "Cross my heart."

"Hope to die?" she shot back, a hint of sass in the curl of her lip. "Stick a needle in your eye?"

There she was, he thought with satisfaction. That was his Sadie. "I wouldn't go that far. Now try not to wiggle, because if you do," he warned gleefully, "it's going to hurt."

She froze, going almost comically still, and he chuckled. If she was able to maintain that level of stillness for more than a few seconds, he'd eat the other shoe.

He held her gaze for another moment, relishing the wariness and the fear in her eyes, letting her see the anticipation in his, then dropped his gaze to take in the rest of her.

She was a picture.

Her hair was a bright halo around her head, the strawberry-blonde a sharp contrast to the black leather ottoman. Her face was still damp with sweat, and though the tears had stopped, their silvery tracks were visible on her flushed cheeks. Her neck and chest were flushed, too, right down to her nipples. Despite her obvious arousal they were soft, the areolas puffy from the rug burn. He traced a finger around one gently, delicately, delighted when it puckered and reddened. She started to squirm in reaction, then froze once again.

"Nice catch," he chuckled, and slid his hands to her thighs.

The ropes were pressed into her legs, snug against her soft skin. He glanced at the clock on the wall across the room, calculating the time she'd spent in bondage. He laid a hand on each of her feet, checking her skin temperature. She was warm, and her feet didn't appear to be swelling—he could still see the delicate tendons running from her instep to her toes. Satisfied that her circulation wasn't yet a concern, he gave her toes a reassuring squeeze and turned his attention to her pussy.

"Goddamn, that's a pretty cunt," he drawled, and continued to ignore his erection while he took in the sight before him. The delicate folds of her labia were trapped in the padded clamps and stretched wide, revealing the deep pink of her inner flesh. The delicate opening was bright red, and all of it gleamed. She was so wet there was a literal puddle on his ottoman. Even as he stared, entranced, her cunt pulsed, the muscles contracting in an unmistakable invitation.

One he was only too happy to accept.

He dropped his head, moving slowly to savor her reaction, and swirled the tip of his tongue around her clit.

She let out a high-pitched whine and jerked, yanking at the clips holding her pussy spread, and the whine morphed quickly into a short, sharp scream.

He glanced up, noted the color in her cheeks had deepened by several shades and that her breasts were bouncing in concert with her ragged breaths. "I guess that hurt, didn't it?"

"How…did you guess?" she panted and managed a weak glare.

"Well, this isn't my first rodeo. And that being the case," he continued, "I'm guessing it also felt good."

"Oh, God," she wheezed.

"Is that a yes?"

"Does it matter?"

"Of course it does," he chided. "Your pleasure is my goal, Sadie."

"It doesn't feel like it at the moment."

"And your pain," he continued, lowering his head once again so his lips hovered over her clit, "is my pleasure."

He waited a beat, savoring the tremor that raced through her, then sucked her clit into his mouth.

She spasmed under him, her whole body jerking against her restraints as she came. He kept still, feeling the pleasure and the pain zipping through her, hearing both in the broken cries that slipped from her lips. There were incoherent pleas for more, for less, curses and prayers in equal measure. She called his parentage into question, insulted his ancestors all the way back to the flood, and vowed such violent revenge that he wondered if he should wait until she was unconscious to untie her.

Her clit pulsed between his lips, under his tongue, but still he didn't let go. He brought one hand up, wanting to feel the pulse and pull of her flesh, and when he slipped two fingers inside her she went off again. She was so slick he decided to add a third finger, stretching her wide and fucking her hard through the orgasm, his only regret that he was feeling the desperate clench of her pussy on his fingers instead of his dick.

As the orgasm faded, he lifted his head, wanting to see her face for this next part. He kept his fingers buried deep, brushing his beard back and forth over her clit to keep her stimulated, and with his free hand reached for the first clamp.

When he touched it, she froze. "No." She shook her head, sending her hair flying, her eyes wide with fear. "Don't, please don't."

"They have to come off," he reminded her, anticipation rising even as he sought to soothe. "You know that, Sadie."

She let out an anguished cry, tears making her eyes shimmer. "Jack."

"I know, darling," he crooned, sliding his fingers into position on the clamp. "I know."

"Do it fast, okay?" A single tear spilled down her cheek. "Please do it fast."

He pushed to his feet and leaned over to lick the tear from her cheek. "I will, I promise." He slipped his thumb up to her clit, pressed down, and looked deep into her begging eyes. "Breathe deep, Sadie."

He waited until she'd obeyed, sucking in a hard, shaky breath, and popped open the first clamp.

He was so close, barely a breath away, so he saw the first flare of relief. Then the pain hit, agony firing in her eyes, and she opened her mouth to scream.

He kissed her, swallowing her frantic cries, pinning her with his body as she writhed. Pressed against her he could feel the frantic beat of her heart, every pulse and spasm of pain, and when her pussy contracted once again around his fingers, nearly came in his pants.

He kept his mouth on hers when he released the second clamp, savoring the guttural groan that rumbled up through her chest. He released her mouth and leaned back to spring the third and watched her come again. She was still coming when the fourth fell away, and he didn't think he'd ever seen a more beautiful sight.

When her pussy stopped pulsing around his fingers, he pulled them out and reached for the plug still nestled between her spread cheeks. She gave a helpless little moan and shivered when it slipped free, her open cunt spasming anew, and he found himself wishing he'd pulled it while he'd been releasing the clamps. Next time, he thought and dropped to his knees to untie her legs.

Her breath was coming in raspy little moans, her body limp and unresisting while he worked, and her eyes, wide and frantic during her orgasms, had drifted shut. When the ropes fell away from her left leg, he straightened it gently, hooking her knee over his shoulder for support, and went to work on the right.

When it was free and draped over his shoulder, he ran his hands up her thighs. The rope had dug furrows into her supple flesh, but they would fade. Moving slowly, giving her muscles time to adjust, he eased her feet to the ground. Her eyes fluttered open, her eyes searching him out as he leaned over her to undo the wrist cuffs.

"Jack?"

"I'm here," he assured her and, slipping his hands under her, drew her slowly to a sitting position. "Move slowly now, there's no rush."

She made a little humming sound in the back of her throat, like a satisfied cat. "Jack."

"I've got you." He kept his hands on her back for support. He suspected if he let go, she'd simply pour onto the floor like a spilled drink.

"You sure do," she said, and she sounded so pleased that he looked up.

Her eyes were surprisingly alert—a little swollen from the tears, a little hazy from the orgasm, but tracking well enough. Still, she swayed in his hold, and wore the soft, goofy smile of the very drunk—or of a submissive riding one hell of an endorphin buzz.

"Feeling good?" he asked.

"Yep," she said, smacking her lips so they popped on the end of the word. "Golly, you're cute."

He stifled a snort. "Is that right?"

"When you don't have resting dick face," she amended and grinned when he barked out a laugh. "But even when you do, it's pretty hot."

"I'm glad to hear it," he said, still chuckling. "Can you stand up?"

"Prolly. I think my legs work," she said cheerfully, and kicked out a foot to demonstrate. "Oops, sorry."

He grunted and shifted to pull her foot out of his armpit. "It's fine."

"Good thing that wasn't between your legs," she pointed out, and kicked out her other foot to connect solidly with his elbow. "I'd hate to hurt your dick."

"That makes two of us," he assured her, and to save his body any more bruises, rose to his feet, sliding his hands down to grasp hers. "Let's try standing, all right?"

Agreeable, she staggered to her feet. "See? Told ya."

"So you did." He wrapped an arm around her and tucked her close, not wanting to take a chance on a fall. "How about a hot shower?"

"'Kay." She slid her arm around his waist, hooking her fingers through his belt loop. "You stayed dressed again."

He was eyeing the stairs. She was pretty steady on her feet, and he didn't want to risk carrying her, so he was hoping she could manage them with his help. "Did I?"

"It's very disappointing," she informed him soberly. "Are we going up the stairs?"

"That's where the shower is."

"Okay." She started up, him matching his pace to hers. "Jack?"

"Yes?"

"We're done playing, right?"

He glanced at her. "For now."

"So, if I were to ask a question that was forbidden during the scene, it would be allowed now?"

His lips twitched. "Yes."

"Good. Will you fuck me now?"

He laughed. "Let's get upstairs first, all right?"

"Okay," she said eagerly and sped up.

He managed to keep a hold on her through his laughter, matching his pace to hers. When they reached the top of the stairs, she shoved her hair out of her face and looked at him expectantly. "Well?"

"Keep going." He urged her forward with a hand on her butt. "You're not too sore?"

"No," she said, twisting around to look at him as they walked through the bedroom. "I will be later, but right now I'm buzzed."

"Fuck drunk."

"Technically, I'm finger-fuck drunk."

"What's the difference?" he asked.

"The difference," she said, enunciating each word with careful precision, "is *dick*."

"I wouldn't have taken the clamps off first," he informed her, and she stopped dead at the foot of his bed.

"You wouldn't?"

"Nope."

"That's..."

"Sadistic?" he offered when she trailed off.

"Yeah." She shoved at her hair. "Like, really a lot."

"I didn't know if you could handle it. Next time, I won't be so careful." He nudged her forward. "Keep going."

He herded her into the bathroom, crossing to the shower. She slipped away from him to turn in a circle, her expression avid. "This bathroom is nice."

He crossed to the shower, opened the door, and stepped in to turn on the taps. Water pumped from the jets on the wall and streamed from the rainhead fixture in the ceiling. "Thank you," he replied, and reached for her hand. "In you get."

Sadie stepped into the glass enclosure, taking care not to bump into the slatted teak bench that took up half the long wall. "Wow. You could have orgies in here."

"I'll keep that in mind. How's the temperature?"

"It's good." She stepped into the jets, taking care to avoid the rainhead. She was reluctant to get her hair wet, not knowing what kind of shampoo he had. His hair was long and thick and always looked nice, and that was a good sign, but previous experiences in dudes' showers had made her wary. "Do you have shampoo and conditioner?"

"In the niche behind you."

She picked up one of the bottles from the tidy little shelf built into the glass-tiled wall, noting the brand with surprise. She popped the cap and took a sniff. It smelled like him. "Is it okay if I wash my hair?"

"Sure. Take this first."

"Oh." She took the bottle of water he held out. It was chilled, and she realized he must have a mini fridge hidden away somewhere. She twisted off the cap, suddenly parched. "Thanks."

"You're welcome," he said, and stripped off his shirt.

She choked on the water, spitting it out, and goggled. The shower enclosure was starting to fog up, rendering him slightly blurry, but she could see enough. "What are you doing?"

"Getting naked," he replied, and reached for his belt buckle. "Isn't that what you wanted?"

"What?" she asked, distracted by the sight of his bare chest. He was furrier than she thought he'd be, and thicker, and the tattoo on his right forearm went all the way up his arm, over his shoulder, down the right side of his torso before disappearing beneath the waistband of his jeans. "What?"

"I said, isn't that what you wanted?"

"Uh-huh." Her gaze was glued to his hands which were slowly, methodically, popping the buttons on his fly, one by one. *Dear God, he's not wearing underwear.* "Yeah."

"Do you still want to fuck?" he asked and shoved his pants down and off.

"Hang on," she said, and chugged the water. When the bottle was empty, she lowered it and gasped, "What was the question again?"

"I said," he drawled, "do you still want to fuck?"

She tore her eyes away from his penis to look at his face. He was laughing, probably at her, but she didn't care. She dropped her gaze back down, straining to see detail through the foggy glass. No, she didn't care at all. "I really do."

"Good," he said, and stepped into the shower with her.

The enclosure was so big she didn't have to move out of the way for him to get in, which was good because her feet seemed to have been glued to the floor, and her eyes were glued to...all of him.

He was rolling on a condom, which compromised her view of his penis, but she'd seen that before. The rest of him, on the other hand, had been a mystery until just a moment ago, and she was far from done looking. "Can you just stand there for a minute?"

He opened the shower door, tossed the condom wrapper at the trash can, and shut it again. "Why?"

"I haven't seen you naked before," she said, trying to see all of him at once. Shoulders, pecs, arms—dear God, the arms—abs, waist, legs. "I want to take it in."

"I feel so objectified," he said, and dragged her under the rainhead. "So cheap."

She sputtered, swiping her now thoroughly wet hair out of her eyes. "That's a joke, right?"

"Yes, Sadie," he said, clearly amused, and plucked the bottle of shampoo she still held out of her hand. "That's a joke."

"I keep forgetting you have a sense of humor," she said, grabbing his arms when his hands slipped around her waist and pushed her backwards.

He backed her up until her back hit the tile, cool against her heated skin. She blinked the water out of her eyes.

"I get that a lot," he said, then hitched her off her feet, angled her hips, and shoved his cock into her.

Chapter Thirteen

She gasped in shock and pain—her pussy was really sore—and wrapped her arms reflexively around his neck. "Shit, Jack. Give a girl some warning."

He grunted, sliding his hands from her waist to her ass. "I did. I said, 'do you wanna fuck'."

She let out a breathless laugh and wiggled, trying to get comfortable. She was still swollen from her earlier orgasms, making his dick feel impossibly, deliciously thick inside her. "That's not a warning," she told him, and, delighted with the opportunity, rubbed her breasts into the fur on his chest.

"Want me to stop?" he asked and began to lift her off his invading length.

"Don't you dare," she said, and dug her nails into the back of his neck in warning.

"None of that," he warned. "Or I'll take you to the bedroom, tie you to the bed..."

She sank her nails a little deeper into his skin. "I like it so far."

"...and fuck you so slow it'll be midnight before you come again."

"Bastard," she managed and, swallowing a laugh, pulled her hands from around his neck and tucked them behind her, pinning them between her back and the wall. "There. Satisfied?"

"Getting there," he said, eyes gleaming as he looked down. Her breasts were thrust up by the position, the nipples hard and pink. "Keep your hands behind you," he ordered and bent his head.

Her sigh held both delight and disappointment. Delight, because his mouth on her breasts felt amazing, sucking and nipping with just the right amount of pressure and sting. Disappointment because when he bent over to suck and nibble, his hips shifted back and his dick slipped out of her. "No, come back."

"In a minute." He released her nipple, sliding down the slope of her breast to the tender underside. He nuzzled, then bit down, making her squeal. "Busy, here."

Frustrated, she started to pull her hands from behind her back, intending to grab his head and...well, she wasn't sure what she was planning to do, but as soon as she shifted, his head came up.

"Ah-ah-ah," he warned, eyes narrowed. "Keep those hands behind your back, or I'll cuff you to the wall."

"It's glass tile," she scoffed, though she kept her hands behind her back, just in case.

He merely smiled his cartoon-villain smile. "Didn't notice the rings, did you?"

"What rings?" she demanded and followed his gaze up the wall to the steel rings mounted in the tile two feet above her head.

"Oh. Those rings." She swallowed. "Jesus, Jack, who puts hard points in their shower?"

"Who doesn't?" he asked and shoved his dick back into her.

She had a snappy come back all ready, but then he started fucking her and she didn't care anymore. It hurt when he banged into her bruised pussy, but it felt good, too, the friction and penetration perfect.

But after a few moments, it wasn't enough.

"Can you go a little faster?" she asked, trying not to let her head bang back against the tile.

His pace didn't vary. "If I fuck you any faster, you're going to get a concussion."

"I'm not sure I care," she admitted, tits bouncing.

"I do," he countered, punctuating the words with a swivel of his hips that ground his pubic bone against her clit and almost, *almost* did the trick. "Nobody will want to play with me again if they find out I gave my last play partner a head injury."

A valid point. "Can I touch my clit?"

He continued to fuck her at the same, steady pace. "No."

"Dammit, Jack," she moaned.

"I'm sorry, who?" he asked, slowing down.

"Dammit, Boss," she amended, panic flaring when he slowed even further. "I meant please, Boss."

"Better," he allowed, but he didn't pick up his pace.

She wiggled in his hold, trying to use her legs to bring him in closer, but he was stronger than she was, and all it got her was another decrease in speed.

"Keep it up and I'll go get my cuffs," he warned her.

"Why are you so mean?" she whined.

"Were you unclear on the definition of sadism?" he asked, the laugh lurking in his voice again.

She ignored it. "I'm about to safeword this slow-ass fuck."

"Technically it's a *slow-pussy* fuck," he countered, still laughing. "You took your ass off the menu, remember?"

"I will use my safeword," she threatened, teeth gritted in frustration.

"And I will honor it," he assured her. "You say red and I stop. Completely. Totally. No more play, no more fucking. No orgasms."

"So *mean,*" she wailed.

"Maybe if you asked nicely…"

"You just want me to beg," she accused.

He beamed at her like a teacher whose pupil has just gotten a particularly difficult concept. "Of course I do."

"Bastard," she choked out, determined not to laugh.

"That doesn't sound much like begging."

"No, no, no, don't slow down *more,*" she wailed as he did just that. "I'm going to start crying in a minute."

"I do like crying," he admitted. "But tears are a keep going signal for me, so probably not the way you want to go."

She'd have sworn she felt tears well up. "I'm terrible at begging."

"Let me give you some motivation," he offered, and like the sadistic jerk he was, pulled all the way out.

"You sadistic jerk," she said, and tried to impale herself on him.

"Still not begging," he told her, and hitched her hips higher so her pussy was planted against his belly. "Try again."

"God, Jack, please," she whined. "I need to come so badly."

"Getting better," he decided and shifted so his forearm was braced under her ass, freeing one hand while still holding her up. "What else?"

"What do you mean, what else?" she asked, bewildered.

"I can see I'm going to have to give you some help." He let out a disappointed sigh. "Try this. *Boss, please let me come. I promise I'll be good.*"

"Boss, please let me come," she parroted. "I promise I'll be good."

"I need it so badly."

"I need it so badly," she repeated dutifully.

"If you let me come, I'll do anything you ask."

"If you let me come, I'll do *almost* anything you ask," she said, and made him laugh.

"Clever girl."

"I hate you."

"You were better at this when you were tied up and clamped. It was probably the pain," he mused. "It's a great motivator."

"Trust me, I'm in *agony* right now."

"Yes, but is it enough?"

"It really is." She bit her lip, struggling to let go. She was so used to playing a role in these scenes that it was hard to drop the act and let herself just *be*, but he wasn't going to settle for less. "Please, Jack. Please fuck me hard enough to make me come."

"Nice," he murmured, the teasing light leaving his eyes as they bored into hers. "Give me more."

"I need to come so badly," she continued, letting all the frustration and need pour out in her voice, holding back the snark that she so often employed as a shield. "Even though my pussy hurts when you do, I need you to fuck me harder."

The gleam in his eyes took on a glittering edge. "Are you telling me that so I'll fuck you faster, just to make it hurt?"

"Yes, but it's still true." She swallowed hard and put every ounce of need into her next words. "Please, Boss. I need you."

She'd meant to say *I need it,* not *I need you,* but the words were out now, and she wouldn't take them back even if she could. His eyes burned into hers, the dark brown almost black now, and a flush bloomed high on his cheekbones.

"Say it again," he ground out, fingers digging into her butt.

She had to swallow twice to be able to talk. "I need you," she whispered. "Please, Boss."

The growl he let out made her flinch, then he spun her around. Her hands fell away from the small of her back, reaching for him instinctively before she caught herself. "I'm sorry," she cried and tried to snatch them back.

"Above your head," he ordered, and she lifted them up just as he laid her down on the bench. "Hold on."

She barely had time to comply before he shoved her legs back and drove into her, jolting her entire body, then he was pounding into her hard and fast, just like she'd wanted.

It hurt, his pelvis slamming into her tender, bruised labia, but he'd angled himself so his pelvic bone dragged at her clit, pleasure building with every stroke, and the pain just didn't matter.

She held on to the bench for dear life. Water streamed from the wall jets, hitting him in the side and sending up a fine spray that blurred her vision. His hair swung forward, wet and curling, to curtain his face.

Water dripped from his beard onto her bouncing tits, and she stared, fascinated, as his lips peeled back into a snarl.

"Come, dammit," he growled, hips hammering. "I want to feel it."

She tried to spread her legs wider in response, only to bump up against the shower wall. He took the hint, shoving her knee higher and hooking his arm under it. It opened her up, letting him go deeper, but it still wasn't quite enough. "Oh, God, I need…"

"What? What do you need?" He shook the hair out of his eyes, sending water raining down. "Tell me."

"Pin me down," she choked out, arching up into him. She needed his weight, the force of it wrapped around her, smothering her. "Hard."

Understanding lit his dark gaze, and he shifted, rearing back. She started to protest, to tell him no, that was the *opposite* of what she needed. Then he laid his forearm across the tops of her breasts and leaned into her, and oh, it was *glorious.*

Pressure and heat and a deep, almost sublime feeling of helplessness rolled through her. She bucked against it, instinctively trying to throw off the thick bar of his arm, but he simply pressed down and kept pounding into her. Her head went light, her vision dim, and deep inside, she felt the first, tentative flutters of her orgasm.

"There you go," he muttered. His face was set, his eyes fierce. "No, baby, don't look away," he ordered when her eyes began to slide shut. She forced them back open. "That's it. Keep watching me, Sadie, look right at me when you come. I want to see it. I want to feel it. Come for me, you beautiful brat, come—"

She let out a choked cry, her body jerking under him as the orgasm hit, rolling through her like the tide, mowing down everything in its path. There was a roaring in her ears, like rushing water, and though she wanted to close her eyes to savor the tingle and the rush of it all, she kept them locked on his.

"Good girl." His voice was like gravel, his hips grinding into hers, turning her clit into fire. "That's a good fucking brat."

Then he lowered his forehead to hers, and keeping his eyes open, came.

Two hours later, she snuggled into the pillows in Jack's big bed with a sigh. "This was a good idea."

Jack stretched beside her. "Are you talking about the scene, or dinner?"

"Both," she decided and yawned. "But next time, we have to get two pieces of cake. You ate more than your half."

"I'm bigger than you," he pointed out. "I need more cake."

"That's not how cake works. Vegetables, yes. Cake, no. Everybody knows that," she said and turned to look at him.

He was watching her, a strange expression on his face. "Do I have frosting on my chin or something?"

He shook his head. "No."

"Then why are you looking at me like that?"

"You look good in my bed," he said.

"It's a good bed," she decided, brushing a hand over the curved headboard. "Surprising, though."

"Oh."

"Not many hard points on a sleigh bed."

He grinned. "Looks can be deceiving," he said and kissed her.

Warning bells clanged in the back of her head, but she could barely hear them over the pounding of her heart. She met the kiss with enthusiasm, eager to get back on familiar footing. This sneaking warmth she suddenly felt was confusing. She didn't understand it, and it made her uneasy. But desire—that she understood and knew what to do with.

"I have two questions," he murmured against her mouth.

The kiss had left her feeling faintly lightheaded, and though she was pretty sure she didn't have another orgasm in her, pleasantly buzzed. "What are they?"

He shifted to nuzzle her neck. "Am I going to have to arrange some kind of demonstration every time I want to see you?"

She jerked, startled. "What?"

He traced his tongue over the curve of her jaw. "Don't get me wrong, the demos are fun," he assured her, and nipped at her chin. "But I'd like to have a normal date sometime, too."

"You would?"

He pulled back to smile into her eyes. "Yes. Would you?"

"I guess so," she managed, trying to talk around the lump in her throat. "Do you mean like a play date, or a date-date?"

"A good question. What do you call today?" he asked. "The demo notwithstanding."

"Um…" His hand had snuck up to snuggle her breast, scrambling her thoughts. "I'm not sure."

"Well, whatever this is, is what I want to do again." His expression was curious. "Is that all right with you?"

"Yes," she decided, and another wave of that sneaky warmth flooded through her, all the way up to her cheeks this time.

"Good," he said. "Now, second question. Are you staying tonight?"

"Oh." She blinked. "Tomorrow is Sunday."

"You have plans?"

"Ah..." She fought to think. "I'm supposed to go to my folks' for dinner."

"What time?"

It's Sunday dinner," she explained. "They eat right after Mass."

He cocked an eyebrow. "You're Catholic?"

"Lapsed—much to my mother's chagrin."

"Just think how she'd feel if she could see all your Catholic schoolgirl outfits," he said and nipped at her tongue when she stuck it out. "What time is Mass?"

"Eleven-thirty, I think? Dinner is at one."

"I'll kick you out by eleven," he promised. "And I'll make you breakfast before you go. Waffles."

She liked waffles, and she didn't really want to get out of this big, warm, comfortable bed to get dressed and drive home. "Will you show me how you use the rings in the shower before breakfast?"

"It's a deal," he said, and sealed it with a kiss.

* * * *

Sadie stroked her hands, slick with fragrant oil, down Amanda's arms one last time, then eased back. "Okay, Amanda, we're all done."

Amanda blinked her eyes open on a sigh. "Sadie, you're a goddess."

"That's what they all say," Sadie quipped and dug a bottle of water out of her bag. "I'm putting your water on the nightstand, okay? And—"

"Drink it all," Amanda finished. "I know the drill."

"Good." Sadie laid a hand on Amanda's arm, keeping her voice soft. "Your robe is on the bed, and you take your time getting up. I'll be downstairs."

"Okay. Hey, Sadie?"

Sadie turned back at the door. "Yeah?"

Amanda sat up, holding the sheet to her breasts. "Do you have to rush off to another client?"

"You're my last massage today. Why?"

"James won't be home for another couple of hours, and I've got a lasagne in the oven. Want to join me for dinner?"

"I could go for some lasagne," Sadie decided.

"Good." Amanda slid off the massage table, taking the sheet with her. "I'm going to grab a quick shower, you pour the wine. There's a bottle of red on the counter."

"Fine, but you only get a glass if you drink all your water."

"Yeah, yeah," Amanda muttered but grabbed the bottle on the way to the bathroom. "Ten minutes."

"Take your time," Sadie called back, and, to save herself a trip, broke down the massage table before making her way downstairs.

Ten minutes later, she was halfway through the single glass of wine she allowed herself when she had to drive, her mouth watering from the smells coming from the oven, when Amanda padded in. Wrapped in a long green robe, her dark hair sleeked back and her skin dewy from the shower, she all but floated across the floor. "God, I feel good. Loose and relaxed."

"That's how you're supposed to feel," Sadie told her and handed her a glass of wine.

"Scheduling a weekly massage with you is the best thing I've ever done," Amanda declared, and tapped her glass against Sadie's just as the oven timer dinged. "Oh, good, it's done. I'm starving."

"Can I help?" Sadie asked as Amanda circled the kitchen island.

Amanda slipped a pair of oven mitts on her hands and opened the oven door. "Grab plates and silverware, will you? And there's a spinach salad in the fridge."

Sadie dutifully got out the plates and flatware, laying out two places at the stools that lined the kitchen island, then opened the fridge. "That smells amazing. Where'd you get it?"

Amanda set the pan on the hot pad she'd set out on the kitchen island. "You don't think I could've made this?"

"Amanda, I love you," Sadie said, setting the salad down. "But if you made that, I'll eat my massage table."

"Brat," Amanda accused, laughing, and boosted herself onto a stool. "Julia made it. Our new housekeeper."

"Since when do you have a housekeeper?"

"Since I got promoted." Amanda grabbed a spatula, dug out a slice of lasagne, and laid it on Sadie's plate. "I'm spending so much more time at the office, it just made sense to have someone come in to handle the housework. She comes in three times a week, and I swear, I don't know how we ever got along without her."

Sadie grabbed the salad bowl and dished up a serving for each of them. "Work's keeping you that busy?"

"I'm hoping it'll calm down once I finish cleaning up the mess the last director left behind." Amanda picked up her fork. "But even if it does, I'm not giving Julia up. I always have clean underwear, I don't have to dust or vacuum, and I've never eaten better."

Sadie swallowed her first bite of lasagne. "Me neither. Whatever you're paying her, it's not enough."

Amanda's mouth was full, so she just nodded and forked up another bite. When she'd swallowed, she picked up her wine. "Are you going to Nick and Rebecca's for Thanksgiving next week?"

Sadie shook her head. "I have to go to my parents' house for dinner. But they always eat early, so I told Rebecca I'd swing by after."

"Is Jack going?"

Sadie poked at the salad. "Rebecca invited him, so probably."

"You haven't talked about it?"

"No." Sadie reached for her wine glass, saw it was empty, and got up to help herself to a bottle of water. "Why would we?"

"It seems like it would come up, since y'all are dating."

Sadie rolled her eyes. "We're not dating."

Amanda snorted. "Right."

"We're not," Sadie insisted, and resumed her seat. "We just hang out sometimes, that's all."

"And fuck, and play, and go out to dinner, and spend the night at each other's homes—"

"He has not spent the night at my apartment," Sadie interrupted.

"But you've slept over at his," Amanda pointed out.

"Have you seen his place?" Sadie demanded. "He's got thousand-thread-count sheets and a bathtub you could drown in. It's like staying in a five-star hotel."

"So you're just there for the sheets and the tub," Amanda drawled.

"And the sex," Sadie admitted, twisting the cap off her water. "That's pretty good, too."

"Sounds like dating to me."

"Well, it's not."

"I guess you'd know," Amanda said, and set her wine back down. "How's the sadist thing working for you?"

Sadie sipped her water, hoping it would dissolve the sudden knot in her belly. "He's pretty mean."

Amanda snickered. "Most sadists are."

"But he's sneaky about it," Sadie went on. "By the time I realize he's doing something awful, I'm either already coming or about to, so I don't care. He brought out an actual stun gun the other night."

Amanda dropped her fork with a *clang*. "You're kidding."

"Nope. He said the zapper thingy he used the first time I went to his place had such an, and I quote, 'amusing effect', he wanted to see how I'd react to an upgrade."

Amanda's eyes were wide. "And?"

"It hurt like a son of a bitch," Sadie said, then laughed. "But I came so hard I saw God. Fucking Doms."

"Bastards, every last one," Amanda said and tapped her wine glass against Sadie's water bottle. "Here's to 'em."

Chapter Fourteen

On Thanksgiving Day, Sadie helped her mother divide the leftovers into Tupperware. "Mom, why don't you buy some new containers?" she asked, scooping green beans out of a casserole dish. "These are all stained."

"That's because I used them for spaghetti sauce once," Jennifer Bloom replied, elbow-deep in the big pot of mashed potatoes. Her dark brown hair was tied back in a braid, the streaks of silver that had begun to appear in the last few years gleaming. "But they're still good."

Sadie shook her head, knowing better than to argue. "Do you want me to save room in these containers for anything else, or should I fill them up?"

"Fill them up." Jennifer plopped a spoonful of mashed potatoes into the container in front of her. "I can stick anything left behind in the freezer. Is this enough for you, or do you need more?"

Sadie eyed the mountain of potatoes. "Mom, don't give me all that. It'll go bad before I can eat it all."

"So, put some in the freezer." Jennifer set her spoon down and grabbed a lid. "I hate to think of you ordering in every night."

"I don't order in *every* night," Sadie protested. "Sometimes I eat cereal, or macaroni and cheese. And I recently learned to make waffles."

"Sadie, taking a package out of the freezer and shoving a frozen hunk of bread into the toaster is not 'making waffles'."

Sadie laughed. "Not freezer waffles, real ones made with flour and butter and milk—"

"Wait a minute." Jennifer held up a mashed-potato-flecked hand, the hazel eyes Sadie had inherited wide with shock. "You mean *actual* waffles?"

"A friend taught me," Sadie said haughtily and began snapping lids on the green bean containers.

Jennifer's smile went sly. "A naked friend?"

Sadie groaned. "Mom."

"What? You think I don't know about naked friends?" Jennifer scoffed. "Please. When I was your age, I had naked friends coming out of my…ears."

"When you were my age, you were married with two kids," Sadie countered.

"Okay, so I only had one naked friend by then," Jennifer said without missing a beat. "But I had plenty when I was younger."

"Gee, is that the time?" Sadie exclaimed and reached for the ties on her apron. "I have to go."

"You do not," Jennifer said. "You just don't want to tell me about your naked friend."

"It's halftime," a voice boomed, and Sadie looked up as her father bounded into the room. "Where's dessert?"

"You get no dessert until my kitchen is clean," Jennifer informed him, and pointed to the pile of Tupperware on the counter. "Pick something and put it away."

"Okay." Always agreeable, Michael Bloom began spooning gravy into a container. "What's new, Sadie Lady?"

Smiling at the nickname, Sadie opened her mouth to answer, but her mother beat her to it. "She has a naked friend, but she doesn't want to talk about it."

"Why not?" Michael asked, his shaggy mop of ginger curls bouncing as he shook the last of the gravy off the spoon. "Is he weird?"

"Not weirder than you," Sadie shot back, fumbling with the apron ties. They'd wound themselves into a knot, and she couldn't get it undone.

"You should've brought him to dinner," The gravy handled, her dad reached around his wife to pick up the turkey platter. "We could judge for ourselves."

"Screw it, I'll wear the apron," Sadie decided and leaned over to kiss her mother's cheek, then her dad's. "Thanks for dinner, Mom. Everything was great. Dad, you got gravy on your tie."

Michael scowled down at the stain. "Nuts."

"You're not staying for pie?" Jennifer asked, digging her fingers into Sadie's arm when she tried to slip away. "I made lemon meringue."

"I told you, I promised my friend Rebecca I'd stop by her house for dessert." She twisted neatly out of her mother's grip, snagging the giant container of mashed potatoes as she swung back toward the door.

"You could stay for one slice and spend some time with your brothers. You barely got to talk to them at dinner."

Sadie hurried over to the hooks by the back door to find her coat and purse. "They were busy with the kids."

"The kids are napping now," Jennifer pointed out. "We could get out the Scrabble board, play a game. All of us, like we used to."

Sadie finally unearthed her purse under six layers of coats. "We'd be screaming at each other in twenty minutes."

"That's true," Jennifer muttered. "You kids never could play a civilized game."

"And besides." Purse in one hand, potatoes in the other, the coat draped over her arm, she turned to beam at her parents. "I have to go."

"But what about the pie?"

She reached for the doorknob, mouth open to respond, when her brother Brian wandered in from the living room. "Hey, Ma, when's dessert?"

Sadie opened the door. "Brian can have my piece."

"Your piece of what?" Brian asked, staring at the ceiling.

"Lemon meringue." Jennifer frowned at her son. "Why are you staring at the ceiling?"

"I can't look at Sadie," Brian said, his cheeks ruddy. "She knows why."

"Is this about that accidental sex dial?" her mother demanded.

"Accidental what dial?" her father asked, finally looking up from his gravy-stained tie, and, choking on a laugh, Sadie made her escape.

* * * *

Half an hour later, Rebecca opened the door to the loft she shared with Nick, a welcoming smile on her face. "Hey! How was dinner with your folks?"

"Good, until my mother asked me if I have a naked friend," Sadie said, stepping inside.

"Your *mother* asked you that?"

"And my father asked if my naked friend was weird." Sadie closed the door behind her. "How are things going here?"

"Well, nobody's asked about naked friends, but that's probably because both my parents and Nick's assume we've already seen each other naked."

"You're doing better than me." Sadie peeled off her coat. "Where should I put this?"

"I'll take it—we're putting them in the bedroom." Rebecca paused. "Why are you wearing an apron?"

"The strings are knotted, and I had to make a strategic retreat."

"There she is," Jack said, walking up with a drink in his hand. He wore gray slacks and a white dress shirt with the cuffs undone. His hair was loose, his beard freshly trimmed, and his eyes were crinkling with his smile.

"I'll just go put this away," Rebecca said, and slipped away with Sadie's coat.

Jack drew to a halt in front of Sadie and dipped his head to kiss her. "Hi."

"Hi, yourself." She kissed him back, then pointed at the drink in his hand. "What's that?"

He tilted the glass so the light bounced through the amber liquid. "Scotch, neat."

"It'll do," she decided, and taking it from his hand, knocked it back. "Shit."

He whacked her on the back. "You're supposed to sip it."

She wheezed. "Now you tell me."

"Rough day?"

"Not really. I'm just being dramatic."

His lips twitched. "All right. Want another drink?"

"Yes, please. Preferably one that won't set my throat on fire."

"It wouldn't have, if you'd sipped it." He slipped a hand around her waist, over the knotted apron strings, and looked down. "Why are you wearing an apron?"

"It's part of the being dramatic," she told him. "Plus, the strings are knotted and I can't get them undone."

"Want me to do it?"

"Yes, please."

He set his glass down on the entry table and moved behind her. "Hold still."

She looked around the big open living room as he worked. "Lot of people here."

"There were more before," he said. "Rebecca's parents went back to their hotel, and Nick's parents left too. But your old boyfriend is still here."

"Old boyfriend?" she echoed, confused.

"Nick's brother?"

"Nate's here?" She spotted him by the windows, standing next to his twin and laughing, one arm wrapped around a pretty brunette. "He was never my boyfriend."

"Hmmm," he said.

"Don't start," she muttered, and caught Nate's eye. She returned his cheerful grin, then cut her eyes deliberately to the woman at his side and gave him an exaggerated thumbs-up.

Nate grinned back and tugged Kit closer, bending to whisper in her ear. Kit turned, her face lighting up when she spotted Sadie. She waved, a little waggle of her fingers, and Sadie replied with a smile and a wink. Kit laughed along with Nate, then turned back to their conversation.

A yank on the apron strings almost jerked her off her feet. "Hey!"

"This is a very stubborn knot," Jack remarked, all innocence. "How did dinner with your parents go?"

"Well, my brother Brian still won't look at me because I accidentally called him this summer while I was having sex, my mother asked me if you were my naked friend, and my dad asked me if you're weird and if that's why I didn't bring you to Thanksgiving dinner."

His hands had gone still on the apron strings. "You told your mother about me?"

"I told her a friend taught me to make waffles," she explained. "She inferred the naked part."

"Uh-huh. And your brother won't look at you because…"

"Apparently every time he looks at me, he thinks about me having sex, and it breaks his tiny little twelve-year-old brain."

"You called your twelve-year-old brother while you were having sex?"

"He's not *actually* twelve, that's his emotional maturity level," she explained. "He's twenty-two. And I told you, it was an accident."

"And your dad thinks I'm weird."

"He *wonders* if you're weird," she corrected him. "I neither confirmed nor denied."

"I can't tell if you're making this up or not," he finally said.

"I'm not creative enough to make this up," she assured him.

"Oh, I don't know." His arms circled her waist, drawing the now untied apron strings forward. "You're plenty creative when it counts."

"That's mostly you," she reminded him, and for a moment, let herself lean into him. He was warm and solid, and he smelled like the shampoo he kept in his shower, and the thought drifted through her mind that it wouldn't be a hardship to just stay there forever.

"Your curses are inventive," he offered.

"That's true," she allowed. "I'm a very good curser."

He chuckled, his breath stirring her hair. "Are you up for some cursing tonight?"

"I could be." She angled her head to see his face. "What did you have in mind?"

He merely raised an eyebrow. "Now, what kind of a Dom would I be if I told you what I was going to do?"

"A nice one?" she ventured. "Kind? Courteous? Accommodating?"

"I don't think so," he said with a laugh. "But I am willing, this one time, to give you a hint."

She eyed him warily. He was wearing a broad smile that she didn't trust for a minute. "What kind of a hint?"

"Before I answer that, what do you have on your schedule for tomorrow?"

"Nothing," she replied, confused.

"No clients, no plans to go shopping?"

"No clients, and I'd rather walk on Legos than go shopping the day after Thanksgiving."

"Good." His smile broadened, morphing from genial to cartoon villain. "Then it won't be a problem if you're a little gassy."

It took a moment for the pieces to fall into place. "You want to do butt stuff."

"Correction," he said. "We're *going* to do butt stuff."

Sadie was torn. On the one hand, she really loved anal sex. But the stuff that came with it was such a pain in the…well, ass. "I don't know, Jack."

The eyebrow rose again. "Are you safewording?"

Dammit. "No."

"Do you have a reason to say no?" he continued. "Other than the ones already discussed?"

She sighed. "No."

"Well, then."

"Fine." She grumbled it to hide her delight. "You can fuck my ass tonight."

"Why, thank you. I believe I will." He dropped a kiss on her pouting mouth. "Do you need anything from me to, how did you put it? Get yourself 'company ready'?"

"No, but I'll have to stop by my place to pack a bag." She sent him a scowl. "I'm staying over, and spending all day tomorrow at your place."

"Are you?"

"If I have to suffer through the aftermath, the least you can do is suffer with me."

"Looking forward to it," he said, chuckling when she scowled harder, and grabbed her hand. "Come on. Let's get some pie."

Chapter Fifteen

They stopped at her place to drop off her car and pick up an overnight bag, then continued to his apartment. Sadie disappeared into his bathroom as soon as they arrived, calling out as she ran up the steps that she wasn't to be disturbed on pain of death. Amused, he put away the leftovers Rebecca had pressed on him, plus an enormous container of mashed potatoes from Sadie's mother, then visited the guest bath before following her up the steps.

He kept an ear out while he changed his clothes, slipping into the black pajama pants he favored for lounging. With the occasional burst of running water the only sound coming from the bathroom, he worked on setting the scene.

He stripped the bed down to the fitted sheet, laying the duvet over the footboard so he could reach it easily later, and stacked the pillows on the chair in the corner. Rope came out of the storage bin under the bed, along with a pair of wrist cuffs in supple leather, and the small tool kit he needed to open the hidden panels in the headboard.

He opened the first one at the upper left corner, revealing the eye bolt that served as a hard point. He flipped the mechanism that extended it past the opening and locked it into place, then did the same on the other side. He attached a length of rope covered in a thin PVC sleeve to each, leaving the ends to trail on the mattress. They'd be tied to her cuffs, but he'd do that when she was in them.

He dipped back under the bed for the custom pillow he'd had made for the headboard. The thick slab of memory foam was three feet wide, five feet long and had been custom fit to lie against the curved headboard, providing extra padding for anyone who found themselves bound to it.

He fitted it into place, attaching it to the hooks that sat below the mattress in the front, pulling it over the top of the headboard and fastening it to the hooks on the back side. He stepped back to eye the setup, then grabbed a pillow from the pile on the chair. The mattress was soft, but she'd be on her knees for a while, and some additional cushion wouldn't hurt.

He laid the pillow in the center of the mattress, right in front of the headboard pad. Satisfied that the bed was ready, he picked up the toy bag he'd pulled out of the closet.

He opened it and considered the contents. With his plans for the scene in mind, he selected a wooden paddle, a riding crop, and two floggers—one in deer hide, the other in buffalo. He added a leather vampire glove to the pile, and one covered in soft rabbit fur for contrast. He picked out a cane, just in case, then tossed the bag back in the closet and draped the duvet over the pile of toys so she wouldn't see them.

He dug the bottle of lube he preferred for ass play out of the nightstand and tucked it and a pair of condoms next to the toys. He was tying his hair back when the bathroom door opened.

Sadie stepped out, naked, her hair still in the loose waves she'd worn earlier. She started to smile at him when her gaze dropped, and she blinked. "Damn. Olivia was right."

"What was she right about?" he asked amused.

"That black pajama pants season is almost as good as sweatpants season."

"What?"

She waved a hand, her eyes still trained on his pants. "Never mind, it's not important."

"Okay."

She shook her head, like a woman coming out of a dream, then stepped forward. She stood straight, her hands raised and out to the sides, palms up and slightly cupped, and in a deep voice that rang with ceremony, announced, "I have performed the ritual, and the path is clear. You may now bugger me."

Delighted with her, he laughed and scooped her up in a fierce hug. He swung her around just to hear her squeal, burying his face in her hair. "God, you are something else."

"I keep telling you that," she reminded him, her hands clinging to his shoulders.

"And I believe you every time," he assured her. He held on to her for one more moment, savoring the simple joy of her in his arms, then set her back on her feet.

"You're in an awfully good mood," she observed, brushing at her hair. "That usually means you have something terrible planned for me."

"Oh, not so terrible," he assured her, and reached up to gently tug a lock of hair from where it clung to her cheek.

Her eyes were dancing with anticipation, even as they narrowed in suspicion. "That's what you said when you brought out the stun gun," she reminded him.

"And didn't you like it?" he countered.

"No. It hurt like a motherfucker."

"You came so hard you were speaking in tongues," he reminded her.

"Oh yeah," she murmured, her eyes going dreamy at the memory, and he stifled a laugh.

He circled around to stand behind her and nudged her toward the bed. "You'll be fine. Trust me."

"I do," she said, surprising him. "But we might have different definitions of 'fine'."

Amused, exhilarated by her easy declaration of trust, he dropped a kiss on her nose. "Oh, we absolutely do. Now be a good girl and get on the bed."

Five minutes later, Sadie was finally starting to relax.

She'd been nervous at Nick and Rebecca's—it had felt so much like a couple thing, being there together—and the nerves had stayed with her on the ride back from her apartment. But being on her knees with her wrists cuffed felt familiar, and comfortable.

Unlike all the strange and unsettling *feelings* fluttering around inside her, she knew what to expect from this.

Determined to put the flutterings out of her mind, she focused on what he was doing. He'd buckled the cuffs into place and positioned her on the bed, and now he was tying a length of rope to the cuff on her left wrist, the other end of which was attached to an eyebolt she'd never noticed before.

"Was that always there?" she asked. "That eye bolt?"

He pulled steadily on the rope, stretching her arm out along the headboard. "Yes."

"Was it visible?"

He tied off the rope and rounded the bed to the other side. "No."

"Oh." She looked closer, realizing that a whole square of wood was missing from the headboard. It was cherry wood, with dozens of intricately carved panels, each about eight inches square, and she'd assumed they were merely decorative. But now…

"Are all of these little panels hiding a hard point?"

"Some of them," he said, threading rope through the cuff's D-ring. "Some of them are hiding other things."

She looked up at him. "Like what?"

"Terrible things," he said with a sinister eyebrow wiggle, and stretched out her right arm before tying off the rope. Stepping back, he nodded. "That'll do," he decided and disappeared from view.

She could hear him rummaging around at the foot of the bed but didn't turn to watch. She was too busy wondering just what all those wooden panels hid, and how she could find out.

"Before you think of snooping around my headboard," he announced, "you should know it takes a special tool to remove the panels."

"I wasn't going to snoop," she protested.

"If someone were to try to pry a panel open with anything else, like a screwdriver, it would be very noticeable."

A screwdriver was a terrible idea, she thought. The panels were fitted too tight for that. But a butter knife might do, or one of those thin metal nail files.

"I mention this only because I think you should be aware," he went on casually, "that if any damage is done to my headboard, you can expect similar damage to your ass."

She huffed out an affronted breath. "I'm not sure why you're telling me this. I have absolutely no interest in your wood."

"Well, that is a disappointment," he said with a chuckle, and she realized what she'd said.

"You know what I meant," she said, turning her head to the right to try to see him.

"I know," he said, his voice in her left ear, and she jolted. "You're jumpy."

"A little," she admitted, knowing a lie would only draw more attention to her nerves.

He drew his hands up her back, slowly, leaving goosebumps in his wake. "Why?"

Maybe just a little lie. "I'm not sure," she breathed, shivering when he delved his hands into her hair. "I guess I'm just edgy."

"Hmmm. Maybe you've had too much time to think."

He was massaging her scalp, and it felt good. Really good. "Maybe."

"Well, let's fix that." He ran his fingers through her hair, his big hands surprisingly gentle. "I need this out of the way."

She was silent as he gathered up her hair, wrapping an elastic around it so it sat on top of her head in a loose replica of his habitual bun.

"There," he murmured, and planted a kiss on the base of her neck. "Did you know you have a little cluster of freckles, right here?"

"I have freckles everywhere," she managed.

"Not everywhere," he replied. "A sprinkle here, a dusting there. One of these days, I'm going to play connect the dots. With a blade."

She blinked at the wall in front of her. *A blade?*

"But that's for another time," he went on, stroking his hands down her back. Big and warm, slightly rough, the rings he wore cool and smooth in contrast. "Tonight, I want to keep things simple."

"That's a change." She tilted her head back. She wanted to lay it on his shoulder, but he was too far away.

"Sometimes, you have to get back to basics." He skimmed his hands over her hips, down her thighs. "I need these a bit wider, I think."

She inched her knees apart, balancing on the pillow he'd put under her knees to cushion them. "Like that?"

"A little more," he said, urging her legs apart with his hands on her inner thighs. "There, that's good. How does that feel?"

She wiggled, assessing as she settled into the new position. Her legs weren't so far apart that her thighs were straining, and she felt steady enough. "It's fine."

"Good." He dropped a kiss on the base of her spine. "Let's get started."

She tensed, anticipating a blow. But all he did was run his hands up her back again, spreading them out so it seemed he covered every inch of her skin. He drew them down, stroking over her hips, her ass, her thighs, then did it all over again.

She fought down impatience, knowing from experience that he couldn't be rushed. She'd tried sassing him to move things along—something that had always worked very well for her in the past—but he was immune to her tactics, no matter how much she bratted it up. More than once he'd drawn out a scene until she was ready to scream with frustration. He would move at his pace and no faster, no matter how much she begged—something else she'd gotten a lot of practice at over the last few weeks—so she closed her eyes and drew a deep breath, forcing her tensed muscles to relax, and ordered herself to go with it.

She timed her breathing to his stroking hands, letting herself settle into the rhythm of it. His strokes grew heavier, firmer, the pressure pushing her forward so she rocked back and forth. It was relaxing, almost hypnotic—until the first hit came.

The slap on her back didn't hurt—in fact, it might not have registered at all except that it broke the rhythm she'd gotten into. But then the next one came, and the next, the rapid smacks moving up and down her back, butt and thighs, gradually increasing in intensity. He was warming her up, bringing blood to the surface in preparation for harder blows. She wondered dimly what he'd use—the way he was concentrating on her back made her think flogger, but he could just as easily choose a crop or a slapper. Even a whip was a possibility, though it would have to be a short one. There wasn't enough space in the room for anything long.

Her thoughts were interrupted when the bed shifted behind her, and something heavy stroked over her shoulders. It was soft and carried the unmistakable scent of well-conditioned leather.

"Flogger," she murmured.

"Good guess."

"Heavy," she said, trying to picture it in her mind. The leather falls felt wide rather than thin, and thick as they trailed over her ass and hips. "Buffalo?"

"Have you been peeking in my toy bag?" he wondered.

"I might have, if I'd thought of it," she admitted.

"I can see I'm going to have to invest in a lock," he said. "How are you feeling?"

"Good." She said it automatically, but it was true. She felt warm and loose, and even though arousal was beginning to build, oddly content.

"Color?"

"Green, green, greenity-green," she sang and let out a low laugh.

"All right, then," he said, amused, and slid a hand around to her belly. "Lean back a little, love, and roll your shoulders forward."

Her body felt heavy, and not quite her own, so she let his hand guide her, pulling her where he wanted her. "Like this?"

"Perfect," he murmured, his beard tickling her shoulder as he brushed a kiss there. "I want you to try to maintain this position. If you get tired or need to move, let me know."

"Yes, Boss."

She felt his lips curve against her skin. "Good girl."

His hand slid away from her belly, leaving behind a lingering warmth. She was wishing it back when the flogger fell.

Her breath gusted out, more from surprise than from pain, and she blinked the haze away from her eyes.

"Tell me how much that hurt, Sadie, on a scale of one to ten."

She tried to think. She knew by ten he meant the point when she'd use her safeword. "Um. A four, maybe?"

"Good to know. You ready for more?"

"Yes, Boss," she replied, the honorific sliding smoothly off her tongue.

"Don't forget to keep breathing," he instructed, and the flogger fell on the exhale.

There was no pause this time, no break between blows. The flogger struck over and over, dancing over her back in a steady rhythm. They weren't hurting yet, not really—it felt like someone giving her a congratulatory pat on the back with a little too much enthusiasm, a comparison that made her giggle out loud.

"Something funny?" he drawled, not missing a beat.

"Congratulations to me," she said and laughed again.

He didn't respond, just kept the flogger moving.

The leather falls moved down, skipping over her lower back to her ass. He hit her a little harder there, the layer of fat over dense muscle making it an ideal target for the heavy buffalo hide. Her butt and thighs warmed under the blows, heat and sting building, then he moved back up.

She lost track of time. The steady rhythm of the flogger was lulling, even when the hits started coming harder. She registered the pain in an abstract sort of way, as though it was happening to someone else, even as her blood pumped and her nerves sang. Some dim part of her recognized that she was in sub space, the happy endorphin-soaked phase of the scene where nothing hurt, even when it did.

There was a pause in the flogging, but it didn't register until Jack's arm slipped around her from behind. "What's your color, Sadie?"

"Green," she murmured, and pressed her back into his chest. His skin was damp with sweat—flogging was hard work—but he felt delightfully cool against her battered back. "Oh, that feels nice."

His low chuckle had a shiver running down her spine.

"Do you know," she said dreamily, "when you laugh like that, you sound like a cartoon villain?"

"Do I?"

"One of those old black-and-white ones where the girl gets tied to the railroad tracks," she continued, tilting her head back onto his shoulder. Floating, and more than a little buzzed, she turned her face into his neck and breathed him in. "You sound like that guy."

"You're endorphin drunk," he announced.

"I know." She sighed. "I'm starting to hurt, though."

"How much?"

"Mmmm. Prolly a six."

"I'm going to push that," he warned her.

"Bring it on, Boss-man," she purred and giggled.

"You got it, brat," he replied. His arm slid away, and the flogger began its hammering beat once more.

She rocked forward with every blow, little grunts and cries slipping from her lips. Pain blossomed and spread through her back and butt, the backs of her thighs stinging. She pulled at the restraints on her hands, not because she wanted to be free, but because she needed to *move.* A deep, crawling itch had settled under her skin, spreading like a rash, and she knew from experience that the only thing that would ease it was more pain.

"I need more," she mumbled, pushing her butt out. "Please, Boss."

"Does it itch, baby?"

"Yes." She squirmed, seeking his touch. The itch was arousing, maddening. "Make it stop."

"Hold still," he commanded.

She bit her lip, her body shaking as she strained to obey him instead of her own desperate needs. "Please, please, please," she chanted, her breath coming in shallow pants. "Jack, I need you."

"I'm here," he assured her, and she heard leather snap as pain exploded across her buttocks.

"Oh, thank God," she breathed, her face damp with sweat and tears. The pain was like fire, sharp and bright and burning, but it eased that horrible itch. "Again."

Leather snapped again, sending flames licking over her skin, bringing relief and agony in equal measure. "It hurts," she groaned, and tried to pant through it.

"I know, baby," he crooned.

His voice was a song, his arm a steel band across her belly as he came up behind her, and fresh pain bloomed. It wasn't soothing now, the press of his skin against hers, but a buffet of torment. His silk pants felt like burlap against her tenderized butt, his chest hair a boar bristle brush against her raw back. It overwhelmed her, scattered her senses, and for a moment it was so jagged, so searing, it was all she could feel.

Then his hand slid down her belly to delve between her thighs, and it flipped like a coin.

She felt like a sauna, wet and hot, her pussy pulsing against his fingers. He knew she was hurting—it was in her voice, in the way her breath stuttered in her lungs. Her hands were clenched on the headboard, her knuckles nearly white. Her back and butt were red, the tiny welts from the thinner, nastier falls on the deer hide flogger standing out like crimson flags. She was near the limit of what she could take, though she likely hadn't realized it yet, her brain too fuzzy from the endorphins, thoughts too scattered by the pain.

One hand cupping her pussy—God, it was like a furnace—he slipped the other up between her breasts to close around her throat. He wanted that connection with her heartbeat, with her breath. With her soul.

"You're wet, Sadie," he said and sank his teeth, slowly and with careful restraint, into her shoulder. She jerked against him, her pulse leaping under his hand, a thin whine vibrating in her throat. He was sweating, but her back and butt were radiating heat, and no doubt highly sensitive from the beating.

Testing, he rubbed his chest against her back, and was rewarded when she gave a full-body shudder and flooded his palm.

"So fucking wet," he whispered. "My bratty little pain slut."

She let out a breathy laugh, a giddy, needy sound that went straight to his dick. "I know," she gurgled and swallowed, her throat bobbing against his palm, and rasped, "Who knew?"

"I didn't," he admitted. "But I'm very happy to make the discovery."

She laughed again, but this time the sound cut off on a sob. "Jack."

"What, baby?" He cuddled her close, knowing it hurt, knowing she loved it. "What do you need?"

"You," she choked off, her hands clenching into fists. "I need you."

He licked the teeth marks he'd left on her shoulder, fighting to bring himself under control, and pushed her forward. "Lean against the cushion."

She obeyed, turning her face to the side and pressing her body into the memory foam. Her cheeks were flushed, her eyes heavy and glassy. Her lower lip had multiple teeth marks, and the remains of her eye makeup was smeared like bruises under her eyes. With her back and ass all but glowing, she was the sexiest, most beautiful woman he'd ever seen.

He reached behind him for a condom, quickly rolled it on, then picked up the lube.

Sadie shivered when he slipped a lubed finger between her butt cheeks but didn't move away. Hell, if her hands had been free, she'd have reached back and spread her cheeks to make it easier.

She couldn't remember ever feeling like this before. Her entire body felt like one big exposed nerve, throbbing and twitching at the slightest touch, the faintest breeze. Her back and her ass were a symphony of pain, her head swimming with endorphins. And her pussy…

She'd been so preoccupied with the pain that it simply hadn't registered at first, but when he'd slipped his hand between her thighs, all the hurt had faded to the background, and staggering arousal came rushing in.

Her body felt heavy with it, her blood thick. The stinging, throbbing pain was feeding a roaring, boiling need that left room for nothing else. And when his slick finger breached her asshole, it ramped up a notch.

Primed and eager, she pushed her hips back and concentrated on forcing that tight ring of muscle to relax.

"Eager little butt slut," he murmured, and though it hadn't been a question, she nodded.

He worked a second finger in alongside the first, adding more lube until they were gliding back and forth with ease.

"Should I try to add a third finger," he wondered out loud, "or just get on with it?"

"Do I get an opinion?" she panted. She was clinging to the headboard, hips undulating into the thrust of his fingers.

"Oh, I can guess what that would be." He slapped her left butt cheek, laughing when the resulting burst of pain made her tighten on his fingers. "But you know, I have a couple of toys I didn't get to use."

He started to withdraw his fingers, and she almost burst into tears. "Oh, please, Boss."

He stopped moving, his fingers barely breaching her tightest hole. "Please what, brat?"

"Please don't make me wait," she said, the words tumbling over themselves in her rush to say them.

"Wait for what?" he asked silkily.

"For you to fuck my ass," she said, and tried to recapture his fingers by pushing back. Maddeningly, he moved too, keeping them where she could barely feel them. "Please, fuck it now, Boss. Please don't make me wait."

"Your begging is getting better," he remarked, and pulled his fingers completely free. Her protest died in a hiss of pain when he grabbed her ass in both hands, fingers digging into the bruised and battered flesh, but she didn't care. He was pulling her cheeks apart, and that could only mean one thing.

She held her breath when she felt his latex-covered cock glide though the slick, heated folds of her pussy. He was shockingly cold and incredibly slick—he'd used a heavy hand with the lube, something she was sure she'd be grateful for in a moment.

She wouldn't have been surprised if he'd chosen to linger, just to torment her, but thank God he didn't. Instead he slid quickly upward, bumping over her taint before pressing firmly against her asshole. And before she could so much as draw breath to brace herself, he'd slipped inside.

"Jesus Christ, Sadie," he marveled, a tinge of awe in his tone. "You sucked me right in."

She'd have said something smart, something witty—surely she would have—but she was far too busy remembering how to breathe.

God, he felt huge. He wasn't, of course—he had a perfectly reasonably sized penis—but even fingers felt big in her butt, and he was way bigger than a finger.

He slid forward with ease, lube and her eagerness easing the way, and slid back out again. "Fuck, you feel like a furnace."

"You feel like a telephone pole," she countered, closing her eyes to concentrate on the feeling. It hurt, the burn and the stretch and the unbelievable pressure as he worked himself deep. She loved it.

"You love it," he declared. There was a blast of cold when he added more lube, then he was all the way in, his pelvis pressed against her ass. "Say it."

"I love it," she parroted, unable to do anything else. She swore she could feel every single one of his pubic hairs scraping against the raw skin of her butt, and when he leaned into her, pushing her hard into the cushion and rubbing his chest against her, her back lit up like the Fourth of July. "Fuck, Jack."

"I am," he assured her. He inched back, then forward again, grinding against her ass. "Believe me, I am."

She got lost in the pain, in the pleasure. He seemed to be in no hurry, fucking her with a slow, steady pace that seemed specifically designed to push her to the outer edges of control. She was so worked up that she would've gladly accepted a pounding, even welcomed it, but he ignored her enticing wiggles and kept to his snail's pace.

"You're killing me," she groaned out, nearly sobbing with frustration. Her orgasm tickled the edges of her consciousness, just out of reach. If he'd only fuck her just a little bit harder…

"Killing you?" he repeated, and it sounded to her buzzing ears as though he was laughing. "I thought I was being very considerate. If I fuck your ass hard and fast, won't that only exacerbate the…aftereffects?"

It took her a moment to figure out what he was talking about. "Yes, but…"

"But what, brat?" he whispered in her ear, low and silky smooth.

"But I need to come," she whined. Arching her back, she gave a little butt wiggle, pressing her ass into him. The resulting flare of pain made her suck in a breath—man, he'd beaten her ass *good*—but she welcomed it. Needed it. "Please, Boss. Fuck me harder."

"Such good begging," he praised, and obligingly picked up the pace.

God, it hurt. The lube cut the friction to almost nothing, and though the sense of fullness every time he bottomed out was intense, she had no complaints. But her back and her butt felt as though they were on fire, and every time he stopped to add lube, he pulled out completely, which meant that when he drove back in, he breached the tender ring of muscle anew, and no matter how ready and eager she was, it always closed down just enough to make reentry pinch, just enough.

It was so fucking good she could hardly stand it.

It went on and on, pain and pressure and fullness until she wanted to scream. Sweat streamed down her back, making the welts sting anew, and his grip on her ass had turned almost punishing. The orgasm was gathering like a storm in her belly, her cunt, but it was still just out of reach. She needed something else, something more.

"Oh, please," Hands clutching at the headboard, she turned to look at him. "Please, Jack."

"What is it, brat?" he asked, a hitch in his gravel-like voice, and she was perversely pleased to note that he didn't sound so smooth anymore. Didn't look it, either. He was sweating, his teeth gritted, and his eyes were blazing. "You need something?"

She tried to shift her mouth into a pout, but she was too far gone for pretense. "Yes."

Satisfaction gleamed in his eyes. "What?"

She shook her head, the loose bun flopping, and pressed her face to the cushion in front of her. "I don't know. I can't...I don't know."

"More of this?" he asked and pushed hard into her.

It stole her breath, had fresh sweat breaking out on her skin. He kept going, hammering her with short, sharp thrusts that made his balls swing forward and slap against her wet pussy. "Is that what you want?"

She would've answered him, but her voice had stopped working, and all she was capable of doing was moaning.

"Or do you want more of this?" he continued and dragged his hand down her back.

A scream ripped from her throat and her vision went white as her back erupted in agony. She dimly heard him laugh, full of triumph and delight, but all her focus was on the sharp, stabbing pain that couldn't possibly be just from his hand.

Her suspicions were confirmed when she managed to look behind her and saw he'd slipped on a black leather glove. He saw her looking and waved at her, the tiny metal teeth embedded in the palm gleaming in the light.

Vampire glove, she thought, blinking through the tears, then closed her eyes on a fresh wave of anguish washing over her when he stroked it, oh so gently, over her hip. Her whole body seemed to clench, and she fought to ride the pain, to let it carry her.

"You like that," he observed.

"I hate it," she choked out, only half lying.

"Liar," he accused.

"Sadist," she countered, and tried to gather her scattered wits. She was so close now, the orgasm almost within reach. Her asshole was clenching around his dick, her pussy around nothing, and an insistent throb had taken up residence deep in her belly. "Boss, please."

"Again?" he asked and raised his hand.

"No, no, no," she chanted, flinching away. She yanked at her hands, forgetting they were tethered in her desperation to avoid another stroke of that glove. Part of her recognized that it would bring the orgasm closer, that every time he hurt her, pleasure followed pain, but her lizard brain was overloaded, and all she could think was *please.*

"Please," she said, putting all the frustration and fear and longing inside her into the word. She twisted to look him in the eye, hoping he'd see the plea there as well, and licked her lips. "Please."

"Please what, pain slut?" he asked. He was holding himself still, his dick pulsing inside her, his groin pressed hard against her ass. His gloved hand hung at his side, the other clamped on her hip in a death grip. "What do you need? Ask me, and I'll give it to you."

"My pussy," she said, the words ripped from her belly. "I need to touch my pussy."

"But your hands are cuffed," he pointed out, all reason.

"Undo it," she begged, lifting her left hand as high as she could. "Please, Boss, undo it. I need it to come, please."

"I'm sorry, baby," he crooned, and a purely evil gleam lit his eyes. "I can't do that."

Her breath gushed out on a sob, and her pussy gave a hard, desperate clench.

"But since you asked so prettily," he continued, the cartoon-villain smile curving his lips, "I'll touch your pussy for you."

Relief and gratitude rushed in only to be cut off by horror when he lifted his gloved hand, and realization dawned.

He moved slowly, pressing himself into her back, crooning and shushing in response to her babbled cries of *no, please, don't.* His hand slid around her hip to her belly, the leather smooth against her sweaty skin, and for a moment she was confused. Then he turned his wrist, and with deliberation, he closed his hand over her soft, wet pussy and ever so gently, squeezed.

Pain was a living, breathing thing, snaking under her skin and into her blood in little licks of flame. But through it was the insistent throb of arousal, the pulse and hum of need, and amazingly, the ball of tension in her belly began to tighten. And when he began to pound into her…

"Oh God, oh God, oh God." She pressed her forehead to the cushion, all her focus on that roiling, churning ball. It was picking up speed, spinning harder and faster. "So close, I'm so close, please."

He was hammering into her now, hard, fast thrusts punctuated by growling grunts and the slap of his balls into the back of his hand. He squeezed her labia harder, sending the pain spiking, and with a thrust that jammed her into the headboard ordered in a harsh, almost guttural growl, "Come."

And with a scream, she obeyed.

* * * *

They were curled up on the sofa, watching a movie, when for the third time in the last hour, Jack heard a sound like air being let out of a squeaky balloon.

He bit his lip to hold in the laugh, grunting when Sadie poked him in the ribs.

"Don't you dare laugh," she warned him, though he could hear the laugh lurking under the grumpy demand. "This is your fault."

"How is it my fault?" he wondered and earned himself another poke.

"I told you anal makes me gassy, but did you believe me? Noooo."

"I believed you," he corrected, and snagged her hand so she couldn't poke him again. "I just didn't care."

"God, you're an asshole."

"Excuse me?" he said, twisting to look down at her. She was dressed in a pair of paint flecked yoga pants—her most comfortable, he'd been informed—and one of his sweatshirts. Her hair was down, still damp from the morning shower they'd shared, and her face, bare of makeup, wore a smugly impish smile.

"You're not excused," she said with a haughty sniff, and turned red when the balloon let out another burst of air. "Dammit, it's not funny."

"I beg to differ," he said, not even bothering to hold back his laughter. "I think it's hilarious."

"You would," she accused, and squealed when he plucked her off the sofa and planted her on his lap. "Hey!"

"Hey, yourself," he said, and before she could gather herself enough to struggle, dragged her hands behind her back. "Now, what was that you said?"

"That you're an asshole?" she answered with a smirk, then jerked. "Don't!"

"Don't what?" he asked innocently and danced his fingertips over her ribs again. "Don't do this?"

"Oh, I hate being tickled," she wailed, twisting on his lap. But he anticipated the move and countered it to dig his fingers into her armpit. "Jack! I'm going to pee on you!"

"We haven't negotiated water sports," he informed her, laughing almost as hard as she was. "But I'm game if you are."

"Stop, you sadist," she gasped. "Red!"

He dropped his hands to her waist, and since she'd nearly managed to twist herself off, hoisted her back onto his lap.

"You don't safeword when I grab your pussy with a vampire glove," he marveled, "but a little tickle does it?"

"I *hate* being tickled," she informed him breathlessly.

"That should probably go on your limits list," he informed her soberly.

"Believe me, I'm making that change as soon as I get home," she informed him, her hair curtaining her face as she scowled down at him. "Stop grinning at me, you goof."

"I'm not allowed to grin?"

"It's unnerving. I still expect to see Resting Dick Face staring back at me."

"You'll get used to it." He lifted a hand to toy with the ends of her hair. "Your eyes are still a little puffy from crying."

She sniffed, her mouth twisting into a sneer that was completely belied by the happy twinkle in her eye. "You like that, don't you, you pervert?"

"Hell, yes," he said, and nearly fell over laughing when she farted again.

She slid off his lap and skipped away, shouting, "Asshole!" over her shoulder, and a moment later he heard the bathroom door slam behind her.

Still chuckling, he aimed the remote at the TV and paused the movie, then rose to go into the kitchen for a bottle of water. He grabbed two and carried them back to the sofa.

She emerged a moment later, her hair smoothed into place. Shooting him a haughty look, she strode past him to the front door, plucked her purse off the hook by the door and carried it back to the sofa. He watched, amused, as she hauled out a pack of tissues, a small bottle of nail polish remover, and a bottle of sparkling gold nail polish.

She glanced up, caught him staring. "What? I need to touch up my pedicure."

He waved a hand. "You just carry all that around with you?"

She tugged off the fuzzy socks he'd given her to wear. "No. I took it to my mom's thinking I could fix it there, but between helping with dinner and the drama after, I didn't get a chance."

"Ah." He watched her pull her left foot up to prop it on the edge of the sofa and uncap the bottle of remover.

"And dammit, I forgot to give my mom that bottle of anise extract."

He eyed the purse warily. "It's in there?"

"It can't hurt you," she said, amused.

"You never know." He nudged her bag away with his foot and picked up his water. "Are you going to the meeting next week?"

"Sure," she said, carefully removing the polish from her big toe. "Well, the party anyway. The board meetings are boring, so I usually skip them."

"I don't blame you," he muttered. He'd joined the board of the BDSM club because he'd wanted to be involved in his community, and for the most part he didn't regret it. But there were times when he absolutely wished he didn't have to be there. "What are you going to wear?"

She glanced at him, curious amusement in her hazel eyes. "Since when do you care what I wear?"

"I don't, unless it interferes with my scene plans," he said. "In which case I'll just make you take it off."

She set the remover on the floor and reached for the bottle of polish. "What if I want to keep it on?"

"I guess you'll have to choose between fashion and orgasms."

"Harsh," she said, and carefully painted a sparkly gold strip down her toenail. "I might be able to play in it. What kind of scene?"

"Nice try," he drawled, enjoying the impish twinkle in her eyes.

"Fine," she muttered, mouth twitching as she fought a smile. "If I can't play in it, I'll take it off. But can I have two hours to look cute in it first?"

"I have no problem with that," he allowed. "So long as it doesn't interfere with the collar."

She dipped the brush back in the bottle and turned back to her toes. "What collar?"

"Your collar."

"I don't wear a collar."

"You will on Saturday."

She jerked, the brush skidding across her toes. "What?"

He sat up and plucked the bottle of remover from the floor. "Here."

She reached out to take it, her gaze locked on his face. "That's a joke, right?"

He kept his expression calm, his voice mild. "No. You seem surprised."

"I am," she admitted, and grabbed the pack of tissues.

"I don't know why." He eased back against the sofa, fighting to stay relaxed while she soaked a tissue in remover and attacked her gold-streaked toes. "It's basic protocol. The collar makes it clear we're together, that you're under my protection."

"I don't need your protection," she interrupted, tossing the tissue aside.

"You have it anyway," he countered, refusing to rise to the bait. "Collar or no collar."

She picked up the polish again, her head bent, and resumed painting. "Then why wear it?"

"Because wearing it makes it clear to everyone else. And it's appropriate."

"I've never worn a collar before," she said, looking like a deer in headlights.

He resisted the urge to tell her he'd never collared anyone before. "Does it scare you?"

She frowned. "No. But it feels…weird."

"Weird, how?"

"Like we're…together. *Together,* together."

This time he couldn't hide his smile. "Sadie, what do you think we've been doing for the last month?"

"Fucking?" she ventured.

"Is that all it's been?" he asked quietly and watched her squirm.

"No, not all," she finally admitted, and relief flooded through him. "But collaring…that's a big step."

She turned to him with troubled eyes. "Isn't it?"

"Not necessarily," he said, and forced a casual shrug. "It means whatever we want it to mean. In this case, it's a play collar, and it means we're going to the party together, and leaving together."

"That's it?"

He spread his hands. "That's it."

She took her time capping the bottle of nail polish, then bent over to blow on her toes. "Is it cute?"

"Is what cute?"

"The collar," she said and turned her head to meet his gaze. "If it's not cute, I'm not wearing it."

He laughed and snagged her hand, hauling her down to rest against his chest. "I promise, it's at least as cute as you are."

"That's pretty cute," she decided.

He handed her a bottle of water and picked up the remote. "Want to keep watching the movie?"

"Sure. Turn it up though, I can barely hear the dialogue."

"You just want the sound up to drown out any more farts."

"Shut up," she said, laughing, and farted.

Chapter Sixteen

The week flew by in a blur of work. Thanks to referrals from Amanda, Sadie booked three new clients, and was pleased to see her bank account grow accordingly. She hosted Wine & Whine Wednesday, and though Sam couldn't make it this time, she had a full house. Nikki was there, her foot nearly healed, and announced shyly that she'd had a second date with Kody, and they'd asked her to play at the party on Saturday.

With everyone occupied with reassurance and advice for Nikki, Sadie decided not to bring up the whole collar thing.

She wasn't even sure what she'd say. It felt like a huge step for her to wear Jack's collar, even just as a sign of protection, but he'd been so…so *casual* about it. It confused her, and though she would have liked to talk to her friends about it, she didn't know how. So she focused on reassuring Nikki and said nothing.

She was behind schedule on Saturday night, thanks to one of her new clients running late, and since the outfit she'd planned took a while to put together, she was still putting on her face when the knock sounded at her door.

"Coming," she called from the bathroom, and set down her makeup bag to hurry down the hall.

She flipped the locks and opened the door. "Hi, sorry. I need two minutes."

"We have time," Jack said, a smile creasing his beard as he stepped over the threshold and shut the door behind him. He wore his fancy camel overcoat, but she could see he'd broken out the leathers again. "You probably shouldn't open the door like that. You might have given your neighbors a show."

She was already hurrying back to the bathroom, her laugh trailing behind her. "I forget sometimes that not everyone has seen me naked."

"Their loss," he called, and she laughed again and dug into her makeup bag.

She worked quickly, playing up her eyes with sparkly shadow and dramatic liner, and had just begun to add a layer of mascara when a thought occurred to her. "Are you going to make me cry tonight?"

"It's not my primary goal," he said from the doorway, and she jumped. He grinned in response. "But it's always a nice bonus. Why?"

She uncapped the mascara on a half laugh and leaned into the mirror. "I'm going to start buying cheaper makeup if it's just going to end up in streaks on my face."

He chuckled. "Don't worry, I'll clean you up afterwards."

"Great, a paper towel facial," she muttered and gave her lashes a quick coat.

"I have makeup wipes in my toy bag."

She paused, her gaze flicking to his in the mirror, the mascara wand forgotten in her hand. "You do?"

"Sure." He flicked one of her pigtails, his lips curving when the curls bounced. "Part of the job."

She capped the mascara and replaced it in the makeup bag. "Your job is to clean up my makeup?"

"When I'm the reason it's running down your face, it is."

She risked a glance up and found him watching her in the mirror. His eyes were warm, his smile soft in a way that made her belly clench and her toes want to curl inside her boots. She forced herself to speak past the lump in her throat. "You could just, you know, not try to make me cry."

"Where's the fun in that?" he wanted to know. "And speaking of fun…"

"What?"

"This outfit."

She laughed and chose a lip gloss. "You like?"

"'Like' is a very tame word for what I'm feeling," he said. "I assume it lights up?"

"Of course," she said and slicked color on her lips. She smacked them together, pleased with the cherry-red color, and dropped the tube back in her makeup bag. She reached up and straightened the festive red bows she'd tied around each curling pigtail before bending down to flip the switches on the battery packs hidden in her boots. Then she turned to face him, hands on her hips, and struck a pose. "Well?"

He dropped his gaze to her feet, encased in shiny red vinyl boots that came to mid-calf, and slowly traveled up. Where the boots stopped, the lights started. She'd wound the strings of Christmas lights around each leg in a spiral pattern all the way to the crotch, then up over her hips to wrap around her torso. They wrapped around her back, crossing over her belly and again between her breasts before going up over her shoulders. She'd brought the ends together and taped them down with medical tape at the center of her back, and besides the boots, it was all she wore.

"Sadie," he finally said, "I think you've outdone yourself."

She beamed, looking down. "The lights have different settings, too. I can set them to static, twinkle, or chaser."

"Chaser?" he echoed, and she bent to make the change. When the lights switched from a steady glow to a running wave, he started to laugh.

"You look like you're auditioning for a holiday-themed porn parody of *Tron*," he said, leaning against the doorway with a delighted grin.

"I know, right?" She switched them to twinkle. "I can't decide which setting I like best."

"Let me see the back," he said, and she obediently turned. "Can you sit in that?"

"Sort of," she admitted, craning her neck to look down at her butt. The strands wound around her ass, leaving it bare, but the lights on the backs of her thighs had proved very uncomfortable when she'd done a test sit in her desk chair. "A stool will probably work best."

"A backless one," he advised, running a hand over the lights crisscrossing her back before crouching to skim his palms down her thighs. He paused when he hit a patch of tape. "You taped it down?"

"Medical tape," she said. "I tacked it down in a few places, mostly on my legs and hips. Because, you know."

"Movement," he finished and rose to his feet.

She scooped her makeup bag off the sink. "I figure it'll last my allotted two hours."

"And the lights will look charming," he said, stepping into the bathroom, "reflecting off this."

She stared at the circle of metal in his hands. "Oh."

The collar was an unbroken circle of rose gold, with a small rectangular tag in the same warm tone hanging off it. There was writing on it, but she couldn't see what it was. She swallowed the lump in her throat and ignored the urge to touch it. "How does it work?"

"There's a hinge, so it can go around your neck." He demonstrated, pulling the two sides of the collar apart. "The screw fastens with an Allen wrench."

"Isn't that dangerous?" she asked, still staring. She couldn't take her eyes off it. "I mean, what if you have to get it off fast?"

"It's not designed to be snug," he explained and draped it around her neck. The metal was warm where his hands had been, cool where they hadn't. And when the open ends came together with a tiny click and it lay heavy against her collarbones, her mouth went bone-dry.

"See?" He gave it a tug. "Plenty of room."

She swallowed and lifted her gaze to his. He was watching her, his dark eyes assessing, and she managed a smile. "How does it look?"

He laid his hands on her shoulders and turned her toward the mirror. "See for yourself."

The collar lay around her neck, glowing softly in the light, the small rectangular tag hanging just above her breastbone. She could see it clearly now, and though the letters were backwards in the mirror, she recognized their order quickly enough.

"Jack's", she read aloud, her fingers creeping up to toy with the tag before she could think better of it. "Did you think I'd forget your name?"

He chuckled, his eyes on the collar as he fastened it into place with an Allen wrench. "You never know," he said, and with a final turn of the wrench, dropped his hands and raised his eyes to hers in the mirror. "Well? Is it cute enough?"

It was lovely, almost stunning in its simplicity. But she couldn't say that. "It'll do."

"Brat," he said, and gave her an affectionate pat on the butt. "Do you have something to wear over this, or are you going commando under your coat?"

"I have a dress," she said, fighting to keep her tone even. "It's on my bed."

"I'll get it," he offered, and stepped out.

"The green one," she called after him, and with one last lingering look in the mirror, picked up her makeup bag and followed him out.

* * * *

At the warehouse they used for official club events, Jack escorted Sadie into the party area. "I'll see you after the board meeting."

"Okay," she said, scanning the room. There weren't many people here yet, as the party wouldn't officially start until the meeting was over, but there were always a few early arrivals.

"Sadie."

"Hmmm?" she asked absently, still looking around. Rebecca was likely here already, since Nick was on the board, and she was hoping to talk to her before everyone else got here and things got—

"Sadie."

"What?" she said, exasperated, and turned to look at him.

He merely raised an eyebrow. "I want to go over the rules."

"Rules?" she said blankly.

"For tonight. You're wearing my collar, and that comes with responsibilities."

"Oh, God, you're not going to make me wait on you like some servant, are you? Because if that's the case, we can just get rid of this right now," she told him and reached for the collar.

"You can't get it off without the wrench, remember?" he said, laughing, and drew her hands down. "And no, I'm not going to make you wait on me."

"Then what are we talking about?"

"Just some basic guidelines," he soothed, still holding her hands. "You've never been to a kink event with someone."

"Of course I have," she began, but he was shaking his head.

"I meant, you've always been responsible for yourself," he explained.

"Oh. Well, yeah."

"Tonight, I'm responsible for you. So, rules."

Her hands tensed in his grip, and she knew he felt it, because he smiled. "Stop panicking. I'm not implementing high protocol."

"Maybe you should tell me what you *are* doing," she suggested.

"It's simple. I don't want you to go anywhere without telling me first, and if someone bothers you or asks you to play, you'll let me know."

She frowned. That all *seemed* reasonable, except… "Can I go to the bathroom without telling you?"

"No," he said, his smile growing when she scowled. "Naturally, that doesn't apply while I'm in the board meeting."

"Oh, naturally."

"But otherwise, yes. I'm not saying you have to ask permission," he said before she could blast him. "But you do need to give me the courtesy of telling me where you're going, and when you'll be back."

When she stayed silent, staring at him, he gave her hands a squeeze. "Can you do that?"

There was no reason for the panic suddenly licking at the back of her throat, she thought, and swallowed it back. "Yes."

"Yes…?"

She swallowed again. "Yes, Boss."

"There, was that so hard?"

"Yes," she muttered, and with a laugh, he kissed her.

Eager to be on familiar ground, she kissed him back, her blood quickly heating when he sucked her lower lip into his mouth and tugged. Then he eased away, nudging her gently back when she would've followed. "I have to get to the meeting."

"Right. The meeting." She dropped back to her heels, rocking a little, and tried to understand why she was suddenly so desperate for him not to go. "Okay."

He shrugged out of his coat, revealing the snowy white button-down he'd paired with the leather pants. "Hang this up for me, please?"

She took the coat. "Sure."

"I'll keep my bag with me," he told her, bending to pick it up. "Don't want you peeking."

"Ha," she said with a smirk and nipped playfully at the finger he flicked down her nose.

"Behave," he ordered and gave her a quick, hard kiss. "I'll see you in about an hour."

"'Kay." She took a moment to watch him walk away—she really loved what the leathers did for his ass—before she started across the room, his coat draped over her arm. Halfway there she realized what he'd done and stopped dead. "Dammit, Jack!"

His rolling laugh echoed through the space. "If I come back and it's on the floor, you will be, too."

"Sneaky bastard," she muttered, and started walking again. She turned left at the restrooms, heading for the small storage room they used as a cloakroom. Grumbling to herself and wondering just how she could get back at him, she selected a hanger off the rolling rack and carefully draped the expensive wool over it. She hung up her own coat, then slipped off the T-shirt dress she'd worn over her costume and hung it as well.

"Should've had Jack put it in his bag," she murmured and made a mental note to come back for it when the meeting ended. She'd want it after they played.

The reminder that they were going to play together had nerves jumping in her belly, and she didn't understand why. They'd been playing and fucking for a month now, and though he managed to surprise her nearly every time, she'd stopped being worried about it. They'd found a nice rhythm, and she trusted him. So there was absolutely no reason to be nervous.

"None at all," she declared out loud, and bent to turn on her battery packs. She set the lights on chaser, double checked that both strands were lit, and headed back out to the main room.

It had started to come to life in her absence. A dozen or so people milled around, gathered in the conversation areas and dancing to the music that had been switched on. Someone had opened the bar, which consisted of setting out a couple of cases of soda and juice and a bin of ice on the repurposed reception desk in the corner. Deciding that hydrating would help her nerves, she headed in that direction.

She'd filled a glass with ice and was trying to decide between juice and soda when Rebecca stepped up next to her.

"You're here early," Rebecca observed, her pretty gray eyes focused on Sadie's lights. "And dressed so festively. Love the boots."

"Thanks." Decision made, Sadie grabbed the can of soda closest to her, popped the top, and poured. "You look cute."

"I do not." Rebecca grimaced. "I had to go into the office today for an emergency meeting, and Nick didn't give me time to change when I got home."

Sadie sipped her soda and grimaced. Dammit, she'd grabbed a diet. With the taste of aspartame burning on her tongue, she turned to face her friend. "It's a little conservative," she allowed, taking in the trim pencil skirt in quiet gray, matching pumps, and tailored black blouse. "But it has potential."

"Point that out to Nick, will you?" Rebecca leaned over to grab a cup and fill it with ice. "He's grumpy because he wanted me to vamp it up tonight."

Sadie snorted into her cup. "Vamp it up?"

"Well, he said 'slut it up'," Rebecca said, selecting a soda.

"That sounds more like Nick." Sadie eyed Rebecca's clothes and considered the options. "I can help you with that, if you like. Are you particularly attached to that blouse?"

Rebecca glanced down at her clothes. "No. Why?"

"What about the stockings?"

"They have a run," Rebecca said, annoyed. "They're going in the trash as soon as I get home."

"Good." Taking Rebecca's free hand in hers, Sadie began towing her toward the cloakroom. "Come with me."

Ten minutes later, Sadie sat back on her heels with a sigh. "This isn't going to work unless you hold still."

"I'm sorry, it tickles." Rebecca tightened her grip on her skirt, held up around her waist. "Are you sure this won't smudge?"

"Not without makeup remover," Sadie said, and went back to drawing a careful line up the back of Rebecca's calf with her liquid eyeliner. "You could sweat buckets, it won't move."

"Okay." Rebecca peered down at her. "How high are you going?"

"What are the chances of Nick getting you out of this skirt at some point?"

"Excellent."

"Then I'm going all the way up to cheek," Sadie said, and carefully skimmed the eyeliner up the back of

Rebecca's thigh, coming to a stop at the edge of her lacy boy shorts. "There, one leg down."

"Gimme a second," Rebecca said, and did a full-body wiggle that made her hair bounce in the ponytail Sadie had put it in. "Okay, go ahead."

Sadie bent to apply the liner to the back of Rebecca's other heel. "Don't move this time."

"I'm telling you, it tickles," Rebecca said, huffing out a breath. "I need a distraction."

"I could sing," Sadie offered.

"How about you tell me about your new accessory instead?"

"What new accessory?" Sadie asked, dragging the line up the back of Rebecca's knee, then she remembered. "Oh, right. That accessory."

"Is that all you're going to say?" Rebecca asked after a moment.

"It is until I get this line drawn," Sadie replied, carefully dragging the liner up. When she hit panties, she rose to her feet. "There, all done. Keep your skirt up for a bit—it needs to dry."

Rebecca turned around. "Well?"

Sadie dropped the eyeliner in her purse. "It's just a play collar, Rebecca. It's no big deal."

"Honey. You're wearing a collar with Jack's name on it. That is the very *definition* of a big deal."

Sadie grimaced. "I thought it was, when he first brought it up. But then…I guess it wasn't."

"I'm confused," Rebecca said.

"Yeah, me too." Sadie shook her head. "You can drop your skirt now."

Rebecca let it go, smoothing the fabric down her legs without taking her eyes off Sadie's face. "Okay, let's figure this out. Start from the beginning, and don't leave anything out."

"I'm not sure where the beginning is," Sadie mused and eyed Rebecca's blouse. "How's the shirt feel?"

"Huh? Oh." Rebecca rolled her shoulders. "It's tight. I think you took it in too much."

"Tight is the point." Sadie reached out and undid three of the buttons marching down the front of the shirt that was indeed straining across Rebecca's ample breasts. "There, how's that?"

"Better." Rebecca looked down at the black lacy bra now visible. "And sluttier."

"You're welcome."

"Okay, back to you." Rebecca stepped carefully into her shoes. "He called it a play collar?"

"Yep," Sadie replied. "Here, use this."

Rebecca accepted the tube of red lipstick and the small compact. "Thanks."

"I mean, I know play collars are a thing," Sadie went on, poking around in her makeup bag. "I see them all the time."

"True."

"But it felt…thin," she decided.

"What did?"

"The way he explained it." Sadie looked up at her friend. "He said it was basic protocol, just a way to let people know we're here together, and that I'm under his protection."

Rebecca rubbed her newly reddened lips together and frowned. "That is thin. What'd he say when you called him out on it?"

Sadie bit her lip. "I didn't."

Rebecca lowered the compact. "Sadie."

"I know, I know." Frustrated, Sadie reached up and gave her pigtails a yank. "I should've said something."

"Why didn't you?"

"Because I didn't want to hear him say it meant nothing," Sadie admitted, and dropped her hands. "I've never thought about being collared, Rebecca. Never. It just wasn't on my radar, you know?"

"But you're thinking about it now."

Sadie nodded, fighting back the sting of tears. "Yeah. The moment he mentioned it, I wanted it," she went on. "I wanted what it meant, you know?"

Rebecca nodded. "I do know."

"But he was just so *casual* about it," Sadie went on. "Like it was no big deal, and I was afraid to say anything because…"

"Because if you did, he'd know it was a big deal to *you*."

"Yes." Sadie brushed at her cheeks, relieved to find them dry. "Silly, right?"

"Human," Rebecca corrected her. "Can I ask you something?"

Her throat thick, Sadie could only nod.

"Are you in love with him?"

"I think I am," Sadie admitted and let out a shuddering breath. "Oh God, I think I'm going to be sick."

"Okay." Rebecca grabbed a chair from the stack in the corner and nudged Sadie into it. "Sit, put your head between your knees."

Sadie obeyed, breathing deeply until the wave of nausea passed. "What the hell am I going to do, Becca?"

"You're not going to like this, but you have to tell him."

Just thinking about it had nausea threatening again. "I'm not ready for that."

"At least about the collar," Rebeca said, easing Sadie upright. "You're going to feel like shit if you don't."

"I feel like shit now."

"And you'll keep feeling like shit until you tell him."

"I hate it when you're right," Sadie grumbled, one hand on her still unsteady stomach. "I feel like I ate spoiled meat."

"Yep, that's love, all right."

"You don't have to sound so fucking cheerful about it," Sadie said with a scowl.

Rebecca hauled her to her feet, laughing, and wrapped her arms around Sadie in a fierce hug. "You know I love you."

"I love you, too." Sadie felt some of the rough edges inside her smooth out. "Rebecca?"

"Yeah?"

"Don't tell anyone about this, okay?"

"Not even Nick?"

"*Especially* not Nick." Sadie drew back to look her friend in the eye. "Hoes before bros."

Rebecca laughed, her gray eyes sparkling. "Okay, I won't tell him. But let me know when I can, will you? He owes me twenty bucks."

Sadie let out a watery laugh. "You bet on me?"

"Of course."

Sadie leaned her forehead against Rebecca's, just for a moment. "Bitch."

"Slut," Rebecca said, and made Sadie laugh. "Come on. We've got about half an hour before the meeting is over. I'll buy you a ginger ale."

"I'll take it," Sadie said as they started out, arm in arm, and hoped half an hour was enough time to pull herself together.

* * * *

Jack walked into the party space with a spring in his step. They'd made quick work of the only new business on the agenda, and their newly elected board president hadn't seen the point in drawing the meeting out. So he'd gaveled the meeting adjourned, to the gratitude and relief of all in attendance, and Jack was eager to get on with the fun portion of the evening.

"That was the best meeting we've ever had," Nick announced, falling into step beside Jack.

"It was the shortest meeting we've ever had," Jack corrected him.

"Which makes it the best. We should've elected James as board president years ago."

Jack chuckled, scanning the room. It was considerably fuller than it had been when he'd dropped Sadie off forty minutes earlier. "You know he only agreed to run because the alternative was Joel."

"And thank God he did," Nick muttered. "It's bad enough he's on the board—could you imagine him as president?"

"No," Jack said. "I can't."

"Rebecca would probably refuse to come to parties if he was in charge," Nick said, keeping his voice low as they moved through the room.

Jack glanced over. "Not a fan?"

"That's putting it mildly." Nick shook his head. "You know, when he first started coming to club events, I thought he just needed some direction, maybe some seasoning. But now…"

"He's gotten worse," Jack agreed. "Sadie can't stand him."

"Not surprised. He asked her to play at the Halloween event, and she handed him his ass," Nick said bluntly. "He complained to James, said she should be reprimanded for insubordination."

"You're kidding."

"That went nowhere, of course. She was actually fairly polite—though Rebecca was there, and she said the unspoken *fuck you* was pretty clear."

Jack laughed. "I'll bet."

Nick shook his head. "If it was anybody else, I'd try talking to him. But that guy—"

"A brick wall," Jack agreed as they approached the bar. "Save your breath. Do you see Sadie?"

"No, but I see Rebecca," Nick said. "At least, I think I do. Excuse me, miss, but have you seen my girlfriend?"

Rebecca spun around on the bar stool she was perched on and beamed a smile at Nick. "Hello."

"Hello, yourself," Nick said, taking her hands and drawing her off the stool. "What happened to you?"

Rebecca laughed, her ponytail swinging. "I told Sadie you were grumpy because I had to come in work clothes, so she did a little styling."

"I'll say," Nick said with a grin. "Give us a spin, Ms. McBride."

Rebecca pursed her lips in an exaggerated pout and gave a slow twirl. Jack didn't know what Rebecca had looked like prior to the makeover, but now, with the seams running up the backs of her legs, the gaping blouse, pouty red mouth and jaunty ponytail, she was secretarial porn come to life.

"Ms. McBride," Nick said, his voice a low rumble of appreciation.

Jack watched, amused, as Rebecca fluttered her lashes. "Yes, Mr. Saint? Do you need me to come into your office and take dick…tation?"

Nick burst out laughing and grabbed her by the hand. "You bet I do. See you later, pal."

"Sadie just went to the bathroom," Rebecca called over her shoulder as Nick dragged her away. "She'll be back in a minute."

He lifted a hand in acknowledgment then turned in the other direction. He'd use the restroom himself while he had the chance, then find Sadie and have some fun.

He swung through the restroom door, smiling when he saw the man standing at the sink. "Hey, Cade."

"Jack." Washing his hands, Cade gave him a head jerk in greeting. "Board meeting over already?"

"Short and sweet." Jack crossed to the urinal. He took care of business quickly, running his plans for the evening in his head. He wanted a public spot, but not in the center of the room. Knowing Cade often helped James with equipment, he asked, "Do we have a St. Andrew's cross set up tonight?"

"Two of them." Cade tore off a strip of paper towel. "Plus the spanking benches, bondage table, and we set up an area for wax play."

"Nice." Finished, Jack zipped up and crossed to the sink. "I was going to take the cross, but now I might switch and go for the wax play."

"You playing with Sadie tonight?" Cade leaned against the wall. "How's that going?"

"It's going good," Jack murmured, thinking back to the look in her eyes after he'd fastened the collar around her neck.

"I see we've moved past the 'it's too early to say I'm in love with her' stage," Cade said, and Jack glanced over to see him smiling.

"Is it that obvious?" Jack asked, the water running while he scrubbed his hands.

"Probably to everyone but her."

Jack laughed and rinsed his hands. "She's too busy trying to convince herself she's not in love with me."

Cade tore off a paper towel and held it out. "Do you think she is?"

"I'm almost sure of it," Jack said, taking the towel. "She just hasn't realized it yet."

Cade opened his mouth, then turned when the door swung open.

"Well, well, well, if it isn't our resident sadist."

Jack twisted off the taps and tossed the paper towel in the trash. "Hello, Joel."

Chapter Seventeen

Sadie came out of the bathroom, purse in hand, and ducked into the cloakroom. She was feeling a lot better than she had an hour ago, her good humor mostly restored by the talk with Rebecca. She still didn't know what the hell she was doing, but at least now she didn't feel so alone.

Shivering, she set her purse on the floor below her coat. She should've remembered how cold the warehouse could feel when she was planning this outfit and saved it for the smaller party James and Amanda always threw at the holidays. Their house was always kept warm in deference to naked or nearly naked submissives, and though they cranked the heat in the warehouse to try to do the same, twenty-foot ceilings made it a challenge.

She was contemplating putting her coat on over the lights and reimagining herself as a Christmas flasher when Sam walked into the cloakroom.

"There's my best girl," he said, and enveloped her in a warm hug. "Jesus, you're freezing."

She laughed, returning the hug. "I know. I was just trying to decide if I care more about looking cute or staying warm."

He eased back, rubbing his hands down her arms. "What'd you decide?"

"Warm," she decided, reaching for her coat, then drew her hand back. "Hmmm."

"Change your mind?" he asked, slipping out of his jacket and grabbing a hanger.

"I'm going to wear Jack's coat. It's warmer."

"And sexier." He hung up his own jacket before slipping the long sweep of camel-colored wool off its hanger. "You can be a Christmas flasher."

"Sam, you just get me," she said, sliding her arms into the satin lined sleeves and wrapping the heavy wool around herself. "What do you think?"

"It's huge on you," Sam said, "but it works. Go on, give me a flash."

She thrust out a hip, grabbed the lapels and flung the coat open. He laughed, delighted. "Fantastic."

"Good." She folded the coat closed. "I'm glad to see you. I thought you might have to work tonight."

"It's my weekend off," he told her and dragged a hand through his short crop of silver-streaked dark hair. "I almost didn't come, to be honest."

"Tired?" He looked it. There were bags under his eyes, and an air of fatigue around him, like if he sat down for two minutes, he'd be snoring in one.

"Exhausted," he admitted. "And Collette had a faculty thing tonight she couldn't get out of, so I'm flying solo."

He looked so forlorn she wanted to cuddle him like a puppy. "I'm sorry, sweetie."

"It's no big deal," he said with a smile that failed to reach his eyes. "I'm glad I came, if for no other reason than to see you in that outfit."

She laughed, because she knew he wanted her to, and bobbed a quick curtsey. "Happy to be of service."

"Speaking of which," Sam drawled and tapped a finger on his own neck, "is this new, or have I been that out of touch?"

"It's new," she confirmed. "You don't seem surprised."

"Sadie, you getting together with Jack is the least surprising thing that's happened this year."

"It surprised the hell out of me," she muttered, and he laughed.

"That's because you don't pay attention," he began, then paused. "Do you hear that?"

"Hear what? Oh. That's the men's room."

"The men's room?"

"Something about the venting," she said. "You can hear just about everything that goes on in there from here. That's the faucet running."

"I'll be damned." Sam marveled and tilted his head. "Someone's talking, too, but I can't hear who."

"You will when they turn off the water. What do you mean, I don't pay attention?"

"You don't," Sam said, then a voice came through the vent, clear as day.

"Hello, Joel."

"That's Jack," Sam said.

"Shhh!" Sadie hissed and strained to hear.

Joel nodded at Cade. "Cade."

"Joel," Cade said, and nodded back. "How was the board meeting?"

The genial smile on Joel's face faded, irritation twisting his otherwise handsome face. Though the board election had taken place months ago, Joel wasn't close to forgetting—or forgiving. "Fine," he bit off. "Though I think we need to reevaluate this annual charity donation. It's unnecessary."

A sentiment, Jack thought, that Joel had brought up no less than three times during the meeting. "It's good community relations, Joel. And a good cause."

"We could be putting that money to use for the club," Joel insisted. "More education, more demonstrations. There's a Gorean Master in Chicago I've been wanting to bring in to do a lecture on training—"

"Put together a proposal for the board," Jack interrupted smoothly and had to bite the inside of his cheek to keep from smiling when he saw Cade roll his eyes. "We'll take a look."

"Well." Cade cleared his throat and pushed off the wall. "I'm going to go find Olivia. Good to see you, Joel."

"I need to track down Sadie, too," Jack said and started to follow Cade to the door.

"Yes, I understand congratulations are in order there," Joel said, stepping aside to let them pass.

Cade paused at the door. "Congratulations?"

Joel kept his gaze on Jack. "She's wearing his collar."

Jack ignored the way Cade's jaw dropped in shock—though he committed it to memory to share with Sadie later—and sent Joel a bland smile. "So she is."

"I applaud you," Joel went on, the genial smile back on his face. "I didn't think anyone could tame that brat."

In the storeroom, Sadie snorted. "Tame the brat. This isn't Shakespeare, asshole."

"Shhh!" Sam said. "I can't hear when you're talking."

"Thank you," Jack said gravely, even though a laugh tickled the back of his throat.

"Now that you've got her declawed, you should give the rest of us a chance."

"I'm sorry?" Jack, who'd turned for the door, slowly spun back around.

"Well, what else are you going to do with her?" Joel sauntered over to the sink and flicked on the faucet. "You obviously can't keep her."

"Dammit, he turned the water on," Sam grumbled. "I can't hear."

"Give the rest of us a chance?" Sadie seethed as the sound of rushing water muffled the conversation taking place in the men's room. "I ought to give him a shot to the balls."

"I think Jack will take care of that for you," Sam said.

"He better," Sadie muttered, and strained to hear.

"Can't I?" Jack asked.

"God, no. Woman like that's only good for one thing." Joel flicked his hands and combed them through his hair, water still pouring into the sink. "Use her up and pass her on."

"And you'd like to be next in line?" Jack asked while Cade choked beside him. "What makes you think she'll give you the time of day?"

Joel scowled. "She won't have a choice if you order her to."

"She always has a choice," Jack corrected him quietly. "That's what makes her submission a gift."

"She's got you wrapped around her little cunt, doesn't she?"

"That doesn't even make sense," Cade muttered.

Jack just smiled. "Sadie makes her own choices, Joel, and I highly doubt she'd choose you if the alternative was a moat full of hungry crocodiles."

"I could make her my slave in less time than it would take you to pick out a new suit."

"I have my suits made," Jack told him. "And no, you couldn't. But you're welcome to try."

"And when I do," Joel said, and turned off the water with an angry twist of his wrist, "you'll transfer ownership of Sadie to me."

"Absolutely," Jack said, trying not to laugh. "I'll just go let Sadie know you're coming for her."

"You do that," Joel called after him as he ducked out the door, Cade hot on his heels.

"Does he actually believe that?" Cade wondered as they walked down the hall.

"I don't know, but I can't wait to see the look on Sadie's face when he comes to find her," Jack said. "And after that, we're going to have a serious discussion with James about getting rid of Joel."

"Amen to that."

In the storage cloakroom, Sadie stared at Sam, her shock mirroring his. "Did Jack just agree to *give me to Joel*?"

"We must have misunderstood," Sam said. "I could hardly hear anything when they had the water running. Just something about women only being good for one thing, and…having a suit made?"

"Joel said, 'you'll transfer ownership of Sadie to me', and Jack said 'absolutely'." He said *absolutely*, Sam."

"I'm telling you, we misunderstood. First of all, Jack doesn't *have* ownership of you, collar or no, so how could he transfer it?"

"He said he'd tell me Joel was coming to get me," Sadie went on, gathering steam. She was so *mad*, but under the boiling anger was a hole, dark and deep.

"This doesn't make any sense," Sam insisted. "We had to have missed something important. He *collared* you, Sadie."

"It's just a play collar," Sadie said, desperate to believe it. "It doesn't mean anything."

"You have to talk to Jack," Sam began.

Sadie shook her head fiercely and tried to ignore the weight around her neck. "I can't."

"Okay." Sam turned toward the door. "I'll go talk to him."

"I have to go."

Sam swung back, panic in his blue eyes. "What? Sadie, you can't leave."

"I want to go home," she said, and had her purse in her hand before she remembered. "Shit, he drove. I'll take a cab."

"Sadie, you're wearing Christmas lights under a man's coat," he pointed out. "You can't get into a cab like that."

The reminder that she was wearing Jack's coat had her shrugging out of it. Leaving it in a puddle on the tile floor, she yanked her dress and coat off their hangers. "Happy now?" she asked when she'd dragged them on.

"That's really not much better."

"Sam, I can't stay here." She grabbed his hands, pleading. "I can't. Please."

He stared at her, concern bright in his eyes, and nodded. "All right. I'll take you."

She sagged with relief. "Thank you."

"But you have to let Jack know you're leaving. You have to," he said when she shook her head.

"I'll text him when we're gone, all right?"

Sam hesitated. "As soon as we're in the car?"

"Before I even buckle my seatbelt," she promised, and held her breath.

Sam nodded, eyes troubled. "Okay."

She flung her arms around him and choked back a sob. "Thank you, Sam."

"You're welcome. Hey." He eased her back to peer into her face. "It's going to be okay."

"I know." She swiped at her cheeks, but they weren't wet. They were dry, and cold. So cold. "I know."

* * * *

She sent the text when she got into Sam's truck, as promised, and knew Jack would get it when he checked his phone. Though since his phone was in his toy bag and turned off per play party rules, it might take a while for him to do that. But she didn't mention that to Sam.

He took her home, where she turned down his offer to walk her upstairs. She knew as soon as he left he was going right back to the party to talk to Jack, so she didn't have much time. She went straight to her closet and dragged out a suitcase and began throwing clothes into it at random. He'd come looking for her, when Sam told him what they'd overheard, and she didn't intend to be here when he did.

The suitcase filled, she swapped out the thin T-shirt dress for jeans and a loose sweater that hid the lights better—she didn't have time to take them off. A check of the time told her Sam was probably back at the party now, or would be shortly, so she dragged the suitcase to the living room. She had her makeup bag in her purse, so she bypassed the bathroom and grabbed her portable massage table.

Within twenty minutes, she was loaded up and pulling out and, right on cue, her phone rang.

She didn't have to look at the screen to know it was Jack—she'd assigned him his own ringtone, a sharp wolf whistle that never failed to get her attention. Hearing it now made her want to throw her phone out of the window. Instead, she silenced the call, sending it to voicemail, and half a minute later her phone pinged with a new message.

She knew she shouldn't, but when she stopped at a red light, she hit the button to listen to it.

"Sadie, it's Jack. Sam told me he took you home, and he told me why. I'm on my way. I'll be there in fifteen minutes."

"But I won't be," she sang softly. She turned off her phone, then shoved it to the bottom of her bag—and jammed her thumb on the bottle of anise extract she had yet to get rid of. Cursing and shaking her hand, sitting at the red light with her thumb throbbing and her heart breaking, she had a terrible, wonderful idea.

* * * *

Jack left Sadie's apartment building, his phone to his ear. "Sam."

"Jack. Did you talk to her?"

"She's not here." Climbing into his car, he switched to hands-free mode, hit the ignition, and pulled into traffic. "Did she say anything to you about going someplace else?"

"No, probably because she knew I'd tell you." Sam cursed under his breath. "I shouldn't have taken her home."

Jack thought the same, but he bit the words back. "She'd have left anyway, and she was safe with you. Do you know where she'd go?"

"Normally I'd say to Olivia or Rebecca, but they're both here."

Jack drummed his fingers on the steering wheel, his foot holding the gas pedal almost to the floor and tried to think.

"Hold on a second, I'm getting a text. It's her."

"Where is she?" Jack demanded.

"Hang on, I'm still reading. It says, *I'm safe. I'm not going to tell you where, because you'll just tell Jack –* "

"Hell," Jack muttered.

" *– and I don't want to talk to him. But you should tell him to check his apartment. I left him a present.*"

Jack gunned the engine and flipped the car in a U-turn, ignoring the honks from the cars he'd just cut off. "Dammit, I didn't even think of my place. Did she say anything else?"

"*I love you, traitor,* but that was probably for me."

"Yeah," Jack agreed, and hoped he hadn't ruined any chance he had of hearing those words directed at him—minus the traitor. "Call me if you hear anything else, and bring the others up to speed, will you?"

"Will do. Jack? I'm sorry."

"It's not your fault, Sam," he said. *It's mine.* "I'll talk to you later."

He disconnected the call, then concentrated on getting to his apartment as fast as possible.

At first glance, his apartment looked the same as it had when he'd left it. The doorman had confirmed that Sadie had indeed been by, though she'd stayed less than twenty minutes. By his calculations, she'd been leaving his place about the same time he'd been arriving at hers.

He glanced around the living room, saw nothing amiss, and headed for the stairs. His bedroom was neat and tidy, as was the bath, but he noticed the pair of fuzzy socks she'd left on his dresser were gone, as was the packet of makeup wipes and the bottle of moisturizer she kept on his bathroom counter.

Though his heart sank to see the empty spaces, he didn't think that's what she'd meant when she said she'd left him a present. Sadie just wasn't that subtle.

He did a thorough sweep of the second floor, and finding nothing else out of place, went back downstairs. He was crossing the room when the smell hit. Faint and unwelcome, he recognized it immediately.

"Oh, she wouldn't," he breathed, horror curling in his gut along with nausea as the scent of licorice filled his nostrils.

His phone rang, and though he knew better than to hope, his stomach dropped a bit when he saw Cade's name on the readout. He answered on speaker. "Hey."

"Find her yet?"

"No, but she texted Sam, said she was safe."

"Yeah, he told me. He also said she left you a present at your place?"

"Yeah."

"You might want to have the bomb squad sweep before you go in," Cade said, and Jack thought he was only half joking.

"I think I found it," he said, and began methodically sniffing all his couch cushions.

"She leave a pile of shit in your bed or something?"

"No," he muttered, confused when the smell faded instead of getting stronger. "I'm smelling licorice."

"Okay," Cade said, clearly not understanding.

"I hate licorice," Jack told him and began sniffing the pillows.

"And I take it she knows this."

"It's come up," Jack said drily and moved into the kitchen. But he couldn't smell it at all there, so he went back to the sofa.

"You think she went to a store, bought licorice, and hid it in your house?"

"I think she took the bottle of anise extract that she had in her purse and poured it on something," he countered. "I can smell it, but it's faint, and I can't tell where it's coming from."

"Why did she have a bottle of licorice extract in her purse?"

"Long story," Jack said. "Dammit, I can't find it."

"Maybe you can get a licorice-sniffing dog," Cade suggested.

"Fuck you," Jack said. "And call me if you hear anything."

"Will do," Cade said and clicked off.

Jack spent the next thirty minutes sniffing every corner of his home. The smell was undetectable on the second floor and the kitchen, and strongest in the living area, but he couldn't find the source. He took the couch completely apart in case she'd done something like soaked cotton balls in the vile stuff and tucked them between the cushions, but he found nothing. There was nothing under the rug or in the drawers of the end tables—he even checked the lampshades.

"I know I smell it," he muttered and considered trying to call her again. She wouldn't answer, and though yelling at her over voicemail would make him feel better, it wouldn't help in the long run. She was pissed and, from what Sam had said, she was hurt.

He went over what Sam had told him they'd overheard while he put his couch back together. Even with the running water obscuring part of the conversation, Jack found it hard to believe that Sadie would actually think he was planning to hand her over to Joel on a silver platter, and Sam had reluctantly agreed. *"I thought it was pretty clear we'd missed something important,"* he'd told Jack. *"But she just wouldn't hear it."*

Jack couldn't understand why she hadn't simply confronted him. He'd never seen Sadie back down from a fight, and she wasn't afraid to cause a scene either, something she'd ably demonstrated when Olivia's ex had attempted to talk to her at a party.

He was missing something, and he didn't know what. But until she decided to answer her phone, he could do nothing but wait.

Frustrated that he couldn't immediately fix the situation, he crossed to the bar. He'd pour a drink, and take it upstairs—he wanted a shower, and not to smell licorice with every damn breath—and try to figure out his next move.

He selected a crystal decanter of brandy, pulled the stopper, and was immediately assaulted by the smell of licorice. He reared back as though to avoid a blow, then brought the decanter to his nose for a careful sniff.

"Jesus, she poured it right in," he realized, and stared at the rest of his bar. Twenty-plus bottles, and he'd bet his best flogger that she'd hit every single one of them—including the two-thousand-dollar bottle of Bunnahabhain 1980 Canasta that he'd only had a single glass out of.

He set the decanter down, carefully replaced the stopper, and walked backward until he could no longer smell licorice. Then, helpless to do anything else, he sat down on one of the bar stools lining the kitchen counter and laughed himself breathless.

* * * *

Sadie knew her parents would already be in bed, so she used her key to let herself in. She'd made a quick trip to the basement to raid her father's tool drawer and dragged her suitcase to her childhood bedroom on the second floor. Her mom had turned it into a guest room years earlier, but the floorboard still creaked in the same place, and the street light cast the same shadows on the wall that they had when she was a child, and she took comfort in those small things as she used her dad's Allen wrench set to take the collar off.

Then she stripped off her Christmas lights, crawled under the covers, and tried to sleep.

She must have managed to nod off at some point, because the next thing she knew the sun was streaming through the window. Groggy and bleary-eyed from the restless night, she got out of bed in search of coffee.

The kitchen was empty, but the full coffee pot told her someone else was up. She helped herself to a cup, then sat at the counter and turned on her phone.

She went through the texts first—and there were a lot. The ones from her girlfriends had gone from *where are you?* and *are you okay?* to *call me when you can* and *I'm here if you want to talk,* and had her blinking back sentimental tears.

The ones from the Doms were much sterner, though the sentiment was the same. Still, she knew if she texted any one of them, word would make its way back to Jack almost before she could put her phone away. Which was fine with her—he'd know she was safe without her having to actually talk to him yet—but it meant she had to be careful with the information she shared.

With a deep breath for courage, she tapped on Jack's name, surprised to see there were only three texts from him. The first one from last night read *Sam said he took you home, but you're not here—please let me know you're safe, Sadie.* The second read *SERIOUSLY?!?,* and she barked out a laugh. From the time stamp, she assumed it had come after he'd discovered her sabotage. And the third, which had arrived six-fifty-three a.m., read simply, *I missed you last night.*

She stared at those five words until they started to blur, then blinked her vision clear and switched to her voicemails.

She frowned. Though she had several missed calls from Jack, he'd only left one voicemail. It had come in shortly after the first text, and after a moment's hesitation, she hit play and raised the phone to her ear.

"Sadie, I need you to pick up the phone," he said, his voice echoing slightly. She could hear traffic noises in the background, and the thump of his fingers tapping the steering wheel, the way he did when he was agitated, or thinking. "Sam told me what you overheard, and I promise you, Sadie, I was *not* giving you to Joel."

There was a pause, and in the background, the honk of a car horn.

"I don't know if you actually believed that's what I was doing," he went on, "in which case, we really need to talk, or if something else has you running scared. In which case, we really need to talk."

"No, we don't," she muttered.

"I'm not going to get into it over voicemail," he continued, "but there are things I haven't told you. And I see now that I should have.

"I'm on my way to your place now, and I'm hoping you'll let me in. If not..."

He trailed off on a curse. "If not, then we'll talk when you're ready."

There was another pause, another curse. "And if you decide you want me to leave you alone, I'll respect that. But I'll be here when you're ready to talk, whether that's in a day or a year. I'll be here."

The voicemail ended, and Sadie lowered her phone to her lap. Ignoring the coffee, she opened up a new text to Sam.

You up?

Almost immediately, those three little 'I'm typing' dots appeared.

Yes. Are you okay?

Fine, she replied. *Can I call you?*

This time, instead of the dots, her phone rang. She answered. "Hey."

"Hey," he replied, his voice hushed. "Are you okay?"

"I'm fine," she assured him. "Why are you whispering?"

"Collette's asleep," he told her. "Hang on, I'm going into the kitchen."

She looked at the kitchen clock, realized it was just past nine. Early for a Sunday morning. "Sorry, I wasn't thinking."

"I was awake," he assured her at normal volume. "And I needed coffee anyway. Where are you?"

"Um, I'd rather not answer that."

"Better for me anyway," he said. "I won't have to lie."

She smiled at that. "Sorry I put you in a bad spot last night."

"I can handle it. Jack was more worried than mad, especially when I told him what we overheard."

"About that," she began. "Did he fill in what we didn't hear?"

"Oh, yeah. You want verbatim, or the gist?"

"The gist will do."

"Joel is still pissed you turned him down on Halloween, and went on some wild rant about how he could make you his slave girl or some shit. Jack told him you'd rather wrestle naked with crocodiles, but Joel was welcome to try. That was right before the whole 'transfer of ownership' nonsense. Cade backed him up—he was in there, too."

"Oh."

"He was really upset, Sadie," Sam said. "You should call him."

"I know, and I will." Sadie winced and imagined she could feel her friend's disapproval through the phone. "As soon as I figure out what to say."

"I'd figure fast if I were you," Sam said. "The longer you put it off, the harder it's going to be."

"I know."

"I'm going to tell him I heard from you, that you're okay. You all right with that?"

"Yeah," she said, knowing if she asked, he'd keep quiet.

"Keep me posted, sweetie."

"I will. Bye."

"Bye. Oh, wait!"

Sadie lifted the phone back to her ear. "What?"

"What surprise did you leave for him at his apartment?"

Sadie winced. "I may have, possibly, sabotaged all of his liquor."

There was a moment of stunned silence, then, "How?"

She chewed her lower lip. "Did you know that Jack really hates licorice? And that last month, I ordered some massage oil and got a sixteen-ounce bottle of licorice extract instead?"

"Holy shit."

The stunned shock in his voice made her wince. "I know. It's bad, right?"

"Honey, the technology does not exist to measure the shit storm you've landed yourself in with this one."

"I left the really expensive bottle of Scotch alone," she protested feebly.

"That may save you," Sam said, and began to laugh. "*All* of his liquor?"

"Except the expensive one," she reminded him. "Turns out, sixteen ounces of extract goes a long way."

He was still laughing. "Remind me never to piss you off."

She found herself smiling for the first time since last night. "I love you, Sam."

"I love you too, sweetie," he said. "Call me if you need me, okay?"

"I will. Bye."

She got up to freshen her coffee and snagged a banana from the bowl on the counter. She'd just sat back down when her brother Brian wandered in. As soon as he saw her, his gaze shot to the ceiling.

She would've rolled her eyes, but she wasn't in the mood. "Grow up, Brian."

"You grow up," he shot back, and crossed to the coffeepot. "What are you doing here?"

"I came to talk to Mom."

"She went to early Mass."

"I know that, jerk face." She shook her head. He was trying to pour coffee into a cup and keep his eyes on the ceiling, and she could already see it was going to end badly. "You're going to burn yourself."

"Am not," he said and cursed when hot coffee splashed over his hand and onto the counter.

She snickered into her coffee. "Told you."

"Yeah, yeah," he muttered, shaking his hand. He glanced at her, apparently forgetting not to. "You look like shit."

"Gee, thanks."

"What's wrong?"

She glanced at him, expecting him to be staring at the ceiling once again. But he was looking right at her, concern in place of the brotherly disdain he normally displayed. "I had a rough night, is all."

He picked up his coffee. "Need me to beat him up?"

"Beat who up?"

"Whoever made you feel like shit."

That made her smile. "I made myself feel like shit, but thanks."

He studied her for a moment. "Well, if you change your mind, you know where to find me."

"Thanks, Bri."

"No problem." He lifted his coffee mug in a toast and ambled out.

"Aren't you going to clean this up?" she called after him.

"You do it," he yelled back. "I can't look at you anymore without my head exploding."

"Jerk," she muttered, but she got up for a paper towel. She was just tossing it into the trash when the kitchen door opened.

"Sadie!" her mother exclaimed and hurried over to wrap her up in a hug. "I told your father that was your car out front when we left for Mass."

"I told you," Michael countered and leaned in to plant a smacking kiss on Sadie's cheek. "How's it going, kid?"

"It's going," Sadie said.

"Did you sleep here last night? What's wrong?" Jennifer asked, easing back to look at her daughter. Then her eyes narrowed. "Ah."

Michael wandered over to the refrigerator. "Ah, what?"

"Never mind." Jennifer kept one hand on Sadie's arm as she turned to her husband. "What are you doing?"

Michael turned from the refrigerator, a pack of deli meat in one hand, a loaf of bread in the other, and a bottle of mustard tucked under his chin. "Making a sandwich."

"No, you're not." Hurrying across the room, she took the food from him. "You're going to go watch the football game."

"It's not on yet."

"Watch the pre-game."

"I hate the pre-game," Michael said, adorably baffled in his rumpled Sunday suit, his wild mop of ginger hair springing out around his appealingly craggy face. "And I'm hungry."

"Michael." Exasperated, Jennifer dumped the food on the counter and planted her hands on her hips. "Look at your daughter's face."

Michael glanced at Sadie, then back at his wife. "What about her face?"

"Never mind. Just go watch TV," she told him, and started pushing him out of the room. "I'll make your sandwich and bring it to you."

"You don't put enough mustard on," Michael grumbled, resisting. "Why can't I make my own sandwich?"

"Because I need to talk to Sadie."

"About what?"

"Her sex life," Jennifer said bluntly.

"Oh." Michael's face flushed, and he was almost out of the room before he remembered his priorities. "The mustard—"

"I'll use the whole damn bottle if you'll just get out of here," she promised, exasperated, and finally managed to push him through the open doorway.

"That man is going to drive me to drink," Jennifer muttered and reached for the apron on a hook by the stove.

"Want me to make it?" Sadie offered, half rising from her stool.

"No, I've got it." Settling the apron neatly over her dress, she pulled a plate down from the cupboard and reached for the loaf of bread. "Are you hurt?"

"No," Sadie said, a warm glow spreading in her at the question. Of course that would be the first thing her mother would ask. "I'm fine."

Her gaze steady, Jennifer laid bread on the plate. "What happened?"

"I think I screwed up," Sadie admitted, and just saying the words out loud made her want to burst into tears.

"Do you want to talk about it?"

Sadie ran a hand over her head, grabbing onto her ponytail like an anchor. Then she let it go, sucked in a deep breath, and talked. "I've been seeing someone."

"The weird guy you didn't bring to Thanksgiving."

Sadie sputtered, half laugh, half sob. "Yeah."

Jennifer picked up the package of deli meat. "What's his name?"

"Jack," she murmured. "His name is Jack."

"Is he hot?" Jennifer wanted to know.

The question made her want to smile. "He is. And he's funny, and kind, and generous…"

"What else?" Jennifer prompted gently, layering ham on bread.

"He listens to me. Really listens, you know?" Sadie toyed with the handle of her coffee cup. "I'm not sure anyone ever has before. Not like him."

"Is that why he scares you?"

"He doesn't scare me." The protest was knee-jerk.

"Beautiful girl." Setting aside the ham, Jennifer reached across the counter to lay a hand over her daughter's. "I've known you every minute, every second of your life. And right now, you're absolutely terrified. And I'm not surprised."

Baffled and miserable, Sadie stared at her mother. "You're not?"

Jennifer patted her hand and eased back. "You've been seeing him for what, a month?"

"Five weeks," Sadie confirmed. "How did you know?"

"Because that's your pattern." Jennifer continued to build the sandwich. "A month, six weeks—that's your limit. I thought that might change when you discovered BDSM in college, and those needs were finally getting met, but…"

She trailed off with a shrug while Sadie sat there, shocked to her toes, and tried to keep her head from exploding.

"You know…" She had to clear her throat before she could get the rest of the words out. "You know about that?"

"Of course." Jennifer turned to the fridge, coming back with a head of lettuce and a package of Swiss cheese. "You think you're sneaky and subtle, Sadie Lynn, but you're really not."

"Oh, my God," Sadie mumbled and, putting her head down on the counter, prayed for God to strike her dead.

"We were concerned, of course," Jennifer went on cheerfully. "But you seemed so much happier, so much more at ease. And after we did a little research—"

"Research?" Sadie croaked. She didn't dare raise her head. "We?"

"Your father and I," Jennifer elaborated and chuckled when Sadie let out a long, low wail of despair. "Stop moaning into my counter."

"That wasn't a moan, it was a death rattle," Sadie countered, keeping her head down. "Because I'm dying."

"You're not dying. You're just being dramatic."

Sadie braced herself and lifted her head. "Dad knows?"

"You know I don't keep secrets from your father," Jennifer chided. "Unless I need to, of course. We talked about it, did some research, as I said—"

"I can't think about that," Sadie said, and screwed her eyes closed as if it would help.

"—and concluded that you were an adult who was capable of making your own decisions," Jennifer finished.

"Um. Thanks?"

"You're welcome." She slapped a slice of Swiss onto the ham and reached for the mustard. "Now, where was I?"

"I can honestly say I have no idea."

"Oh, yes, I remember now." Turning the mustard bottle upside down, she began to shake it. "You're scared. The question is, are you scared of your feelings or his?"

Sadie kept her gaze fixed on the sandwich. "I don't know what his feelings are."

"Well, that's just nonsense."

Sadie forgot herself and looked up. "What?"

"It's nonsense," Jennifer repeated and squirted out a huge glob of mustard. "He might not have told you how he feels, but that doesn't mean he hasn't *told* you."

She paused to slap a piece of bread on top of the sandwich, turn it over, peel back the bottom piece of bread, and squirt mustard on the other side. "Actions speak louder than words. So what are they telling you?"

"I know he likes being with me," Sadie said. "That's obvious. But I don't know what he *wants*."

"What do you want?"

"I don't know that, either," Sadie admitted. "Mom, what if he breaks my heart?"

"If he breaks it, he's not worthy of it," Jennifer said briskly. Then her voice softened. "But what if he doesn't?"

"I don't know if I can risk it," Sadie choked out, stunned to find herself near tears.

"Darling girl," Jennifer smiled. "You've already done that."

While Sadie sat reeling from that revelation, Jennifer added a layer of lettuce to the mustard-soaked bread, slapped the sandwich together, then picked up the plate and hurried out. She was back in moments, rounding the counter to perch on the stool next to Sadie's. "Now. I'm going to tell you something, and I want you to listen to me."

Sadie scrubbed her hands over her face. "Okay."

"All your life, you've been afraid of getting hurt. Not physically," she amended. "Scrapes and bruises, even broken bones, they never bothered you. But emotional hurt…that's a different story."

Sadie stared at her hands. "I'm just being careful. There's nothing wrong with that."

"Except you're not careful, you're avoidant," her mother corrected. "And there is something wrong with that, especially when it keeps you from letting yourself be loved."

"I let myself be loved," Sadie protested, feeling hollow.

"By family, by friends," Jennifer agreed. "But we're not talking about them, are we?"

Sadie's vision blurred. "It's hard, Mom."

"I know it is." Jennifer leaned in to press her forehead to her daughter's. "It's the hardest thing ever, to open your heart to someone. But I promise you, it's worth it."

Sadie sniffed. "Really?"

"So worth it," Jennifer insisted. "Does Jack get you? I mean *really* get you."

Sadie knuckled away a tear. "Yeah, he does."

"Do you get him?"

"I think I do."

Jennifer lifted her hand to brush at Sadie's wet cheeks. "And the sex is good?"

It was a relief to roll her eyes and laugh. "Jesus, Mom."

"Sexual compatibility is important," Jennifer insisted. "For example, if your father didn't like to eat pussy, we wouldn't have lasted a month."

"What the hell, Mom?" Brian cried from the kitchen doorway, a look of abject horror on his face.

"Oh, grow up, Brian," Jennifer said, annoyed. "It's not like you've never eaten pussy before."

Sadie nearly choked when Brian went red, then white, then red again.

"And if you haven't," Jennifer went on, "then I feel sorry for all your girlfriends."

Brian just stared, mouth agape. "What is *wrong* with you two?" he wailed, turned on his heel, and fled.

"He'll be fine," Jennifer said with a dismissive wave as Sadie continued to laugh. "And if he tries that 'I can't look at you bit' on me, well, I just won't feed him."

Sadie shook her head, still laughing. "I love you, Mom."

"I love you, too." Jennifer skimmed her fingers over Sadie's cheek before gathering her in for a hug. "My beautiful child."

Sadie laid her head on her mother's shoulder with a sigh. "My beautiful mom."

"You deserve to be loved," Jennifer said fiercely, holding on just a little tighter, then eased back to cup her daughter's face in her hands. "Don't deprive yourself of that, okay?"

Sadie nodded. "I'll try."

"Try hard." Jennifer patted her cheek. "So?"

Understanding the question, Sadie pushed off the stool. "I'm going to go talk to him."

"That's my girl." Jennifer rose to her feet and untied her apron. "And you'll tell him what you want?"

"After I apologize," Sadie said with a wince.

"Apologize?" Jennifer began, confused, then her eyes narrowed. "Sadie Lynn Bloom, what did you do?"

Sadie tried to look innocent. "Just a little sabotage."

"If it's bad enough to bring out the big eyes, you better save them for him," her mother said and sighed.

"Well, if he forgives you, bring him to Sunday dinner next week."

"We'll see." Sadie leaned in for one last hug. "I gotta go."

"I have to go, too," Jennifer said, raising her voice slightly. "I need to check the tracking on the sex toys I bought last week. I want to make sure nobody's home when they get here, so your father and I can break them in properly."

"God, why?" Brian wailed from the hall, followed by the sound of running footsteps.

"You're terrible," Sadie accused, laughing.

"Where do you think you get it from?" Jennifer winked. "Good luck, darling girl."

Chapter Eighteen

She could use the luck. Standing outside Jack's door, her palms sweating and her heart pounding, Sadie wished she'd raided her mother's liquor cabinet for a shot or two of liquid courage. Then she remembered what she'd done to Jack's liquor and winced. She wasn't sure what she should apologize for first, running out of the party without telling him or poisoning his booze.

Knowing the longer she stood there, the harder it would be, she closed her eyes, took a deep breath, and rapped her knuckles on the door. When it opened almost immediately, she took an instinctive step back.

He wore jeans and a black sweater, his hair loose and his feet bare, and his expression was set to Resting Dick Face. It surprised her, and she realized she hadn't seen him look like that since the demo a month ago.

God, had it only been a month?

"Hello, Sadie," he said, and she winced at his formal tone.

"Jack," she replied, and swallowed her pride. "Can I come in?"

He stepped back wordlessly and waved a hand, gesturing her inside. She stepped forward, moving carefully past him, her heart rate picking up speed as the scent of his shampoo tickled her nose.

He closed the door behind her, the click of the latch like a gunshot to her anxious ears, and stepped around her. "Would you like to sit?"

"Thank you," she said, and moved into the living area. She perched on one of the chairs, her purse on her lap, and waited for him to take the chair opposite her before she spoke. "I owe you an apology."

"More than one, by my count," he drawled, anger creeping into his tone, and she nearly sagged with relief because that awful formality was gone from his voice.

"I know."

"And an explanation," he continued.

"I'm not sure where to start," she admitted. "Did Sam…?"

"He told me what you heard," he told her. "I want to know what you were thinking when you heard it."

"I don't know what I thought. That's not a cop out," she hurried to add when his eyes narrowed. "At first I was just pissed at Joel, for being such a jerk. And Sam was shushing me so he could hear better, but the water was running and we couldn't hear anything. And when it shut off, that's when Joel said that thing about transferring ownership of me over to him."

She swallowed. "And you said, 'absolutely'."

"Did you think I meant it?"

She hesitated, gathering her courage. "Now it seems ridiculous, but I did then."

"Why?"

She licked her lips. This was the hard part. "Because the collar didn't mean anything to you."

Surprise flared in his eyes. "What?"

"I didn't really expect it to mean what it usually means," she said, the words tumbling over themselves as she rushed to get them out. "It was fine that it didn't. But I thought it would mean *something*."

"It did," he murmured, but she was still talking.

"You said it would be appropriate," she reminded him. "Because we were going to the party together. Basic protocol. It felt like, I don't know, like a box to check."

He surged to his feet and paced to the window, staring out into the bright winter sunlight, and she rushed to finish.

"So, when you said 'absolutely', and your voice got the way it does when you're trying not to laugh out loud..." She trailed off, taking a moment to screw up her courage. "I knew I'd overreacted, even when Sam was driving me home, but I couldn't stop. I think I'd been quietly freaking out for a while, and I used what happened as an excuse to finally do it out loud."

He turned to look at her, backlit by the sun. "Freaking out about what?"

She waved a hand helplessly. "You. Me. Us. I don't know what you want from me."

"You don't know what I want?" he echoed.

"You've never told me," she said simply, and wished she could see his eyes. But the sun at his back cast his face in shadow.

"No, I never did," he murmured, and scrubbed a hand over his face. "It looks like I owe you an apology, too."

"Huh?"

He shoved his hands into his pockets. "If I said I'd wanted you to wear my collar to the party last night as a symbol that we were together, in a committed relationship, what would you have said?"

"I would have been…surprised."

"Surprised, or spooked?"

The lie was on the tip of her tongue, but she couldn't bring herself to say it. "Spooked," she admitted.

"I shouldn't have asked you to wear it." He dragged both hands through his hair. "You're not ready, and I guess when it comes down to it, neither am I."

She shook her head. "I don't understand."

"The reason you don't know what I want—the reason I haven't told you—is because I was afraid if I did, you'd bolt." He angled his head. "Was I wrong?"

"I don't know." She licked her lips. "I guess it depends on what you want."

"I'm in love with you."

The air whooshed out of her lungs, leaving her feeling lightheaded and giddy. *And yes, fucking terrified.* "I think I'm going to be sick."

"Well, that's reassuring."

"Give me a damn minute, for God's sake," she said on a wheeze, and dropped her head to hang between her knees. "You love me?"

"It seems I do."

"Don't be cryptic," she said, irritated, and sat back up to glare at him. Her heart was still beating like a scared rabbit's, but she didn't feel like puking anymore. "Okay. What does that mean?"

"What the hell kind of question is that?" he demanded, in full resting-dick-face mode.

"A valid one," she shouted back and leapt to her feet. "You said you love me, but I don't know what that means. Do you want to date? Move in together? *I don't know what you want from me."*

"You want to know what I want?" He stalked toward her, moving so fast she barely had time to squeak before he was gripping her upper arms, all but lifting her off her feet. She could see his eyes now, and they were blazing. "I want us to be together. I want you to be my submissive and wear my collar. I want you to love me back, dammit!"

"I do love you back, dammit!"

He blinked. "You do?"

"Yes!"

His grip on her arms tightened, shock replacing the anger in his expression.

"I know," she said, answering the question in his eyes. "It surprised the hell out of me, too."

"You love me," he repeated.

"I just said so, didn't I?" she demanded, then she didn't say anything at all because he was kissing the hell out of her. When he broke free, it was to swoop her up in a hard hug that all but squeezed the breath out of her.

She squeezed him right back.

"I'm sorry I was trying so hard not to spook you that I made you think you didn't matter," he murmured into her neck.

"I'm sorry I left the party without telling you and poured anise extract into your liquor bottles," she replied.

He hugged her all the harder. "You're going to pay for that one, you know."

"Don't I get points for leaving the really expensive one alone?"

"Half a point," he allowed, and pressed a gentle kiss to her neck before easing back to look her in the eye. "And you can thank Sam for telling me about that, because I was ready to dump it down the sink with the rest of them."

Sadie made a mental note to send Sam a thank-you gift. "So, what do we do now?"

"We have some talking to do," he said. "And I think we need some new rules."

She blinked. That wasn't what she'd expected to hear. "Rules?"

He nodded. "If we'd been communicating well, this misunderstanding never would have happened."

She winced. "I know."

"Not all your fault," he reminded her, and gave her ponytail a gentle tug. "Turns out, I've got some insecurities that need addressing, too."

"Oh."

"We'll work out the rules together, all right?"

There was a squiggle in her belly, but she decided she liked it. "Okay. Together."

"But first," he said, and holding her hands, stepped back.

"What?" she asked, confused when he sat down on the couch. Her eyes widened in surprise when he grabbed the waistband of her leggings, dragged them to her knees, then yanked her forward so she sprawled ass-up over his lap.

"This," he said over her shocked squeal, "is for not telling me where you were going last night and making me worry about you."

She bit her lip. She had done that, and deliberately. "Okay."

"Once I think you're sufficiently contrite, I'm going to take you upstairs, tie you to the bed, and make you come so many times you can't remember your own name. When you've regained the power of speech, we'll discuss your punishment for the licorice."

"Do I get any vote here?"

"No."

"Is this how it's going to be from now on?" she demanded.

"Of course. I'm the Dom."

She pressed her cheek to his leg and smiled. "Just checking."

Epilogue

Three months later

Jack walked through his front door, shut it behind him, and shucked his coat. He didn't bother hanging it up, just tossed it over a chair on his way to the stairs. He took them two at a time, coming to a stop outside the closed bathroom door.

He checked the time, frowning. He was a little earlier than he said he'd be, but not by much. She should be ready by now. "Sadie?"

"Hi," she replied, her voice faint through the closed door. "How'd it go?"

"Fine," he called back and crossed to his closet. The shirt and jeans he wore were grimy from helping set up the various apparatus needed for the party in James and Amanda's basement, so he stripped and tossed the clothes in the hamper. "Nick and Cade both showed up, so the four of us made quick work of it."

"That's nice."

"How did your new client go?"

"Good, but she was a talker. I just got home fifteen minutes ago."

Every time she called his apartment 'home', it gave Jack a warm glow of satisfaction. They weren't living together, not yet—she was insisting on a full year of dating before she'd agree to give up her lease. But they spent most nights together, either at his place or hers, and he was counting down the days on his calendar before they could make it official.

"How long is it going to take you to get ready?" he asked, checking the time again. They weren't due at James and Amanda's for another hour, but he had something to do before they left.

"Two minutes," she promised, and he would have scoffed, but when Sadie said two minutes, that was exactly what she meant.

He pulled the polished wooden box off the top shelf on his side of the closet and set it on the bed. He dressed quickly in black slacks and an emerald-green sweater that Sadie had given him for Christmas and was just slipping on his boots when the bathroom door opened.

"Ta-da!" she exclaimed then squealed with delight. "Oh, you're wearing the sweater!"

"You're not wearing anything," he said, looking at her costume with amusement.

"Hey. There are stickers," she pointed out haughtily, then frowned. "I got body glitter, too, but that shit gets everywhere, so I decided not to use it."

"Thank you for your restraint," he said, eyeing her nipples. She'd pasted two glittery green shamrocks over them. "What, no rainbow?"

"What do you take me for?" she demanded, and spun around to present him with her ass.

"I stand corrected," he said, eyeing the rainbow that curved from the top of her left hip and down, disappearing into the crack of her ass. "Is that paint?"

"Yeah. Nikki came over to help me," she admitted. "I couldn't quite get the hang of doing it in the mirror."

"Uh-huh. One question."

"What?"

"Why does the rainbow end *in* your ass crack?"

"I was hoping you'd ask," she said, and bent over to reveal the gold butt plug nestled between her cheeks. "Voila, the gold at the end of the rainbow."

He was laughing as she straightened and turned back to face him. "We were going to do one pointing at my pussy, too, but we ran out of time."

"It's perfect," he told her, still chuckling.

"Thanks," she said and, stepping closer, rose on her toes to press her lips to his. "Hi."

"Hi, yourself." She'd left her hair down, so he buried his hands in the silky mass. "I missed you today."

"I missed you, too," she said and sighed. "I wish I had fewer clients on Saturdays."

"Me, too," he said. "But you're clear tomorrow, right?"

"Right."

"Good, because I have plans for tonight."

"Oh, really?" she purred, and leaned into him. "Would you like to share these plans?"

He chuckled. He rarely told her what he had planned for a scene, and though she grumbled about it, she liked being surprised. This time, though, was different. "As a matter of fact, I would. Kneel, please."

A curious light came into her eyes, but she sank to her knees without a word, and he felt a surge of pride and affection. Their trust had come a long way in the last few months, and it showed in the easy way she obeyed the simple command without even a glimmer of suspicion or fear.

He turned away to pick up the box he'd taken down from the closet, then faced her once again. Her gaze flicked down to the box once before rising to meet his again. "We've come a long way in the last few months, don't you think?"

She nodded, a curious light in her hazel eyes. "Yes, Boss."

"We've gotten better at talking to each other," he continued, "and I feel as though our trust has grown. Would you agree?"

"Yes, Boss."

"Good," he said, then faltered. He hadn't planned this part, wanting the words to come from his heart, but now that the time had come, he was fumbling for the right ones.

"Boss?" she said tentatively, and he looked up to see her watching him, worry shadowing her eyes.

"I love you, so much," he said, wanting to erase that worry, that doubt. "Do you love me?"

The smile she gave him lit her face. "Yes, Boss, I do."

"Enough to wear this again?" he said, and with his heart in his throat, opened the box.

"Oh," she breathed, and her eyes shot to his. "You kept it."

"Of course I did," he said, shocked to see the sheen of tears in her eyes. "Did you think I hadn't?"

"I didn't know." Her gaze fell to the circle of rose gold inside the box. "You haven't mentioned it."

"I was waiting until the time felt right," he said and lifted it out. Setting the box aside, he held the collar between them. "I've thought about how I wanted to do this, and what I wanted to say when I did."

She looked up at him, waiting, her heart in her eyes.

"But, really, it all comes down to just one thing." He drew a steadying breath. "Sadie, will you be mine?"

She was nodding before he finished asking, laughing, her smile lighting up the room. "Yes, Boss. Yes, yes, yes!"

"Lift your hair up," he told her and waited until she'd gathered the bright mass in her hands before slipping the collar around her throat. When he locked it in place with the wrench, he'd have sworn all the pieces of his life fell into place.

"There," he said and leaned back to see tears streaming down her cheeks. "Sadie?"

"I'm sorry," she said, laughing through the tears. "I'm just so happy. I wasn't sure I'd ever get this back."

"It was always yours," he murmured, drawing her to her feet and kissing the tears from her cheeks. "It was just waiting for you to be ready."

She met his mouth with hers, sighing into the kiss. What started as a tender expression of the love he felt for her turned into something more and when he raised his head, they were both panting.

She licked her lips. "Boss?"

He tried not to think about how those lips would feel around his aching cock. "Yes, love?"

"Do we have time for you to fuck me before we go to the party?"

"Hmmm," he said and nearly laughed when her eyes narrowed. "I suppose, but it'll have to be quick and dirty. And I doubt you'll have time to clean up after."

She arched an elegant eyebrow. "Are you saying if I want you to fuck me, I'll have to go to the party with your come dripping out of my pussy?"

"That's exactly what I'm saying."

"You, Sir, are a filthy pervert," she declared, then grinned. "What are you waiting for?"

Want to see more from this author? Here's a taster for you to enjoy!

Sun, Sea and Satisfaction Guaranteed

Hannah Murray

Excerpt

Clio Reed closed her eyes, drew in a deep breath, and reminded herself that she was on vacation.

The little cabin was perfect. Nestled in the woods on the edge of Lake Michigan, it was accessible only by an unmarked dirt road hidden so well that even the people who owned the cabin would have trouble finding it. The wide porch was screened to keep the bugs out, and held a pair of thickly cushioned lounge chairs which were perfect for lazy summer days. She could stretch out after a morning swim in the lake with Cecil, snuggle into the thick cushions with her e-reader after lunch, and watch the sunset over the lake with a glass of wine after dinner. Cecil would stretch out on the deck's wooden planks, snoring as he slept off a day of romping in the water. She'd sleep cozy and comfortable in the king-sized bed, and the next morning, they'd get up and do it all again.

She could take leisurely walks, play with her dog and read as many romance novels as she wanted, blissfully alone. If she concentrated hard enough, she could almost smell the lake and the rich, loamy scent of the woods.

The knock on the door made her concentration waver, but she ignored it and drew another deep breath. She imagined she could hear the sounds of the woods, the chirp of crickets and the gentle rush of the wind through the trees, the creak of the porch boards under her feet as she walked to the lounger and settled in to read—

Knock, knock, knock.

Her vision wavered, nearly disappearing at the three hard raps. She grunted, an annoyed rebuke for whoever was pounding on her door forming on her tongue. She swallowed it down, wiggled to settle more firmly into her cross-legged position, and pulled the image clear into her mind once more. There was her cabin, lovely and perfect. She was lying on the lounge chair, Cecil's furry bulk on the chaise beside her, no one around to inter—

Knock, knock, knock. "Come on, Clio. I know you're in there."

"Leave me alone," she mumbled under her breath, eyes still closed, mentally in her lakefront paradise, an e-reader in her hand and her dog at her side. "I'm on vacation."

"Mom wants everyone out on the upper deck for a family meeting. She sent a message on the family chat, so I know you got it."

No, I didn't, she thought smugly. Because her phone was tucked away in a drawer, turned off as a hedge against just such a maneuver.

"You were supposed to be there ten minutes ago. You're holding everything up."

This floating nightmare isn't even underway yet, and it's already started. Ignoring her younger brother—and the small pang of guilt—with the ease of long practice, Clio rolled her shoulders, straightened her spine, and tried to find paradise in her mind once again.

"Dammit, Clio." *Bam! Bam! Bam!* "I've got better things to do than be Mom's errand boy."

"Tell her no," she shot back, then bit her lip.

"I heard that," he crowed.

"Shit," Clio muttered and opened her eyes.

Instead of the rolling waves of Lake Michigan lapping at a sandy shore, she saw the industrial carpet, cream-colored walls, and impersonal décor that made up her stateroom on the *Duchess Dream* cruise liner.

Since it was a third of the size of a budget hotel room, *stateroom* was a stretch, but calling it a floating cell had earned her a disappointed look from her mother. Cam knocked again, then rattled the knob. "Come on, Clio. You know if I go back up there without you, she's going to come to get you herself."

"I'm coming," she called, resigned and resentful, and slid off the too-soft bed to open the door.

Her brother's handsome face wore a predictably smug smile, which went perfectly with his frat-boy-on-spring-break outfit of a Ron Jon Surf Shop T-shirt, board shorts, and flip flops. "What took you so long?"

"Ha," she replied, and walked back into the room, leaving him to follow.

"Wow," he said, looking around. "This is small."

"I know." She sat down on the tiny couch, which was really just a wide, shallow chair with two small, hard cushions. The couch was too hard, the bed was too soft—she felt like Goldilocks on the cruise from hell.

"Mom says it's my fault for making my reservations at the last minute."

"She's not wrong." He wandered over to look out of the porthole over the double bed. "If you'd booked when Tara and I did, you'd probably at least have a window."

"I was hoping Mom would cave."

"What an optimist." Cam sat beside her, wincing as he settled on the hard cushion. "It won't be so bad. She's been pretty mellow, actually."

"Which is why she sent you down here to fetch me."

"Okay, so mellow is probably an exaggeration." Cam patted her knee in sympathy. "But I've got something that might help."

"A prescription for tranquilizers?" she asked hopefully.

"I'm not medicating our mother."

"I meant for me."

"I'm not medicating you either." He pulled a small velvet box out of his pocket and flipped the lid open. "I'm going to ask Tara to marry me."

"Holy crap, Cameron." She stared at the ring. "Is that Grammy Reed's ring?"

"Yeah." He turned the box so the diamond caught the light. "Dad gave it to me when I told him I was going to propose. I wanted to make sure that was all right with you."

She blinked in confusion. "You want my blessing?"

"No. I mean, I'm happy to have it, but I'm talking about the ring. You're older than me, so technically, it should go to you."

"Technically, it should go to Carter," she countered. "He's the oldest."

"Dad said he'd offered it to him when he and Gabe got engaged, but they didn't want it."

Clio looked at the ring again, its delicate gold filigree and central stone gleaming in the light. "Yeah, I don't think it would fit Gabe."

"Dad told them they could keep it for their kids, but Carter said he was fine with it going to one of us."

"Cam." She reached up to cradle his face in her hands. "I'm so happy for you."

"Thanks." He squirmed a little, delighting her. "You're not going to get mushy, are you?"

"Hell, yes," she said, and pinched his cheeks for emphasis. "It's absolutely okay with me if you give Grammy's ring to Tara. It's perfect for her."

"Yeah." He looked down at the ring again, his smile going sappy. "Yeah, it is."

"When are you going to ask her?"

He snapped the box shut and tucked it away. "Tonight, at dinner. I can't wait to see Mom's face."

Clio started to point out that it wasn't their mother's moment, then bit her tongue. If Cam and Tara didn't mind, it was none of her business. "She doesn't know you're planning to propose?"

He shook his head. "I asked Dad not to say anything. You know she can't keep a secret."

Clio snorted. "He better hope she doesn't find out about that."

"I know."

"Although if she's mad at him, she won't have time to nag me this week," she mused. "Would it make me a terrible daughter if I threw him under the bus?"

"Yes." He pushed to his feet and held out a hand. "Speaking of which, we better go."

She made a face and allowed him to pull her to her feet. "Can't you just tell them I took a sleeping pill and I'm too groggy to come out on the deck because I might lose my balance and fall into the ocean?"

"No." He dragged her to the door.

"Wait!" She tugged her hand free and ran the three steps back to the bed for her long-sleeved shirt and wide-brimmed sun hat. "Okay, I'm ready."

"You know it's ninety degrees out, right?"

"Believe me, I'd prefer fewer layers." She hated covering up the cute pink top, and could have gone without the sweat she knew would gather under the brim of the hat and soak into her hair. Shorts would've been nice, too, instead of the loose cotton pants, but at least this way, she wouldn't fry to a crisp in the Florida sun.

Being a natural redhead, with the accompanying pale-as-Casper skin, could be a real bitch. Especially when both of her brothers, her parents, and every other member of her family except for Great-Aunt Francine looked like they'd just stepped out of the pages of a surfing magazine after five minutes of sun.

"Can't you just wear sunblock? You look like somebody's grandma."

She smacked him on the arm. "I'm wearing sunblock, you ass. I still burn."

"Like a vampire," he muttered, wincing when she smacked him again. "Ow. Quit hitting me."

"Quit being a dick," she shot back and smacked him one more time for good measure. "Let's get this over with."

"Wait." He turned back at the door. "Tara asked me to get her a bottle of water. Can I have one of yours?"

"I don't have any bottles of water."

"What's that?" he said, pointing past her to the nightstand.

"That's distilled water."

"So?"

"So, it's for my CPAP."

"Your what?"

She pointed at the sleek little machine on the nightstand. "The thing that helps me breathe while I sleep?"

"Oh, right. Can't you refill it at the sink?"

"No, jackass, I can't. I have to use distilled water, or the minerals in the tap water fuck up the machine."

He frowned. "That sounds made up."

She shoved him out of the door. "You can't have the water, Cameron."

"Then I have to go back to our room to get one of ours."

She checked her pocket to make sure she still had her key card, then pulled the cabin door shut behind her. "So go. I'll meet you up there."

He narrowed his eyes, suddenly suspicious. "Give me your key."

"What? No."

"I don't trust you not to go back in there and bar the door."

She rolled her eyes as though she hadn't been considering exactly that. "Get a grip, Cameron."

She headed down the narrow hallway, Cam on her heels. "Listen, our room is on the deck above you. Why don't you come with me? You can have a bottle of water, too."

"I don't need a bottle of water, I'm very well hydrated." She bypassed the bank of elevators in favor of the wide central stairwell and began to climb. "Go, Cam. I promise I won't run away."

"Okay. Tell Mom I'll be right there."

She waved a hand and continued up the stairs as he veered off. Half a flight later, she heard footsteps behind her again and stopped climbing with an aggravated sigh.

"Cam, I said I would go," she began, turning to confront her brother, and found herself face to face with a stranger. "Oh. You're not Cam."

"No, I'm Fox," he said, and smiled. "Hello."

"Hello," she replied automatically, while her brain sounded the hot-guy alert.

Seriously hot guy. He was big, towering over her even though he stood two steps lower, and handsome. He had dark hair curling over his ears, misty green eyes, and a jaw covered in dark stubble that looked like a vacation beard in the early stages. He wore a plain black T-shirt, khaki cargo shorts and flip flops, and a smirk on a beautiful mouth that, aside from his hair, looked to be the only soft thing about him.

She blew out a breath and tried not to drool.

She didn't speak, and would've sworn that her expression didn't change even a smidge. But his smirk deepened and his eyes lit with amusement, and it made her want to kiss him and punch him at the same time. To prevent herself from doing either, she said, "What kind of a name is Fox?"

"Family name." His gaze flicked down then up again, and she fought the urge to squirm in her long pants and long sleeves and grandma hat. "It's Foxworth, but since that makes me sound like one third of a tight-ass accounting firm, I just go by Fox."

"Good call," she said, and with nothing to say besides *can I sit on your face?*, turned and began climbing the stairs again, automatically keeping tight to the rail so he could walk past her.

He didn't.

"Who's Cam?"

She paused and turned to frown at him, still two steps below her. "What?"

"Who's Cam?" he repeated. "You said, 'you're not Cam', so who's Cam?"

"My brother," she said absently, trailing her gaze down his body again. His shoulders were broad, his chest and arms thick. He had actual, visible muscles in his forearms, which were tan like the rest of him and dusted with dark hair. *Forearm porn of the highest caliber,* she thought hazily and turned to continue up the stairs, holding on to the railing so she wouldn't fall, trip him, and drag him on top of her.

"What's your name?" he asked, keeping pace behind her.

"None of your business," she replied automatically, because really, it wasn't.

"True," he said easily, her don't-fuck-with-me tone having no effect on his friendly cheer. "I only asked because it's expected. Social niceties and all. I don't really want to know."

That was just what she needed, sarcasm from a hot stranger. She sniffed and kept climbing, trying not to be annoyed because her ass looked flat in these pants.

"I don't need to know, anyway," he continued. "It's not like we're family or anything. Hell, we'll probably never see each other once we get out of this stairway."

"If there's a God," she muttered, already mourning the loss of his forearms.

"Unless we want to see each other outside of this stairway, of course."

"Why would we want that?" she blurted out without turning around.

"I don't know." He was, annoyingly, not at all out of breath from the climb. "Maybe because you think I'm hot."

She missed the next stair and stumbled, barely catching herself on the railing in time to keep from falling on her face.

"Careful there," cautioned a young man in a crew uniform coming down the stairs. He had soft brown eyes, a pretty face and what looked like a pleasingly muscled form under his crisp uniform. "You all right?"

"Yes, thanks." She smiled at him, and his smile broadened in return.

"Here, let me help you." He stepped closer, holding out a hand.

"She's fine," Fox said from behind her and hauled her up with a strong arm around her waist. "Aren't you, darling?"

"Peachy," she said through gritted teeth and resisted the urge to kick him.

"Right." The young man's smile went from warm and interested to coolly polite. "Keep hold of the railing, now."

"Thanks," she said, watching as he continued down the stairs, taking her first prospect of a shipboard hookup with him. Annoyed, she turned to glare at Fox. "Do you mind?"

"Sorry," he said, not sounding sorry at all, and pulled his arm from around her waist. "Just trying to help."

"Cockblocking me from the cute sailor is not helpful," she muttered under her breath and started climbing again.

"Sorry, what was that?"

"Nothing." She stopped on the stairs again and turned to glare at him. "What did you say?"

"I said 'sorry, what was that?'," he replied with a frown. "Did you hit your head?"

"No, I did not hit my head. Before that, when I fell. You said something."

"Oh." His frown faded and the smirk reappeared. "The part about you thinking I'm hot?"

She tried not to stare at the way his shoulders moved in the black t-shirt. Or the way his forearms flexed as he shoved his hands into his pockets. And she certainly didn't remember how it had felt around her waist, thick and hard and deliciously restraining. "I don't."

"Don't what?"

"Don't think you're hot." *Liar, liar, pants on fire.*

"You don't?"

She planted her hands on her hips and scowled. "No."

"Oh." He shrugged and smiled, unconcerned. "Sorry. My mistake."

"Don't mention it," she replied, oddly disappointed, and started up the stairs again.

"I probably shouldn't have assumed that," he continued, "just because you were staring at me."

I wasn't staring. In fact, I made a point not *to stare.*

"The fact that I checked you out doesn't mean anything either," he went on blithely as she ground her teeth together. "I mean, I did check you out, but that certainly doesn't mean I find you hot."

Clio kept silent as she reached the top landing, biting her tongue to keep quiet, and crossed to the doors leading out to the deck.

"Not that you're not attractive." He followed her out, unfortunately catching the heavy door before it slammed in his face. "You seem lovely, even in those clothes. Are you a member of some kind of religious order that prohibits shorts or something?"

She jerked to a stop and turned to him, her scowl not at all feigned this time. "Yes, actually. Sister Theresa

Grumpy Pants of the Order of Perpetual Boob Sweat. Nice to meet you. Would you like a brochure?"

He flashed a grin, quick and delighted. "Hey, you *do* have a sense of humor."

"I'm a fucking laugh riot," she muttered and kept walking, completely unsurprised when he fell into step beside her. "Is there a reason you're following me?"

"I'm not following you," he told her. "I'm meeting my family up here."

"Right."

"Seriously. Not everything is about you, Theresa. Can I call you Terry?"

She refused to smile. "Sure. Foxworth."

"Touché." He leaned forward to peer at her face, keeping pace with her easily. "Are you sure you don't think I'm hot? We could have dinner later. Maybe play a game of shuffleboard."

"Are you using 'shuffleboard' as code for some deviant sexual act?"

"Would you say yes if I was?"

She just might. He *was* hot, and charming, and she figured he owed her an orgasm or two for cockblocking her with the sexy, brown-eyed crewman. The possibility of a shipboard romance with a handsome stranger—and by romance, she meant wild sexual romp with absolutely no feelings involved—was the only thing keeping her from diving over the side of the ship and making a break for it. Well, that and the knowledge that her mother was a very strong swimmer, and would no doubt come after her.

She sent him a speculative glance, taking in his cheerful grin and handsome face. There was a slight breeze out on the deck, making his hair float up around his head like a dark halo. And his forearms were still flexing, porn-like.

He caught her eye and sent her a saucy wink. "Okay, just dinner. We'll find a secluded table for two and you can tell me all about perpetual boob sweat. Who knows? Maybe I'll join the order."

"I only have to get two more recruits to win the toaster oven." She refused, absolutely refused to laugh. "Are you always this chatty?"

"Depends on how much the other person talks," he said easily. "Though I am sometimes very, very quiet."

She gave a skeptical snort. "When?"

"When I'm sleeping, eating, or performing cunnilingus."

The laugh burst out before she could catch it, and he grinned.

"There it is," he said. "I knew you had at least one in you."

"Have you been trying to make me laugh?"

"Sure. People are always more willing to say yes to things when they're in a good mood."

"What are you trying to get me to say yes to?"

His grin was wicked. "Me."

"Of course," she said, more than tempted to say yes to dinner and cunnilingus. A tongue that got as much exercise as his did was bound to have stamina. But she could see her family ahead, her mother's blonde head next to her father's blond head, her other blond relatives nearby, and the anxiety that had been surprisingly absent since he'd said, *"No, I'm Fox,"* in the stairwell was creeping in again.

It was remarkably difficult to say, "I'm afraid I'll have to pass."

"You sure? Satisfaction guaranteed. I'll even wear a gag if you want."

She managed to choke back another laugh. "Intriguing, but yeah. I'm here with my family."

"Ah. Well, if you change your mind, I'll be around. It was nice to meet you, Sister Theresa."

"Likewise, Foxworth."

"And who knows? Maybe our paths will cross again."

They were only a few feet away from her family now. She shook her head. "I doubt it."

"Never say never," he said with a wink, just as a tall figure with bright red hair broke free from the crowd.

"Darling, *there* you are!" Aunt Franny, resplendent in a flowing orange caftan with purple flowers and gold trim, came flying toward them. She wore chandelier earrings that brushed her shoulders, blue eyeshadow, and her bright red hair—cut in the same Dorothy Hammel hairstyle she'd been wearing for as long as Clio could remember—was topped with a tiara that sparkled in the late afternoon sun.

"Aunt Franny," she began, then stood stock still, her mouth open in shock, as Franny's outstretched arms wrapped Fox in an enthusiastic hug.

"Hi, Mom," he said and winked at her over Franny's silk-covered shoulder.

About the Author

Hannah has been reading romance novels since she was young enough to have to hide them from her mother. She lives in the Pacific Northwest with her husband—former Special Forces and an OR nurse who writes sci-fi fantasy and acts as In-House Expert on matters pertaining to weapons, tactics, the military, medical conditions and How Dudes Think—and their daughter, who takes after her father.

Hannah loves to hear from readers. You can find her contact information, website details and author profile page at https://www.totallybound.com

Home of Erotic Romance

Sign up for our newsletter and find out about all our romance book releases, eBook sales and promotions, sneak peeks and FREE romance books!

www.ingramcontent.com/pod-product-compliance
Lightning Source LLC
LaVergne TN
LVHW050925080826
845145LV00001B/214

9781802505634